Revelations

Richard C Pizey

Other titles by Richard C Pizey

Ripples
Echoes of Andalucia

For updates and information on forthcoming publications
check online at
www.augfifth.com

R e v e l a t i o n s

Richard C Pizey was born in London and educated at the Nautical College Pangbourne.

After leaving college, Richard pursued a variety of courses including hotel management and catering, and electronic engineering and telecommunications, typically spending most of his time with more like-minded people in the art department of Colchester Technical College.

After a spell in Australia, constructing boilers, selling encyclopaedias and playing guitar with a rock band, he returned to London - via life as a disc jockey in Munich and Copenhagen - eventually taking up a career as a recording engineer. During thirty years of pushing faders in the studio profession, Richard also wrote scripts and jingles for radio and television commercials.

Having spent his childhood in exotic locations such as Bombay, Valletta, and Portsmouth (the UK version), and formative years in Australia, Germany and Denmark, it is perhaps little wonder that Richard still travels extensively. His interests include cosmology, tennis, music (especially classical and jazz funk), and wine.

Revelations (sequel to *Ripples*), is the third novel from
Richard C Pizey, author of *Echoes of Andalucía*.
Available from bookshops or at
www.augfifth.com

Set in 11 / 14.5pt Garamond

ISBN 978 0 9566452 2 7

Printed by Copytech (UK) Limited, Peterborough, England

Revelations

Richard C Pizey

AUGMENTED FIFTH
ANOTHER DIMENSION

For Jean and David

in respect of their belief, honesty and stimulus

Many thanks

to Debby,
without whom . . .

to Lady Jane -
proof-reader, supplier of coffee, chocolate and wine,
and friendly encouragement to get the job done

à Adela
En vérité, la splendeur de toutes les choses possibles

and to Doris Kouba
for expanding and correcting my foray into the German language

Chapter One:

Up

1

Simon sat in quiet contemplation. It was something he did with great frequency these days. Of course, in a previous life he'd been a pharaoh; perhaps not one of the famous pharaohs but one of those attached to an almost unpronounceable name. He'd been the governor of thousands of Egyptians engaged in constant battle against the Phoenicians, Canaanites and Babylonians, laying waste to hundreds of square miles of already barren land. And now he was reduced to sitting outside, reminiscing about his long-lost greatness and fortune when his every whim had been attended to by legions of slaves.

He had a problem and he found that it helped to come out here to the calm though frigid atmosphere of the balcony. For several days he'd been wondering about the changes in his life, the Coriolis-type forces that had whispered through the two bedrooms, the bathroom, the kitchen and the living room of the normally placid apartment. Coriolis – he purred at the thought of such a word, mysterious and difficult to quantify. He had no idea as to its meaning but, having heard it somewhere – probably on one of those scientific programmes the stranger liked to watch – reckoned it was educational and intelligent and decided to sort of just leave it bouncing around jumbling his thought processes.

The twosome had become a threesome. Overnight, as it seemed, a stranger with a strange way of speaking had made a meaningful intrusion. It was as though the planets had altered their courses, though Simon was well aware that the analogy was extreme. They maybe swerved, just a little, an occasional bumping here and there but nothing that amounted to a change of orbit in the far-flung reaches of swirling space. Not really.

He scratched behind his left ear and raised his sight to the horizon, where a jet aircraft was playing hide-and-seek with the skyscrapers that made this new Babylon famous. How times have changed, he thought. Then it started snowing, lumpy flakes adding to the layers of frozen whiteness that covered everything. From below came the muffled noise of traffic and an occasional outburst of laughter as stalwart citizens followed their daily routines. Simon stretched his neck and looked down at the street, where a series of brown lines defiled the pristine blanket – two in the centre, especially dark, where successive waves of cars took it in turns to transgress the slippery surface; and a hotchpotch of tracks along the sidewalks where intrepid pedestrians paced out the vagaries of life. To Simon, it was all a mess, the mass wandering of humanity in its constant search for an uncertain future. He licked his lips and stared at a pigeon that was skillfully navigating an urgent eddy of snowflakes. Blimey, he thought, vague computations of aerodynamics, wind velocities and weight-ratios flitting annoyingly through his head, these birds must be equipped with extremely large *cojones*. And when the beady-eyed aviator performed an awkward landing only a few feet away, he stared disdainfully at the unwelcome visitor cloaked in religious shades of purple and grey.

Laid-back in moral vicissitude, due mainly to the fact that he knew there was nothing he or anybody else could do to change anything, Simon was indifferent about most of the stuff that happened in his immediate domain. But this was different. He felt put out by the untimely arrival of this unwanted invasion. Simon and bird, two entities adrift in a sea of whiteness several stories above street level. He began to wonder what the bird would be thinking, tried to investigate the space behind the small red dots that glared evilly through strange light. The bird, sensing imminent catastrophe, twisted its beakiness towards Simon in a gesture that spoke volumes. Two seconds later the creature took off, its tiny feet raising a mini whirlwind of snow that reminded Simon of the snow-storm-within-a-globe that sat collecting dust on a shelf in the living room. While large wings propelled the pigeon towards new adventure, Simon decided he'd been sitting outside for quite long enough. He stretched his back and thought of dinner.

It was 1988, becoming 1989, the disembodied week between Christmas and the New Year; the maddening, annoying, frustrating week; the week during which nobody really knew whether it was holiday time or work time, muddled confusion heightened by the all-enveloping layer of glistening snow. Alex stood looking out of the plate-glass window while Eve busily ironed some clothes; not one of her favourite occupations, although she didn't mind so much so long as there was music, inspirational music, heavy powerful music which seemed always to give added impetus to the movement of iron across fabric. Today, the chosen accompaniment was rock, loud rock, loud American rock played with passion, flair and technical ability. She had the ironing board assembled in its regular position behind the sofa so that the loudspeakers, set equidistant some eight feet or so from each other and from the front of the sofa, were ideally located to send the irresistible waves of music crashing straight towards her. Van Halen were asking the question *Why Can't This Be Love*, as they had for a couple of days, and Alex was playing air-guitar, as *he* had for a couple of days, when a stripy vision of flying fur launched itself into Alex's lazy line of sight. The animal landed with aplomb and marched purposefully towards the door.

'Do you suppose it's time to bring your pussy in from the cold?' Alex asked over his shoulder.

'Yes, definitely, he'll be frozen,' Eve answered with verisimilitude and without succumbing to the bait.

'No, he's alright, he's a US Navy Seal, trained to climb tall buildings and survive in silly temperatures.' Alex flipped the latch, opened the sliding door and stepped outside. It was cold, freezing cold. He shuddered as his bollocks shot upwards and relocated to the back of his throat for warmth and protection. 'Simon, get the fuck inside. Now.'

While the cat sat and went through the pros and cons of entering or not entering, Alex looked left and right and straight ahead at winter wonderland. It had been snowing almost without stop since Monday, and now, two days later, the city was at a virtual standstill, although on the street far below something was banging and clanking as though trying to tear itself to pieces. Intrigued, Alex stepped to the parapet and peered over. An unenlightened dribble of traffic had come to a halt, a dozen or so snow-clad vehicles lined up fore-and-aft with a rubbish-guzzling monster advancing in mechanical solemnity. It was four in the afternoon and dusk had mantled everything except the myriad patterns of light, radiating from offices seemingly suspended in the sky, which shone brilliantly through the icy air. Alex breathed deeply and coughed as the chilly intake of breath stung his lungs. 'C'mon cat, hurry it up,' he invoked the small tiger-type animal that with tail held high was wandering towards him.

Alex and cat entered the living room, and Alex, having quickly shut the door behind him, turned to look again at the magical scene etched against the dark sky. It was fantastic. He was certain there could be no other place on the planet with such a majestic skyline. Lights twinkled in a firmament of steel and glass, fabricated as though in some rectangular extension of the Christmas tree that stood just inside the wall of glass marking the boundary of Eve's apartment. They'd decorated it together, helped of course by Simon, who, having found the baubles and the tinsel irresistible, had calmly managed to break one of the fragile silver balls while playing a complex game of one-a-side football with Basile the household rabbit – stuffed, French, and overtly amiable. Eve had decided to keep it simple – silver baubles, silver tinsel and tiny white lights – there was enough colour out on the streets, where stores, shops and delicatessens were vibrantly resplendent in abundant representation of the festive season. Here, Alex thought, Christmas was Christmas, and now, with the added bonus of snow, the scene took on the long-forgotten aspect of amazement, forgotten since his days of dangling from apron strings.

He moved across the room and sat on the sofa, placing his feet solidly on the floor either side of Simon, who was importantly cleaning himself, and gazed distractedly at the panoramic vision of New York. The music, punctuated by an occasional angry hiss from the hard-working iron, prevented him from drifting into sleep, so he picked up a collection of photographs that lay balanced on a neighbouring arm of the sofa and began idly to flick through them. It was something he did often and he was therefore familiar with the subjects on display. The pictures, dozens of them, were before-and-after photographs of a series of seven paintings – pre Prentiss and post Prentiss – which had been lovingly restored by Terry, a picture-restoring colleague from London, who, in photo-graphing all the various stages of metamorphosis, had been meticulous in recording the transitions. It was amazing, Alex thought, the variety that made up the collection – an eclectic range of artists, most of whom were unknown to him. He'd heard of Vermeer, of course, but the others were a total mys-tery. However, inspired by snippets of knowledge gleaned from Terry, he'd done some homework regarding two or three of the pictures that he'd found to his taste. In particular, a sombre landscape by Emil Fila, and an equally sombre snowy scene by Friedrich, loaded with darkly mysterious fir trees, a stark crucifix and ghostly outlines of a Gothic church. As so often before, he shuffled the photos backwards and forwards, pausing every now and then to stare at a print already familiar.

'It's no good,' Eve said, coming to sit next to him, 'there's nothing you can do. *Fait accompli.*'

'I know,' Alex replied, looking at the pictures in his hands and wondering at their history, 'but there are still so many unanswered questions.'

'But do they need answering?'

'No, probably not, but it's . . . it's like walking along a country lane, you always want to know what's around the next corner.'

'Or behind the next hill, or beyond the horizon; or where do you go to when you get to the edge of the Universe?'

'Yes,' Alex agreed, full of admiration. 'Exactly.'

The question at the top of the list was why had these paintings come to America in the first place? Hidden away in a rambling New York mansion, a veritable depository owned by an enigmatic Mrs Carmichael, they'd been discovered in a roundabout sort of way following the death of a lawyer, Charley Meyer, who, it transpired, just happened to be Eve's grandfather. Documents found in his desk had sent one of his partners, George Michelstraub, overweight but cheerful and rather cuddly, on a mission from the company offices in upstate Binghamton to the dusty labyrinths of the Carmichael domicile, where he'd run straight into a problem. There were only six paintings. There should have been eight.

'Where are the others?' Michelstraub had asked, red faced and spluttering, surrounded by dishevelled dustsheets.

Mrs Carmichael, prim and proper, and her maid, whom Michelstraub eyed with deep suspicion, stood motionless. 'Where are they, then?' he shouted at the girl. 'Huh? Why don't you speak to me? What are you hiding?'

'If they're not here, Mr Michelstraub, they're not here,' Mrs Carmichael reasoned.

'No, no, they're here, they must be. Look,' he argued, stabbing an elderly sheet of paper with a wrinkled digit. 'Here . . . it says one, two, three . . .'

'Yes, yes,' Mrs Carmichael agreed, swinging an elegant pair of spectacles onto the front of her face, 'I can see what it says, eight paintings, but if they're not here, they're . . .'

'They must be, they have to be.'

They weren't. Despite his best efforts and those of the maid, Michelstraub was faced with a shortage. With the figure '8' burning large in his conscience he carefully inspected the gaudy paintings in front of him, and no matter how hard he pushed his imagination the total number of framed pictures remained steadfastly fixed at half-a-dozen. Out of breath and out of sorts, he fashioned the dustsheets into a soft landing place and proceeded to slump onto them. The maid was dispatched to brew some coffee and, while Mrs Carmichael sat on a chair and drummed four well-manicured fingernails, Michelstraub glared at the documentation and tried to draw inspiration from faded ancient print.

The coffee had arrived at the same time as his tired eyes had latched onto the word 'Europe'. The quick-witted solicitor blinked behind his glasses and treated his mind to an American-tourist-type excursion around foreign cities. Like a dandelion seed he followed an erratic course until he snagged himself on the horns of a dilemma. Realising that the collection had materialised in Europe, he persuaded his mind to construct visions of the missing paintings stranded somewhere in the cultural mist of the far-removed continent. He sipped coffee and crunched biscuits and came to hit upon the idea of using a native European, a sleuthy, crafty type of European; and, through a devious method of selection, succeeded in dragging Alex out of blissful ignorance.

The Atlantic had been crossed and re-crossed and the Londoner's ex, Jessica, who'd welcomed the homecoming hero with unbridled sex, had proceeded to mould herself onto the quest. The team had been formidable. Alex's enquiring journalistic mind, paired with Jessica's perfect psychological probings, had turned Europe upside down and the elusive paintings had been unearthed, almost accidentally, in an abandoned mansion in southern Germany.

The disc ground to a halt, Edward hung up his guitar – Alex's had melted into the land of wishful thinking as soon as he'd picked up the photos – and the silence became profound. Sensing some divine intervention, Simon jumped onto the sofa and sat on his haunches, upright, the classic Egyptian Cat God. They sat, the three of them staring through the window, each lost in thought – two humans, one God. It was snowing again and six eyes watched the flakes, drifting and dancing, obedient to the vague caprices of architectural-driven wind.

Alex pulled all the photos into some sort of cohesion and returned them to the arm of the sofa. 'It's funny, you know, when I think back to that goose-chase; the good times, the bad times, the euphoria when the paintings were found and the surprise that they turned out to be.'

'Why funny?' Eve asked. 'Surprising, yes, I can understand; even amazing, perhaps. But now it's all under control, the photos tell the story and George is over the moon with his prize possessions.'

'I know, I know, but there has to be more, there must be some sort of meaning behind the collection.'

'Well, perhaps there is, or rather, was. It was a long time ago, you know, that these paintings were brought together . . .'

'Mmm . . . General von Über Alles of the Third Reich.'

'Exactly, and he must be long since gone! End of story,

no connecting threads. *Finito.*' Eve got up, stalked into the kitchen and collected a couple of bottles of Corona from the fridge. She opened them and brought them back to the sofa, where she sat on curled-up legs and leaned against Alex.

'But . . . but why?'

'Vhy vhat?' Eve raised the bottle to her lips and sucked at pale nectar.

Alex smiled at the woman's ability to keep up with the circular meanderings of his mind. 'Why did he send them here?'

'He didn't, remember? He sent them to Argentina. At least, that's what you told me.'

'Yes, and the ship was sunk and everything with it. But still, the pictures ended up here. It's weird, mysterious . . .'

'It's your journalistic curiosity, the desire to bag everything into neat little parcels, all the boxes ticked.'

'Maybe, maybe, but that was more Jessica's department.'

'Ah, yes, Jessica's well-organised mind, the ever-ready oracle.'

And it had been Jessica's idea to visit London's National Gallery. It had been a good idea, a productive one which had yielded the golden egg – a letter written by the high-ranking general – that had transported them to Bavaria and the defunct kindergarten that in an earlier existence had been the general's home. The outcome, however, had been the result of luck rather than sophisticated detective work. It was an expedition that had been laced with conundrums and suspicions, an uneven pathway that had led eventually to magnitudes of heartbreak.

Having found the two missing paintings in a dark dusty vault beneath the mansion, the mystery had deepened. Prised open, Pandora's box had revealed Rembrandt nestling in the company of a saucily erotic Prentiss. The discovery had sent Jessica's mind on a voyage of supposition and gave cause for Alex to begin wondering at the relevance of the name 'Prentiss'. Jessica's hypothesis, revolving around red herrings, was proved correct when Terry, the specialist, revealed Vermeer lurking beneath the iffy *Prentiss Pose*, as the paintings had come to be labelled.

Whilst Jessica had stalked off with Vermeer under her arm, the Rembrandt had been transported to Binghamton and reunited with Michelstraub's dodgy collection. Terry, likewise, had been transported to the lawyer's offices, where he'd revealed the true identities of the remaining *Prentiss Poses*. The collection that somehow had wound up in New York suddenly became infinitely more important than anyone had imagined.

Frustratingly surrounded by uncertainty as to their origin, Alex once again found himself in a state of limbo. 'There has to be a link,' he stated. 'There . . . Well, shit, there just has to be.'

And then the phone rang, startling the comatose watchers of hectic flurries. Eve left the sofa at the same time as the cat. They went in different directions, the four-legged feline slinking towards the kitchen to inspect his food bowl, Eve circling behind the sofa to collect the phone from its home on the bookshelves. 'Yes?' She was straightforward. 'Oh, George.' She looked at Alex, questioningly, as if she thought the call would be for him. It was.

'George?' Alex asked, hesitatingly; then, mellowing, 'How are you?'

Simon marched back into the living room, disgruntled,

tail swishing menacingly through disinterested air.

'I thought he'd finished?' Alex queried. A pause, then, 'Oh? Really?'

Eve walked through the room in the direction of the kitchen with Simon, performing a Thatcher-type turn, hot on her heels. Hearing the metallic sound of a can being opened, Alex smiled at the receiver while Michelstraub rumbled on.

2

The meal was simple, the candles made it special: cold chicken and salad with baked potatoes and a bottle of Chenin Blanc, ice cold. The fowl had done them well and, four days after Christmas, there were still the drumsticks to contend with. At home in her kitchen, Eve always manages to rustle up the most amazing meals from whatever she finds in the fridge, and, Alex was quick to realise, with never a tantrum in sight.

Eve placed her knife and fork on her empty plate, wiped her mouth with a napkin and arched her brows, quizzically.

'It goes on,' Alex responded to silent interrogation.

'The chicken?'

Alex chuckled. 'No, the mystery.'

They ferried the plates and empty dishes into the kitchen and Alex ran some hot water into the sink. He always made a point of washing up immediately after a meal, a trick he'd learned through trial and error, mostly error, and a small degree of laziness, when he'd discovered it was much easier to clean everything before the remains had a chance to congeal into stubborn resistance. He lowered the plates into the hot soapy water and while he brushed them clean and stacked them on the draining board, he outlined the facts that George Michelstraub had told him.

'It's amazing!' he exclaimed. 'There they were, the seven paintings, all lined up side by side, all of them in pristine condition, restored to their former glory.'

'And?'

'Well, just imagine. Terry had gone over those paintings in minute detail, patiently swabbing away with his cotton buds, examining each carefully executed stroke as the *Prentiss Poses*, layer by layer, gradually revealed their inner secrets.'

He paused, lost in thought, hands submerged in murky water, one holding a plate, the other gripping a sudsy brush. Eve stood behind him and put her arms around his waist. 'Come on, hon,' she said, 'finish the dishes and then you can concentrate on what you're trying to tell me.'

'Hmm,' Alex muttered, sloshing water over the plate and setting it to one side before groping about at the bottom of the sink, trying to locate items of crafty cutlery lurking in the depths.

Eve collected the cat's bowl from Simon's eatery beside the fridge-freezer. 'Give that a rinse,' she said, placing the empty bowl at the edge of the sink, 'but only after you've done everything else.'

'Yeah, I know,' Alex commented, 'your hatred of cross-contamination. Yuk, humans and animals.'

Eve looked at him. 'Well, you know . . .'

'It's okay, honey, me too,' Alex quickly agreed. 'I mean it's not exactly hygienic, is it?'

Simon stopped cleaning his paws, looked up at his flat-mates and wondered what all the fuss was about. Inspecting the place where his bowl had been and satisfying himself that it hadn't actually returned, he placidly continued his pedicure.

'*Für Elise*,' Alex stated as they returned to the comfort of the sofa.

'*Für Elise?*' Eve asked.

'Mmm,' Alex confirmed. 'Beethoven. Isn't it?'

'Beethoven it is,' Eve answered.

'And two letters, initials,' Alex added. 'K. M., written in ink on the back of one of the wooden frames.'

'K. M.?' Eve asked. 'What's K. M.?'

'No idea.'

'So that's that, then, no further forward.'

'No.' Alex took a gulp of wine. 'But . . . Bugger, the documents that galvanised George onto the picture trail in the first place were found in your grandfather's desk.'

'Charley, yes, of course, and his name was Meyer. Maybe he's connected to the "M"?'

'Yeah, maybe, but then we're stuck with the "K". And why *Für Elise?*'

'You know, your ex would be the perfect person for all this.'

'Jessica?' Alex asked.

'Yes, Jessica; of course Jessica. She was pretty analytical, wasn't she? I mean, from everything you've told me she'd love to get her teeth into something like this. You know, sorting out the pictures and what to do with them?'

'Yeah, you're right,' Alex grinned, 'but perhaps not so much the 'ytical'. She was very matter-of-fact, dogmatic to the point of being obsessive about pigeon holes and what goes into them.' He fell into a reverie regarding the woman's organisational skills, her ability to be always one step ahead of everyone else; and then he remembered her fuse, short and fiery. Theirs had been one of those strange relationships, strong on the inside and strong on the outside, yet loaded with dangerous unknowns. Both had been mulish from the outset, but it had been an accepted state of affairs and any contretemps had been swept aside by an unfailing sense of humour. The European project, founded and funded by George Michelstraub, had pulled them together, Jessica having been the driving force behind the unveiling of the truth. She'd also been the unremitting wedge that had split the relationship, laying it open to writhe about in unhappy complexity like a worm that suddenly finds itself in two pieces.

Alex had weathered a roller-coaster ride of emotions, a performance witnessed and modified by his allies from Manhattan, Mandie and Dan, the samaritans who'd listened when Alex had ranted and were supportive when he'd raved, teetering on the precipice of a ragged horizon. While he'd zigzagged to and fro across troubled waters, a silver lining, bursting forth from behind successive layers of grey, had directed him to roost in Queens – an English alien in the lives of Eve and Simon.

'I have to talk with Michelstraub,' he stated.

'No you don't.'

'I do, I do, he's the cause of all this . . . uncertainty.'

'There isn't any uncertainty, it's a done deal. Anyway, if you feel you have to talk with someone you'd do better talking to Mrs Carmichael. I think there's more to her than meets the eye.'

'That's true, there's something lurking behind that woman's poise. I seem to remember it was as though she was challenging me to ask penetrating questions.'

'So why didn't you?'

'Aw, honey, I was dead-beat. It was my first visit to this crazy city and I'd only been here for twenty-four hours and she was kind of haughty, you know? Like a politician thinking himself above humanity.'

'That bad?'

'No, perhaps not, but it was a strange situation. Also, I didn't know then what I know now.'

'And what do you know now?' Eve taunted, aided by a wide grin.

'Less,' Alex answered truthfully. 'Really, it's like mankind setting foot on the Moon and then doing nothing about it. A footprint, a flag, a heap of scrap metal, and intriguing boundaries loaded with endless possibility which no one bothered to cultivate.'

'So, sweetheart, this has to be your New Year's resolution. Go talk to the lady who may be the central cog.'

The next day, braving sub-zero streets and over-heated stores, Eve went shopping, happily gathering bits and pieces from favourite haunts including a little-known Italian deli, dangerously located only two-blocks from the apartment.

Alex spent the time mooching, and discovered an unopened pack of cigarettes. Wedged into deep security between a cushion and one side of the sofa, it hadn't really been hidden, more sort of lost or mislaid, having slid inadvertently into darkness. He paced around the room holding the packet in his hands as though it had some magical power, some life-force all its own that would connect to a logical explanation. He added up the weeks: five, five weeks and a couple of days and no hint of a cigarette, no whiff of smoke and no nasty stale odours emanating from warp or weft.

The door opened and Eve breezed into the living room wearing an aura of freshness and a wide grin above an arm-load of flowers. Alex came to a halt in his peregrinations around the sofa and, Montezuma-like, held out the cigarette packet in overblown greeting to the unknown.

'Shit, where'd you find that?' the healthy apparition enquired.

'In the folds of the sofa.'

'God, it must've been there for years.' Eve draped her coat over the back of the sofa and transported the flowers towards the kitchen and resuscitation under the tap.

'But you don't smoke,' Alex stated, sort of avoiding a direct question.

'I don't,' Eve agreed over the sound of running water.

'Then, who does?' Alex asked, realising a question was necessary.

'No one,' Eve giggled as she returned to the living room. 'But I used to, briefly, several years ago.'

'Ah, you never told me.'

'It never came up in conversation, honey, and like I said, it was a long time ago. I was pregnant.'

'Pregnant?' Fearing some sort of contamination, Alex hastily deposited the cigarettes onto a table.

'Yes, pregnant, or . . . how do they say it in English? "With child".' Eve smiled sweetly.

'Pregnant?' Alex's mind was stuck in a valley of nappies and baby food. 'But you're not s'posed to smoke when you're . . . pregnant.'

'This was afterwards when I realised I wasn't. Some sort

of strange reaction kicked in, I stopped eating food and started to smoke.'

'Well, that at least explains why you're so slender,' Alex said, placing his arms around Eve's body. He leaned his head against hers and inhaled the frost still captured in the long dark hair.

3

During the intervening days between Christmas and New Year's Eve the temperature refused to budge, obstinately remaining several degrees below zero. However, this didn't deter Alex and Eve from making daily excursions through the frozen city. They'd stormed 5th Avenue, almost from one end to the other, visiting Mark Twain's House, the Frick Collection and the Guggenheim. They'd also carved invisible lines through the gelid air during a frenetic thirty minutes of Frisbee-throwing in Central Park. Each expedition had been aided and somewhat abetted by frequent halts at hot dog-selling kiosks. The week slid rapidly through a squelchiness of love and affection. Alex was beside himself with happiness, his star was on the ascendant and his soul tingled with delight in receipt of all the attention bestowed upon it by an equally rapturous Eve.

All of a sudden it was Old Year's Night, and eight o'clock found them stamping on impacted snow and ice at the top of a Manhattan stoop. Alex, housed in a well-padded navy blue parka – a Christmas present from Eve – and an excessively long light-grey scarf wrapped three or four times around his neck, exhaled large volumes of white vapour into the frigid atmosphere. Eve, also wearing a parka, arctic white, and with her neck encased in a similarly long scarf, only of a different colour – some strange hue between red and maroon – smiled in sweet anticipation. Laden with enormous paper carrier bags, clinking and clanking in glorious rhythm with the stamping feet, the pair resembled a couple of Eskimos returning from a serious visit to a supermarket.

With a chunky mitten, Eve pressed the buzzer and the door opened almost immediately. Warmth and light gushed around the familiar form of a radiant Mandie and spilled out onto the snowy scene.

'Happy New Year's Eve,' she announced, arms spread in wide welcome, her face creased with customary smile.

Eve and Alex stumbled across the threshold and Mandie closed the door behind them.

'What on earth have you got there?' she asked, staring at the bags that were being deposited onto the floor.

'Supplies,' Alex answered, unwinding his scarf as Mandie bent forwards to pick up a couple of the carriers. 'Careful,' he warned, 'the contents are fragile.'

Divested of their outer layers, Alex and Eve collected the remaining bags and followed Mandie into the kitchen, where they received joyous bear hugs from Mandie's partner, Dan, who then thrust glasses of steaming mulled wine into their cold hands.

'We started already,' Dan stated unnecessarily, turning to pick up his half-empty glass. Holding it by the foot of the stem he raised it towards the newcomers, 'Happy New Year's Eve,' he announced, before asking, 'Hey, honey, where'd those baby sausages get to?'

'Here,' Mandie answered, handing him a dish piled high with skewered food, 'take it through to the lounge.' With a smile at Alex and Eve she said, 'Come on you two, people to meet.'

The atmosphere sparkled with seasonal gaiety. In the window stood a giant Christmas tree, pinprick blue lights enhancing its sharp green needles, some of which had been selected to support threads of silver tinsel. An assortment of burning candles occupied an assortment of locations, the accumulated brilliance enough to spread golden lustre in all directions. Alex stood in dumfounded amazement as he quickly realised that he'd stepped into a gathering of all his friends from the New World.

George Michelstraub, fat and jolly, embraced Eve, using his left arm to pull her slender form against his generous girth, while his right hand located and shook Alex's right hand for all it was worth. 'Hey,' he said, 'hey.'

Alex smiled at the lawyer's lack of vocabulary, recalling with something approaching affection the contrasting verbiosity of previous meetings.

'Hey,' said another voice. 'Hey, Alex!'

Alex turned. 'Bry!' he exclaimed, untangling himself from Michelstraub's grasp and stepping across to shake hands with Dan's buddy from the force. 'Good to see you.'

'Yeah, and this is my lady,' Bry grinned, placing an arm behind an attractive brunette. 'Penny,' he said, introducing his partner, 'but you can call her Pen.'

Alex suppressed a smirk, recalling his ex's distaste for shortened names. Hmm, he thought, she'd have had a field day.

'This is the guy from London,' Bry explained to the dark-haired woman at his side. 'I met him last year and we went eating crawfish.'

'You did?' Penny exclaimed, somewhat surprised.

'Yeah, we all did,' Bry expounded, sweeping an arm in a giant circle to include most everyone present. 'In the snow.'

Dan and Mandie and Eve had disappeared, but soon returned carrying dishes and plates laden with tempting morsels.

'Didn't we?' Bry asked Dan. 'In the snow?'

'On the Island,' Dan explained a little more succinctly, 'by the boardwalk, you know, in that great seafood restaurant? Alex had just arrived at JFK and needed cheering up.'

'Yes,' Alex agreed, 'I did, and it was a great reception.'

'Hey, we're renowned for our hospitality,' Dan chuckled.

'Hey you guys, you brought champagne?' Mandie questioned Alex and Eve.

'Of course, it's New Year's Eve,' Alex explained.

'Yes, it is,' Mandie agreed, laughing, 'and we've got champagne coming out of our ears.'

'And,' Eve added, 'it's Alex's first New Year New York style, so we thought we'd bring some more.'

As the evening coiled itself towards midnight, the conversation, which had been drifting backwards and forwards over a plethora of subjects including the treacherous act of planting a bomb on board a Pan Am jet, turned towards Michelstraub.

'George?' Alex asked. 'You didn't bring a partner with you?'

'Will that be a statement or are you asking?' Michelstraub countered, ever the lawyer.

'One very rarely sees him with a woman on his arm,' Mandie revealed, 'although there is a reputation following him around that he's quite a ladies' man.'

Alcohol consumed during the evening had already caused Michelstraub's face to lean towards the colour purple, and Mandie's statement, as well as deepening the rich hue, caused the man to smile.

'Yes,' he chortled, 'I do like female company. And luckily, it seems to like me.'

'It's the *bon vivant* aspect they relish,' Dan opined.

'Mmm,' Mandie added, 'that, and his sagacity.'

'So, George?' Alex asked. 'Has your sagacity shed any light on the inscription you found?'

'Wasn't actually me who found it,' Michelstraub answered, 'it was Terry's discovery. Having finished the task of removing the layers of pigmentation that covered the originals, he'd begun to clear his work area.' Michelstraub paused to take a gulp of stone-cold mulled-wine and looked over the rim of the glass to make sure his audience was hanging on his every word. He swallowed. 'Whilst leaning the paintings against the wall, face-in to protect them from excessive daylight, he bent down to pick up a stray cotton-bud and the writing just happened to converge with his line of vision.'

'*Für Elise*,' Eve said. 'And K.M.'

'Yup,' Michelstraub affirmed.

'Any ideas?' Alex asked.

'Apart from a piece of music by Beethoven? No.'

'And the initials?'

'Well, no,' Michelstraub answered.

'We think they could be my grandfather's,' Eve suggested.

'Really?' Michelstraub asked. 'I can understand there might

be a connection to the name Meyer, but your . . .'

'What makes you think it's Beethoven?' Penny cut in across the table, causing everyone to look in her direction.

'It's a piece of music, honey . . .'

'I know, I know,' Penny acknowledged, looking at her partner.

'Well . . ?' Bry pushed at the envelope.

'It might be a name . . .' Penny suggested.

'It is a name!' Mandie exclaimed, laughing.

'Yes, but it might be a name referring to a person. This man, Eve's grandfather?' Penny paused, looking up for confirmation as Eve and Alex nodded in tandem. 'Well, maybe he had this particular painting earmarked for a client, or a colleague . . . Or a friend?' She looked at each of the faces gathered round her and grinned in the silence that accompanied the digestion of this riveting piece of information.

'Penny,' Alex stated, being the first to recover, 'you're a genius, complete and utter.'

'I am?' Penny asked, slightly embarrassed at Alex's endorsement, slightly embarrassed that he'd called her by her full name.

'She's *my* genius,' Bry announced, laughing. 'Dan, if she were working with us, we'd have to promote her.'

'If it were up to me,' said Dan, 'I . . .'

'Who?' Eve asked.

'What who?' Alex questioned her.

'No, which who?' Eve continued her line of enquiry. 'Elise who?'

'Hmm,' Michelstraub mumbled, attacking a plate of cold roast beef, 'there's the rub. Beethoven, or some mysterious woman?' He dolloped some horseradish sauce onto his plate and the clock started to chime midnight.

'The appointed hour,' Mandie stated.

'The anointed hour,' Dan added jovially, opening a bottle of Clicquot. The cork crashed into the ceiling on the twelfth stroke while, despite every effort of thick double glazing, muffled sounds of multitudinous fireworks could be heard as the Big Apple flexed its celebratory muscle.

Alex found himself the centre of attention as Eve and Mandie planted kisses on either side of his face and congratulated him on his first New Year's celebration in New York.

Michelstraub, unwinding himself from his position of placid seniority, ambled over to grasp Alex firmly by the hand. 'Happy New Year, Alex,' he said. 'Here's to moving onward and upward.'

A little unsure of the meaning behind the remark, Alex grinned inanely and shuffled his feet.

Dan, meanwhile, had finished pouring the champagne and everyone took a glass, raised it shoulder high and looked at Mandie, expectantly.

'Out with the old, in with the new,' she said, and smiled radiantly as Dan moved behind her and put one of his arms about her waist. He kissed her on her neck and whispered something that caused her to giggle.

Bry and Penny were wrapped in a tight embrace and Eve had both arms clasped round Alex's neck, while Alex was astonished to realise he was still holding on to one of Michelstraub's hands. No one was left out of the equation, everyone an equal: friends, relations and lovers united in the age-old act of initiating the birth of another year. And then there came the sound of the doorbell, furious and insistent. The seven celebrants unlocked themselves from intimate embraces and froze in shocked uncertainty.

'Who are we expecting?' Mandie asked the assembled tableau.

Startled expressions volunteered no answer.

'I'll go,' said Dan, walking stoically towards the door, 'it could be Sol. Told him he'd be mighty welcome if he happened to be free.'

The door was hauled open and, sure enough, there he stood, Sol, big, black and happy, clutching a guitar case. 'Hey everybody, what's up?' His smile was wide and infectious and had the effect of starting the party all over again.

'Happy New Year, Sol,' Mandie greeted the newcomer, leading him towards food and drink. 'What'll it be? We're onto champagne, but I think there's just about everything else.'

'Yeah? I'll have a beer then, a Mexican one with my name on it.' He grinned hugely and plonked himself solidly onto a wooden rocking chair, which squeaked with surprise and stalled on its backward swing. Placing the guitar case onto the floor beside him, he took a moment to tune into the occupants of the room. 'Hey, the traveller from England,' he said, acknowledging Alex and leaning forwards as if to leave his chair until, deciding against the effort, he allowed the curved bearers to resume their enforced attitude of rest. Sol's job as a security guard, first at the docks and more recently at J.F.K., had sharpened his acumen at people recognition. Beaming at the man who had the appearance of a lawyer, the man who was demolishing layers of sliced meat, he said, 'I know you, from the airport.'

Michelstraub tore his eyes from the wealth of food stacked on his plate and smiled at the newcomer. 'You do?'

'Sure I do. You were there to greet Alex, last time he flew

30

in from the UK.'

'Actually, Sol,' Alex broke in, 'I've been backwards and forwards several times since then, but you're right, George was at the airport on one of those occasions.'

'Too right he was,' Sol nodded, happily receiving a bottled beer from Mandie and raising it in general approval. 'So, here you stay?'

'Here he stays,' Eve responded, fluttering her eyelids at the foreigner from London.

'Yeah, looks like it,' Alex concurred, putting his arms around Eve.

Mandie, busily occupied in lines of communication to and from the kitchen, drifted into focus and lowered a heaped plate onto Sol's lap. 'You got some catching up to do,' she told him, 'but don't worry, there's plenty left.'

'So, who are you?' Sol asked Bry, directing the question around a mouthful of cold chicken on rye.

'Bry,' said Bry. 'I work with Dan, and this here's Pen.'

'So you're another detective?'

'In the making, so to speak,' Bry answered. 'Another coupla years.'

'We're safe, then,' Sol announced, 'surrounded by the force.'

'Sol!' Mandie exclaimed. 'Stop talking and eat.'

'Yeah, yeah,' Sol retorted, 'I'm just enjoying myself. So now I know who we all are, maybe I'll concentrate on the food.' Hoisting his half-empty bottle, he asked, 'And can I get me another of these?'

'Comin' up,' Mandie said, turning towards the kitchen, the fridge, and a life's supply of Mexican beer.

With a half-demolished pastrami sandwich on the plate in front of him, Sol flipped open the case and extracted a honey-coloured six-string guitar. 'Thought I'd play a little soul,' he said, 'you know, to welcome the New Year?' Striking a few harmonics, he quicky tuned the instrument and launched into a funky rendition of *Stand By Me*. 'You can join in,' he announced over the twanging strings, '. . . if you want. Help me along kinda thing.' He grinned at the assembled company, all of whom appeared startled that anyone should think they could sing. The shared embarrassment quickly evaporated when Sol's voice lifted above the easy chords: it was evident that the maestro required little help from an untrained chorus. Effortlessly his rich voice hit all the notes, the high ones as well as the low ones, and he ran through a repertoire of classic numbers. Time stretched through a montage of thoughts and imaginations, observations of the past and aspirations for the future, as the gathering savoured the textures of a newly born year. Between each song, while grinning at splatters of eager applause, Sol relaxed with his friends, joining in with the various topics of conversation, laughing at merry memories and splashing his vocal chords with ample helpings of beer.

'Do you know that song from *The Music Man*?' Alex enquired during one such break. 'You know, um, what's it called? Shit.' He rubbed a hand across his face, trying to remember.

'Tell me what it's called and I'll play it.'

'It's, um . . . the Beatles covered it, years ago.'

Sol started playing some notes, a pair of dreamy triplets. 'You mean this?'

'Yeah, great, that's the one.'

'Nope.' Sol ceased to play and grinned widely. 'Never heard of it.'

It transpired that Sol did indeed know the ballad and he proceeded to air it in his own soulified version, dusky tones lending heartfelt depth to the words, the six metal strings accentuating the simplicity of the song. 'S'pose that'll be for your beautiful young lady, then?' he surmised, setting the guitar to one side.

'Too right,' Alex enthused. 'Beautiful lady, beautiful song.'

'Yeah, they don't write 'em like that anymore. But, hey, who cares when there's such a rich collection to pick from?' Sol reached for another sandwich and dragged it onto his plate. He was happy and in his element. 'Say, anyone else care to play?'

Alex thought about producing a rendition of an old Dylan song to which he knew the chords. His technique rusty and his vocal ability poor, the thought was short-lived. Dan, however, came to the rescue with an hilarious version of *The Streets of Laredo*. With an occasional incorrect chord and substituted lyrics, the performance, with everyone joining in, fell to pieces as raucous laughter filled the room. This was the true spirit of Christmas, the joy and vivacity of shared moments and happy experiences.

Dan handed the guitar back to Sol and set to work opening another couple of bottles of bubbly. Mandie, meanwhile, disappeared on another of her forays into the kitchen, reappearing a few moments later with a dishful of something on fire.

'Come on,' she said, eyes full of mirth and glad tidings, 'everyone grab a plate.' Setting the burning dish onto the coffee table, she announced, 'We have pudding!'

'Pudding?' Sol asked.

'Christmas pudding,' Mandie explained. 'It's an English invention. Alex and Eve brought it with them and it's been cooking for hours.'

4

A couple of hours later, Alex went flying, arms and legs akimbo.

Before leaving Dan and Mandie's home they'd tried to order a cab. However, being New Year's Eve, it had been impossible to get through to any of the companies on the list. After the sixth or seventh failed attempt, Eve had suggested walking. 'It's not far,' she'd said, 'just over the river. Shouldn't take more than thirty minutes.'

'Mmm,' Alex had readily agreed, 'a quick sniff at fresh air, might be good for us and maybe it'll clear our heads.'

Having said their goodbyes and successfully negotiated the steep steps down to street level, they'd encountered a section of sidewalk that was little more than a sheet of ice. Although alcohol hadn't helped his sense of balance, it did enable Alex to see the funny side of being flat on his back on a New York City sidewalk. Eve, once she got over her initial alarm, also burst into laughter, and as she struggled to help Alex to his feet the street echoed to the sounds of merriment. Clinging to one another for support, they staggered away towards Eve's apartment in Queens.

As they approached the river, the going became a little easier. The sidewalk had been cleared and they found themselves walking between three-foot mounds of piled-up snow.

'Um, I seem to recall that Mrs. Carmichael lives somewhere round here, doesn't she?' Alex asked.

'Yep, two or three blocks away,' Eve confirmed. 'Why?'

'We need to pay her a visit, remember?'

'We? You.'

'Yes, okay, me.'

'You and your never-ending curiosity.'

'Well . . . I've just remembered something else.'

'Hmm, must've been the fall.'

'No, it's serious, it's something George said, I think during my first meeting with him.'

'What? What serious thing did George say?'

'Well, I'm sure he referred to Mrs. Carmichael as Ellie.'

'And?' Eve queried. 'This'll be going somewhere?'

'Maybe,' Alex replied enigmatically. 'Maybe.'

They walked on in silence, holding hands and looking at the lights across the water. It began to snow and from somewhere the sound of a car began to make itself audible. Strangely, it was the first vehicle they'd encountered since leaving the party, and, instinctively, Alex put his arm around Eve's waist. They stopped walking and watched the automobile as it manoeuvred slowly along the slippery street. When it drew level, the car came to a halt, its windows were opened and the occupants cheered and shouted and sang '*Auld lang syne*.' They were all waving balloons and streamers and Alex noticed that the driver had a kazoo stuck in his mouth at which he was blowing furiously, its sound nasally strident above the noise of the engine. He watched, fascinated, as the rolled-up paper attached to the kazoo extended itself towards the windscreen, the feathered tip brushing against the laminated glass, and then, when the driver momentarily stopped blowing, the whole thing zipped backwards, rolling itself up in the blink of an eye.

Eve and Alex grinned stupidly and waved at the revellers. It was a scene borrowed from a fairground or a circus, slightly bizarre, slightly surreal, an episode played out against the winter backdrop of snow and ice. Strangers in a strange world, engaged in some sort of ritualistic interplay, caught in the frozen hours between one year's dying embers and the uncertain birth pangs of the next.

The people in the car began hauling their festive banners into the interior and the driver eased the vehicle forwards. One of the balloons broke free and hovered undecidedly in space, and as the car slowly pulled ahead, Eve disentangled herself from Alex's arm and went to retrieve the gently spinning globe. Crouching and lifting one leg after the other, she clambered through the protective railing that was positioned at the edge of the sidewalk. Sudden headlights illuminated her face and the world became full of sound – the scream of a racing engine and the scraping of a solid object across ice. Veering out of control, a second car, screeching out of nowhere, snagged Eve on a wing mirror and smacked sideways into the railing, slithering along it for several yards. A flailing foot became caught on an upright stanchion, but not for long. Attached and unacceptably part of the vehicle, Eve's body was dragged along the railing, her feet, ankles and legs twisting at impossible angles, her back flexing grotesquely against the steel bar. An eternity later, the car came to a halt and the silence was profound.

One second, two seconds, that's all it took; in slow motion or in real time there was no difference. One moment Eve was standing on the road trying to catch a balloon, the next, she'd been pinned like a butterfly to the railing. As in one of those horror movies set in a funfair, everything lurched in dizzy disarray, a world of make believe, unreal and frightening. Alex blinked, and the tumult of madness dissolved. Across the street a door opened and a figure became silhouetted against escaping light.

'Help!' Alex yelled. 'Fucking help!'

The figure moved back into the house and the door slammed shut.

'*Jesusfucking Chris*t,' Alex yelled as he lunged towards Eve. She wasn't going anywhere. Wedged like an ornament between car and railing, her head hanging down above the car's roof and her left hand vaguely holding the upper section of a radio antenna as though for additional support, she was immobile. Alex removed his coat and placed it as best he could over her shoulders. Strange noises started leaching into the silence, amongst them the sound of steam hissing angrily around broken gaskets; and pieces of hot metal, realising they were no longer functioning, began a creaky lament in the frozen air. Before Alex had time to work out his next move, the door re-opened and the figure re-appeared, running this time, running across the street.

'An ambulance is on its way,' the stranger called out. 'Is she conscious?'

'No, no way! Fuck me!'

'Okay, okay,' the man replied. He was carrying a thick blanket, which he draped over Eve's shoulders already covered by Alex's coat. 'Can you hear me?' he asked the pinioned woman.

' 'Course she fucking can't,' Alex screamed, waving his arms in despair.

'Okay, okay,' the man said, 'we have to try. Can you hear me?' he repeated, more loudly.

Another door opened, this time on the same side of the street as the accident, and more light spilled onto the tableau. Then another door opened, and another, and people began to emerge warily from the safety of their homes.

'Where the fuck's that ambulance?' Alex asked, unaware of the passage of time and oblivious to the fact that no more than thirty or forty seconds had elapsed. 'Fuck,' he said, stamping his feet with impatience.

People stood and stared, six of them, maybe eight. One or two were a little unsteady on their feet, a consequence of seasonal celebrations, festivities so rudely interrupted by this uncalled-for, impromptu performance. Someone, a woman, having deduced that Alex was the victim's partner, pressed a glass of brandy into his hands. 'Right now, that's what you need,' she told him.

'I do?' he asked in bewilderment, nonetheless raising the glass to his lips.

'Yes.' The answer was vehement and left no doubt.

Alex looked up to the skies and noticed a snowflake descending towards him. He watched as it fluttered lazily through the air, then something else caught his eye, the balloon. He found himself staring at it and saw that it was coloured blue and that it was suspended almost exactly above Eve, as though keeping some sort of vigil over her body. They were trapped, both of them, one stuck between snowy wooden branches, the other, gripped in a steel embrace. He looked at the car, dented and ugly, and wondered about the occupants. There was no movement and, save for an occasional musical '*ping*' of protesting metal, there was no sound from within the useless mass of stalled conveyance.

Chapter Two:

Down

1

'There's nothing you can do,' he was told.

Alex looked at the inert body on the bed and wondered at the statement. Could it be true?

'There's nothing anyone can do,' one of the nurses added, while making adjustments to some tricky-looking piece of equipment.

Tubes and cables wound themselves indecently around Eve's body, modern technology connecting patient to computer and causing little green blobs to slide across a flickering screen. Alex shook his head and tried to clear his mind. He was still in shock, still having a problem coming to terms with reality. 'There are more tubes here than beneath the whole of London,' he mumbled, panicking and wondering at the scene before him.

Crammed into the small cubicle the medical staff looked up at the stranger in their midst, doubt on their faces. 'It's a matter of time, we just have to wait,' a doctor informed him, ignoring or perhaps not understanding Alex's odd comment. 'She has a couple of broken ribs, a broken wrist, and a small but worrying fracture to the skull. There could be brain damage. But we won't know until she wakes up.'

Brain damage? Finally, someone knowledgeable, someone who appeared to be in control of the situation, someone who seemed to be in charge; and Alex clung to the words as if Eve's life depended on them. Then, with the doctor's statement smacking into the anvil, reality slammed home. Brain damage? Fuck! The concept brought him back to earth with a bang. Suddenly he was aware of noise, the clamour of the busy ER – electronic beeping from an array of life-supporting machinery, air being viciously sucked into greedy ventilators; and voices, professionally subdued yet urgent. From everywhere came strange metallic sounds, annoying and impossible to identify, while close at hand the gentle rustle of clothing became the roar of an earthquake as frantic workers swarmed around the cocooned queen. It was bedlam, it was traumatic, and with everything spinning in time-honoured bewilderment, Alex slowly became conscious of another sound, a steady rhythmic beat with a heavy thump. His heart was still trying to keep pace with the rush of adrenaline that had been sustaining him since the drama unfolded, twenty, thirty minutes ago. Brain damage?

'Okay. Right,' he muttered, noticing the medics, a team of five or six people kitted out in green tunics and bending over Eve's body like a series of welder-robots on an automatic assembly line. He looked again at the mass of tubes, clueless as to what any of them were for, although some dim memory informed him that one of the pipes would be administering a saline drip. He had no idea why, it was a mystery, some random piece of knowledge that had probably communicated itself to him from a long-forgotten television drama.

Someone was coming towards him, taking hold of his

arm and turning him away, walking him like some appre-
hended prisoner along a succession of sterile shiny corridors.
Bright lights in the ceiling were reflected in the highly polished
surface of the floor, however they weren't quite bright enough
to overpower the yellow line that Alex and his guide seemed
to be following. He began to wonder about the Wizard of
Oz, but then, suddenly, the line slid beneath a swing door and
deposited them in a yellow room.

'Wait here,' said the orderly, pleasantly yet firmly.

He sat on a plastic chair and watched the man confront a
unit made of shiny stainless steel, a cabinet which seemed to
do nothing. But no, the machine came alive and began filling a
plastic cup with something that resembled coffee. He watched
as the man emptied four sachets of sugar into the black liquid.
He watched and listened to the rasping of a plastic spoon as
it was twirled to and fro, back and forth against the ribbed
container.

'Drink this and wait,' the orderly directed, passing him
the cup of hot, sweet coffee. 'Someone will be along in a
moment.'

Alex sat, sipped and waited, staring nervously straight
ahead of him. It was quiet here, and peaceful, the only sound
coming from a wall-mounted clock. Ten minutes past four.
He remembered it was New Year's Day, which meant . . .
Christ, last night had been New Year's Eve and they'd been
. . . Where had they been? He scraped his fingernails against
the ridges of the warm cup and stared at the clock. Ah, slowly,
slowly, the long pointer moved from dot to dot and time
became relevant . . . They'd been celebrating with Dan and
Mandie . . . and . . . He shivered and drank some more coffee.
The door swung back on its hinges and a voice said, 'Alex.' He

looked up and the room was full of Dan. But . . . Dan? How, Dan? What was he doing here?

'What are you doing here?' Alex asked, his speech catching up with his thoughts.

Dan hastened across the room, hauled Alex out of his chair and gave him a bear hug.

'Ouff,' Alex exhaled, and from the corner of one eye he watched coffee fountain out of his inadvertently-squidged cup and onto the floor. He felt weak, he felt nauseous. He sat.

Dan pulled a chair from a stack in the corner and sat next to him. 'They called me,' he explained, 'the emergency services. There was an accident on my turf and they asked if I was available. I reminded them it was New Year's Eve, but then they told me about this crazy English guy who wouldn't stop swearing at everybody.'

'Shit.'

'See? it just had to be you.' Dan smiled, briefly, then asked, 'Eve?'

'She, she . . . Jesus, Dan, she's a mess. She's all tied up, tubes, wires, cables, drips, everything. Multiple fractures and brain damage, everything.' The words just tumbled out, one after another. At last there was a friendly face, someone to talk to, someone solid and reliable.

'Brain damage?'

'Maybe, they're not sure. They don't know.' Alex paused. 'Jesus, it was horrible, a fucking nightmare. The noise, Christ, screeching metal sounding like a thousand shrieking Valkyries and then . . . then silence, a terrible eerie silence.'

Dan stood up and gently removed the collapsed cup from Alex's hand. 'Come on,' he said. 'Come with me.' Placing a steadying arm around Alex's shoulders, he guided him along corridors and into an elevator, high speed, straight down to the lobby, through a pair of entrance doors and out, out into the freezing night. Across the street a pair of headlights was switched on and a car began moving sedately towards the two men. It came to a halt in front of the hospital and Dan pulled open a rear door, pushed Alex inside, walked round to the other side of the car and let himself in. Speech wasn't necessary, and they sat in silence as the patrol car pulled away and sped into the night.

*   *   *

The tiles were black, the tiles were white, the tiles were black, the tiles were . . . They weren't tiles, not here, they couldn't be, there'd be too many germs cunningly concealed in the cracks and crevices; interstices invisible to the human eye, but to a speck of dirt they'd be things of interstellar dimension. Alex thought it weird that he'd managed to crawl through one of these gaps and when he looked down, trying to locate the source of his entry, he saw that the whole floor was on the move, everything melding to become one complete joint-free surface. The material was expanding in all directions, ahead of him and behind him, and even as he watched it began curving upwards either side of him, meeting in a seamless coagulation above his head and simultaneously extruding itself into the form of a tube. The walls appeared to be made from a substance that was wet, shiny and slippery, but when he reached out to touch the surface his hand went straight through the edge of the tubular construction. He had no idea where he was going or where he'd come from, and all he knew about his method of travel was that it seemed to be accelerating.

One minute he'd been standing, looking at the floor, next, he was on his back and attached to something similar to a camp bed on wheels. Although his vision was thereby somewhat restricted he had a perfect view of the area immediately above his face, curving metal furnished at equidistant points with small openings that pulsed with bright, painful light. He tried to count them, the shafts of light, but gave up when it became obvious that his momentum was increasing.

Suddenly no longer on his back, he was sitting cross-legged, staring straight ahead. The hollow tube stretched seemingly forever towards infinity, beams of light penetrating the steely darkness like golden wormholes threaded through a fabric of space and time. Alex craned his neck and looked behind him. The whole cylindrical edifice had disappeared and there was nothing, not a thing, just a field of pitch-black emptiness. Shit! He turned to face the front and there, too, the tunnel had ceased to exist. He looked up into a funnel of brilliance and a great big eye stared back at him and held his vision. Wrestling against the power of the eye he managed to tear his line of sight to one side and, gaining control, peered down to find that he was sitting on thin air. He was still cross-legged but there was nothing underneath him, no visible means of support. *Nada.*

'There's nothing you can do,' a voice said, shivery, as though floating through thick syrup, a veritable sea of the stuff in expectant palpitation. 'Nothing.'

And there it was again, from above, softer and not so frightening. 'It's okay, Alex, it's nothing. Just a bad dream.'

Alex forced his mind upwards through golden mist, upwards towards the warmth of a shining sun, upwards, upwards . . . He opened his eyes and found Mandie looking down at him, her face haloed in radiant tresses.

'Mandie?'

'It's okay, Alex. It was just a dream.'

'Eve?'

'No news, not yet.'

Alex searched the face in front of him, tried to look behind the eyes. He saw the pain, the worry, the evident tiredness and anxiety. He noticed the smile, reserved and minimal, the sort of smile used when gearing oneself up to launch into a manifestation of bad news. 'And?'

'No, Alex. Really. It's still too soon. Dan's been on the phone all morning . . .'

'Morning? What time is it?'

*   *   *

Eve wakes up, adjusts her eyelids and wonders why the world is hazy and populated with green people. Unable to move her head, she rolls her eyes to the corners of their sockets and peers at wishy-washy surroundings. Everything is unfocused, ethereal shape-shifters with waving appendages, long ones and blobby ones, moving randomly, near and far. It's funny, she thinks, being in a sea world with strange slimy things gyrating slowly through forests of giant seaweed. Suddenly, becoming aware of tubes and cables and a really annoying beeping noise, she panics, her pulse rate sending unseen messages to something box-like above her head. A red lamp winks on-and-off, on-and-off, and she hears distant footsteps, urgent footsteps and perhaps not so distant. She looks at the tubes again and knows they'll be full of oxygen, a lifeline to keep her breathing in this strange new world. She tries to move but her limbs are made of lead and nothing happens and after a while she forgets the necessity.

Hours later she opens her eyes and stares at a green person who's fiddling with a tube; everything's jumbly but she thinks it's probably one of hers. 'One of my tubes,' she mouths, but no sound emerges. She smiles weakly and the green person says, 'Hello, you're with us, then?'

Eve tries to swallow but her mouth is devoid of saliva. 'Dry,' she croaks, at least she thinks she does, but the green person does nothing so she tries again. She licks her lips with something that feels like a loofah and the green person smiles, knowingly, and says, 'I expect you're thirsty?' Eve realises it must be an angel, until she remembers that angels are white and have large wings, so she starts to think about apprentice angels and how maybe they start out a different colour. Like swans. The green person returns, looking more like a woman, and Eve recalls the question about being thirsty, how the voice had seemed kind of female. And then gentle hands hold her chin and open her mouth and the taste of lemon floods her senses.

Again, she tries moving and her left leg twitches. She thinks it's her left leg but it could just as well be the right, everything is so confusing and she starts to laugh, but that hurts, really hurts, so she stops. The woman, because that's what it must be, brushes an appendage against her forehead, something damp and clammy but comforting and somehow reassuring. She remembers her fingers and tries to flex them, left hand and right hand. The digits respond and grope about, hesitatingly, drawing her hands across some sort of material and Eve is happy and delirious until the creeping movement jars something in the back of her hand, something which stabs at her. The pain is excruciating and the red light starts to blink. Shit, she thinks, as nausea rises and strange lights that remind her of the aurora borealis flicker behind her eyelids, I'm buried in a fish tank.

*   *   *

Sometime later, Alex is admitted into the intensive care unit and is unsure whether to sit on the edge of the raised bed or lean over it, like some ancient professor of medicine involved in arcane practice. Deciding against both, sitting or leaning, he stands instead with arms folded, head slightly bowed and brain whirring.

'She woke up,' a green-smocked nurse informs him. 'At nine o'clock.'

'Oh.'

'But not for long.'

'I see.'

'Seemed to be having some kind of panic attack.'

'Panic attack?' Alex asked, head spinning round to look at the nurse.

'It's okay, it's okay,' she quickly assured him, 'it's quite normal. RTAs often wake up disoriented and struggle to break free. We put her back to sleep.'

'Oh.' Alex's vision returned to Eve's body, the bed and the network of complex equipment, while his auditory system monitored electronic clicks and beeps and faint squeaks from rubber-soled shoes on gleaming flooring.

'There's nothing you can do.'

'Yeah, so everyone keeps telling me,' Alex responded, looking round to see where the male voice had come from.

'She's through the worst of it,' the doctor said, bright honest positive eyes regarding Alex in a fatherly manner. 'Everything is functioning normally.'

'Yeah, but she's on a life-support machine,' Alex protested, realising the doctor was young, younger than himself, much too young. The fatherly component had probably manifested itself out of authority, medical authority. 'And what about the damage to the brain?'

'No, no, there is none, her brain is okay, shaken, but okay, and the machinery is just a precaution,' the doctor – A. Martinez, according to the label attached to his chest – replied. 'She'd be perfectly okay on her own, but we like to keep the assist switched on. And,' he added, pointing at the box of chocolates that Alex had deposited on the bed, 'she won't be able or allowed to eat those for a while.'

'A while, Doctor?' Suddenly Alex had some respect for authority. Everyone likes to believe in experts, even when they have no idea what they're talking about; experts and listeners both.

'She's tough, she's young, she's in remarkably good shape. Battered, bruised and broken she may be, but she'll pull through. And with her level of fitness the recovery will be complete.'

'That's fantastic, that's fantastic,' Alex said twice in happy reception of the news. 'Incredible.' And then he stopped listening, his mind closing in on itself while the doctor went on to explain that he was in fact the surgeon in charge of the operating procedures. Medical terms floated in the ether and parts of the anatomy reverted to Latin origins, while beeps and squeaks played on.

'Pregnant?' Alex's subconscious had been craftily tracking

the surgeon's soliloquy, registering alarm and maximum alertness at the mention of the word. 'Pregnant?'

'Excuse me?' The medical man faltered in what he deemed was turning into rather splendid oratory.

'Pregnant, you said she was pregnant. Eve. Pregnant.' Alex's Adam's apple was becoming restrictive, glottal tension causing his voice to escalate a couple of octaves and his sentences to curtail themselves.

'No, no. Not pregnant.' The expert on everything smiled and whirled a stethoscope through the air, rather in the manner of a propeller on an aircraft waiting for permission to leave a tricky situation.

'Oh.'

'It's one of the first things we check for with RTAs, you know, in case we have to make a critical decision? Female patients, of course.' The propeller increased from idling towards full throttle.

'What? Oh, yes, of course,' Alex agreed, grinning like an idiot. 'Naturally.'

'So you'll be okay then?' the surgeon asked grandly, taxiing towards a pair of swing doors.

'Yes, yes. I'll come back tomorrow.' Alex headed towards the room of yellow desperation, the placid room of nervous contemplation where visitors go to huddle and make impossible decisions. There were no visitors, just a grouping of empty chairs bathed in winter sunlight and clinical reflections. He shoved money into the vending machine and took occupancy of a chair backed onto a radiator. Lifting the plastic cup to his lips, he breathed onto the coffee's hot dark surface and listened to the timed click and spacey hiss of an automatic room freshener.

2

Alex walked slowly along the street, muttering. 'It's a disaster,' he told himself, 'a total fucking disaster.' As he walked, he thought some more and realised it was worse than a disaster: it was a sacrilege. 'Life,' he complained, 'one minute you're living it to the full, next, you're gone, gone big time. Shit.'

He'd been wandering the streets for an hour-and-a-half, longer, and had lost his sense of direction and now had little idea as to his whereabouts. It didn't matter. Bollocks, he thought, life is so fucking precious. And, as the theory took hold, he began to look around him with renewed interest. Everything became the focus of his attention: shop windows, people, traffic, even the piles of dog shit randomly scattered across the sidewalks, islands of excrement on walkways of icy slush.

Passing an antiques shop, he noticed a model of Romulus and Remus, the chubby twins greedily sucking at the swollen teats of a huge black wooden wolf, and, in an adjacent window, a painting portraying a bunch of Greeks busily trying to slaughter a bunch of Romans – a panorama of horses, spears, shields and dead bodies.

The next shop happened to feature a proud display of teas from all over the world, a complete assortment of tea leaves – Lapsang Souchong, Darjeeling, Oolong, Assam, green, white, orange, black – ranged in a line of wafer-thin, porcelain oriental bowls. What's that all about? Alex wondered, trying to decipher the strange names and finding he was familiar with none of them. 'A whole world of tea,' he said to his reflection peering at him from the foothills of the Himalayas, 'and I know nothing about it.'

Next, he came to a travel agency offering discount package deals to Paris, London and Rome, according to a poster exhorting the populace to 'Discover Europe'. He crossed the busy thoroughfare and entered a small park, an oasis of tranquillity, stark contrast to the grey cubism of the city pulsating insomniously in every direction.

A solitary beam of sunlight escaping from the leaden sky gave Alex cause to become absorbed in deep examination of the shadows of trees and buildings, shadows that stretched blackly across a sea of glistening snow. He tortured himself trying to remember what a blade of grass looked like; not its outline or colour but its intensity, its fibre and fragile network of thread-like capillaries. Like some manic dog, he scraped at the pristine covering until he reached the mantle of compressed grass and then knelt in something approaching benediction, a deep-seated connection with Mother Nature. Thirstily, his eyes drank it all in, he wanted to savour every detail, every nuance down to the level of atomic particles. He needed to remember everything, to experience, feel and taste life and all it had to offer. He sought out the texture, the flavour, the interplay of light and shade; he wanted it all so that when his time came, when some projectile came hurtling out of an unknown future to strike him down, he'd be able to lie back in his box, content to play and replay the images that were, this very moment, being etched onto his retinas and transmitted to a place of storage deep in his soul. Then, remembering Simon, he reckoned he'd better stop dawdling; by now the cat would probably be half demented with hunger and starting to chew its bowl.

Simon was cleaning himself in the meticulous fashion peculiar to felines. He'd just finished inspecting his groin to see if by any chance his bollocks had been returned to him, and was in the precarious act of preening his rear left leg, when Alex entered the kitchen. The cleaning process temporarily suspended, Simon looked up at the intrusion through half-closed eyes and imperially forgot to withdraw his tongue, its little pink tip pointing accusingly at the familiar stranger who'd come to a halt in front of the worktop.

'Hey, Simon, what's happening?' Alex asked as the animal resumed the never-ending task of fur conditioning.

Suitably unimpressed, Simon ignored the question and stretched his tendons, opening his claws for easy access.

'You're not impressed, are you? I can tell,' Alex told the cat, while he opened and closed cupboards searching for cans of cat food. 'I wouldn't be either,' he admitted, more to himself than to the agile creature with a paw in its mouth. 'Forty-eight hours and no one to feed you,' Alex went on, pulling open drawers until he located a tin-opener and stabbed the sharp point into a can of Whiskas' chicken-and-beef. The noise of tearing metal had an immediate effect on Simon's ears and legs and he launched himself across the tiled floor to perform a series of figure-of-eights between Alex's legs, miaowing and shoving his back against the supports of "the one who feeds me", regardless of the fact that it was "the other one who's feeding me now".

'Okay, okay,' Alex said, bending down with a saucerful of quite tasty-looking food, 'I know you love me, but I also know it's only for the food.' He stood up and wondered how it is that cats are able to purr and eat at the same time. Leaning his lower spine against the worktop, he watched the cat and realised that he also was hungry; hungry and tired.

Alex stepped out of his jeans and placed them on the chair, noticing how they settled, sort of just sitting there, retaining the shape of his buttocks and hips as though he hadn't really undressed but was sitting on the chair, invisible, filling out his trousers as per normal. Wondering why he'd never noticed it before, this moulding of clothing, the retention of shape and volume despite empty containment, he climbed onto the bed. Pulling back the duvet he slipped his legs into the welcoming space . . . and froze, instantly, when something crashed to the floor.

He leaned to the left and saw nothing. He leaned to the right and then leaned further to the right and was rewarded a nagging twinge from some under-worked lateral muscle. Putting up with the discomfort he leaned further, until, losing his balance, he had to support his weight with one hand resting on the floorboards. With his head skimming the surface of the floor and blood pressure expanding his eyes to the size of footballs, he viewed the seldom-visited world under the bed. And there it was, the prize, lying in pristine innocence. Almost. Alex stretched out, his left hand crawling towards the object while the twinge nagged some more. And then he had it, the article was clasped in his hand. With supreme effort he pulled himself back onto the bed. Twisting his body into a sitting position, he drew his knees up between his arms and inspected the present he'd given Eve for Christmas.

* * *

It had been mid-morning on Christmas Day, before a late breakfast of scrambled eggs, smoked-salmon and well-chilled Chardonnay. They'd sat in bed exchanging gifts, the stuff they'd bought in a crazy, hectic pre-Christmas scramble.

Alex had wanted to present this particular gift on Christmas Eve and for several days he'd tossed the idea backwards and forwards, initially pleased at the conjunction of his girlfriend's name with the appropriate title of religiosity, and becoming delirious when he realised he'd be able to say, 'Merry Christmas, Eve.' Perfect! Then, his mind racing ahead through seven days, he'd grinned stupidly at the thought of wishing her, 'Happy New Year's Eve, Eve.' Further deliberation eventually made him decide against the idea, undue haste might give the impression that the package, carefully wrapped and resembling a giant pen, or small torch, was more probably a gift to himself.

Eagerness and frustration had combined to cause troubled sleep, but, on Christmas Day when he'd woken up at nine o'clock, a split second before the alarm clock realised it should be doing something, he'd leapt from the bed and loped to the pile of gifts that lay scattered beneath the tree. He knew exactly where to look and quickly located the present, resplendent in its distinctive cotton candy-pink wrapping-paper. As the clock suddenly burst into mind-shattering life, he picked up the parcel and returned to bed.

'You look smug,' Eve said sleepily.

'I do?'

'You're up to something,' she said, stifling a yawn behind a collection of sleep-puffed fingers.

'I am?'

'It's a give away,' Eve giggled, moving an elbow into support position.

'It is?' Alex asked. 'What is?'

'Mornings. A morning person you are not, although earthquakes and World War Three might possibly induce you to open an eye.'

'Doubtful,' Alex grinned.

'So?' Eve's eyes widened as Simon landed on the duvet.

Alex brought his right hand into view, the slim, candy-coloured rectangle held horizontally. 'Open,' he said, leaning forward to plant a gentle kiss on Eve's mouth. 'And Merry Christmas.'

'Merry Christmas, honey,' Eve responded. 'Happy New York Merry Christmas.' She hefted the present to check its weight and smiled when she realised it probably wasn't a pen – despite its shape and size the object was too heavy. She removed the ribbons and eagerly began to unfold the paper, and then feminine curiosity caused her to start tearing at the protective layers of pale pink tissue paper. Discarding the wrappings, she looked at Alex as she opened the black velvet pouch that had been exposed. As the object slid into view, she started giggling, bursting into peals of laughter when she realised she was holding a perfect representation of a penis, in glass. Shaking with mirth, she asked Alex if there was a problem.

'Problem?' he'd queried, grinning like a guilty Cheshire

Cat.

'You know, of the sexual variety? Am I too much for you? Have I worn you out?' She placed her arms around Alex's neck and kissed him deeply.

'No,' Alex answered, 'you're not too much for me, you're just about right. In fact, pretty damn perfect.'

'And . . ?'

'Nothing. It's just something . . .'

'A little variation?' Eve suggested. 'I'm open to variation, I'm open to everything.'

'I know,' Alex agreed. 'You're amazing.'

'Yeah, well, it takes two to tango, honey, and we'll try this model out later. Think you can keep up?'

'My inventiveness knows no bounds,' Alex assured the American woman as she unfolded her legs, ducked into an overlong T-shirt and drifted towards the kitchen. He looked at the pristine prick sparkling in virginal ignorance. 'None at all.'

Confronted by an *après*-breakfast confusion of empty plates and coffee cups, they'd left the kitchen to look after itself and taken up residence on the sofa. Eve got up and switched on the Christmas tree lights and stood looking at the presents, while Alex ferried glasses and the remains of the Chardonnay.

'What else do I got, English?'

Eve liked the endearment and used it often, much to the bewilderment of others. She found Alex's London accent cute, smiling at the long a's and giggling at the Cockney expressions which he aired from time to time for no apparent reason. She had no idea what the rhyming phrases were all about and would wait for some explanation. But none came. Alex would just grin inanely, pleased at his patter, pleased at his enunciation and happy to maintain some tenuous form of connection with the Little Apple, despite the fact that Victoria Park and Bethnal Green's Museum of Childhood, crammed with teddy bears, toys, games and model railways, formed the extent of his knowledge regarding the East End.

'Open this,' he said, smiling at Eve's happy countenance.

Before starting to unwrap the flat square object, Eve handed Alex a long, envelope-shaped packet, thin and floppy, with a label addressed to "My Smart Londoner". She smiled as he prised open one end of the packet and drew out a tie. 'Just in case you might think about looking for a job,' she told him. 'You know, impress the powers that be?'

Alex unfolded the tie and draped it around his neck. 'Great,' he announced, tying it into a loose knot above his sweatshirt, 'the colour's incredible. It'll go really well with my suit.'

'I know.'

'It's exactly right,' Alex enthused. 'Smart, but not too businesslike. You know, not drab like some executives wear. And what sort of colour is this?'

'It's the right colour, English. Goes with your Atlantic eyes.'

'Atlantic eyes! Bloody hell, that's a new one. No one has ever referred to them as Atlantic eyes. Conjures up deep dark depths and . . .'

'There you go then, the strength of deep foundations and the icy calm of regal blue. Together with your impeccable accent you'll go far, young man.' Eve grinned into an upended glass and then set about opening the present sitting on her lap. 'Brilliant!' she exclaimed. 'Van Ha . . .'

Grabbing the CD, Alex leapt off the sofa and twiddled

with the hi-fi. Moments later a voice said 'Hello Ba-by' and the opening bars of *Good Enough* washed like a tidal wave across the parquet flooring. Responding to auditory stimulation, Eve unwound her legs and elevated herself into action.

$$- // -$$

It had been the first night they'd met that Alex had learned of Eve's career as a professional ballet dancer. He'd been lost for words, dragging non-sequiturs out of a crazed atmosphere after being introduced to the elegant woman who'd been waiting for them at the ticket-returns office in the Lincoln Center. Having managed to sneak crafty glances at the slim figure, before, during, and after the concert, he was able now to appreciate her ability to maintain such trim fitness. Dan and Mandie, who'd instigated the evening, the meeting, and just about everything, had chaperoned Alex and Eve as though they were two puppets, which, because of Alex's momentary lapse of *compos mentis*, was a pretty accurate description. To be honest, he'd been in a complete spin and had no inkling of his friends' intentions and had no idea that they, Mandie, had spoken to Eve. Such is life, and it was only natural that with the girl's inspired sense of fun, the introduction had been arranged.

They'd been exiting the auditorium, after witnessing an incredible concert performed by the Chicago Symphony Orchestra, when Alex had asked the universal question obligatory to conversational preamble.

'Really? Wow, that's amazing!' he'd responded, when Eve informed him that she'd been a member of a ballet company.

And then, relaxing in the comfort zone of a candle-lit

bistro, Eve had popped the universal question obligatory when testing unknown waters, 'Do you think you'll be staying in New York City?'

It had been one of those special moments, a juicily delicious moment of suspended breath, the elongated pause between yes and YES, when uncertainty falls on stony ground and the ecstasy of realisation broadens the veins. Alex's fingertips had dabbled in spots of wine, while fireworks eclipsed his brain. The mix had been astonishingly perfect – classical music, jazz music, conversation and the easy camaraderie of trusted friends. He knew of other questions that would have been infinitely harder to answer.

Although it hadn't been coincidence that had brought them together, Alex knew he'd been lucky in finding this woman. Even though outwardly he may have shillyshallied at the idea of coming to live in America, he'd known in his heart that he would. This, after all, is where his friends were, his new friends, Dan and Mandie.

During the past eight months, Alex had added considerably to his collection of air miles, indeed, he was almost on first name terms with some of the crews, and, whenever his bank statements permitted, he'd flip-flopped joyously across the ocean. Unfortunately, because he'd been unable to pick up more than one or two promising stories for an ever-decreasing output of newspapers, the monthly account seldom climbed out of the doldrums and the flips and the flops became random affairs separated by lengthy spells of introspection.

A few days after the magical evening at the concert hall, he'd returned to the UK in a strange mood. He didn't really want to be returning. America had taken on a new aspect and nothing seemed impossible. Life, suddenly, was full of exciting prospects. Alex's head had become a hive of industry, a melting pot seething with neurons, a birthplace of ideas and aspirations shaped ingeniously, though secretively, by emergent thoughts of Eve and the questions posed by Dan and Mandie.

Each time he came home, he'd stare morosely at the neatly stacked packing cases that seemed to be in every room; he'd wander the streets of London, lingering on corners that resounded with painful memories; and he'd dream of escape. Once, finding himself on the wrong Tube, he'd justified a visit to the pub he'd used as an office in the good old days, the days when he'd actually been employed to write articles. It had been like stepping back in time, nothing had changed, but everything seemed smaller. Even the landlord, Jack, who'd always been a towering presence, seemed somehow diminished in stature and was still occupied in the never-ending task of filling dishes with an assortment of nuts and crisps.

'Hello, Alex, what's new?'

Time stood still and Alex whirled about to see if Dan and Mandie, somehow impossibly transplanted from Manhattan, were sitting at the table near the fireplace. Raising his left hand he used it to cling to the bar, while relativity and time-travel galloped along the same track, confusingly, but in a mouth-watering sort of way.

'New York, Jack.'

'So they say. Pint?'

'Nothing changes, does it?

'Not really. So that'll be yes, then?'

Alex lifted a peanut from the top of a pile and watched as Jack pulled at a pump. There was something . . . He couldn't think of the correct word. Stuck? Stagnant? He watched as a mug of beer was lifted over gleaming wood and deposited on a mat. Up-the-creek-without-a-paddle, he wanted to say, but even that wasn't quite right. No, it was more like being in a cul-de-sac, a narrow one with no space for turning. And then, triumphantly, he remembered the word. Necrosis.

'Isn't that where your friends came from?' Jack was staring at him oddly.

'Friends?'

'Those people from America. Weren't they from New York?'

'Christ, you've got a good memory.'

'Goes with the territory, know what I'm saying?'

'Yeah, I suppose.'

'So what about it?'

'What about what?'

'New York! What about New York?'

'I'm going to move there.'

'Ah, big decision.'

And then Alex's mind had set about regenerating the diseased cells, clumping them together, formatting them to come to his aid. There was much to be done. 'Not really, mate, the hard part's over, the decision is made. Now it's just a question of how to go about it.'

'Ah, big question.'

'Yep. Any ideas?'

'Just do it. Sell up and go.'

'But I don't have anything to sell.'

'So just go.'

'But there's stuff, you know, things.'

'Excellent opportunity to throw away the stuff you don't

need, be ruthless.' Jack looked up as another customer entered the pub. 'Something I should've done years ago. Blimey, you should see the rooms upstairs, full of clutter, don't know what half of it is.'

Alex had gone home to have a heart-to-heart with himself. It was all perfectly true, there was clutter everywhere; upstairs, downstairs, in his mind and in his life. It all had to be sorted out, and quickly. It shouldn't be too difficult though, he told himself, there was a light at the end of the tunnel, a beautiful slinky light that was a beacon of hope. He thought back to the day after the concert, the day when his mind had been full of Eve, the day when Mandie had invited the woman to an impromptu dinner. It had been one of those evenings that fell over itself with unrestrained happiness, extended hours of cultured conversation around the dining table and relaxed togetherness on comfortable sofas. The following day they'd gone to the zoo, just the two of them, their chaperones having opted out, and visited all the animals, aardvark to zebra, but hadn't really seen any of them; not the smallest insect, not even the largest reptile. They'd been in a private microcosm, ecstatic in their own company and content to wander hither and thither, oblivious to the crowds and the world around them.

Alex looked at the chaos surrounding him, the bits and pieces essential to everyday living that he'd hastily removed from the collection of packing cases. And then he looked further afield, at the detritus that had blocked his mind ever since the split from Jessica. Bollocks, he thought, he needed none of it. He walked to the bay window and looked out at the world, a drizzly day, dull and sort of jaundiced. Yes, it would be easy to leave all this behind.

But first, there was a letter that needed to be written, strong words to the council about the sleeping policemen that had been installed shortly after he'd moved into the house in Southgate; it had been as though the council had been waiting for his arrival. All the neighbours had been busily moaning about the hassles incurred by the lumpy additions to the street, but none had done anything towards having them removed. It was a golden opportunity for Alex to exercise his knowledge of the English language, to set down on paper exactly what he, and everyone else, thought of the . . . the arrested development of the council's collective brain. He found some paper – nice stuff, Three Candlesticks, with a classy sheen that would enhance the inky strokes of his longhand. With a pen-mightier-than-the-sword type of inspiration propelling nib across paper, he was on an upward curve. Had anyone, he asked, imagined how an ambulance would negotiate these unnecessary barriers, how painful it would be for the unfortunate incumbent, especially one suffering from appendicitis or broken bones, or burns, or everything combined? His ingenuity roamed wild, exploring all the negative consequences attached to these monuments of badly thought-out planning. He wrote about elderly people, the doddery ones, and fire engines and excessive damage due to vibration both to vehicles and houses. He wrote about negligence and stupidity and offered an alternative method of traffic calming – one employed by several other boroughs – namely, the expedient use of chicanes to 'choke' the street at various intervals. Proud of his missive, he folded it and placed it in an envelope, and had then spent the rest of the day searching for a stamp.

His mind, occupied with thoughts of Eve and how to get back to her as soon possible, had not ventured in the direction of Jessica. Neither had his feet. It was strange however, knowing that they shared the same town, and he decided to keep a wary eye open in case she hove into view around an unexpected corner. He remembered the last time he'd bumped into her, somewhere near Covent Garden, when initial euphoria had quickly transposed into a sense of grief. They'd communicated via short, clipped sentences; nonsense really, which had gone round in circles and ended up nowhere. Then, he'd still loved her. Then, he would have gone to the ends of the Earth to win her love. But that was then, before America had embraced him with open arms.

$$- \, / / \, -$$

And now it was Christmas and here he was, in Eve's apartment, sitting wide-eyed on the sofa while he and Simon watched the sinuous movement of the ballet dancer's improvisations to the powerful music being provided by Van Halen. It was intoxicating and Alex was rapt. Simon, however, had seen it all before, endless hours of it whenever the boss thrashed her gleaming body through the tortuous routines of sweaty exercise.

And then the music stopped. Three seconds later it started again, the room sinking beneath electronic interpretations of a helicopter chattering into the sexy undulations of *Why Can't This Be Love*. Eve was in ecstasy, her supple body rippling like that of a seal flexing its muscles at a shoal of silvery prey. A perfect coordination of twists and turns, feints and arm-waving abandon, systematically evolved into a series of openly wanton and sexually explicit postures. The stalks behind Alex's eyes greedily extended themselves and the stamen between his legs rapidly followed suit, an extension which didn't escape the notice of the whirling ballerina. With eyes fixed on Alex's rising expectations, Eve gyrated towards him and settled her hot body onto his lap. Leaning backwards, she hurriedly removed her T-shirt and then bent forwards to bring her pulsating body into contact with Alex's chest. She lowered a hand to explore the straining erection, silky fingertips running over and around the areas of arousal, occasionally dipping into the hollow of Alex's anus. She started kissing his mouth, gently, a brushing of the lips gradually developing into an exploration of nooks and crannies with the tip of her tongue. Eve's cool eyes regarded Alex's closed ones, while her lips closed around his tongue and drew it into her mouth. She treated it like a Popsicle, removing the sweet saliva and twisting her tongue around the trapped muscle until, out-of-breath, Alex opened his eyes. Sliding easily from his legs, Eve repositioned herself so that she was lying across his lap, face upward with her ass nestled comfortably against his rigid member. She grappled behind him, delving into the hidden realms of the sofa's contours until she discovered the cool hardness of the glass dildo. 'Now,' she murmured, placing the instrument into Alex's right hand, 'would be perfect.'

'But what about this?' Alex mumbled, indicating his rampant readiness.

'Put it on hold, English.'

'But . . .'

'No buts, just do as I say.' Eve rolled over, raising herself slightly so as to present her perfect ass.

Alex inspected the revealed flesh, the puckered indentation and the split fruit of womanly ripeness. He lowered his face and ran his tongue through the tropical furrow, eliciting a whisper of approval from a mouth pressed into the softness of the sofa. Lightly drawing a finger around the outer edges of slippery folds, Alex teased and tormented, massaging the tender channels with sticky juices collected from the central oasis. Inverting the dildo, he brought the tip of rigid glass into contact with the tight hood enveloping an anxious clitoris. Manipulating the instrument around the mini cone, he encircled it, sometimes journeying north, sometimes journeying south, but always employing the lightest of touches. Sometimes he used the tip of a finger to investigate the twin openings, searching, pressing, testing, but not entering; that would happen later. As though directing some kind of porno movie, a tasteful one, he conducted the entire operation along delicate but artful fantasies, a sexier and more pleasurable version of Bosch's vivid imaginations.

Gradually increasing the radius of circular motion, Alex slowly but surely brought the glass rod to Eve's moist aperture, and tenderly, almost experimentally, began to insert it. The whispers issuing from Eve's distant mouth became moans and she pushed her body backwards in an effort to assist the hesitant, irritatingly hesitant, though delightful, penetration. Uncertain of Eve's secret depths, Alex was reluctant to sink the dildo too far, so he began a cautious withdrawal and became fascinated at the perturbation of fluttering flesh as it slid over the small bead-like prominences attached to the glass penis.

Roused and hard, Alex's real-life weapon of lust was thrusting against Eve's abdomen. There was nowhere for it to go, no receptacle, the only sanctuary being the modest shelter of a bellybutton. But it wasn't modest, it had no scruples, and its owner was greedy. 'Fuck, that feels fucking fantastic, honey, a twofold sensation,' Eve spluttered. 'Shit, shit, just like that, yes, *yes*, don't fucking move anything. Touch my asshole. Press, gently. Ahh, *fuck.*'

Alex sat there, a virtual prisoner beneath Eve's squirming convulsions, his right hand manoeuvering the *objet d'art* in and out of tight spaces, while the middle finger of his left hand roamed around the creased entrance to Eve's fundament. Suddenly he began to feel in charge of things, he was the maestro at the keys, manipulating the sharps and the flats into symphonic rhapsodies. He was the master of melody, the composer of orgasmic crescendo. He was the boss. 'Turn over,' he commanded.

Eve lifted her head from a damp patch on the sofa and eyed him speculatively. '*Je*sus! Why?'

'Just do it,' Alex hissed. 'Obey.'

Eve wriggled her body submissively into position, ass down, belly up. 'Okay, English, what now?' Her face and neck were flushed, her eyes simmering and her smile radiant.

Reinserting the knobby stem, Alex bent his head forwards. 'Thith,' he said, in an awkward kind of lisp, his tongue beginning to tease at the bud that was peeking out of its housing.

'Thith ith good, Alexth, my Englith. It'th vewy good.' Eve was all giggles and it had been impossible to discern whether the spasms she produced were those of orgasm or those of hilarity.

*   *   *

Sitting on the bed, revisiting the pleasure he'd experienced as he'd watched the glass penis slide in and out of Eve's receptive body, Alex's mind became assailed by quirky imaginings. He began to worry that the present had been intended perhaps not so much for Eve as for himself and his own sexual fantasies. Then he told himself, 'So what if it was?' The afternoon of passion that had wound itself over the back of the sofa and onto the floor and ended up between sticky sheets, had been an extended experience of open honesty and shared enjoyment. There had been no holding back, for either of them. The suppleness of Eve's body opened new dimensions to their lovemaking, and the ingenuity of her mind – no, bollocks, both their minds – expanded the horizons of sexual gratification. Anyway, Alex reasoned, nodding to himself, the CD certainly had been bought solely with Eve in mind. Happy at the absolution of all sins, he found himself thinking that the band was prettyfuckingfantastic, especially the track about 'love walking in'. For some obscure reason Van Halen had been an unknown quantity in Alex's previous life and his ears hadn't experienced the pleasure of slurping up the aural excitement. Now, here he was, humming it.

Lifting the slightly curved dildo to his nose he sniffed at it like an errant schoolboy, one who's just discovered his sister's dirty underwear, and was vaguely disappointed at the lack of fragrance. He walked into the kitchen and opened a cupboard, looking for inspiration, when he remembered that someone, probably Jessica, had told him that he spent too much time thinking. So he stopped. Then he started again, pondering the situation he was in – an alien in a big town.

The next day, Alex woke up and wished immediately that he hadn't. Daylight and consciousness meant that his brain kicked itself into action, and the reality of life and all its frailties washed round the corners of his imagination. He climbed out of bed and padded into the kitchen, muttering 'Shit, shit, shit, what the fuck am I gonna do?' Spooning Whiskas' chunky chicken bits into Simon's bowl, he remembered there was a way forward, a plan of action, so to speak. He went into the lavatory, sat down and stared at the floor. It was tiled in one of those foot-square modern designs, all squirly and meaningless until you really looked, and then, with each and every visit, the patterns went through subtle changes – the female flamenco dancer became an elongated coach with funnel and smoke, and the fearsome sabre-toothed tiger morphed into a grinning monk; while the magic carpets remained magic carpets, ferrying rotund pashas to all four corners of the smallest room in the apartment.

Returning to the bedroom, Alex stared at his jeans. As though sculpted, they still retained the perfect denim outline of his ass, maintaining faithful readiness to accept his nether regions and needing only the manipulation of the zip to restore equilibrium to the master's torso.

3

'You're not pregnant,' Alex announced, grinning widely and helping himself to a grape.

'What?' Eve glared at him from her nest of tubes.

'First thing they said; well, second thing.'

'What was the first?'

'That you were alive.'

'Yeah, well I suppose that's pretty important. What about the pregnant bit, though, what's that all about?'

'Oh, it's normal procedure, you know, just in case it looks like you're not going to make it? Then they have to make an impossible decision, doctors playing at being God. "Who shall we try to save?" they ask themselves. "Who's most likely to survive?" Roll the dice and slam the white ball into the pocket.' Alex shoved his hands into his pockets and stared at the box of chocolates he'd bought on his previous visit, wondering when Eve was going to get round to opening it. She didn't, she just lay back in the bed, her right hand resting lightly on the box of temptation. Alex helped himself to another grape. 'I brought you some grapes as well,' he informed her.

'So I see, hon. Do you think there'll be any left for me?'

Alex sat on the edge of the bed and pondered life and existence and realised that he missed the deep meaningful discussions that used sometimes to develop between him and Jessica. He began to ruminate about the strange relationship they'd shared, the mood swings, the impossible question-and-answer sessions and the seemingly insurmountable problems that flared up out of nothing. He supposed that back then he'd realised that the relationship would burn itself out, eventually; it was inevitable. But . . . those discussions, sometimes they'd been momentous. Hmm, like most other people, he'd been dreaming the impossible dream.

'. . . dreaming, you know, some sort of awareness in a sea of nothingness?' Eve was explaining her perceptions at the time of waking up after her ordeal. 'It was like going round in circles, a moth around a light bulb, never varying my orbit and never landing. You know, just going round and round? And though I wasn't conscious of a direction I knew there was some sort of goal to be aimed at, an attraction. Sort of like swimming round the edge of a black hole but never venturing into the vortex.'

'Amazing,' Alex agreed, emerging from his own black hole and shelving thoughts of another time and another place. 'So are you going to eat those, or what?' he asked, glaring edaciously at trapped chocolates.

'Not allowed, English. Doctor's orders.'

'Yeah, well, they don't apply to me.'

'Go on then, I suppose someone has to be my taster.'

Alex restrained himself from tearing wolfishly at the Cellophane seal, thinking "dignity at all times", the maxim that had been one of Jessica's favourites. He even went so far as to lower the well-stocked box into Eve's range of vision and asked her which, from the tempting array, should be the first to be consumed. 'Consideration at all times,' he muttered, adding to the list of epigrams.

'While you're standing there, munching on my chocolates, tell me about life outside these walls. Tell me what you're up to.'

'Oh, nothing,' Alex answered around a particularly tasty cherry swimming in liqueur. 'You know, feeding Simon and stuff? And I get to see Dan and Mandie almost every day.'

'I thought so, they're good people, the best.'

'Yep, Dan got here shortly after you were admitted.'

'Yeah, a nurse told me all about it. Said that when the station house informed him there was an English nutjob swearing at everyone, he knew it was you. Had to be.'

'Nice. But, shit, honey, you'd have been swearing too if you'd been there.'

'I was there.'

'You know what I mean. It was scary, I thought you were a goner. I mean, Jesus, what a thing.'

'Thing?' Eve's eyes opened to their maximum. 'Is this how you relate to it?'

'Disaster, catastrophe, calamity; it was dreadful.'

'But I'm gonna be okay, and then you're gonna have to look after me.'

'I am, honey, I am.' Alex leaned forward and tested another chocolate.

'So, in-between feeding Simon and passing the time of day with Dan and Mandie, why don't you go see Mrs Robinson?'

'Who?'

'You know, Mrs Rob . . .

'You mean Mrs Carmichael?'

'Yes. That's exactly who I mean.'

'Why?'

'Well, I seem to remember that's what you were talking about before I tried to capture the balloon.'

'Yeah, you're right,' Alex beamed, chocolaty fingers grasping Eve's battered hands. 'See, you're better already.'

'And . . . why not go see everybody?

'What do you mean?'

'Your continental buddies, your friends across the water.'

'But . . .'

'Go. Do. 'Cause when I get outta here I'm sure as hell gonna monopolise you.'

4

The wind howled around Alex's head as he held onto the rail running around the ferry's perimeter. The idea of an 'unwind session' round the bay had been Dan's, and Alex had approved as soon as it had been mentioned, yesterday afternoon. It would be just what he needed, although he'd forgotten the probability of being so cold.

Dan passed a cup of steaming coffee through the air and Alex gratefully wrapped his fingers around the polystyrene container.

'So whatcha gonna do?' Dan was upfront and purposeful, the question directed by years of police training.

Alex sipped at his coffee and stared across water at the World Trade Center, twin towers linking heaven and earth in a modern version of Babel.

'You have to spend the time doing something useful,' Dan advised, answering his own question.

Alex nodded towards the shore and the two large exclamation marks. 'Yeah, 's'funny you should say that,' he said, lines of sight skimming over the frilled surface of chilled water, 'it's exactly what Eve told me. She said I might as well

79

make myself useful, told me to go and see Mrs Carmichael.'

'She's right,' Dan nodded affirmation. 'Damn right.'

'You think?' Alex asked, seeking double affirmation.

'Of course, it'll be good for you. Mental agility, Alex, get your teeth into it, find answers and take no prisoners.'

'She also mentioned Jessica and Wolfgang, sort of.'

'She did. She *did?* Dan wheeled round to face Alex at the same time as the ferry carved a new course to starboard. 'There you go then, carte blanche, Alex. What a woman! Still, it's the obvious decision and it's great that her mind is fully functional and up to speed. You never know with an accident like that just what the outcome will be. She didn't lose consciousness, did she? I mean, you know, it's not good when you lose consciousness, that's when all sorts of stuff can go wrong.'

'No, she didn't, not totally, she was in and out of it. She cracked a joke about the balloon stuck in the tree, something about the fact that such a fragile object had escaped any injury. She's a tough cookie.'

'You know she used to be a ballet dancer?'

'Yep, I discovered that on the night we met. In fact I think it was you that told me, either before or after the concert. But hey, you should have seen her the other day, she was on the floor doing these pull-ups and stuff in time to some funky music. She suggested I should try some.'

'You didn't?'

'Nah, I just lay on the floor and giggled. The music was good though and I managed to lift my feet into the air. And that's when she told me how supple she used to be, "flexible and bendy" she said, not missing a beat, working out and speaking at the same time. Incredible.'

'You should do some of that stuff, you know? Even I go to the gym once or twice a week; you never know when you're gonna have to chase a criminal.'

'Yeah, I suppose,' Alex responded, drinking coffee and thinking about doughnuts and pasta.

'Anyway, you're dining with us tonight, it's Mandie's birthday and she's cooking up something special.'

'Mandie's birthday? Shit, I didn't know.'

'No reason you should.'

'But I should get her something.'

'Don't even think about it, buddy, she's not that type of person. She's a giver, not a taker.'

'Yeah, you both are, you've given so much. Without your support I would've sunk without trace.'

'You know?' Dan said, throwing an arm around Alex's shoulders, 'I think you probably would. The doctors and nurses told me you were becoming a menace. They were concerned but didn't know what to do with you.'

'Huh, *I* didn't know what to do with me.'

'But you're okay now.' It was a statement, an understanding, and left no room for dissent.

Bathed in strains of Vivaldi, Alex glanced at the black and white chequered floor tiles. 'I sort of guessed we'd be coming here,' he beamed at Mandie. 'It's a special place, holds a lot of meaning.'

'Holds a lot of memories,' Mandie agreed. 'We come here for special occasions.'

'It's where I proposed,' Dan said, grinning above the menu in his hands.

'It's where you brought me on our first date . . .'

'No, no, we went to the movies . . .'

'Our first date when you ended up coming back to my place.'

'Oh, *that* first date?'

Mandie smiled across the table at Alex. 'Actually, it was the magical third date, the pivotal point at which things either go forward . . .'

'Or stop dead,' Dan supplied. 'We went forward.'

'It's where you brought me on my first evening in New York,' Alex reminded his friends.

'Like I said, Alex, special occasions,' Mandie repeated, rewarding him with one of her golden smiles. She looked up as the Maître d' approached their table. 'Luigi, we have a special celebration, let's start with Prosecco.'

'But of course, madam,' the boss beamed, sort of lowering himself forwards and sideways and scuttling away to locate ice and a bucket.

'And then I think we'll stay on white,' Mandie advised the retreating Italian.

'I'll bring the wine list, madam,' Luigi said, managing to incorporate a quick spin into his gambol towards the kitchens.

'Alex is worried,' Dan announced across an array of gleaming cutlery resting on the crisp white tablecloth. ' 'Bout Eve.'

'We're all worried about Eve, honey,' Mandie acknowledged. 'But she's out of danger now, isn't she? She's on the mend?'

'Yes, no, yes; it's a different sort of worry. Um . . .' Dan looked at Alex. 'Tell her what you told me, old buddy.'

'Well, it's sort of silly,' Alex said bashfully.

'And?' Mandie coaxed.

'I think she might be trying to test me,' Alex owned up, squeezing the words through tight lips.

'How so?' Mandie's smile was disarming.

'Well, she told me to go see people.'

'People? You mean psychiatrist people?'

'What? No,' Alex laughed, 'ordinary people, such as . . . Mrs Carmichael.'

'And that's a problem?' Mandie was nothing if not direct.

'No, no, it's just that, well . . .'

'He doesn't know if he should leave her bedside,' Dan offered, spreading a liberal supply of butter onto a chunky wedge of French stick.

'What can he do?' Mandie asked.

'Exactly. That's what I said,' Dan agreed.

'And that I should visit London and Munich,' Alex added, feeling a little out of centre.

'London? Munich?' Mandie asked, visualising the globe.

'Yes, Europe,' Alex answered.

'London? Does that mean . . ?'

'Jessica. She told me I should go talk to Jessica, in a round-about sort of way.'

'*Je*sus! Maybe she is still ill,' Mandie posited, pinching the bread out of Dan's hand as he was aiming it towards his face.

'I know, that's what I'm worried about.'

'What?'

'Well, does she really want me to go? Alex replied. 'I can understand her being okay about Mrs Carmichael and . . . and about Munich, you know, Wolfgang and stuff, but . . .'

'She's a tough cookie, your Eve, she's a smart kid . . .'

'She certainly is,' Dan nodded, 'that's what I said. Said she . . .'

A glare from Mandie cut him short. 'And, she's right. All she can do at the moment is rest, and sleep, and you can't help her with either. She knows this, Alex, and therefore she also knows it's best you get things done. Hell, she probably wants you to meet with Jessica, you know, to make sure you're completely over her?'

'You think?'

'Of course, I'm a woman.'

'Well, in that case . . .'

'What do you want to see Mrs Carmichael about?' Dan asked, watching Luigi ease the cork from a bottle.

'Oh, it's something to do with her name, Ellie. I had this vague notion that it might be connected to the "Elise" written on the back of one of George's paintings. We were discussing it at your New Year's Eve party, remember?'

'That's right, we all thought it referred to the music by Beethoven.'

'Yup, until Bry's lady suggested it might be nothing more than a name.'

'Yes, of course, I remember,' Mandie agreed. 'So you think the painting was meant for someone called Elise.'

'Well, perhaps, and this is why I want to talk to her, Mrs Carmichael, Ellie.' Alex smiled in satisfaction, happy that his two friends were *au courant*. 'You know, find out if she and Elise are one and the same person.'

Back at Eve's apartment he returned to the safety of the john and was slightly disturbed to notice that one of the magic carpets had become a long thin alien having backwards sex with a slinky female earthling. Wheeling his vision across the other stylish perturbations, Alex was relieved to see that they all seemed to be locked into familiar outline. 'Thank God for that!' he grunted, before his mind dived into the world of tiny things. Recalling his weird dream that had pulled him through floor tiles, he began to think of atoms and the even tinier bits of stuff that whizzed about in their centre. He couldn't remember what they were called, the things that are smaller than everything, the particles that burst out of the sun and zip through space and anything that gets in the way, specifically planets and the creatures that patrol their surfaces, human creatures such as himself. What the hell were they called? not the humans but the . . . Then he had it, nailing the answer to the floor with his lazy-eye vision. Neutrinos, miniature stuff that travels from Sun to Earth in eight minutes and then burrows through skin, blood, bone, earth and rock, without turning a hair. Hmm, he thought, the dream must have converted me into one of these hurtling objects, a microscopic me that can weave my way through the very fabric of stuff that bonds everything together.

And then he turned his mind towards the events of the day, primarily the conversation he'd had with Dan and Mandie. Three out of three, he thought, including Eve. They'd all come to the same conclusion. Go. Do.

Chapter Three:

Mrs Carmichael

1

There was nothing to do but wait, something at which Alex doesn't excel, so he steeled himself himself to watch the Carmichael pooch, some sort of terrier-type model, drag its ass around the carpet. The technique it employed was strange and ungainly. With hind legs pointing skywards, mouth agape and eyes staring inanely, the scraggy animal used its front paws to pull itself along in the manner of a clockwork toy. As it caroomed across the expensive-looking Persian carpet, Alex mentally noted its tracks, reminding himself to steer clear of the more-than-likely worm-infested area when the time came for him to make a move.

'Been expecting you, you know, for quite a long time. I considered you to be a bright young fellow.' Mrs Carmichael swept into the room, shooed the dog out and edged herself onto a faded yellow chaise longue.

'First time anyone's told me that,' Alex confessed, grinning foolishly.

'Don't know what took you so long,' the elderly lady continued, ignoring Alex's remark. 'Where have you been?'

'Oh, here and there,' Alex answered, shuffling backwards

to take advantage of a wooden chair, upright and pretty uncomfortable. He sat and crossed his legs, left over right, and clasped his hands around his left knee. 'I, um . . . Why have you been expecting me?'

'Connections, young man, the tying together of loose ends.'

'Yes, but . . .'

'No "yes but", that's not going to get us anywhere, is it?'

'No, but . . .'

'Really, it's quite simple, logical. There were three of you clamouring around my house, were there not? The lawyer, the girl, and you. The first two came and went, quite happy with their findings, and that was that. You were different, you asked questions, but not enough. You danced around the edge of the puzzle like a ditzy ditherer. So close, young man, the truth was within reach.'

'The truth? What truth?' In listening, Alex had been reminded of the woman's sharpness, her acuity of mind. He re-crossed his legs, right over left, and thought he'd venture a supposition. 'They call you Ellie, don't they?'

'They? They who?'

Alex took a chance. 'The people of the Forties.'

Mrs Carmichael looked at her knees, bony beneath the creased material of her green dress. She took her time, allowing her tired eyes to focus on different elements of the room while she thought about a response. 'Hmm, I think this calls for a drink.' She got up, walked to the door and pressed a small button recessed into an abundance of ornate architrave. On her way back to her seat, she took a battered volume from a collection of books resting on top of a grand piano. Moments later a maid entered the room, listened to Mrs Carmichael who spoke of whisky and water and ice and a suggestion of beer for Alex, and then made a hasty exit on a mission to locate the various components.

'See? I was correct in my assumption, the boy has a quick mind. So, tell me, why the Forties?'

'Just a guess.'

'Really?'

'Yes, really, although some lateral thinking connected you with Charley and some vague tangent extended my deliberations towards the war.'

'Goodness. Which one?'

'The second one.'

'Why?'

'Well, it was during the Second World War, or at least at the end of it, that the paintings went missing.'

'And how does this involve me?'

Alex came to his second supposition. 'The name "Elise", written on the frame of one of those paintings.'

Mrs Carmichael was unmoved. 'And how does this involve me?' she repeated in the same level tone.

'I don't know,' Alex confessed.

The maid returned with a tray of refreshment: two tumblers, a bottle of whisky, a jug of water, a container of ice cubes, a bottle of Molson, and a plateful of baby pretzels.

'Two fingers of Scotch, one of water and two ice cubes,' Mrs Carmichael directed Alex. 'You may as well do something useful if you're expecting the information I believe you're expecting.'

'I believe I am,' Alex responded, unscrewing the top of the bottle of Grouse.

'Hmm . . . '

'It was something you said about Charley.'

'It was? Are you sure? I don't believe I said anything about Charley.'

'About the paintings not being to his taste? Isn't that what you told me?' Alex dropped ice cubes into the tumbler and handed the drink across.

'Yes. I remember.'

'So I'm thinking that perhaps you knew him quite well?'

Mrs Carmichael took a studied sip of whisky, a wry smile lightening her face. Watching her every move, Alex supposed she must have been a very attractive woman. Hell, she still was. With her long blonde hair pulled back in severe approximation of the Scandinavian style and secured behind her head with a tortoiseshell clasp, she had the appearance of an actress, elegant and poised. Alex guessed she must have been around seventy, perhaps a little more, and yet her skin, save for a few laughter lines, was scarcely blemished. Needing little makeup, she'd used just a touch here and there to accentuate her natural beauty, the type sought by the makers of creams and potions that supposedly retard the ageing process. Alex looked at her eyes, piercing blue, and found them staring at him. Having invited himself into her home without really stating his intentions, he began to feel a little uncomfortable. But then, he was himself a little unsure of his intentions. Yes, his journalistic instincts were digging at a story, but he had no idea what the gist of the tale would be. It was just . . . a conviction that there must be some sort of connection between Mrs Carmichael and Charley Meyer, and the paintings. As the woman replaced the tumbler onto the table, Alex lowered his right leg to the floor and decided to soften his approach. 'I didn't take you to be a doggie person,' he observed.

'I'm not.'

The direct answer surprised him. Hadn't he just witnessed a four-legged beast dragging its ass around in ecstatic circles? 'But . . .'

'Not mine, horrid little thing. Belongs to Ulrike.'

'Ah.'

'Ulrike . . . she's like a daughter; talks to me, you know, about things, about so many things. She's been with me for years, says I remind her of her mother. Maybe I do, maybe I don't, but it's sort of a shared existence.'

'Um . . .'

'You're wondering why I'm talking about the maid and why I put up with her animal. Oskar, that's the wretched creature's name.'

'Not really. I mean, it's none of my business.' Uncertain of the strange conversation he'd engineered, Alex was evasive.

'What do you mean?' Mrs Carmichael laughed. 'You're on a mission, young man, I can read you like a book. You're edgy. Look at the way you're sitting!'

Alex inspected his legs, knees pressed together, bent at right angles; all of him was arranged at right angles. His vision collided with the beer and he raised the moisture-beaded bottle to his face. Mrs Carmichael was correct, she'd known he was after something and her manner of speech, direct, unnerved him. Edgy, he thought, just about summed it up.

She'd opened the book and was turning it around so that Alex could view a photograph that had been pasted into the left-hand page.

'It's you,' he stated confidently.

'It's me,' Mrs Carmichael confirmed. 'It's me when I was nineteen.' She turned the page. 'And this is my daughter, Irma, and my husband Pavel. It's nineteen-forty-two, we'd been married for five years. And then the Germans came and knocked on the door and took it all away, everything.'

Alex was stunned. He didn't know what to say. He said nothing. He gazed at the woman in front of him, took another swig from the bottle and waited for her to continue.

'I wish I could remember the name of the street.' Mrs Carmichael looked through Alex and into the distance, into latent memories of another life when everything revolved around the childlike yet passionately dangerous whims of a painter, an artist with short legs, short fuse and moronic moustache. 'But of course! You must look for a face on a corner, low down, almost street level. An incredibly old face on an incredibly old street corner, somewhere near the king's processional route – I think that's what they used to call it. Yes, I'm certain, not far from the river, not far from the bridge. You must go and you must find a map and do a lot of walking. We used to walk, you know, we used to walk everywhere. And in the springtime we'd take a picnic to the slopes beneath the place called . . . Hell's bells, I can see it . . . Yes, Petřín, beautiful place, trees, cherry trees, and we used to spoon beneath the blossom.'

'Spoon, Mrs Carmichael? Are you sure?'

'Of course I'm sure! Ah, but those were the days, we used to call it *obtlávat*, a Czechoslovak word, an old one, rare and full of meaning.'

'*Obtlávat*,' Alex said slowly, echoing the strange word and picturing Mrs Carmichael and her beau *obtlávat*-ing on the side of a hill.

'I know about you and Eve, you know?' Mrs Carmichael fired across a narrow space. 'You see, I've done some investigating of my own.'

A pretzel wedged itself in Alex's throat and he tried dislodging it with an avalanche of beer. 'Eve?' he spluttered. 'Eve?'

'Eve, the woman you're living with.' Mrs Carmichael smiled. 'It's okay, Alex, don't look so worried. I approve, I think. And so too would Charley.'

'Charley.' Alex found himself reduced to repeating peoples' names.

'Mmm, Charley.' Mrs Carmichael tapped Alex on his knee. 'And there's your connection.'

'And the city of cherry trees?'

'Prague.'

'And you went spooning with Charley?'

'Do try to keep up,' Mrs Carmichael admonished. 'The spooning was with Pavel in the halcyon spring of Germany's revival, the years while the storm was brewing, the years before the lunatic finally went haywire.'

'But Charley . . ?'

'Karel. He was a friend of Pavel's, a friend who was a member of the resistance and seemed to have endless connections and was therefore one step ahead of the pack. It was Karel who arranged for our escape.'

'But your daughter . . . and your husband?'

'The escape went wrong and they didn't survive the camps.'

'But . . ?'

'It's a long, painful story, Alex. Maybe some other time.' Mrs Carmichael picked up her drink and drained it. Holding the tumbler towards Alex, she told him to refill it. 'Karel hid me in a boat, downstream from the city where there was less chance of being discovered. I stayed there for three weeks until one day he arrived in the company of a German corporal; frightened me half to death, I thought he'd been turned. Karel explained the disguise and the plan, gave me some British money and waved me goodbye as I was driven away by the fake officer.'

'Blimey, what a story!'

'There are many such stories, Alex, some good, some bad, most of them revolving around the heroism of a few brave individuals. In a couple of generations the stories became legends and then new events came along and produced their own stories, and the legends of yesterday were forgotten. The world goes on and nothing changes.'

'But they're immortalised in print.'

'Maybe, but as Aurelius says, "*For all things fade away, become the stuff of legend, and are soon buried in oblivion*".'

'Says?'

'Ok . . . Said.' Mrs Carmichael sought refreshment in the whisky and smiled bleakly. 'But this is what you wanted, is it not?'

'Yes, absolutely. But where do the paintings fit in?'

'Ah, the paintings. I don't know, I can only conjecture.'

'But Charley . . . and you, you were . . .'

'Friends?'

'Yes.'

'Maybe a little more. They were impossible times, extraordinary times.'

'Did the others know about Charley? About Karel?' Alex suddenly had the impression that his eyes were crossing themselves. There it was, right in front of him, the answer to the conundrum regarding the initials on the back of the painting.

Charley was Karel and the 'K' was Karel and Karel was Charley. So, shit, it *had* been Eve's grandfather who'd scrawled the initials onto the frame. He wondered if Eve knew that her grandfather had originally been called Karel, and then, stupid, stupid, he realised that she couldn't have, otherwise she'd have made the connection right away.

'Others?'

'Um, um . . . Michelstraub and his colleagues at the office.'

'Heavens, no. It was secret and something shared between the two of us. It wasn't necessary for anyone else to know.'

'But . . . he was married?'

'He was, Alex, he was. He came to America, I stayed in London.'

'Amazing!'

'Quite so.'

'And this is why you seem more English than American?'

'Mmm, I worked as housemaid for a family in north London.'

'You did? Whereabouts?'

'Golders Green.'

'Jewish?'

'Of course Jewish. They also were from Germany but had removed themselves from the continent in nineteen thirty-seven.'

'Wise move.'

'He was an opera singer with friends in many countries, so it wasn't too much of a problem to relocate; especially when his colleagues, already in London, pleaded with him to make the move.'

'And Charley? Karel? Why do you call him Karel?'

'It was his name, the Czechoslovak version of Charles.

He stayed in contact, of course, and at the end of the war he made arrangements for me to come here.' Mrs Carmichael laughed. 'In fact, he introduced me to Rudi, my husband, my second husband.'

'Of course, the collector, the Professor.'

'Yes, a man who'd travelled everywhere, seen everything there was to see and had brought most of it back to New York. I was twenty-eight, over-awed by the intelligence of this older man, and fell in love. It was a great time to be in this country, everything seemed possible even though the cold war was just around the corner. Rudi was well respected and people from far and wide came to our house, experts, all of them experts in their own chosen field. We had dinner parties, wonderful affairs where the conversation would range round all manner of topics. I learned so much. Rudi made everything interesting, he made everything live and filled one with such enthusiasm He was a great teacher.'

'But what about the pictures?' Alex asked, trying to bring the conversation back on course. 'Why is the name "Elise" written on the back of one of them?'

Mrs Carmichael looked up from her reminiscences. 'Elise?'

'*Für Elise*, to be exact.'

Mrs Carmichael smiled across an ocean of years, an avalanche of memories that were inevitably pinned to the two words. She crossed the room and rang the bell for the maid. Upon entering, Ulrike was immediately sent off on a mission to make coffee and Mrs Carmichael returned to her seat. 'Karel had a lot of fingers in a lot of pies, to use one of your English expressions. He had the Germans falling over themselves in Karel-induced confusion. His philosophy was that if you make enough noise, people will believe anything you tell them – especially Germans who unfailingly do everything by the book. His trick was to give conflicting orders. The Germans had no idea what was happening and would collide into one another in their urgency to follow Karel's latest scheme. That he was a Jew, they had no inkling.'

'But how did he convince them? How come he was a force to be reckoned with?'

'He was from Vienna and grew up under the controlling strictures of the Habsburg way-of-life. The blinkers were applied at birth and were thus an accepted reality; no one questioned authority. Under this rigorous suppression he quickly learned to keep his mouth shut, but kept his eyes and ears revolving like little radars, evaluating every detail. He applied all this knowledge to maintain his survival during the German occupation of Prague.'

'Yes, but . . .'

'The pictures, I know. Well, no, actually I don't. I can only surmise that he was thinking of the future, his future. We'd often spoken about life after the war, but our ideas were just dreams, fantasies, there was no way of knowing how things would turn out. Countries were falling like skittles and Hitler seemed all-powerful.'

'Yes . . .'

Mrs Carmichael looked at Alex, then looked down and ran the point of a finger around the rim of her glass. 'I loved him.' The announcement was soft. 'He was kind, he was gentle, intelligent and . . . married. But I loved him. He was a man who knew what he wanted from life and he wasn't afraid of the consequences. I respected this and I respected his fight for survival. He protected me, he protected my family, and after my husband and child were taken from me, he brought me under his wing.'

Alex remained silent, there was no reason for interruption. He clasped his hands together and placed them in front of his knees, an acolyte at the feet of wisdom.

'Karel and his wife and me.' Mrs Carmichael nodded, 'Yes, we had a relationship, Karel and I, and I will never know if his wife, Klara, suspected anything. Life was so different in wartime, Alex, people took chances, risks they wouldn't normally consider. We used to meet whenever we could, wherever we could, in bombed-out buildings, in a shed by a tram depot, in someone's garden. It was dangerous but that somehow made it all the more exciting. Of course for Karel it was doubly dangerous, he was a married man, and he and Klara were sheltering a Jewess. Suspicion was rife – a word, a look, a wrong move would end in death. People were afraid to speak. Even in their own homes everyone communicated in hushed whispers. But somehow we got through. I stayed with them for about six months before Karel was able to get me away to the boat, before he found anyone trustworthy.'

'The fake officer?'

Mrs Carmichael nodded and took a deep draught of whisky. 'I don't know how he masterminded the re-routing of the paintings, but he was . . .'

'Seems he was a genius.'

'Yes.' Mrs Carmichael lapsed into silence, some sort of reverie, so Alex quietly sipped his beer and prayed that Oskar the dog wouldn't make a reappearance. He had some sort of aversion to the wretched animals, especially the small yappy type. It was probably a throwback to his childhood, when he'd been bitten by just such an excitable bundle of bones. It was probably also because he detested the way they always went straight for the crotch, in particular his crotch. He found it highly embarrassing and hated it and did his best to stay away from the canine fraternity. And, he remembered, there was something else: the smell of a wet dog, it was disgusting and just the thought of it brought him close to retching. Once, after a long walk through rainy English countryside with an ex-girlfriend and her scraggy pooch, he'd had to share the homeward journey trapped in a small car with the damp creature breathing evilly down his neck. It was vile and all too annoying.

'You'll have to go to Prague.'

'Pardon?' Alex's mind dragged itself out of muddy lanes. 'Prague?'

'Mmm, you need to experience a little of what I've been talking about.'

'And how will I do that?'

'You must walk through the streets and climb the hills and assimilate yourself.'

'Assimilate myself?'

'Absolutely you must. It's a different culture, you have to breathe it and then maybe you'll discover whatever it is you're searching for.'

'I don't know that I'm searching for anything,' Alex smiled and helped himself to another baby pretzel.

He almost spat it straight out when Mrs Carmichael replied, 'So, why are you here?' She helped herself to another large measure of whisky and held out the glass so that Alex could replenish it with more ice. 'Young man, you're at a crossroads – in life, in love; probably in everything.'

'Jesus.'

'America, Eve, paintings, go, stay – everything.' Mrs Carmichael took a gulp of the golden liquid and smiled gently. 'I told you, I can read you like a book. You're in a similar situation to the one I was in all those years ago. Do you give up or do you march forward? Do you crumble in a desperate heap or do you sally forth to find new adventure?'

'Blimey, are you a psychologist?'

'Just ancient, Alex,' came the weary reply. 'Ancient.'

Alex regarded the woman sitting opposite and wondered how someone who'd been through the hell of losing a husband and a daughter to a bunch of demented Krauts, maintained such an air of balanced repose. Maybe it's true, he thought, the notion that these days we're all too mollycoddled, the objectionable nanny state buffering our fragile psyches with layers of cotton wool. He wondered how his contemporaries would cope in a time of national crisis, an era when the world was falling apart at the seams. How do you struggle through life when the people you love are dragged away and never seen again? He decided that the older generation, composed of brave hearts and lashings of spleen, was altogether wiser and far more resilient than its flimsy descendants. And then he thought about Eve, the slender woman who, while recovering from her horrendous accident, had sent him on this mission.

'Well,' he admitted, ' it was Eve who told me that I should come and see you.'

'Eve was right.'

'And that I should go to England and Germany.'

'Again, she was right.'

'Yes, maybe, but . . .'

'There's nothing you can do while she's recuperating.'

'Yes, so everyone keeps telling me . . .'

'And she's receiving better attention and better care than anything you could provide.'

'Yup.'

'So, everything points towards Europe. You've seen me.'

'You make it all seem so easy.'

'It is, it's just a matter of looking at the facts and making a decision based on them. You know all the ins and outs better than I, and I have a sneaky feeling that you also know the answer.'

'Maybe.'

'So you must act.'

'I know. It's just that I'm not sure that she meant what she said, it's as though she's testing me.'

'Eve said what she said, Alex, for a reason. She is testing you. It's up to you to act on it, that's what she's waiting for, something definite, something positive. After all, *she's* not going anywhere.'

2

So now he had another name to add to the list of people insisting he go to Europe; four out of four – Eve, Dan, Mandie, and Mrs Carmichael – and they were perfectly correct, all of them, it was stupid to hang around like an unemployed nurse. It was also true, as everyone kept telling him, that there was nothing he could do.

Spying Simon weaving towards him, he wondered where Eve kept the number for the cat watcher. He pulled open various drawers and cupboards and then came up with the brilliant idea of having a look at the notice board, the object he saw and barely noticed every day, hanging above the kitchen worktop. 'Hair, doctor, dentist, vet, electrician, plumber,' Alex relayed to Simon as he read all the cards and scraps of paper that littered the board. 'Dan,' he read out, continuing his investigation. Then he stopped. 'Dan?' he queried, looking at the cat. 'Why Dan?' He shook his head and shrugged his shoulders and went back to scanning the sea of information. There was only one number, that of someone called Margaret, that looked as though it could be a likely candidate. He picked up the phone and dialled.

'Hello,' said a woman's voice.

'Hi . . . Um, is this Margaret?' Alex shook his head at the stupidity of the question and the Englishness of his voice.

'Yes.' The one word response seemed to lift itself at the end, assertion trailing into hesitant enquiry.

'Okay, good. This is Eve's . . . well, er, Eve's other half.' He raised his eyes towards a ceiling of heavy confusion.

'Alex!' came the friendly reply. 'Yes, I know all about you. How are you? Happy New Year! What can I do for you? Or maybe the question should be, what can I do for Simon?'

'Ah, yes, happy New Year. But, actually, not really. Eve's had an accident . . .'

'Accident? Eve? How? When?'

'A few days ago, she was hit by a car.'

'A car? How? When?'

'A few days ago, she's in hospital.'

'Hospital, you say? Is she bad?'

'Not good, Margaret, not good, not at the moment, but she'll be okay, they say. The thing is . . .'

'Thank *good*ness! What a *fright*, what a *wor*ld. A *car!* My, *my!*'

'Yes, exactly, and that's why I'm calling. You see, I have to go to England.'

'Aha.'

'Yep, and there'll be no one here for Simon. Obviously.'

'Aha. But she'll be okay, you say? Eve?'

'Yes, yes, but she won't be coming home. Not just yet.'

'No. And you're going to England?'

'Yes.' Alex stopped, abruptly, suddenly realising how bad it sounded, as though he were abandoning a sinking ship. 'For a few days, Margaret, only for a few days.'

'You're leaving?'

'I'm leaving, but only for a short while. I'll be back when Eve comes out of hospital.'

'And you want me to feed Simon and clean his tray?'

Thank you God and Socrates and Poseidon and everyone, Alex mouthed at empty space. Thank you, thank you, *thank* you. 'Yes,' he answered breathily, in a heartfelt sort of way. 'Can you start on Friday? I'll call from England and let you know when I'll be back.'

'Yup, yup, no problem, and say hi to Eve. You will be seeing her before you go?'

'Of course. Thanks.' He hung up and smiled at Simon. 'Sorted, mate,' he said, bending down to collect the animal into his arms. 'Your English buddy has to go to the home-land,' he told the creature, 'but he'll be back, and so will your mistress. Meanwhile, your very own nurse will be here to look after you. How about that?' Pretty proud with himself and his powers of organisation in a foreign country, Alex scratched at Simon's neck, pirouetted through to the living room and thought about a travel plan.

Shit, Simon thought, what the hell's going on? Stuck in the arms of a twirling moron and sort of folded forwards over his own stomach, he was beginning to feel a little unsettled. Due to the sagginess of feline flexibility he found himself contemplating his nether regions and, for the umpteenth time, started wondering about the great mystery. It must have occurred a long while ago, the disappearance of his balls, for he had no memory of an accident and was certain there'd never been a medical problem during the short span of his life, thus far. All he knew was that one moment he'd had them, and then they'd gone. The whole thing was truly perplexing. He reckoned he was about twenty-years old, twenty-two, tops, and he thought about sex every day, especially during those times when the humans initiated their horny rituals.

Bugger, now he was starting to feel nauseous, so he waved his legs at the spinning whirlwind, unsheathed his claws and placed what he hoped was an intimidating look on his face, all teeth and drawn-back lips. Goodness, he could feel his chest coming up under his chin and his eyes began to go all sort of bulgy. And then, suddenly, he was the right way around and being lowered to the floor. Thank fuck for that, he thought, marching archly towards the sofa, one of his favourite places. Stretching up, full length, he sank his claws into one of the arms and pulled with all his cat-like might. It felt good, really really good, so he unhooked his talons, reinserted them, and again pulled at the fabric. Simon always made a point of keeping his claws in excellent shape and he knew they were sharp, shaper than . . . he didn't know what, he only knew that his flatmates were never too happy when he forgot himself, while dozing on one of their laps, and accidentally gripped a leg, or a thigh.

Having finished with the stretching business he leapt up and landed softly on one of the cushions, circling two or three times while pounding with his front paws. Settling down for a short nap, he curled his tail up to his nose and thought of female felines. He had a problem with this because . . . Well, because he hadn't met any. There was a definite shortage of female cats, of any cats, in the neighbourhood, especially the immediate surroundings which lay within the apartment and extended no further than the lofty balcony. Sometimes, though, he thought he heard a cat, a wistful miaowing that he knew just had to belong to a beautiful princess of a girl cat. But, what could he do? He was powerless.

His eyelids were getting heavy, drooping to their half-mast position, the stealthy I-look-half-alseep-but-I'm-actually-all-geared-up-for-immediate-action mode, common to cats, the big jungle-busting type as well as the smaller variety that plays with rodents. He slid his eyes from side to side and made a survey of the area in front of the sofa. Everything appeared normal, everything was quiet; the person who no longer was so much of a stranger seemed to have waltzed out of the room. Simon closed his eyes. And then he heard it – *click* – the sound of the button on the hi-fi. He grabbed his head between his paws and wondered which of the many variations of music he was going to be entertained with.

Chapter Four:

London

1

Alex wandered through the echoing extendable device and entered the aircraft that was to transport him three thousand miles to the east and into a completely different life-line, a veritable parallel Universe. This time, though, there was a difference. He was on an expedition, a mission stamped, sealed and approved by Eve. It was as if he had been fitted with a giant rubber band, one that would zing him back to Queens when the enterprise was complete.

The aircraft was a mess of shabby people struggling to find their seats and, having located them, using flabby arms to shove bulging bags into overhead lockers. Over-stressed parents argued about seating arrangements while attempting to pacify noisy brats and silence screaming babies. Cursing under his breath and wondering why he didn't possess his own private jet, Alex inched along the aisle. And then he ran into an obstacle. 'Shouldn't you be in the hold, mate?' he asked the freely perspiring man who was blocking everyone's life.

'Do I look dead, then?' the man responded in challenging manner.

'Nah, just big,' Alex answered in a chummy sort of way.

The outsize shape moved uncomfortably, wheezing and positioning itself to get a better view of its inquisitor. Wedged between two seats, the man peered at Alex through beady eyes and a thick layer of sight-enhancing glass.

'Take your time,' Alex advised thoughtfully, eyeing the queue that simmered along the length of the fuselage.

He surfaced into a cold sweat somewhere above Greenland, subconscious perturbations having led him down alleyways of huge misgivings. He'd read in some glossy magazine – the type that claims to have the answer to everything – that flying is the ultimate release from worldly worries; after all, the article had surmised, once the rubber leaves the tarmac there's no turning back. The oven you forgot to switch off would get hotter, the front door you forgot to lock would remain treacherously obtuse, and, through desperation, the unfed goldfish would leap into the cat's gleeful mouth and there'd be absolutely nothing you could do about it. Lawyers describe the situation by pinching defunct words from an extinct language: *res ipsa loquitur*. Alex described it differently and called it a fucking headache. True, trapped in an aircraft with no connection between heaven and earth and with no possibility of turning off the gas, locking the door or feeding the fish, there is nothing to be done and worry is therefore an exercise in futility. Better by far to order a piña colada and follow your stately procession across the tiny world constantly changing perspective on a miniature television screen. Knowing this, however, didn't prevent him from conjuring up all sorts of wild demons.

'Gin and tonic, please, with ice and lemon, and let's make it two,' he asked the hostess, who'd appeared almost at the same instant that he'd pressed the button above his head.

'Lemons?'

'Gins,' he responded quickly, trepidation standing heavily on something in his head and filling the airspace above Greenland with strange imaginings. 'And some nuts; peanuts, or cashews . . . or crisps, something salty to go with the gin. I think I'm falling to pieces.'

'Sir?'

'You know, panic attack?'

'Aha.'

'And I need an intake of energy to get over it.'

'Yes, sir, of course.' The hostess glided away down the aisle and left Alex in his shroud of doubt. His mind raced through several years, back to a situation in a supermarket when he'd almost started to hyperventilate while standing in a queue at the checkout. Actually, it was something that had happened on several occasions. His stomach would start to feel all peculiar and he'd begin to sweat and wonder what would happen if his body just happened to explode, right there, next to the goodies purposefully displayed to attract the straying fingers of bored brats, the ones who yelled in dismay when they received a wallop from despairing mothers.

He looked out of the porthole, at an unnaturally bright sun in an unnaturally blue sky and at the thick wedge of cotton wool that was effectively separating everything from the planet that was home to every living creature in the Universe. The whole design was so unfuckingbelievable that it managed to capture his fevered mind for more than a few seconds before returning him to the supermarket. It was a strange sensation, he recalled, that of being convinced that one is about to splatter everybody with blood and guts. It was sort of like having an enormous fart bottled up inside you, one that couldn't escape, up or down, and the only way out, the only remedy that the body could come up with, was to explode. And what's more, he suddenly realised, it used only to happen in one specific supermarket. There had never been any problem in Waitrose or Sainsbury's, or Spa, nor even in that German supermarket with the strange name – he was always able to stand in line in these places, feeling no queasiness whatsoever. He tried to remember the name of the dangerous one, the supermarket whose layout was imprinted forever on his mind. Bugger, it was there on the tip of his tongue and he knew it was located in England. It wasn't one of the jaunty places he'd been to in New York, the stores where everyone seemed to be Jewish or Hispanic and much more friendly than their counterparts across the ocean, the broad sweep of bluey-greeny stuff that held the continents apart and above which he was comfortably sitting as the hostess made a return approach along the aisle . . . and walked straight past, obviously on a mission to another passenger in need of sustenance.

Alex turned his mind away from supermarkets and focused on a more immediate issue. Eve. She'd been radiantly positive when suggesting that he should go and visit everybody. 'Go, do,' she'd said. 'Make a plan.' Well, now the plan was unfolding and he was worried about her attitude. What did it mean? Was she genuine in her support, eager that the mysteries surrounding the paintings should be resolved? Was she as cool and laidback as she'd seemed when the conversation had eventually alighted on Jessica? Jesus, he thought, women normally tend to get vexatious around the theme of previous lives and the connotations thereof. Eve, however, had continued without batting an eyelid. 'Go, Alex, go,' she'd told him when he'd returned to her bedside with a rough outline of what he intended to do. 'Say "hi" to all these people I've heard so much about and one day want to meet. The trip'll do you good.' She'd smiled as well, lips and eyes together as if, as if . . . as if she really meant it. Alex flipped down the shelf in anticipation of his drink and nibbly things, and immediately thought about hinges. 'Blimey,' he muttered, 'I'm be*com*ing unhinged.'

'Excuse me?' the hostess asked.

'Oh, nothing,' Alex replied, looking up at a face that was older than its makeup was attempting to present.

The makeup allowed a brief smile. 'That's okay, then, sir,' said the pleasant voice as a plastic cup with a chunk of lemon inside, a small can of tonic, two tiny bottles of Beefeaters and a bag of pretzels, arrived on a tray. 'I've brought you a menu.'

'Menu?'

'Yes, sir. A list of food, hot and cold. Wine too.'

'Ah, thanks,' Alex managed, feeling better and slightly less sweaty as he filled the cup and raised it to his face. 'Menu.'

'Yes, sir. Menu.' The smiling lady walked away down the aisle.

Alex looked out at the surface of cloud, flat and uniform beneath the steely sun. And then an aircraft flashed past in the opposite direction and he was certain it had been at the same altitude. 'Shit,' he exclaimed to the filigrees of ice traced across the blue yonder. 'I hope the skipper knows what he's doing.'

'Nothing to worry about,' said the man on his left, the man who hadn't uttered a word since taking the seat next to him. 'At least a thousand feet.'

'Yes. But on the same level,' Alex replied nervously.

'No, up and down. A thousand feet between opposing flight paths.'

'You're kidding?'

'No, actually, I'm not. When an aircraft reaches cruise velocity it has all these corridors and altitudes to stick to.'

'But what if the pilot forgets?'

'Oh, there's a bunch of computers to organise everything while the pilot stares out of the window.' The man turned to look at Alex. 'Used to be a pilot, air force, but that's a whole different ball game.'

'How so?' asked an interested Alex.

'Speed,' came the answer, direct, military style, 'manoeuvrability also.' Alex's co-passenger chuckled, 'F15s don't got too many passengers to worry about.'

'No,' Alex agreed, 'I suppose they don't.' He resumed his inspection of ice crystals, mouthing 'Got' followed by a question mark, at the blue yonder. 'Hey,' he said, turning back to his new acquaintance. 'What about waste disposal?'

'Excuse me?'

Alex grinned at his neighbour. From some unknown quarter of his troubled mind had come the ancient unanswered question regarding the problem of in-flight waste disposal. 'Sorry,' he said, raising his hand to shake that of the ex-pilot, 'that was a little under par, something that just shot out of my head.'

'You don't say!'

'Yeah, well . . . it's a problem I've been carrying around for a long time and no one seems to know the answer.'

'Waste disposal?' asked the man who, in Alex's helter-skelter mind, should be able to provide an educated answer. 'What kind of waste disposal?'

'Ah, yes, exactly,' Alex responded, still grinning inanely. 'Well, you know when you go to the lavatory and press the lever, does it operate a flap like on a train and let everything drop out of the aircraft?'

'Oh, I see what you mean. No, not any more.'

'So everything gets contained and taken out when the aircraft's on the ground, then?'

'Yes.'

'Oh, that's a relief,' Alex said, taking a large swig from the small cup. 'It's been annoying me for quite some time and though I've asked several people, no one has been able to give me a straight answer, until now.'

'It's not something that most people would worry about.'

'No, I know, but . . . Well, you know how it is when you get something on your mind, it keeps coming back to haunt you.'

'In the old days, of course, everything fell into the sky, just like you said about the trains. But then aircraft started climbing to greater altitudes and the environmental people came along and told airlines to keep everything contained. Anyway, just imagine what would happen if you pressed your lever and opened a flap.'

'Why, what would happen?'

'Disaster. Everything would be sucked out of the airplane.'

'Shit, yeah, I s'pose it would.'

'Well, perhaps not out of the entire plane, but the edges of the lavatory door would be plastered with anything not bolted down in the cabin and there'd certainly be panic in the cockpit.'

'Wow, that's great, thanks. Here, have a pretzel,' Alex said, picking the packet off the shelf and offering it to the man who knew everything.

'No, thanks, I have to go to the head. That's what we call the lavatory in military parlance. Something else you can store in that mind of yours.'

Alex chewed on his pretzel and pondered.

There was some kind of hiatus at Heathrow. A loud traveller, wearing surprisingly subdued apparel, was screaming abuse at the carousel, claiming, 'A bunch of fucking incompetent individuals have lost my baggage. It's a nightmare. It's a disaster is what it is.'

Wandering aimlessly and uncertainly, like a hooligan, Alex sauntered along to see what was causing all the noise. As he approached the scene of battle, he noticed that the upset passenger was none other than the overlarge gangway obstruction that he'd lambasted for holding up the embarkation. Alex shuffled himself to one side and slid between the half-dozen onlookers.

Glowering left and right, the hefty soul walked up and down both sides of the revolving slats yelling 'Bastards' at the empty device. A thud and clatter alerted him to the possibility that at last his bags had been delivered – via a succession of trucks, trailers and conveyor belts – from the womb-like underbelly of the Boeing 757. He rushed to the mouth of the black hole out of which other more fortunate pieces of luggage had tumbled a lifetime ago, only to witness a pram, folded into negligent flatness, and a bag of golf clubs or fishing rods, start their weary cycle on the merry-go-round. 'Bastards,' he yelled at the articles as they crept past and then crept past again. 'Complete and utter bastards.'

Turning his back on the situation, Alex collected his bag from a neighbouring carousel and without so much as a nod toward the wayward hugeness, wandered off towards the Piccadilly Line.

2

Opening the door into musty atmosphere, Alex stepped into the welcoming embrace of an unused dwelling, cold and slightly damp. He threw the keys onto the kitchen table and went through a stack of letters collected from the doormat; bills, nearly all of them. Disgusted, he deposited them, unopened, in a heap next to the kettle. Turning to lean against the worktop, he realised he could do with something slightly stronger than coffee. He opened a cupboard above the sink and stared at a collection of plates and bowls; then he opened another cupboard and discovered cans of tinned food – a miscellany of baked beans, mango slices, raspberries in syrup, haricots vert and diced tomatoes. Running out of cupboards, he looked in the fridge and found memories of the way things used to be. Half a pack of butter, a carton of eggs, two rolls of film, jars of various sauces at various levels and on various levels, and a lost world of rust-coloured broccoli and something nastily indecipherable in the vegetable drawer. The fridge door was more forthcoming, offering a selection of several items: a jar of honey, smooth and untouched; a carton of milk, open and dangerously dated; a bottle of not very much New Zealand Pinot, and a can of Australian lager. 'God bless the colonies,' Alex said, grabbing the beer and shutting the door. He ripped the tab, picked up the mail and slouched into the living room.

It was early evening and the room was unsatisfactorily eclipsed, so he switched on a small table lamp which satisfactorily revealed the dimension of unlived-in chaos. As well as illuminating two feet of the wall behind it, the circle of warm friendly light threw its radiance across the carpet and reached out to the large unpacked boxes that filled the space beneath the bay window, boxes that had been there so long Alex had no idea what was in them. He recalled a saying, some sort of flimsy belief that if you don't use something for a year or so, you might as well throw it away. 'Yeah,' he muttered, raising the beer can to his lips, 'throw it away and then spend the rest of your days regretting it.' Selecting a box at random, he set it onto the carpet in front of the sofa, placed the can on it and sat down to go through the mail. Electricity, gas, phone, a flurry of junk advertising, a letter from the council and a couple of envelopes bearing London postmarks and hand-written addresses.

Alex pursed his lips and ripped into the first envelope. It was from the landlord, a wordy missive in pidgin English, asking, "Please Mister Alex to tell me where you are being, for I am knocking many times on door and no answer am I receiving. I look through windows and I am seeing boxes. I knock on door and windows yesterday and tomorrow and all week I am knocking and never nothing, only boxes. Please to contact me with much hurry. Mr Banergee (your landlord)." Alex read the letter again. In spite of the iffyness, it was beautifully written, and the word "tomorrow" had been neatly crossed out and replaced with "day before". He laid the letter on an arm of the sofa, resolving to get in touch with the honourable Mr Banergee on the morrow.

The second letter, also handwritten, also demanding to know his whereabouts, was from Jessica. "I've been everywhere," Alex read, "spoken with everyone, and have met a blanket of silence. No one is talking. Whether or not they know where you are, they're not saying. Christine . . . remember Christine? Well, she rabbited on about Terry and the pictures and Michelstraub and ended up asking me if I knew what he was going to do with them? Me! Why would she ask me? And then she said something about someone's granddaughter, Elly? Elisa? Something like that, something beginning with E. Yes, E, I'm sure of it. Evelyn? So then I start thinking about you and wondering if you're ok and what can possibly be keeping you in America for so long? No, Eve, that was it, the granddaughter. America! Of all places! Over Christmas, too! And the New Year! Everything's going crazy and I just need to know what's going on, you know? Eileen's being great, remember her? She was the girl who came to the meeting with me, you know, the meeting when everyone told me I had to give back the painting. Well, I'm not going to – I said so then and I'm saying so now. I suppose you've told Michelstraub? Well, I don't care, the picture's as much mine as it is his. So where are you? Have you come back? Can we meet up? You can call me, you know. I don't have your number so you have to call me. Please. J."

Alex raised his eyes to the number scrawled at the top of the page. 'Hmm,' he said, 'another call for the morning.' Aside from the bills, the letter from the council remained unopened. He took another swig of beer, tore open the envelope and scanned the page. It didn't take long – the councillor for traffic thanked Alex for his observations regarding the speed ramps on Samuels Road and went on to say that after due consultation with the department chiefs, the decision had been taken to leave the ramps *in situ*.

'Fuck!' He yelled, slamming the letter onto the packing case. 'This is what you get when you deal with fucking imbeciles.' He had no idea why he was shouting, after all, the room was devoid of almost everything, especially people. Alex didn't care, he had no time for these insensitive bastards, these ignorant peasants who listen to no one but themselves. He'd tried to explain it, rationally, in easy-to-understand English, how it would be far better to slow the traffic via some sort of narrowing at various points along the street. Bollards could be used, as in other boroughs, successfully. He'd written about the emergency services, wondering if the learned councillor had imagined being shaken about in the back of an ambulance as it navigated portly sleeping policemen. 'Bollocks,' he said, crushing the letter into a crinkly ball and sending it on a trajectory which took it through the hallway and into the kitchen. 'I don't know why I bother, it's a brick wall of obsequious ass-lickers, none of whom has the courage to stand up as an individual and face the facts.'

Mortified and raging he thought about ransacking the fridge to see if he could find another beer, and then realised he still had half a can which needed downing. Lifting the can from the box, he shook his head as he thought about the futility of trying to communicate with idiots. 'Fuck it,' he said, and decided to investigate the contents of the packing case; it was there, in front of him, and the time was right. Using the discarded ring-pull to slice through the layers of brown tape holding the box together, he folded back the flaps and discovered a library of music – CDs and vinyl and a few cassettes – and, sitting in the centre, a pack of Waitrose ground coffee, Italian and strong. He looked at the remainder of the boxes clogging the bay window and wondered if one of them contained the *cafetière*. And then the phone rang and went through its rigmarole of automatic answering. Alex picked up the device at the moment it decided to beep. 'Hello?'

'Fuck! You're back, then?'

'Yes, Nick. Here I am.'

'Great! There's a party.'

'A party?'

'Yes, you know, fun thing? Alcohol, women, and more alcohol.'

'Really?'

'Music, women and alcohol. Maybe food, too.'

'Oh, I don't know, it's . . .'

'What are you like? You've been away too long.'

'No, it's just, um . . . Well, I've got this . . .'

'No you haven't, no excuses. Tomorrow. I'll meet you around six, at the Elephant. I may be late, so here's the address.'

'But . . .' The instrument went silent in Alex's hand and he looked at it in dismay and annoyance. 'Bugger.' He sank into the sofa and found his mind wandering back to another Christmas – twelve, thirteen months ago – another place in another time, a desperate time with desperate measures. Actually, the location had been exactly the same, London; but time, having taken notice of Dicken's majestic entry into two cities and clinging with all its hands to the maestro's tenth word, had left Alex reposed on the edge of foolishness. Like a metronome, he'd swung in and out of sensibilities, emotions running amok through faulty penumbras as he'd skated unerringly towards a black hole. There had been no rules, no guidelines, just a wavering path through a giddy mind game of complexities.

Letting his body sag to the left, he lifted his legs onto the sofa and lay flat on his back. Gazing up at the ceiling he noticed a thin crack in the paintwork, just at the point where the wall starts its downward journey, and for some reason that had absolutely nothing to do with religion his thoughts latched onto a well-known confessional, words that might have made sense in yet another place and time. *We have left undone those things which we ought to have done; and we have done those things which we ought not to have done.* Inspecting the paintwork from a distance, he smiled, knowing that the words also had nothing to do with slovenly maintenance. Olfactory senses, conjuring up aromas of cheap perfume and illicit sex, somehow nagged at his dick and brought to mind the speedy spurting into the rubber-protected confines of a young prostitute. *And there is no health in us.* Jesus! He felt his skin crawl at the memory of his meeting with Jessica on a dismal city street, at the frustration he'd experienced when, aware that he was unable to do anything, he'd seen the torment clawing at her from the inside. There had been no relief, for her, or for him. He'd begun to wonder if she was schizophrenic, not deeply and darkly, but just a little, enough anyway to explain her wild mood swings. There was the sweet, lovable, beautiful Jessica, always ready with a smile or a kiss, hyper-intelligent and an equal in the never-ending tussle of word-association. Then, there was the other Jessica, the lost little princess, the vindictive seductress with wild eyes and abrasive tongue. The struggle had pulled Alex inside out, had pinned him to the vivisection table à la Prufrock, his tortured soul wrenched out of his body and left trailing for all the world to see. Recalling their last meeting, early in the previous year at Christine and Terry's apartment in Pimlico, he remembered the look on her face when she'd stated her intention to keep the Vermeer. With an expression like that, Alex knew there'd be no chance of negotiation, and he'd come away empty handed.

3

For twenty miserable minutes Alex kicked his heels outside a centre for alternative medicine on the busy edge of the Elephant. With a confused wind blowing from all directions, but mainly from the east, he fumed, while all feeling ebbed rapidly from his body and his brain. And then, pissed-off with just about everything but most especially with Nick, who'd failed to arrive at the appointed hour, he made the unwise decision to try and find the address that had been transmitted via the phone. Standing outside the herbalist, he peered through the window at all sorts of vegetation – dried stuff dangling from hooks and living stuff growing out of wooden trays – and at row upon row of little brown bottles, some fitted with screw tops and some having those dinky rubber-teated dropper-type things. His eyes latched onto a woman, a tall one with long mousey hair. She was dressed in something resembling a sheet, oranges and purples flowing downwards from the neck, and every now and then he caught sight of sandalised feet that looked a little grimy, though the vision might have been clouded on account of the establishment's none-too clean windows. He watched her giving some money to a crinkly Chinaman and he watched as she walked towards the door, the variety that brushes against Buddha-type chimes every time it's opened and closed. Shutting the dingly-dangly contraption behind her, the woman paused, as though charmed by the sound of splintering icicles, before stepping onto the blustery pavement and clutching her sheet around her thinness. Alex made his move and frightened her out of a cloud of incense-induced Oriental wellbeing. 'Hey,' he said. 'Do you live round here?'

'Um . . .'

'Because I need to know where Doncaster Avenue is.' He smiled to show that he was harmless.

'Um . . .' Vagueness manifested itself somewhere in the pools of the woman's eyes.

'It's okay if you don't, I mean not everyone can live around here, can they?'

'Not far, a couple of blocks away.' Somewhat aided by the breeze, the woman waved a loose part of her apparel in an uncertain direction.

'Great! Thanks.' Alex turned on his heels.

'No, no, wrong way.'

He stopped and looked at the woman who was now pointing the sheet in another direction. 'Well, which one?'

'That's where I live,' the tall thin person stated, pointing towards the setting sun. 'You confused me, I thought that's what you asked.'

'No, no, I wanted to . . .'

'Yes, yes, I realise now, that wasn't it at all.' A small grin of mixed emotion flashed across the woman's face. 'You see, sometimes people ask me if they can . . .'

'Never mind all that,' Alex said, transferring the smile to

his eyes in the hope that the woman would zip back to the planet so they could start all over again. 'Doncaster Avenue.' He said it slowly and meaningfully, as though dealing with an immigrant.

The woman in the sheet burst into a chorus of girly giggles, the tittery kind that sort of makes everything shiver. Turning her body away from Alex, she pointed into a blast of gutsy wind. 'That way, that way, over there.'

Alex squinted across a stream of stranded traffic at a grouping of miserable-looking shops. 'You sure?' he asked.

'I think so, I seem to think it is.' Having ceased her laughter the woman stood still, appearing forlorn, waif-like and lost in the big city. Alex looked at her and wondered what sort of medicament she'd purchased from the eastern apothecary, and what sort of ailment could be locked away within the fragile frame.

'Okay, thanks.' He nodded his head in emphatic approval before venturing into the static traffic.

The area was full of dust and desolation and perfumed with the astringency of melted tar. Running his fingers along a slatted fence that was usefully stopping screes of rubble from crowding the pavement, Alex ended up collecting a splinter and dislodging further aromas, tinctures of resin and creosote. All around, drab terraces were being demolished and replaced with spiky modernity, harsh, metallic and fronted with acres of glass. Diminished rays of sunshine followed his progress as he picked at his punctured finger. Looking up at the surrounding buildings, he marvelled at why people should want to live in boxy fish tanks, fish tanks with views of other fish tanks. He stuffed his finger into his mouth and resumed pacing.

As he came to a crossroads, his attention fully occupied with the problem of applying large teeth to miniscule mote, a small boy came zooming round the corner and crashed into him. Whilst the collision knocked the wind out of him, he was almost emasculated by one of the lad's flying elbows. 'Fuck!' he exclaimed, immediately forgetting the chunk of wood stuck in his digit and using the hand to clutch at his midriff. His other hand wandered into belated protection of his genitals. 'Fucking look where you're going.'

The gamin edged off the pavement and into the street, looking for people his own size. He didn't notice that he was being regarded by the tall stranger, who'd stopped, turned about and was steadily advancing towards him.

'Oi!' Alex called out. 'Do you know where Doncaster Avenue is?'

'Why?'

'It's supposed to be somewhere around here and I can't find it.'

'Keep goin', round the corner, then first left.' The kid grinned slyly and Alex didn't know whether to believe him or not. He had no choice. He was clueless about this area south of the river and had been following vague directions ever since leaving the Elephant.

'Are you sure? You're not telling porkies?'

' 'Course.'

'You are telling porkies?'

' 'Course not.'

'Okay, then. Um . . . thanks.' Alex stood and watched as the lad picked up a pebble and hurled it at a notice fixed to the fence. The metallic *splang* caused by the missile meeting its target seemed to satisfy the boy and he smiled at Alex as if proud of his aim, as if proud of his superiority in knowing where he was. Clutching his crotch, Alex grinned back and unspoken amnesty reached across the hazy street.

Doncaster Avenue was long and tatty, bordered with terraced houses featuring sad façades and neglected pointing, most of them sporting a rich assortment of threadbare fabrics, blankets and stripy sheets to ward off the sun's rays and the enquiring eyes of the collector of rents. As Murphy ordered, and as Alex usually complied, he approached the street from the wrong end and groaned at the thought of tramping along an endless pavement. A whisper of noise, invisibly sourced and faintly ominous, came creeping through the darkening streets from somewhere ahead. It sent Alex's mind reeling back to the hideous catastrophe of New Year's Day, until he remembered that Eve's accident had been preceded by a frosty silence. The sounds began to grow in intensity in the manner of an approaching hurricane, but perhaps more in the form of a mobile circus, volatile clamour reverberating from the enclosing brick walls. Then, wheeling into view, a veritable barrage of humanity, dragging its noisy envelope of home-grown complexities, came boring down the street: adults and children, pensioners and babies and dogs and perambulators, and a pedal-propelled racing car grinding its plastic wheels against the road's dishevelled surface. The whole confusion of babble swept its way towards Alex and sort of flowed around him, leaving him in its wake, stranded as though at low tide. He watched as the amoeba-like entity flooded from portal to portal and wondered where it was going. Maybe they'd been evicted, he thought, maybe the landlord's patience had run out. But there were so many, young and old, an emigration as though escaping from civil strife, an hegira with no baggage and no belongings. There was conversation, Alex realised, convivial and loud, hardly the frightened murmurs of a band on the run. And there were children, laughing and playing and running between the ankles of adults who were oblivious to their raucous offspring. And there was a girl, a glossy teenager dressed to the nines in a skirt the width of a bandage and a top as tight as a bandage, who slackened her pace as the extended family drew level with Alex's presence. In the manner of a frisky colt, the girl's high-heeled pronouncements caught Alex's attention and he quickly noticed the sly smile that issued from the minx's lips when she caught his eyes. Obviously the family slapper, he mused, ogling the skinny legs and the inviting wobble of nubile ass. Every family has its token tart, randomly positioned and incorporated on one of its branches, for otherwise procreation would surely cease and entire families would grind to a complete halt in a time-span of one or two generations.

By the time he reached number 162, he felt and looked like an athlete who'd just completed a marathon; but he had succeeded in the painful withdrawal of the troublesome splinter. After the conflagration with the youngster, he'd removed his jacket, sort of holding it in front of him while massaging his bruised ego and trying to regain equilibrium; and, while walking the length of the deserted street, he'd draped the garment over his shoulders, first the left, then the right, until, engulfed in the sea of refugees, he'd clasped it protectively over his chest. Now, having at last arrived at the designated address, the piece of excess clothing had become something of a burden, so he shrugged back into it. Breathing heavily, in the manner of an over-heated boiler, he rapped his knuckles against the peeling door and waited. A minute later he knocked again and was surprised when the door immediately flew open and a red-haired man, all fiery and angry in appearance, stood in front of him.

'Aye?'

'Number 162?'

Malevolent eyes glared at him before swivelling towards a collection of Roman numerals nailed at eye level to a series of elderly bricks, eroded and wedged between the door and a dilapidated window. 'Aye.'

'This is where the party is?' Alex asked in some hesitation.

'Party? I dinna think so.'

'You know, girls and drink and everything?' Alex tried to remember what Nick had told him and then had the bright idea of asking the man from across the Borders if Nick had arrived.

'Nick? I dinna ken no Nick.' The Scotsman stopped and thought about the matter. 'But I know a Dick. Lives opposite, number one-fifty-nine. Geordie, mad as they come, but a good drinker, aye he's that a'right.'

'Shit.' Frustration crawled across Alex's skin and squeezed fresh rivers of sweat from over-exerted pores. He removed his jacket, again, and held it in front of him like a bunch of wilting flowers as he stood transfixed between northern territories. 'Shit.'

'How about a whisky?'

Alex looked up at the freckled face which had allowed a welcoming smile to connect its eyes.

'Or a beer?'

'What's occurrin'?' a voice called from several doors' distance along the street.

'Wrong house,' Alex responded succinctly. Stepping back from the threshold, he waved his jacket at Nick and thought about a can or a bottle of cool beer.

Nick arrived like a sodden sponge, beads of sweat dripping from his eyebrows. 'Where're the girls? Who's this?' he asked, panting and glaring at the red-haired giant.

'Aye, ye'd better come in, the both o'youse,' the Scot suggested. 'I could use a wee laugh and I guess youse two could use a wee bevvy.'

'What's he talking about?' Nick asked from the depths of confusion. 'Where's the party?'

'There is no party,' Alex explained, 'not here at any rate. Who gave you this address?'

'Someone at work, evidently some fucker who was having a joke.'

'Or maybe you just got the address wrong?' A set of ginger eyebrows arched in lofty amusement.

Alex and Nick looked at their host as if he were some kind of sage.

'Well?' Alex asked.

'Well . . . it's possible . . . anything's possible, isn't it? But I'm sure he said one-sixty-two.'

'It could've been one-fifty-two,' Alex suggested. 'They sound a little alike.'

'Nah, it was definitely one-sixty-two.'

'Well, maybe you got the street wrong?'

'Doncaster? How could I get that wrong? Nothing sounds like Doncaster.'

'Maybe it was Terrace or Close, or Crescent?' Alex was good at supposition. 'Street?'

The Scotsman led them into a dim living room, its window

screened by an unhealthy-looking piece of material draped from a nail above each corner. A shabby sofa and an unrelated armchair fought for space on a circular rug, and improvised bookshelves supported a wealth of reading matter, all of it old and tatty and somehow alluring.

'What are we doing here?' Nick asked.

'It's the result of your directions.' Alex believed in honest answers.

'Yeah, well, what now?'

'Let's drink the Scotsman's beer, you know, since he offered?'

'Ok, but . . .'

'It's polite, it's the right thing to do; besides, I'm knackered after walking all over south London. I think there's going to be a storm. There has to be a storm, even though it's January; there's always a storm when the weather goes all sultry.'

'Alex, you're such a girl.'

'Why?'

'Sultry weather? Who talks about sultry weather?'

'Dunno, the BBC?'

'Here you go, then.' The Scot had returned with an armful of Tennent's lager, tall cans beaded with the bother of refrigeration. 'This'll cool ye down.' He slumped into the leather-upholstered armchair and flung his legs over one of its arms. Ripping open one of the cans, he eyed his visitors who were sitting uncomfortably upright, puppet-like on the sofa. 'Aye, this is a surprise,' he announced, wondering if they had strings, 'I dinna get many visitors.'

'Where do you come from, then?' Nick asked as he, too, opened a can of lager.

'Scotland.'

'Uh-ha.'

'Oh, I see. Edinburgh.'

'Mmm . . . nice place,' Alex offered, his knowledge of the city extending as far as the castle and perhaps the Forth Bridge.

'No it isn't, it's dull, like the weather. Grey and brown, but mostly grey.'

'What about the castle? That's nice.'

'Is it?'

'Stuck on its hill, on a nice summer's day . . .'

'It's a castle, not too different from most other castles.'

'Is that why you're here, then?'

'No, it's the money. Better down here than up there.'

'Yes, but also more expensive.'

'Dinna believe it,' the Scotsman declared, draining his can. 'Edinburgh's bloody expensive and full of Londoners.'

'Everywhere's expensive when you don't have money,' Alex observed thoughtfully and superfluously.

'Aye, too true.' Leaning forward, the host shuffled tethered beer cans across the floor. Selecting one for himself, he sort of gestured to his guests, saying, 'I've whisky if ye'd rather.'

'No, beer's fine,' Alex replied, looking to Nick for confirmation.

'So what about the party?' The Scot asked, sinking back into his throne.

'Yes, Nick, what about the party?' Alex chided his friend.

'I think we'll have to give up on that,' Nick confessed.

'Can't you call someone?' the Scot suggested. 'What about the person who gave you the information in the first place?'

'Colin? I don't have his number.'

'But . . .'

'He's a colleague from work, a nine-to-five friend, not exactly a social buddy.'

'So we're fucked?' Alex deduced in a manner short and concise.

'You're no fucked,' the Scotsman grinned. 'Here, take another beer.'

'This is kinda strange.'

'Strange? No, not really, it's great to have someone to natter with. Like I said, I dinna get too many people knocking at my door.'

'Right.' Nick looked at Alex in a weird sort of way.

'So, who do you support?' The Scot asked, staring chummily towards Alex.

'Sorry?'

'You know, football?'

'Oh, um, I don't really follow anyone, it's . . .'

'Och, so you'll be a poofter, then?'

'I am?' Alex stared back, ready to rebuild Hadrian's Wall in a matter of seconds.

'Well, if you dinna have a team . . .'

'Do you read a lot?' Alex cut in, getting to his feet to make a survey of the volumes stretched along sagging shelves.

'Aye, all the time,' came the answer, slightly cagey, miffed that the channel of inquiry had been diverted. 'Sometimes two or three books at once.'

'How do you do that?' Nick asked, aiming to keep the conversation on a safe level. 'Don't you tend to get the stories all mixed up?'

'I generally revolve around three different genres; it helps prevent confusion. You know, something historical, something classical, and perhaps a novel for light entertainment?'

'Blimey,' Nick observed, 'so this probably means you're gay.' He smiled archly, lifted a can from the metallic forest on the floor and pulled the tab. 'You know, if you've always got your head in a book?'

The Scot grinned and broke into loud guffaws. 'Jesus, no bad for an Englishman.'

'Yep, we Londoners enjoy a good joust, 'specially when the opponent falls off his steed.' Though steely, Nick's reply was delivered with a disarming smile and enough insouciance to bring all global confrontation to a sudden halt.

Alex, having twisted round on his heels to observe the fallout, continued through another one-hundred-and-eighty degrees until the world of literature once again was at his fingertips. He was beginning to forget about the promised party and the lure of loud music and women to match, such things were seldom what they were cracked up to be; at least, that's what he told himself. And anyway, Nick's buddy had well and truly cocked everything up by giving him the wrong address. Shit, then there was Jessica! Arrangements had been made. It was like stepping back in time. Again. All the uncertainties associated with the relationship that had cruised catastrophically back and forth between Scylla and Charybdis came flooding into his head. It was unwarranted, all of it, everything, yet Jessica was sitting there like a great black cloud in the back of his mind and his subconscious began fretting about tomorrow's meeting. Life is so strange, he thought, realising how easy it is for humans to adapt to sudden change. The idea of a raucous shindig now seemed as remote and unnecessary as the splinter he'd sundered from the fence. Fuck, fuck, fuck. Jessica, Jessica, Jessica. He had a sudden urge to spread his wings and fly straight to New York. But then, flapping his imagination like a demented crow somewhere high above Daventry, he understood that closure was necessary.

Can in hand, he continued his inspection of the Scotsman's collection until he came across a copy of Salinger's classic novel. 'One of my favourites!' he exclaimed, breaking the silence that stood between Nick and the Scot. He pulled the book from between its neighbours and held it so that the two men could see the cover.

'Aye, one of mine, too.' The Scot lunged at the chance to redeem himself. 'Read it when I was a teenager and sort of fell in love with, with . . .'

'Holden,' Alex happily supplied the name.

'Holden. Yes. He became my hero and I became a rebel. Still am, 'specially when it comes to governments and politics and authority.'

'Shit, isn't everybody?' Alex stated somewhat unnecessarily. He replaced the slim volume into its berth between Tennyson and Plato, and resumed his passage through the world of literature until the shelving came to an abrupt halt, abutting a cabinet containing a selection of CDs and videos. Having approved of the Scotsman's taste in reading matter, Alex transferred his attention to the array of recorded music. Pleasantly surprised, finding Ravel and Rachmaninov sharing space with Yes and Chicago, he turned to find the Scot looking at him with raised eyebrows.

'And?' The Scot's question was open to interpretation.

'I'm not gay.' Alex returned to the sofa.

'Bit of an issue, is it?'

'Nah, couldn't give a shit. It's just . . .'

'Aye, I ken what you're saying. It was a wee joke, sort of,

kind of. But that's no what I meant.'

'What did you mean?'

'Nothin'.' The Scot paused and scratched his chin. 'Och, you know, us northerners tend to think of all of youse down hereabouts as wussies.'

'So you do think about us, then?'

'But we dinna mean nothin'.'

'Of course, and now you're down here amongst us, one of us, so to speak. It's a big city.'

'Aye, it is that.'

'And full of all sorts, mostly foreigners.'

'Aye.'

'And men who wear skirts.'

'Aye, poofters. But you're no one of 'em.'

'And men who toss cabers.'

'So it *is* an issue?'

'Nah, mate, life's too short, we are what we are and there's fuck all anyone can do about it. People are people; some good, some bad, some short, some tall, know what I'm saying? Everyone's different, it's the way it is. And gays? Ah, shit, it's like everything else. Same as left-handed lesbians and health nuts who refuse to eat meat, and those people whose religion doesn't allow them to go to hospital. They're fine so long as they don't force the issue. Goes for anything really, there's no need to run around like a frustrated minority. Anyway, it's like the rain . . .'

'Rain? I dinna think I . . .'

'Nah, you probably don't. But who gives a shit? You go out, you get wet. Where's the point in faffing about with brollies when it rains most every day? Christ, they'd be up and down like the proverbials.'

'I think we've strayed from the point,' Nick cautioned, lifting a beer can to his lips.

'You do?' Alex asked. 'Fuck, didn't notice. Can't remember what the original question was.'

'Not surprised, mate,' Nick replied round the side of the can, 'but it was a great oratory. Shit, I'll have to get you to give the speeches at my wedding.'

'Wedding? What wedding?'

'In the future, distant future. No need to worry, you'll have time to prepare.'

'So what was the question?'

'It was more of an insinuation.'

'So what was the insinuation?'

'Is gayness an issue?' Nick readily reminded him, tapping his fingernails against the aluminium, slightly agitated in case it sent Alex off on another monologue.

'Oh, fuck. No.'

'Thank fuck for that, then,' said the Scot, edging back into the conversation, having been left high and dry while overlooking the flow of words.

'Yeah, no worries, mate. Anyway there's too much other stuff to think about.'

'Jesus, Mary, I dinna think I can take nae more.'

Alex stared at the Scotsman. 'Well, you need to. We should start worrying about numbers. There's too many of us, we're overrun, the place is bursting at the seams.'

'What place?' asked the bewildered man from heather-clad glens and castle-capped hills.

'London. The world.'

'Oh, right! Yeah, s'pose.'

'No two ways 'bout it. Have you walked down Oxford

Street lately?'

'Shit, yes,' Nick answered, butting into the discussion, 'foreigners everywhere you go. It's easier walking in the street, at least the buses are painted red so's you know to keep out of their way.'

'They're big fuckers, too, so youse can see 'em at a distance.'

'Right,' Nick and Alex concurred simultaneously.

'Och, youse two of a kind, and no bad for southerners.'

'I know,' Alex replied, then, looking at Nick, commented, 'That was masterful, that stuff about bookworms being gay.'

'Verbal parrying, mate, it's my métier,' Nick stated, looking at his beer can. 'Go on then, I s'pose you'd better answer the man.'

'Answer? What was the question?'

'Tell him about his collection, CDs and stuff.'

'Oh, shit, yeah, impressive,' Alex announced, turning to address his host. 'Great stuff, books as well. Truly amazing.'

'What is? That a Scot should have a wide taste?'

'No, no, not at all. It's just that people tell me that *I* have an eclectic taste, so it's always an eye-opener when I discover it exists in other places.'

'Exactly,' the Scotsman agreed. 'You know, I find it really discomforting when I find myself in a house with no books. It's as though something vital is missing, as if . . . as if . . .'

'You go water-skiing without skis,' Alex supplied.

'Aye, although water-skiing is a subject I know nothing about. Tried it once, in the Lake District.' The Scot began laughing, 'It was ridiculous, I had a gravity-defying waterfall shooting up the front of me body and into me face. There was water everywhere and I couldna breathe so I opened me mouth and almost drained the lake. Jesus, it was terrible.' He reached for another can, then, changing his mind, launched himself across the room to a small table crowded with bottles of spirits. 'Will ye no join me in a wee nip?' he asked over his shoulder, pouring Bells as though he owned shares in the distillery. 'But dinna go asking for soda or Coke or ginger ale, we dinna do that here.'

'Here?' Nick asked. 'In London?'

'London? This isna London ye Sassenach, this is the realm of the Thistle. This side of the door everything is Scottish. So, will ye or won't ye?'

'Do you have any ice?'

'Ice we have, I do believe.'

'Okay, then, yes please.'

Me too, then,' Alex grinned at the red-haired Scot. 'And since we've been here for almost an hour, maybe you'd tell us your name.'

'Och, you're a canny wee Englishman, asking my name before you resort to calling me Jock.'

'Well, you know . . .'

'Nay, dinna fash yersel', round hereabouts they all call me Jock.'

'They do?'

'Aye, that and worse. And then they start asking me what a Scotsman wears under his kilt, you know?'

'Uneducated bastards,' Nick surmised.

'So I divert them by saying that if you look real hard you can usually deduce the clan of a Scotsman.'

'What do you mean?' asked Alex.

'Well, I tell them that if he's sportin' a quarter-pounder, stands to reason he's a McDonald.'

'What do you mean?' Alex repeated.

'But if he's only got shortbreads, then it's obvious he's a Walkers.'

'Biscuits? You serious?' Nick asked.

'Aye. And then there's the lads with ginger nuts,' the Scot laughed. 'That usually shuts 'em up.'

'Ginger nuts? Which clan's that, then?' Alex asked, thinking he was beginning to follow the gist of the garrulous Scot.

'McVities, of course.'

'So what's your clan, then?'

'Och, I'm a McDougal.'

'So you'll be strong, yet plain and floury?' Nick retorted, grinning widely.

'No, no,' Alex laughed, 'he'll be self-raising!'

'So, Mr McDougal, what do we call you?' Nick asked.

'Alex,' came the reply as two tumblers of whisky, large and generously charged, were ferried across the room.

'Really? That makes two of us.'

'Are you a Scot as well, then?'

'Don't think so,' Alex answered. 'I was born listening to Bow Bells.'

'So you're a Cockney?'

'No, not really, the folks moved to Chingford. I'm an Essex boy.'

'With Cockney roots,' Nick assured his friend. 'And I'm Nick,' he added, introducing himself to the Scotsman. 'I'm an alcoholic.'

'Are you?' The Scot looked worried and directed a glance towards his stash of spirits.

'No, but that's what they say, isn't it? "Hi, my name's Nick, and I'm an alcoholic".'

'Not round here they don't. Everyone on this street is an alcoholic, but they dinna admit it of course.'

'You too?' Nick asked.

'Use't'be,' Alex the Scot confessed. 'It was messy, and dangerous. That's why I came down south, had to straighten meself out. Took a long time.'

'And now?'

'Never touch the stuff!' Alex the Scot winked above a large smile as he settled back into his armchair with a tumbler half-full of ice-free whisky.

Suddenly it was the following morning, seven-thirty, and the three men were doing their best to order breakfast in a greasy-spoon somewhere near the Old Kent Road. Alex the Scot did most of the talking, and since the owner of the café was also from north of the border, the two Londoners, understanding nothing of the lilting lingo, left them to it. Floundering to an accommodating table, they seated themselves on uncomfortable plastic chairs and supported heavy heads on sets of U-shaped palms. A short while later, after their newfound friend ceased jarring and came to join them, the praying mantises were jolted out of usquebaugh-induced reverie by a gaggle of giggling girls who frothed up to the counter and demanded coffee and scrambled eggs. Six bleary eyes followed the invasion as it settled in vulture-like disarray around three tables. Six ears listened to the shouts of glee and hoots of shrill laughter that reverberated within the shiny confines of the cheap tabernacle. And three brains came to the same conclusion.

'Last night's party!' Nick exclaimed, enthusiasm somewhat dampened by tiredness and something that threatened to dissolve his head.

'The one we missed,' Alex stated over a brave forkful of stabbed bacon.

'The one I saved you from,' the Scottish Alex announced over a suspicious hair-of-the-dog.

The London lads tried to keep their eyes open while the Tube train trundled through darkness. Lucky to have seats, they winced as the world – filling the carriage to five times its capacity – stamped on their toes.

'That was okay,' Nick managed to relate beneath a tabloid hovering above his head. 'Nice of the guy, really.'

'Yeah, he didn't know us from Adam.'

'Nor we, he.'

'No.'

The sentences were short and sort of simple.

'Pity 'bout the party, though,' Alex rallied. 'Those girls looked kind of tidy.'

'In your state, a fish out of water would be enticing.'

'Would it?' Alex asked in a confused, disbelieving sort of way.

'Believe me,' Nick reasoned.

'Believe you? When you're guidance system takes us to the wrong house?'

'That wasn't me, that was . . .'

'Okay, what about Munich, then?'

'What about Munich?'

'When you led everyone into that gay bar.'

'That wasn't me, that was . . .'

'No, no, you can't wriggle off that one, it was definitely you, the rest of us were too far gone.'

'Yeah,' Nick sniggered hopelessly, 'me too.'

'But it was great, wasn't it? I mean all that conversation about space and stuff, and time travel, and nuclear power versus fossil fuel.'

'Was it? What was?'

'Last night, Nick, at the house of the Scotsman.'

'Oh, right. Was it?'

' 'Course it was,' Alex answered, trying to decipher the larger lettering on the quivering newspaper. 'Aren't you interested in that sort of stuff?' he asked, shaking his head. 'It's the big picture, you know? and something the boffins are going to have to answer before too long.'

'Really?'

'Shit yes. How are these things going to work when there's no electricity?'

'What things?'

'Tubes, mate. They'll be stuck in the tunnel when the juice stops flowing.'

'Yeah, but I don't think it's going to happen anytime soon.'

' 'S'what I mean, innit? It's the big picture, it's the future.' Alex grinned at his friend. 'And then there's global warming.'

'Alex, you're talking too much and my head hurts.'

'I know, I know, but someone's got to think about it, haven't they?'

'I'm sure someone is thinking about it, but why does it have to be us?'

' 'Cause no one's doing anything about it, that's why.' Alex shuffled himself forwards on the seat so that he could gain access to his handkerchief. 'It's these papers,' he explained, 'the print gets up my nose, 'specially the stuff they use on crap like that.' He raised his eyes towards the flapping tabloid.

'Makes me sneeze.' Wrapping his nose in the handkerchief, he blew hard. 'Anyway,' he continued, stuffing the damp cloth back into a pocket, 'I enjoyed it, the party.'

'Yeah,' Nick agreed, 'it was okay.' He smiled through his headache. 'And Alex the Scot was kind of alright, wasn't he? I mean, he was pretty generous with all that booze.'

'He was, he was,' Alex nodded sagely. 'Deep too.'

'Deep?'

'Profound.'

'It's all those books, I've never seen so many. Do you think he's read them all?'

'Yeah, why not?'

'Um, dunno . . . just . . .'

'I've read loads of books, mate, hundreds of 'em.'

'But you're not gay.' Nick grinned widely.

'Fuck off.'

'But you're not.'

'Fuck *off*.'

'You're a what's-it-called.'

'Journalist?'

'Nah, you're a cunt.'

'Yeah, I know, but unlike you I'm an educated cunt.' Alex grinned at his superior reasoning as the train shot into a station.

'Shit,' Nick said, getting to his feet. 'I have to get off here.'

'Why, where are we?'

'King's Cross,' came the answer as Nick pushed his way through swirling throngs.

Alex sat back, tired and bemused, while a fresh load of humanity defied the logic of finite space. He closed his eyes and mentally counted the stations until he reckoned the train had made it to Southgate.

4

Alex was feeling itchy. Half of him was in agreement with Jessica's proposal to go to the Barbican, and the idea that music would act as a common ground, a sort of spongy barrier to absorb any premeditated emotions, seemed psychologically sound. The other half demanded that his feet make a rapid exit. Where was she, anyway? He'd already invaded the bar-with-the-sloping-floor and had ordered, and consumed, a miniscule glass of gin-and-tonic with ice and a slice purchased at an exorbitant price.

'When's the last time you got laid?' The question was direct, upfront and to the point, typical of Jessica on the warpath.

'Pardon?'

'Sex, you know, the thing we were good at?'

They were at the bar, exercising their legs and Alex's wallet during a twenty-minute interval, while stage hands busily shoved chairs and music stands to one side, removed the Steinway, and then returned the chairs and the music stands to the exact spots from which they'd just been taken. The

Chamber Orchestra of Europe had filed out of the other end of the auditorium to replace worn-out reeds, squeeze excess moisture from a variety of breezy apertures, cough and blow noses, assess the performance so far, check wigs and hairstyles, and make use of the facilities.

'Can't remember that far back,' Alex answered evasively. 'I could ask you the same . . . but I won't, it's not a man thing, we're not so nosey. We're brought up to understand that it's impolite to ask personal stuff like, "How old are you?" '

'You know how old I am.'

'Yep.'

'So?'

'So . . . how are you? How's the good life this side of the Atlantic?'

'Unchanged, basically. Well, no, perhaps that's not quite right. It gets, you know, more complex?'

'Really? Complex?'

'More things to take care of. More bills seem to come charging through the door and there's never enough time to see to everything. It's . . . monotonous.'

'But you were always on top of everything, little Miss Perfect in control of the Universe.'

'Was I?'

'You know you were.'

'Yeah, well, you were there to help.'

'Was I? I thought I was always in the way?'

'Only sometimes.'

Alex grinned and tore open a bag of cashews, spilling a few onto the venturesome slopes in front of the bar. The ringing of a tinkly bell toppled the alcoholic fraternity into something approaching panic as it hurriedly set about extracting the precious last few drops of social satisfaction. Empty vessels were crammed onto a dearth of receptive surfaces and the well-watered herd proceeded to execute crisscross migratory patterns in search of half-remembered seats.

The second half of the concert included a piece of music by Kodály, someone whom Alex had never known existed. But after listening to the *Háry János Suite*, and particularly the jaunty *Intermezzo*, he was hooked and knew he had to find a CD of this amazing stuff. It was like being at some mad Hungarian folk dance, the musicians well-oiled and delving into dangerous realms of modern jazz. Sometimes the music almost came to a halt and was sort of left hanging on a stringy seventh, tempting and sensual – just long enough to encompass a hurried orgasm should you happen to find yourself sprawled across three or four uncomfortable seats having illicit sex, while the orchestra plays on.

'*Fuck*ing *hell!*' Jessica shouted, standing on the oddly shaped remains of the car's broken window. '*Shit!*'

Alex stepped around the car, looking at the other windows, checking to see if they also had been smashed. 'Just the one,' he said across the roof. 'Give me the keys.'

Jessica fumbled in her coat pocket and handed over the car keys. 'What are you going to do?'

'I'm going to open the car,' Alex answered, leering through the glass of the front door on the passenger's side of the vehicle.

'Fuck, I could've done that,' Jessica grumbled. 'Why does it need to be a man's job?'

'It isn't, it's just that I don't want to disturb any fingerprints.'

'Fingerprints? Sh..t, how can you think about fingerprints?' Jessica stamped her feet, crunching broken glass into smaller fragments. 'Quick, open my door, I need to see if they've taken anything.'

Alex carefully inserted the key and unlocked the passenger door, using a handkerchief-covered finger to swing it fully open. Stretching across the front seats, he used the same method to unlock and open the driver's door. Jessica threw herself into the seat and began rummaging around underneath it, repeating the process under the passenger's seat and in the space between the two. 'Bollocks!' she yelled, twisting round to grope in the well between the front and rear seats. 'Fuck, they're such bastards.'

'Why? What did they do?'

'They fucked off with my bag.'

'Your bag? You left it in the car?'

'Yes, I left it in the car.' Jessica smacked the steering wheel with the flats of her hands. 'Shit! See? It's just like I told you, life is complex.'

'Not that complex, it isn't. I mean, leaving your bag . . .'

'Stupid, huh?'

'Sort of.'

'So what do we do, genius? I'd planned a nice dinner in Soho.'

'You did? Really?'

'Of course.'

'Okay, we still go. Try starting the car, see if it works.'

Jessica turned the ignition and gunned the accelerator. 'It works.'

'Okay, so let's find a police station.'

'A police station? Here? I suppose you know one?'

'No, just drive around, there's got to be one somewhere.'

'Oh, great, just drive around. What sort of plan is that?'

'The best I can come up with. Come on, let's make a move.'

Backing clear of the car park's disjointed chicken wire perimeter, Jessica began threading the car through tight spaces. 'So, where?'

'Dunno. Turn right and circle around a bit.'

'Great!'

'It's all guesswork. Where are we?'

'Um . . .' Jessica peered through the gaping window. 'Aldersgate.'

'Okay, so let's hang another right, then we'll try a few lefts.'

'What, next right?'

'Yep.'

Jessica swore as she swung the car into a narrow street. 'Shit, it's a dead-end. Bollocks.' Reversing rapidly, she twisted the tail end of the car into the road they'd just left and continued to the next right. 'How are we doing?' she asked. 'See any police stations?'

'We're doing fine; *you're* doing fine, great, just keep going. Throw a left, up there at the zebra crossing.'

Jessica cruised over the chunky white rectangles and nosed the car into another street. 'Snow Hill!' she exclaimed. 'Why do I like Snow Hill?'

'No idea,' Alex answered, 'why do you like Snow Hill?'

'Because,' Jessica smiled, pulling into the pavement and stopping beneath a blue lamp, 'it has a police station.'

The desk sergeant was tall and kind of wispy, in an elderly sort of way; not exactly the sort of person to instill much confidence in thin blue lines.

'Evenin'.'

'Yes. We've been burgled,' Jessica stated.

'I see.'

'The car, actually. It was broken into.'

'I see.'

'Outside the Barbican.'

'Outside the Barbican.'

'Yes, we were inside at the time.'

'Aha.' The officer picked up a pencil and licked the pointy end. 'When did you discover the break-in?'

'Ah, well, the concert finished at about ten o'clock, so I suppose it was about ten-fifteen, ten-twenty.'

'Ten-fif-teen,' the officer replied, the syllables all slow and drawn out as he wrote down the information. 'And exactly where was the car parked.'

'Somewhere near, you know, one of those unofficial-type places, all sort of scruffy and surrounded by haphazard fencing.'

'Near where, Miss?'

'The *Bar*bican,' Jessica replied at volume. '*Je*sus!'

'Did you pay anyone, do you have a ticket?'

'Yes, yes,' Jessica answered excitedly, going through all her pockets. 'Here,' she said triumphantly, holding aloft a small piece of crumpled paper as though it would solve all of life's problems and mend the broken window into the bargain.

'And was the person from whom you purchased the ticket still on the premises when you noticed the break-in?'

Jessica and Alex looked at one another and said, 'No,' both at the same time.

'Aha.' The policeman picked up a phone and told the person who answered it to come to the reception desk. A moment later, heavy footsteps were heard clanking down some concrete steps, then, a door at the inner end of the reception hall was thrown open and in walked an altogether more robust officer. Coming to stand alongside Alex and Jessica, he stood with hands on hips and asked, 'What seems to be the trouble?' Square-faced, although rounded at the edges due to a little chubbiness, the man belonged to the capable variety; he also appeared to be cheerfully unfazed.

'Break-in,' everybody said at once.

'The car's outside,' Alex said helpfully, honestly, and accurately.

'Car?' asked the new boy on the scene.

'Yes, it was a car that was broken into,' the desk sergeant responded, beaming as though the problem was no longer his concern.

'Let's have a look, then.'

Alex and Jessica filed outside, following the tread of confident feet. The policeman walked around the car, peered inside and came back to stand on the pavement. 'Anything missing?'

'My handbag,' Jessica answered.

'Handbag? It was inside the automobile?' the officer asked, staring at his boots, or rather at the curve of his stomach that for many years had interrupted the view.

'Yes, yes, I know, I know,' Jessica replied, squirming uncomfortably.

'Okay, we'll need a description, an address and a telephone number,' the policeman said, turning on his heels. 'And we need to fix your window.'

'You can do that?' Jessica asked hesitatingly, wondering if there was no end to the talents of the men in blue.

'We can do that,' came the response, 'a temporary job, but it'll get you home. Now, talk to the desk sergeant while I look for some tape.'

'What about fingerprints?' Alex asked brightly.

'What about them?'

'Wouldn't they help?'

'No, not likely; all the relevant places on a car are awash with fingerprints – yours, hers, mechanics, passengers – and anyway, Prints are out on another job.'

'Okay, just a thought.'

'Anything else we should be doing, you think?'

'Um . . . No.'

The friendly cop lifted a well-polished wooden flap located in the barrier between "Evenin" and "You're nicked, mate", grinned at the desk sergeant whose territory he'd broached and disappeared through a door into the backrooms of the station, a world unknown to the general public.

Left to his own devices, the sergeant grunted and glowered as he wrote down the details of the couple that had returned to bother his watch.

Ten minutes later they were mobile again. The broken widow had been fixed with a mishmash of cardboard and masking tape and Jessica's angst had been ameliorated by the friendliness of the corpulent cop. 'That was really kind,' she said, navigating Holborn Circus. 'Do you think they do that for everyone?'

'Only damsels in distress in the middle of the night.'

'And he didn't make too much of a thing about my leaving my bag in the car.'

'No, he probably knew better.'

'You reckon?'

'He's probably seen it a hundred times, honey.'

'Yeah, but it's such a crazy . . .'

'So, what about Belinda?' Alex asked, swerving away from troublesome topics.

'Who?' Jessica glanced at Alex and tried to work out who Belinda might be.

'Belinda . . . or whatever her name is. You know, the girl you brought with you to the meeting at Christine's place, the last time I saw you?'

'Eileen?'

'Yes, Eileen. Sorry, seemed to remember she was called Belinda.' Alex grinned to himself in a confusion of swirling colours as they dodged the mélange of traffic lights between New Oxford Street and Tottenham Court Road.

'Why?'

'I'm just trying to show a bit of interest in your wellbeing.'

'She's fine.'

'Are you still living there, at her place, with her?'

'It's a safety net.'

'Have you become a trapeze artist?'

'No, it's just . . . Oh, I don't know, I seem to be swinging from pillar to post, one step forward, two steps back. She's good for me, she . . .' Thinking she was offering too much information, Jessica ground to a halt.

'That's okay, then.' Alex paused and contemplated inner space. 'What else? How's work?'

'Fine, just fine. The world will always be full of crazy people.'

'Yep,' Alex agreed, perhaps a little too readily.

Jessica nosed the car around the corners of Soho Square and crawled along Greek Street until she found a parking space between two vans, both white. Getting out of the car, she fussed about the taped-over window, asking 'Do you think it's safe to leave it here?'

'About as safe as at the Barbican,' Alex answered forth-rightly.

'No, I mean with the window in the state it's in. Somebody could easily peel it open.'

'And steal what, exactly?' Alex asked. 'There's nothing for them to take, it's all gone already. Don't worry. Give me the keys and show me where this restaurant is.'

'Are we going to make love, then?' Jessica asked.

They'd ordered a selection of interesting-sounding dishes from an extensive menu, dishes neither of them had encountered before. Their decision making, however, had been helped by an attractive, super-slim Thai waitress, who'd furnished the atmosphere with mouth-watering descriptions. Now, separating paired chopsticks and rubbing them together to rid them of potential slivers, they engaged in the art of catching up on history.

'Are we fuck!'

'Will that be fuck yes or fuck no?'

'It's funny, your choice of words.'

'Why? It's perfectly normal.'

'Well, she, Eve, told me not to "make love" with you.'

'She's American.'

'Yes. American, with a hint of Indian, I think.'

'Indian? Goodness! And you're English.'

'What's your point?'

'They don't go together.'

'They?'

'Races. Shouldn't mix 'em. Like chalk and cheese. Like business and pleasure.'

'But English and Ameri . . .'

'Different cultures, different standards, different beliefs, and they don't have any history. Jesus, we don't even speak the same language.'

'Yes we do, although I'll admit the spelling is a little unusual,' Alex replied, trying to calm the sudden furore.

'I suppose she's beautiful?' Jessica asked, formulating a brilliant statement out of the question.

'She's gorgeous,' Alex enthused.

'Is that it, then, the full summation? Beauty – the only attribute necessary when describing someone's personality?'

'What do you mean?'

'Gorgeous? Is that enough for you? What about other factors such as intelligence, creativity, humour, et cetera?'

'Oh, come on, don't give me all that psychobollocks, leave it for your office or whatever you call it. What *do* you call it? Treatment room? Surgery? Discussion chamber? Anyway, whatever, she trusts me.'

'She must be stupid.'

'Why?'

'To trust you.'

'Why shouldn't she? Did I ever cheat on you?'

'Not that I'm aware.'

'Christ! we were together four, five years, and still you don't know me.'

'So? Did you?'

'You have to ask?'

'I'm asking, for fuck's sake.'

Alex slammed his cutlery onto the table, accidentally knocking over his wine glass and spilling its contents in all directions. Startled diners looked up to see the cause of the commotion and Alex glared back, daring them to utter grievance. Pieces of conversation slid tentatively through the air until, sorting themselves out, they found direction and returned uneasy normality to the Malaysian restaurant.

'No, Jessica,' Alex hissed across the swampy tablecloth. 'I was in love with you, totally, devoid of interest in any other woman, except of course the girl from Ipanema, you know, tall, tanned, young, lovely.'

'She's also American.'

'South American, Latina.'

'You are so shallow.'

'Huh, too open, too honest, more like.'

'You? Open? Honest?'

'Yeah, I tell everybody everything.'

'I never noticed.'

'You never wanted to know.'

Jessica took a long draught from a glass of water and sloshed it around the interior of her mouth, as if attempting to dislodge an unacceptable subject. Placing the glass back onto the damp tabl loth, she changed the direction of the convoluted conversation. 'Eileen has this friend, Beatrice, the sort that floats around in an Indian shift and wafts incense every time she moves.'

'Why are you telling me this?'

'Earlier on you were asking about her.'

'So I was.'

'Anyway, she, Beatrice, comes waltzing around quite often

and insists on baking strange biscuits while listening to folk music.'

'Ugghh.'

'I know, it's terrible, all that nasty nasal off-key chanting stuff. Must be the drugs!'

'Funny mushrooms and herby tobacco.'

'Mmm, that's what she puts in the biscuits. They're a special treat she says, for me and Eileen she says, 'cos we don't smoke.'

'Thoughtful, then?'

'Yeah, very, and she's kind of nice, you know? but she talks incessantly, about nothing. It's galling.'

'It is?'

'Well, yes, that and the fact that Eileen kind of listens. She likes her.'

'And?'

'I don't know, it . . . it sort of makes me jealous.'

'Jealous? Jesus!'

'Well, you know, I don't know that many people, and Eileen is . . . Well, it turns out she's my best friend.'

'Eat your food, the rice is congealing.'

Jessica lifted a sticky mass of rice into her mouth and stared gloomily at pieces of bright green okra, grey-green peas, translucent slices of onion, drab garlic and chunks of pale-yellow chicken, all engulfed in a lurid monosodium glutamate-enriched sauce. 'And now the car's been vandalised. Bastards.'

'I know.'

'What were they doing there? What possible attraction could the Barbican have for people like that?'

'People like what?'

'The fuckers that broke into my car. That kind of people.'

'They probably know that any car parked in the vicinity of a music venue will be a car worth investigating. 'Specially a classic venue, you know, toffs, knobs, lords and ladies, jangling bangles and diamond-laden watches? Stuff like that?'

'Yeah, well they're all bastards and they got my bag. It was the one you gave me, the blue one made from raffia or something. The shoulder bag, you know, with the long blue cord?'

'To drape over your shoulder; yes, I know. But, honey, leaving it in the car is . . .'

'Yeah, well I was late, wasn't I? And I couldn't wait to see you, you know?'

'Please eat your food, Jessica, before they take it away thinking you don't like it. The waiter's hovering.'

'It's what they do, it's what they're good at. They're trained, you know? Anyway, I'll be able to talk to Eileen about it.'

'About hovering waiters?'

'The car, the car! I'll be able to talk about the car! She's good to talk to, she cares, she listens.'

'Blimey, you sound like BT.'

'Well, she does. No one else does, the world is in too much of a hurry.'

Alex regarded the disarray on Jessica's plate and thought about hurry, about how he'd like to rush back to the comparative sanity of life in New York. He watched the woman who used to fill his dreams toy with her food as though it had become something wholly unpalatable, a burdensome truth that as yet hadn't been broached by either party.

The restaurant was becoming suspiciously empty, tables and chairs being wiped and dusted and lined up in readiness for tomorrow's business. Looking around, Alex noticed that the waiters and waitresses had started to conglomerate, sitting around a couple of tables discussing the highs and lows of the day's work, the good tippers and the shoddy manners of finger-clicking idiots. It caused him to think back to the golden days when he'd had some sort of employment as a journalist, albeit a badly paid one, for a newspaper based in one of the city's northern suburbs. At the end of each day, he and two or three colleagues would descend upon a local hostelry and swap yarns in much the same manner as this collection of wilting waiters. Occasionally, the big boss, the editor-in-chief, would hustle his flock of unruly reporters into a Chinese eatery and they'd sit at a round table, spinning a lazy Susan, while one of those toxically over-coloured pictures spilled a stream of never-ending fantasy. And sometimes they'd been lured into the red-flocked interior of an incense-filled Indian, to worry cautiously at the edges of fragile poppadoms and listen to pop-inspired ragas picked from extra bendy strings. The job had been quite interesting, in an amusing sort of way, until about four years ago when the borough's inhabitants seemingly lost interest in the day-to-day capers of their neighbours. The circulation quickly spiralled towards zero and Alex had been launched into the precarious business of freelance journalism, working for any magazine or periodical kind enough to throw crumbs in his direction. The absence of a safety net had encouraged him to tighten his acumen, with the result that his writing had sharpened considerably and he became responsible for self-editing his every article. On one or two occasions this had actually been picked up on by the more alert copy editors of glossy magazines, who took the time and the trouble to thank him for turning in mistake-free copy.

Alex smiled and took a slurp of wine and thought about mistakes and corrections. One thing led to another and he came to ponder on the forgeries created by the unknown Prentiss and, in particular, the revealed Vermeer that Jessica had decided to keep. Perhaps this was the weighty subject that was continuing to dodge the prongs of her perpendicular fork.

'So how's Vermeer, then? What have you done with him?'

'He's hanging in Eileen's living room.'

'Really?'

'Yep, on the wall opposite the fireplace.'

'You're not worried that someone might notice it and start asking awkward questions?'

'Like who?'

'Someone, anyone.'

'Who?'

'I don't know,' Alex answered, cornered. 'But she must have friends who call round, such as this weird . . . What's her name?'

'Beatrice?'

'Beatrice.'

'She's made comment . . .'

'Well then . . .'

'But she wouldn't know the difference between a genuine work of art and a rectangle of framed wallpaper.'

'No, okay, but there must be someone who's asked pertinent questions?'

'Why? Why would anyone be suspicious?' Jessica smiled happily across undulations of uneaten starch. She was enjoying this parrying, this defence of her realm. 'It's just a painting, unknown and worlds away from the everyday concerns of everyday people. And anyway, how many people actually know what it is they're looking at without sneaking a crafty glance at the label, if there is one? And in my case, our case, there isn't.'

'Yeah, I suppose.'

'There's only a handful of people know about it, and none of them, you included, know where I live. And even if you did, you're hardly likely to come barging round and breaking down doors. Are you?'

'No.'

'So there you are.'

'So that's it? The painting is going to remain hanging on your wall, Eileen's wall, a private gallery for the both of you?'

'Yup.'

'You're not going to sell it?'

'Nope.'

'Okay.'

'Unless of course I find it's worth hundreds of thousands. Then I might.'

'But you'd let me know?'

'Alex, I don't think there's an obligation to tell anybody. It's mine, I found it, Terry discovered its true identity lurking under false pretences, and now it's hanging in the front room. Case closed.'

'Can you take me home, then?'

'My place?'

'No, mine.'

'Only if I can stay overnight.'

'Not a good idea.'

'I could sleep on a sofa. You have got a sofa?'

'I do, but you wouldn't stay there, would you?'

'You think you're that irresistible?'

'I was when we started this conversation.'

'That was then, and you've dampened my ardour.'

'So drop me off and go home to Eileen. I'll call you tomorrow, today.'

'Yes, okay, probably best.'

In his fumblings, Alex added a few more scratches to the paintwork around the difficult target of the Yale lock. He shut the door behind him and turned on the hallway light. Peering into the living room he noticed the plaintive flashing of a little red indicator suggesting that there was a message waiting for him. He pressed a button on the phone and listened to the friendly voice of the portly policeman informing him that a bag, fitting the description of Jessica's squidgy blue thing, had been handed in to the station and would someone like to collect it in the next couple of days.

He padded into the kitchen and opened a bottle of wine he'd collected from the local supermarket earlier in the day, yesterday; it seemed months ago. It was French, it was red, and it was cheap, but the selection had not been brilliant and Alex had been content with the price. He poured himself a generous glassful and loped back into the darkened lounge, settling comfortably onto the sofa which had no idea that it could instead have been supporting Jessica's feminine curves.

What a day! What a *couple* of days! A Scottish shindig followed by a Barbican break-in and an offer, recanted, of sex. Damn! The phone was still blinking across space from its temporary home on top of a packing case. Stretching out an arm, Alex discovered he had also to lean forwards in order to reach the silent messenger. Again, he pressed the button and listened. It was Mr Banergee beseeching forgiveness for being so interruptive, his inventive English giving a flowery description of life's tragedies, including the sad demise of an elder sahib and, please to forgive, the escalating costs of maintaining England's most highly treasured properties, especially those in the splendid domains of Southgate. The Indian was most humbly anxious to assure his tenant that he would be doing his very utmostest to keep the rent at a respectful level. Then another voice, Daleky in intonation, informed Alex that the message had ended and that there were no more on the endless loop of tape.

'Thank fuck for that,' he said, swallowing a large mouthful of iffy plonk. He took another gulp to make sure it was as bad as he thought it was, and ended up being quite pleasantly surprised. Picking up the bottle he strained his eyes in the dim yellow light provided by a convenient street lamp and discovered he'd bought something from a region between two rivers, although the French confusingly refer to it as being between two seas. 'Probably why they kept losing wars,' he informed the room, a little uncharitably, quoting *"C'est magnifique, mais ce n'est pas la guerre"*, which turned out to be a bad idea because he spent the next several minutes trying to remember who originally had said it, and why. He thought it was Napoleon and then he thought it wasn't, and then realised that that was the extent of his knowledge of French soldiers, apart of course from that General de Gaulle fellow. But he knew the quotation hailed from a time long before that of the gallant World War II leader and organiser of French resistance.

Then, focusing his mind on the events of the evening, he thought about the topics of conversation that had batted to and fro like defrosted memories of a previous existence.

He wondered what would have happened if Jessica had in fact stayed overnight. Would his feelings for his newfound paramour be strong enough to repel any thoughts of straying from the fold? Alex delved into his personal history and came up with the answer: Yes. Throughout the relationship with Jessica he'd never felt the desire to be with another woman, hadn't even considered it. He'd been content with things the way they were, happy that he'd found the woman of his dreams, until . . . until he'd slid down the slippery path that leads straight to the ever-open gates of Hades. And now he understood what would have occurred had she, by means fair or foul, taken up residence on the sofa. The whole edifice of borrowed time and the structure of tortured friendship would have shattered as effectively as the decimated window of Jessica's car. They'd've drunk wine, this French stuff, and chewed fat until the small hours, and he'd've said something in innocent honesty that would have crawled under Jessica's skin and caused the wrath of God to rain down in the manner of fruit dislodged from a tree struck by an earthquake. It would have been unpleasant and would have left a bitter taste and Alex would have had to lie about the evening's outcome. He didn't enjoy lying and saw no reason for it, believing in the maxim that "truth will always out". He smiled, his butterfly mind latching onto the weird homily, and pictured small jars of truths – contained, preserved and labelled like home-made jams – suddenly jumping out of hidden closets to claim ascendency over the corpse of a discovered fib. God moves in mysterious ways, as does Satan and that bugger Murphy. Again, Alex had the desire to walk through the door and jump on a jet. He drained the glass and poured another and realised it was Thursday, a day to which he was partial, always had been and probably always would be, especially this particular Thursday; for today he was due to fly to Prague.

Chapter Five:

Prague

1

Grabbing his holdall, Alex passed through sliding doors and looked at posters and signs that were totally illegible, and then a series of little loudspeakers started declaiming from on high and he smiled at the thought that he had no idea what was being said. It could have been important, an announcement regarding the imminent end of the world, and he'd miss it, lost in the intricacies of a language that seemed to have no spaces between the words. He noticed someone waving urgently and it seemed the man was waving at him.

'Here, taxi, we go,' the man suggested via a minimal amount of words as he tried to wrest the bag out of Alex's hands and shove it into a yawning boot.

'No, no, I keep bag,' Alex squawked, gamely holding onto it as he lowered himself into an evil-looking vehicle. Doors slammed and the car coughed away from Arrivals, Alex coughing in enforced sympathy due to the cab's overpowering legacy of a million cigarettes. He wound down the window and sucked fresh air tinged with exhaust fumes, which none-theless managed to assuage the choking interior.

The taxi rumbled over uneven surfaces as it headed into

the ancient city of towers, spires, trams and narrow streets; and cobbles, everywhere cobbles. Sitting forward on the edge of the seat, Alex peered all around him, looking at the buildings, statues, parks and people of an alien territory. He had no idea where he was and not much of an idea about where he was going. He knew only the name of the hotel and that it was close to a large square somewhere near the centre, and for now his trust was lumped on the shoulders of the driver.

'Hokey dokey.' The first words uttered since the rattling vehicle had left the precincts of the airport.

'Hokey dokey?' Alex echoed, startled.

'Yes. That's what you say, isn't it?' the cabbie asked.

'Sometimes,' Alex agreed, unsure whether this was one of those times. 'Why have we stopped?'

'Here is hotel.'

'Hah, hokey dokey,' Alex grinned and handed over some money.

'English money not good,' the cabbie assured him. 'Must to change in hotel.'

'Dollars?' Alex asked hopefully, reckoning that a few greenbacks were good anywhere.

'American money not good,' the driver mumbled, shoving another cigarette into his mouth.

'Bugger,' Alex announced, adding to the cabby's knowledge of the English language. 'Wait a moment.' He got out of the car, walked into the lobby and smiled at the receptionist. 'I need to change money,' he said slowly, exaggerating the pronunciation.

'Who you are?'

It was a good question.

'Oh, yes, of course. I have reservation.' Alex pasted a

winning smile onto his face and wondered why he always devolved into strange English when conversing with foreigners. Then it occurred to him that it was he who was the foreigner.

'Prentiss,' he said. 'Alex Prentiss.'

'Hokey dokey,' said the girl. 'How much? You have passport?'

'I have passport. Um, twenty pounds?'

'Hokey dokey,' the girl repeated, snatching money out of Alex's hands in the manner of a leaf-grabbing gale. 'Five, ten, fifteen, twenty,' she announced triumphantly, folding the notes into a hidden drawer. 'And passport?'

Alex handed the little blue book across the formidable counter and watched as it was deposited into the same drawer. 'But . . .'

'When you go you get back,' the blue-eyed blonde explained sweetly. She closed the drawer, snappishly. 'We keep.'

'Money?'

'Yes?'

'Um, Czechoslovak money for twenty pounds English money.'

'Twenty pounds?'

'Yes, I gave you twenty pounds,' Alex said, holding all his fingers and thumbs in the air, twice.

'Change?'

'Change money, yes,' he nodded vehemently, wondering why he'd come to such a difficult place. 'I give, you take,' he grinned.

'Yes,' came the agreement attached to a dazzling smile. Opening another drawer, the girl gathered a mishmash of notes and coins and handed the collection to Alex. 'I give, you take,' she stated with stunning sincerity.

Alex held out his hands and received the financial reward. 'Okay, thank you.'

'Hokey dokey,' the receptionist said brightly.

Alex picked his case off the floor and strode across the lobby, an area that believed itself to be a set for a Tarzan movie. Greenery sprouted in all directions – up, down, sideways, and sort of wriggly, creeping through the matrices of a network of assorted trellises. Yet more verdure, dangling in ropey confusion from a glass ceiling, tinted the sun's rays, illuminating everything as though at the bottom of a shallow sea. The elevator, a modern slinky affair attached to four stout metal pillars, was encased in a tower of plant-surrounded glass. '*Ding*,' it said, its automatic doors wheezing together. Two seconds later, an inbuilt female voice decided to inform Alex that, 'The leeft ees goink up.' Well spaced and well enunciated, so that no one could be uncertain as to the direction of travel, the words were delivered in Eastern European English. Alex wondered if he'd be informed that the lift was 'goink down', when he returned to ground level, and it was then that he remembered he hadn't paid the taxi driver. 'Shit!' he exclaimed, frantically pressing knobs until he managed to hit a button stamped with the figure zero. The lift stopped, opened its doors, closed its doors, and began descending to the lobby. Sure enough, the voice brightly announced that 'The leeft ees goink down.'

'Bugger, bugger, bugger,' Alex muttered, fighting his way back through the jungle and noticing that the taxi driver was in earnest conversation with the receptionist. 'I'm sorry,' he said, dropping the holdall to the ground while rummaging through his pockets for the foreign money the girl had just given him, 'it's um . . . how much?'

The cabbie extracted all the notes from Alex's outstretched hands and took a couple of coins as well. 'Hokey,' he said with a minimal smile. 'You American?'

'No,' Alex answered sharply.

'*Anglicky*,' the receptionist said, informing the man who reeked of tobacco. 'He is having English pass.'

'Yes,' Alex concurred, 'English.' Looking at the girl and then at the man who'd taken all his money, he tried to follow the rapid exchange of sentences that followed his avowal. It was a complete jumble, wishy-washy stuff, all wound up and delivered on a furious monotone. And then it stopped, and the taxi driver ambled towards the door and his fume-filled chariot. Apparently the conversation had come to an end. Alex picked up his holdall and returned to the friendly elevator.

Having been told that Room 42 was located along a corridor to the right of the lift, he stepped out of the talkative device and creaked along a pokey passage that seemed to connect two sections of the elderly hotel. Furnished with one small window, allowing an unimaginative view of tired walls and snow-covered roofs all cramped up and sheltering under a leaden sky, the room was comfortable and complete. Alex stepped into the en-suite and turned on the shower.

2

Karolíny Světlé is the name of a street with a kink in it and sort of connects the National Theatre to Charles Bridge almost as effectively as the river, which flows past one and under the other. The street also features several restaurants, one of which, Století, has an extensive menu with each dish named after a famous individual. Although the festive season had given way to January blues, the small dining room exuded a warm welcoming atmosphere kept alive by oodles of flickering brilliance leaping joyously from an open fireplace. The presence of a highly decorated Christmas tree, standing shoulder to shoulder with some green pointy-leafed tropical plant, helped also to maintain the credence of goodwill. Alex chose a table for two in a corner next to the tastefully lit pine tree. Hanging on the wall adjacent to the table, a painting of strangely shaped vases – or perhaps jugs – sitting on a block of white wood, gazed wistfully across the wooden floor at shoals of snowflakes intermittently visible through the glass-panelled door. Tucked between table and wall, the ribs of a radiator efficiently produced lateral warmth. Alex was content.

Placing his elderly copy of *The Odyssey* on top of the radiator, he browsed the menu, wondering if by any chance they had some mouth-watering dish labelled after John Lennon, or perhaps John Updike. They didn't. But there was a main course, consisting of grilled rump steak with pepper sauce and banana slices, which for some strange reason had been named after Somerset Maugham. Alex's stomach, growling in the void beneath the table, reminded him that he hadn't eaten since breakfast. He was starving. Then it grumbled again, pleasurably activated by his eyes and their discovery on the menu that *Tempranillo* happened to be one of the house wines. He spoke to the attentive waiter, ordered a glass of the Spanish red and set about choosing something to eat.

A loud clicking and whirring caused him to glance up at a small dishwasher that had stirred itself into action in front of him. Not exactly in front of him – in that it wasn't sitting on the chair across the table – but some twenty feet away, slotted into a gap at the side of a well-stocked bar. Finished in bright aluminium the machine was highly visible, as was a red garbage bucket and a red dustpan and brush. To one side of the Miró-esque display of domesticity, a short curtain, abandoned and waiting for someone to drag it across the great divide, hung in concertina'd idleness.

Remembering Odysseus' never-ending struggle to get home, Alex reached for the book and moved the table candle to one side. Before he was able to find the correct page, a plate of fried Camembert atop a slice of toasted French bread atop a bed of green salad, the whole drizzled with cranberry sauce, arrived. The heroic voyage foundered atop the radiator.

A middle-aged couple, sitting in stony silence at a table near the cheerful hearth, looked across at Alex as he began to investigate the delights in front of him. Returning their gaze, he smiled and wondered why it is that some people thrive on taking their homespun atmosphere with them, everywhere they go. However, the combination of cheese and wine seemed to alleviate the situation: four beady eyes returned to their contemplation of a gulf devoid of conversation, and Alex, his mind massaged through gastric ecstasy, fell into idle introspection of the previous year, a time of mighty despair and broken dreams. Recalling endless rounds of verbal swordplay, he muttered 'Bollocks' to his surprised empty wineglass and was relieved when the waiter arrived with the main course, forming a new focus of attention. Scooping up the empty glass, the waiter scurried away to collect a replacement, while Alex, happily aware that the intricacies of the English vernacular would not be understood in these quarters, leered at a couple of grilled chicken breasts in a sea of sweet chilli sauce, accompanied by four rounds of rösti potatoes and a side dish of mixed vegetables. He tucked in and promptly forgot the name of the famed figure who'd been identified with a plate of spicy chicken tits.

The meal was yummy and scrummy and the second glass of wine made it more yummy and more scrummy and paved the way to Alex's brave decision to gild the cherry – hot sour ones, all mixed up with vanilla ice cream and muesli. Normally not a great fancier of ice cream, he'd been lulled into attacking the dessert menu at the idea of hot cherries, a fruit that ranked high amongst his favourites. And the bonus, the big mouthwatering deciding factor, resided in the belief that with the extension of the meal he could possibly justify another glass of the red stuff and eke it out on friendly terms with a coffee or two. 'Sorted,' he informed the smiling waiter who

brought a tall dessert-containing glass to the table. 'Um .
. . *dobry, děkuju,*' he added, assassinating the assortment of
strange words. He was on a roll and the vases and jugs above
his head contorted themselves into surreal agreement. He
swept a quarter-spoonful of sweet frigidity into his mouth
and became aware of another painting, silvery, sort of, a medi-
aeval face in yellow, green and orange, with an erect goatee
and a pale crescent moon silhouetted against an ochre background. Alex focused on the moon while hot cherries shuffled with muesli and ice cream. And when the dessert came
to an end he tinkered with a long-handled spoon, endeavour-
ing to rescue a few stranded nuts and dried fruits from the
bottom of the glass.

Sitting at the centre of the table and sheltered in a holder
of thick stubby glass, the tea light flickered, expiring at about
the same instant that the dishwasher was opened by one of
the waiters. Fascinated by coincidence and the strange properties of time, Alex watched the removal of clean glasses and the
installation of dirty ones. Meanwhile, the non-communicative
couple had been galvanised into action and were busily taking
photographs of one another, the noise of the camera making
up for their lack of speech. *Flash, click, flash, click* – a veritable
hubbub, electronic and mechanical but a hubbub all the same.

Alex looked dispassionately through the bottom of his
wine glass and realised it was time to make a move. More than
pleased with the meal and the attentive service, and happily
relaxed on Spanish wine, he left a generous tip which was graciously accepted by the wide-smiling waiter. Accompanied
by a strange yet familiar taste of the spicy sweetmeats that
had been served with the espresso, Alex left the restaurant
and stepped into cold air, his cobbled footsteps echoing

from the confines of a narrow street. Almost immediately, he found himself engulfed by a small dumpy woman who, in the manner of Alecto, seemed to float out of the shadows.

'You want sex?' she asked. 'I give good sex.'

'Pardon?' Aided and abetted by just the right amount of wine, Alex grinned in startled darkness.

'Everything you want. Good sex.' The woman raised an arm and inserted a hand into Alex's jacket.

'Go away,' he said, pulling her hand out of his interior and backing out of the woman's reach.

'I want. Give money.'

'Go away,' he repeated, stepping off the miniscule pavement and dodging between a couple of cars that happened to be parked across the entrance to a short, interesting-looking alley. 'You're too big, you're too old, I'm not interested,' he informed the stocky lady scuttling along behind him. After a few metres the alley opened into a square, small and unfamiliar. Alex halted. A split-second later, the clippety-clop of ridiculously high heels also came to a standstill.

'Fuck!' The expression of angst, a mixture of frustration at his dismal sense of direction and peevishness at the proximity of the squat shadow, wafted into the frozen night. Alex spun around and raised his arms, Christ-like, as though in readiness to bestow some kind of blessing. 'Listen,' he shouted. 'Go *away*. Pick on somebody else and stop following me.' The shadow, understandably, showed no sign of understanding and even less of complying. Turning on his heel, Alex vocalised a hastily considered suggestion over his shoulder. '*Fuck off!*' Reverberating backwards, the two distinct syllables passed over the head of the persistent woman and disappeared into the alley.

Not really being in the mood for any of this, Alex took it out on an empty beer can that just happened to be in the right place at the right time. The can, believing it had been accosted by Lineker, gleefully bounded into the air and shot through space. Finding little in the way of resistance, it homed in on a white and yellow car and landed with splendid efficiency a couple of yards from its perceived goal. Aimlessly following the course of flying aluminium, Alex sauntered into the square and noticed that the front door of the vehicle was being opened. It had big letters printed on the panel, VB, in black paint, and the large man easing himself into the frosty air was all dressed up in uniform.

'Shit,' Alex hissed under his breath, 'it must be the secret police.' Twisting his neck, he checked the lane to see if his shadow was still in hot pursuit. The woman had gone, vanished; the alley and the whole world were devoid of life. 'Fuckity fuck,' he muttered, 'I wonder what the penalty is for kicking a beer can?' Feigning innocence and maintaining the plausibility that he knew what he was doing and where he was going, he resumed his walk across the square that suddenly seemed wider and infinitely more dangerous than the area of no-man's-land between east and west.

'You, English.'

He stopped, one leg in front of the other, uncertain if the words formed a statement or a question. There had been no upward inflection on the "English" bit so perhaps it was a statement. But, as he surreptitiously slid his feet together, he began to think that in any case it was a pretty stupid thing to say. Realising that there was nothing and nobody else in sight that could possibly be construed to be English, he turned to face the plod.

'You, English.' The policeman, who seemed to have a habit of repeating himself, was standing protected behind the car door. Leaning against the edge of his chariot he lit a cigarette, and before the match was extinguished Alex could see that the man had a chubby genial type of face, and so he decided to come clean.

'Me?'

'Yes, of course.'

Alex looked around to make sure there was no mistake. The square was empty, an area of hard cobblestones gleaming in damp surprise. 'English?' His reasoning was going round in circles, causing him to ask silly things. 'Me?'

'Yes, you are English, no?'

This was it, this was what he'd been waiting for – a question, an enquiry with a "yes" at the front and a "no" at the tail. 'English. Yes,' he replied. Manoeuvring himself towards the chugging automobile, he remembered that he'd left his passport in the safety of his hotel room and wondered if he could survive torture in a cold prison cell. They were all communists here and they did terrible things and he would never be heard of again. He began to despise whoever it was who'd left the beer can in such a tempting location.

'You, English, you like football.'

There it was again, the question that wasn't a question, the statement with no inflection.

'Football? No, not really.' Hoping honesty would be the best policy, Alex started to wonder if these people had any connection to the Scots.

'You, drunk.' The policeman took a long drag at his cigarette and moved towards Alex. 'Drinking, drunk. You English always drinking.'

'Lost,' Alex confessed, wearing his best friendly I'm-just-a-stupid-helpless-tourist type smile.

'Ah, lost footballer.' The policeman dropped his cigarette onto the ground and stamped it into submission. 'Lost,' he said, summing up the situation.

'Yes,' Alex agreed. 'I was in a restaurant back there.' He pointed across the square. 'And I can't remember where my hotel is,' he added, turning the corner of desperation in the belief that a discourse would be the best, if not the only solution. 'It's, it's near the Town Hall and that big square, Staro . . .m, mes,' he said, grinning foolishly and trying to pronounce the unpronounceable.

'But Staroměstská is not this way,' the policeman informed him, rolling his R in the European manner and seemingly forgetting all about football and footballers; or maybe not. 'We take you in car, talk about football.'

'Um . . . thank you, but I like to walk, you know, walking?' Alex moved his right hand through the air, wiggling index and middle finger to explain what he meant. 'Walking is good, after meal, digestion, helps it,' he continued like an idiot, using easy-to-understand pidgin English.

'Yes, walking, with beer can,' the policeman smiled in benign fashion. 'You like Praha?'

Definitely a question, Alex realised, and asked one in return. 'Praha?'

'Praha, Prag, Prague. You like?'

'Oh, yes, very much I like,' Alex nodded profusely.

'We too,' the policeman agreed through dangerous eyes. 'Follow.'

Alex followed the weaponised gentleman around the car and it seemed as though they were heading towards the final resting place of the metallic football. Picking up the can the officer changed direction and moved towards a circular concrete waste bin, coming to a halt in front of it. Alex hesitatingly strolled over to stand beside him, the two of them positioned as though in some sort of ritual, a formal benediction to the world of waste. The policeman handed the can to Alex and motioned for him to place it in the bin. Alex did as bade, resting the offending article on top of a mountain of takeaway wrappers and containers.

'So,' said the policeman. 'Now you can go. That way. Five minutes.'

Alex breathed out deeply and smiled thankfully, feeling as though all the gas of the Universe was being expelled from his lungs in one mammoth effort. Freedom. He almost tiptoed across the cobbles, his footsteps light as air, and for some unknown reason he started humming *September*, the funky title from Earth, Wind and Fire. He walked for about five minutes, until he found himself at the edge of the river and realised he was going in the wrong direction. Prague is a confusing city, full of small streets and winding alleys that, despite guidance from a policeman, have a tendency to transport one in unwanted tangents. Alex glared at the river, cold, dark and uninterested, and shrugged his shoulders. Retracing his steps, he hustled back across the police-supervised square, nodded and smiled inanely to allay suspicion, and deftly avoided contact with any football-minded beer cans.

Drifting out of the square and into yet another of the city's narrow passages, he rounded a corner and found himself in a slightly wider street. And then he stopped. Something lumpy, an excrescence that seemed to be growing out of a wall, attracted his attention and brought him to a standstill.

Peering into the gloom, he shuffled forwards and inspected the well-worn stone carving. Dismal street lighting did little to enhance the situation, but he perceived that this must surely be the figure that Mrs Carmichael had been on about. He looked up at the surrounding walls and noticed a street sign, Liliová, a name, thankfully, that wasn't too complex when compared with most other appellations found in this linguistically difficult capital. Stepping away from the object, he repeated the name of the street, several times, hoping he'd be able to find it again in the morning, when daylight might inspire further revelations.

Fate, conveniently, had led him in the correct direction, and after a few metres the street brought him to Karlova, a tourist bottleneck of endless souvenir shops, busy even at this late hour. Recognising his whereabouts, he turned right and followed the ancient thoroughfare until it deposited him in a small triangular square overlooked by ridiculously tall buildings.

The lift greeted Alex with customary dictum, slithering shut its doors to trap him in its warm embrace and inform him where it was going. He smiled with happiness, he'd made it, he'd escaped from the clutches of the dreaded NKVD, navigated the cramped streets of the old town, ducked beneath the waves of a very strange language and had managed to return to the comforts of the hotel.

Entering his room he shut the door and switched off the lights that the chambermaid, presumably, had left burning so as to give comfort to stressed furniture. He removed his shoes, lay on the bed and thought about America and everything American; from ridiculous soap-characters such as Callie, the blonde bimbo who, draped around the neck of Mr

Big Oil, had whimpered, 'But J.R., I feel so passionate', to the scientific and perfectly precise landing of the Space Shuttle's first return to planet Earth. Mainly, though, he thought about Eve and the relationship they'd forged together after the contrived introduction masterminded by Mandie and Dan at the Lincoln Center. And then his mind flipped through the connections – Mandie, Dan, Eve, Eve's grandfather, Michelstraub, Mrs Carmichael, Rembrandt, Vermeer, Jessica . . . and a troublesome Nazi officer. Twenty minutes later, he sat up, reconnected with his shoes and left the safety of Room 42. The darkened hotel room had given him his moment of epiphany, a revelation so elegant and utterly obscene that it sledgehammered his cerebral cortex and rearranged the interior of his brain. He needed a drink, another one, something strong and alcoholic in order to focus all the divergent threads linking Binghamton to Bavaria, Eve's grandfather to a retired general, and Wolfgang and Terry, both of whom would have to be engineered into doing the right thing.

Finding a bar in Prague is no more difficult than locating a Chinaman in Shanghai. Alex exited the hotel and immediately found one; bar, not Chinaman. Following some curving stone steps, he descended into a series of arched cellars, selected a tall stool in front of a shiny counter, asked for a double Jack and proceeded to push the limits of the barman's English by asking to borrow a pencil and paper. Unfazed, the barman splashed a quantity of whiskey into a tumbler, loaded it with chunks of ice, collected a biro from a ledge by the till and placed glass and pen in front of the strange customer. The swift service came with a suggestion and an inclination of the head. 'Use beer mat.'

Good idea, Alex thought, nodding in agreement and, in

the nodding, discovering a stack of beer mats sitting smugly within easy reach. An epoch and several Jacks later, he'd lost track of time, run out of his supply of koruns, covered a platoon of the small cardboard rectangles in symbols and arrows – some straight, some curving – and had managed to connect all his convergent ideas. By now, after exchanging silly smirks in lieu of foreign words and after exchanging handfuls of coins for generous refills and international détente, he'd become effusively pally with the barman. Clutching his precious beer mats and uttering alcohol-aided attempts at *děkuju* – the strange backward-looking word that means 'thank you' – Alex allowed gravity to ease him from the stool and then fought against it on the stairway to street level, where fresh air smacked him in the face, widened his vision and pointed his feet towards the hotel.

3

Sprawled along the edges of the wide Vltava, Prague is a city of ancient splendour; perhaps not as ancient as some, but certainly as crowded with architectural delight. Old and new, stapled together with bastions of brickwork, the town bustles with the magic of music. Every church excels at ringing its Angelus at every opportunity, while buskers of all abilities stroke, fiddle, pluck, blow and squeeze in surprising places. In a city where whole streets get to be closed by armies of film-making directors and producers – dodging the prices commanded by cities such as London and New York – the narrow quarters are unhealthily choked by tourists, the faithful followers of umbrella-touting guides. At a time when Shakespeare was heavily occupied populating the Elizabethan stage with historical characters, Prague was a honey pot of attraction for philosophers and scientists, bright individuals who swarmed to the cultural centre of Europe to assist in formulating the chapters of the future. While Brahe and Kepler set about organising space, architects and stonemasons constructed beautiful buildings in an effort to reach it. King Rudolf II, busily sinking into a world of academe, surrounded himself with a phalanx of erudite alchemists, pushing them to unlock the secrets of transmutation. Amidst scenes of decadent feasts and orgies of wine, women and song, the castle became a vast pleasure dome, a citadel in which everyone was encouraged to support the impossible dream.

Alex stepped out of the hotel and tried to retrace yesterday's footsteps. But, with last night's alcohol still flooding his system, his feet guided him unerringly to the town's focal point, an open space bounded by pastel-coloured houses and fairy-tale towers and turrets that would feel quite at home in Disneyland. Although inspiring and magnificent, this was not where he wanted to be, so he walked back to the hotel and set off in the opposite direction, into lanes that squeeze themselves, via an intricate design of Daedalus-type complexity, through the narrow confines of European history. Everything was different, as is day from night. The confrontation with the police had taken place in another dimension, dim and deserted, but now, brushed with daylight, the city was a place transformed, seething beneath the tired feet of international tourism. The area contained a maze of tiny shops bulging with a wealth of trinkets, over-priced souvenirs that happily circle the globe and wind up gathering dust on a million mantelpieces and sideboards, keepsakes that outlive their collectors and test the imagination of impartial descendents. A snippet of snatched conversation alerted Alex to the fact that he was following the Royal Route, a processional way blessed across the ages by the steady passage of nobility. While his feet automatically propelled him onwards, sleepy neurons clunked into action and trod lethargic inroads to the recent conversation with Mrs Carmichael. There had been a connection, something that linked this river of bustling humanity to the weathered figurine anchored at street-level. Avoiding a troupe of garrulous Italians, Alex swerved to the left and found himself in Liliová, last night's escape route from the Gestapo. Here there were no tourist attractions and therefore no tourists, and there, on the other side of the street, was the ancient head, little more than a face roughly hewn into the corner of a dilapidated building. Beaten into submission by the weight of years, the gnarled features had done well to remain attached to the elderly façade. Guarded by the figure's eyeless stare, a narrow lane enticed Alex towards a set of tall wooden gates, intimidating despite their evident age. Quickly scanning the emptiness of the cobbled lane, he hauled himself to the top of the barrier and peered into a small courtyard. Encircled by plain walls there was no visible access, save the gate from which he was dangling. Fearing another entanglement with the law, he lowered himself to the ground and strolled back to the street. Following a tall brick wall around three corners, he came across another lane and another gate. In marginally better condition, this gate had been allotted some sort of protection beneath a yellow-painted brick arch. Squinting between woodwork and brickwork, Alex discovered another courtyard, larger, containing a car and a truck. On the far side of the yard, a small area of well-tended garden featured perhaps half-a-dozen trees espaliered against the brick wall. At the back of the yard, to the left and partially out of eyesight, an imposing four-storied house completed the layout.

Alex stood back and stared at the gate. Recalling everything he'd learned in New York, he was convinced he was standing on the edge of enlightenment, that this building had been the epicentre of the general's greedy hoarding of stolen art; it had to be. Here was the courtyard that had seen the valuable convoys come and go. Here was the place where the loot would have been sorted, bagged and tagged in efficient German manner. This was the arena wherein the general would have strutted his elegant uniformed stuff, the stage upon which his word would have been sacrosanct, as convincing as that of God. Precious articles, looted, confiscated and ripped out of the hands of terrified victims, had been pored over in the confines of this very building, the general deciding their destiny, including that of the six paintings that had surfaced in New York and the two that had been discovered in Bavaria.

Short of climbing over the wall or pulling at a rusty handle that looked as though it was connected to an old-fashioned bell-ringing mechanism, Alex realised there was little he could do. And then he came to understand that he'd done enough. He'd come to this country of the strange language to identify the source, the collection point of priceless artifacts . . . and he'd found it. He thought of Charley, brave Charley, known here as Karel, who'd not only survived the persecution delivered by arrogant foreigners but had found a way of turning it around and using it against them; Charley, who'd rescued Mrs Carmichael; Charley, who, having learned of the general's plan, had managed to divert the outcome.

Turning away from the gate, Alex strolled along the cobbled alley until it opened out into a small square, triangular in shape and watched over by empty houses. Deeply engaged in a world of war-weary contraband, he almost tripped over a low-slung chain and was amused to discover that it was the scene of his near-arrest, when the police officer had sought to engage him in conversation about football. Another narrow street brought him to the edge of the river and the approach to the monument-lined Charles Bridge. Crossing the teeming walkway, he passed through an ancient archway slung between two impressive towers and entered the square known as Mala Strana, where he surveyed busy trams stopping and starting under the lengthy shadows of the Church of St Nicholas. Leaning against a narrow shelf affixed to the front of a stall festooned with sausages of every description, he munched on a spicy version that came supplied with two hard slices of bread and a sexy thread of German mustard.

He'd come to think of the town as arty, but not farty. It wasn't some manifestation of the modernistic domains of western cities, it was the real McCoy, with a history that was old before America had been invented. Fought over and conquered time and again by hosts of uncouth invaders, the city had come to rely on its unfailing ability to ignore the charlatans of successive raids, right up to and including the Russians, who'd brought with them their monstrous Stalin in the form of a concrete statue. Plonked atop the hill at Letná Park, the obdurate leader spent seven years in stony contemplation of the fair city before being reduced to rubble in 1962.

Through centuries of turmoil the city had gone quietly about its business, its importance at the hub of trade between east and west and north and south never diminishing. Pretenders came and went with embarrassing regularity, while the city, under a stream of characters such as Charles II, Holy Roman Emperor of everywhere, steadily moved from strength to strength, its castles, cathedrals and palaces being constructed in stunning elegance and in ever-widening circles around its famous bridge, allegedly held together by mortar mixed with eggs.

It was no wonder then, Alex deduced, that the German

general had decided to drag himself from the rural splendour of Bavaria and billet himself here, at the point about which the whole of Europe revolved. At the centre of this vast web he'd've had ultimate control over the stolen wares that were paraded before his eyes, and it would have been a matter of consummate ease for him to transport the stuff hither and thither. Alex was impressed at the efficiency of the operation, its network penetrating far and wide into the wealthy hearts of captured nations. He was even more impressed by the cunning with which Charley had managed to undermine the general's artistic efforts.

Energised by carbohydrates, he consulted his map and set off along the strangely named Újezd. After a while the houses on the right gave way to a large park, an area of tree-covered slopes rising to the lofty area called Petrín, another place that had been referred to by Mrs Carmichael. Recalling the woman's story about a love affair conducted beneath cherry trees, Alex decided to stretch his legs and started climbing towards the distant skyline. About two-thirds of the way up the hill, he came upon a row of benches thoughtfully arranged in anticipation of aching muscles. He sat and viewed the city sprawled in front of him, an array of red roofs surprised here and there with the spires and domes of antiquity. Reflected from the river, occasional sparklets of sunlight burst through the trees, pinpointing the elongated curve of the watery highway that in times gone by had brought commerce and riches from far-flung lands. Leaning into the uncomfortable curvature of the bench, Alex thought about his moment of inspiration from the night before, and then his mind drifted to the song of the same name and the Beatles under attack from the whole British Army on Salisbury Plain. The filmic episode had been shot in the depths of winter, sung lyrics emerging in cocoons of freezing breath in the same manner as the clouds of white air escaping from Alex's lungs, overworked on the steady uphill climb. He stopped humming half-remembered words, suddenly realising that Wolfgang would have to be the lead actor if the audacious plan was to have any chance of success. He smiled at the word "audacious", until awareness of the amount of organisation that lay ahead curtailed his moment of self-congratulation. 'Bugger,' he breathed into the cold air of communism, 'it could actually work.'

Protected by Mother Nature, the hill was dotted with patches of melt-resistant snow, light dustings here and there, with pockets of the stuff gathered around the boles and in the junctions of naked branches. Surveying the steep slopes, Alex imagined the park in springtime, lush grass and blossom-filled trees beneath puffy white clouds and spikes of occasional sunshine – just the way Mrs Carmichael had described it. Of course, everything had been different then, a nation under the fascist jackboot; although perhaps not too different. Now the country was under the yoke of communism, another blinkered excess of heavy-duty control.

Ten minutes later he reached the summit and struggled to stay upright on layers of fragile ice that had formed around the feet of a mini Eiffel tower. Deciding not to expend already depleted energy on climbing the skeletal frame, he slithered through an archway in a tall brick wall and wandered into a formal rose garden. Ferociously pruned against the ravages of winter, the rows of spiky plants, each possessing a circlet of snow at its foot, gave the impression of an avalanche of split arrows embedded in a field of bull's eyes. Uneven pathways, liberally sprinkled with assorted ice-filled pits and potholes, made for balletic movement, and as he pirouetted widely out of control across the frozen arena, Alex was content to be the sole occupant.

4

Filled with dynamic enthusiasm to launch his fiendish plot, Alex arose the following morning before the sun had even begun to think about broaching an unseen horizon. He peed, showered and shaved, threw his few belongings into the hold-all, which he left neatly at the end of the bed, and went in search of sustenance.

Breakfast was quick and snappy. A large table in the centre of a medium sized room had been liberally laden with all manner of breakfasty things. He helped himself to some crunchy stuff purporting to be muesli, poured some milk onto it after taking a cautionary sniff at the jug, and returned to the table he'd selected for himself near the entrance to the kitchens. Being so early, there were few occupied tables and just a smattering of people – one or two business types in suits and shirts with ties, who'd sloughed their jackets and placed them over the shoulders of the chairs they were using. The peaceful gathering was kept amused and awake by occasional squeaks from a pair of swing doors, opening and closing with the important ingress and egress of young waitresses. Alex tried to keep his munching tuned to the two-way traffic, crisp kernels of cereal exploding between his teeth in the fashion of raw celery.

After consuming several cups of coffee and a selection of breadrolls, which he coated in butter and jam, he returned to his room and phoned Wolfgang. A few minutes later, part one of the master plan was in place – his Bavarian friend would be only too happy to see him. Language, the essential means of communication, gave vitality to the German's involvement. The preparation and final dénouement would depend on fluency, and Alex's knowledge of German, restricted to 'Good day', 'How are you?', 'I love you', and 'I'm not going to work tonight 'cos I'm too drunk', would hardly drag the project up the garden path, let alone guide it through the front door.

'How do I get to Germany?' he enquired. He was standing, half awake and full of food, in front of the beautiful Queen of Reception.

'When?' the steely-eyed blonde asked.

'Now.'

'Now? But you have two more days.'

'Yes, but I want to cancel them.'

'Oh, hokey dokey. You don't like hotel?'

'Yes, I like hotel very much but I need to get to Germany.'

'Hokey dokey.'

'Munich.'

'Munich?'

'Uh-ha.' Alex was oblivious to the fact that the Czechoslovaks have different names for countries and cities, even for themselves, changing them at a moment's notice. Less. For example, Lenka, a popular name for a Czechoslovak female, becomes Lenko, Lenku, Lenky or Lence, at the merest whim. Five names for one person! Tragic. 'So how do I get to the station?'

'You take taxi.'

'Can you call me a taxi?' Alex grinned and waited for a quick response.

'Taxi is outside.'

'Oh.' Alex's grin diminished, the receptionist's reply speedier and more serious than anticipated.

'Taxi is always outside. But first you must pay bill.'

'Yes,' Alex agreed. 'Bill must be paid, *c'est la vie*.'

'*Život*,' the girl announced. '*To je život*.'

'Exactly,' Alex nodded, tapping all his pockets as he searched for plastic payment. 'Whatever.'

The fat controller played with his levers and switches and the train slid out of the station, obediently snaking across a variety of tracks before plunging into a long dark tunnel beneath the city streets. Alex found an empty compartment, threw his bag onto a seat and sat with his legs forming a bridge between opposing sides. He was happy, the hotel had given him a doggy bag, of sorts, containing some interesting-looking bread rolls and individually wrapped slices of cold meat and cheese. Enjoying his favourite form of transport, he immersed himself in Odysseus' continuing hassles and fed his face, errant crumbs adding to the legendary problems of the ancient Greek.

It was an express on a mission from east to west, a journey which included minimal stops. And in the blank spaces between hubs of humanity, the train sped like a thing possessed, countryside of blurred extravagance filling the double-glazed windows with vistas of snow-flecked grey-green vagueness. Alex's literary sojourn on the eastern fringe of the Hellespont was disrupted only occasionally, when passengers, lost in transit, erringly entered his compartment. One-sided, short-lived attempts at conversation helped to pass the confinement of five hours. At each interruption he stood up and braved the elongated world of the corridor, stretching his legs from one end to the other of the gently swaying carriage. Twice, like an astronaut floating into another capsule to pee into some strange apparatus, he entered the surprisingly bright and antiseptically clean lavatory. And once, in order to purchase a container of life-sustaining water, he ventured beyond the forbidding narrow neck connecting his carriage with the next.

Finally, as the lights of the compartment began to usurp the power of a waning sun, the train pulled into München Hauptbanhoff. Quickly appearing from nowhere, lines of parka'd passengers filled the corridor and effectively stalled any chance of exit, not only on account of their considerable bulk but with the added detritus of baggage of all shapes and sizes. There was noise, too, as excitement flowed along the lines of impatience. Alex sat and twiddled his thumbs and thought of similar situations in aircraft, those moments of chaos when unruly hordes are wont to inexplicably activate their disjointed muscles in an all-out attempt to leave the cabin, almost as soon as the wheels paint burning kisses onto the Tarmac.

Realising he was going nowhere, he gazed out of the window at the huge expanse of station and wondered at the antics of scuttling humanity. In and out, it was always the same – people imagining they were on the wrong side of the door. If they were out, they struggled to get in, and vice versa. Not unlike Simon, although he usually took his time while deciding where he wanted to be. Cats are like that, relaxed and unhurried most of the time but, even when sleeping, having an unfailing ability to be alert at the sound of a falling pin. Even more so at the sound of a can being opened.

Alex grinned at the memory of being in charge of the stripy feline while Eve had been incarcerated for a week, or had it been two, as a hospital guest. And then, trapped in logical connections, his mind wrapped itself around the contours of Eve's body and he wondered what his raison d'être was doing at this very moment.

Chapter Six:

Eve

1

Eve was stretched. Stretched, as it happens, over the back of a sofa, devising her own particular brand of physiotherapy, harsh and unforgiving in order to restore power and agility to her damaged body. Her T-shirt, patched with excess sweat from beneath her breasts, from under her arms, neckline and the small of her back, was miniscule and rippled in faithful representation of overworked muscles. When Eve exercises, she exercises hard, a habit cultivated from a lifetime of bends and stretches at the *barre*. Setting her own standards, higher than anyone else's, she fervently pushes the envelope of her physicality.

As usual, she was exercising to rock music – Survivor, telling the tale of a young girl who was a star – loud and forceful, the tempo a perfect match for her movements, the aggression ideal for her attitude. While her muscles complained at the contortions through which they were being forced, her mind was suffering from a serious grappling. For several days she'd been questioning her decision to send Alex on his jaunt to the vagaries of England and Europe. Normally at home with her decisions, she couldn't help wondering about Alex's ex,

Jessica, with whom, at her own behest, he was on a collision course. It was unnerving, it was crazy. Arms stretched at full extension, she paused and pictured herself in the hospital bed, propped up, stuck and immobile. 'Go,' she'd commanded. 'Go. Do.' It must have been the drugs, she thought, recalling the chilling belief of being encased in a fish tank while flurries of green-clad beings had attended her other-worldly body. The picture was crystal clear, her memory accurate to the last detail. She could hear the words and visualise their impact on Alex's interpretation. He'd stood there, hesitant, stuffing chocolates into his mouth, the chocolates he'd brought for her.

'Damn it,' she breathed as the doorbell chimed in feeble competition with screaming guitars and tight harmonies. 'Shit!' Throwing a towel over steaming shoulders, she glided to the door. 'Dan!' she said, greeting the detective with a generous smile and a warm kiss. 'It's good to see you, it's *great* to see you.' Her emotion was genuine.

Dan threw his arms around the slender body.

'Hey, I'm all sweaty,' Eve giggled half-protestingly.

'Don't bother me none,' Dan grinned widely. 'I like my women a little sweaty.'

'Yeah, so Mandie tells me.'

'Yep,' Dan readily agreed, 'she'll be one who knows.'

'By the way, where is she?'

'She went out with a bag of cameras and stuff, another of her artistic forays.'

Eve and Mandie had been good friends ever since meeting a couple of years ago, at the time of Charley's death. It had been at the funeral, when she'd raised her eyes from the whirring motor that was straining to lower the coffin into the Earth, that Eve had caught her first glimpse of the lanky blonde standing uncomfortably close to Dan's uniform-clad body. Of course, she'd known that Dan was living with someone, had been for several years, but to see them standing there like an institution had somehow caught her off guard. The introductions had come later in the day, at the wake, over glasses of sherry and islands of matzos under resplendent toppings of prawns, smoked salmon, pastrami, and boiled eggs all chopped up and mixed into a chive-based cream cheese laced with vicious slivers of chilli. She'd noticed – it hadn't been hard – how the couple had wandered through the proceedings like those babies, what are they called, the one's born joined at the hip? Inseparable. 'We must talk sometime,' the woman, Mandie, had said. 'Not now, but maybe, I don't know . . . next week? Would that be good for you? We could meet perhaps for coffee? Somewhere, anywhere?' Dan, attentive Dan, had been silent, though his eyes, flashing backwards and forwards between the two women, had volunteered volumes. The coffee rendezvous had been a fact finding exercise and from the get go, almost as soon as the waitress had moved off to procure two espressos, Mandie had shown zealous interest in Eve's life, every itsy-bitsy teeny-weeny corner of it. At the time, Eve had had only one thing on her mind – well, two things: dance and Charley's death. Actually, there had been a third, a large chunky man of a thing – Mandie's partner. Nevertheless, she'd kept her wits about her, managing to field all the enquiries with a certain amount of reserve and a mountain load of dignity. And, surprise, surprise, the man thing had never came up, had never entered into what was basically a one-way conversation.

Now, thinking back, remembering the questions about

Charley, about the paintings and the associated documents that had been found in the rambling spaces of the Carmichael residence, small shivers of guilt shimmied through the mechanisms of her mind. She recalled her responses, remembering how they'd been vague and sort of disconnected. There had been something else as well, a crucible of secrecy hovering in suspended animation.

Leading Dan into the kitchen, she felt kind of squirmy and decided to lighten the load. Allowing him to keep his arm around her waist, she filled the kettle with water and wondered how best to broach the subject. 'You know?' she began. 'I've been kind of silly.'

'You have?' Dan asked, opening a cupboard and lifting out a *cafetière*. Frequent visits had furnished him and Mandie with inside knowledge of the whereabouts of just about everything. 'Join the rest of humanity.'

'There's something I should've told Mandie, you know, the first time we met? She and I?'

'Jesus, you as well?'

'As well?'

'You sound just like Alex, last year. He said what you said, almost word for word, when we were trying to keep him on his feet after that Jessica woman fled from Scotland and left him floundering.'

'Yeah?'

'Yeah. His worry was that he hadn't told us what he and Jessica had discovered about the pictures.'

'Crazy.'

'Yeah, sort of.'

'No, crazy because my silliness revolves around the same goal posts.' Eve smiled and loaded the *cafetière* with finely ground coffee. 'Now we have to wait a couple of minutes,' she advised, leaning awkwardly against the worktop, 'otherwise the water will scald the coffee and spoil the taste.'

'Goal posts?' Years of detective work allowed Dan to be *au fait* with just about any situation. Hard and pushing or laid back and gentle, he knew all the manoeuvres, all the tried and tested methods of extracting knowledge. This, though, was a little different. He knew and cared for this woman, had been present when Mandie had introduced her to Alex and had been encouraging in their relationship. He was a master at knowing when two people were made for each other, especially when one of them was about to be involved with Eve.

They sat at the small kitchen table, Eve drumming the fingernails of her left hand against its surface while they waited for the water to cool its heels. 'The goal posts regarding Charley and the paintings, and Mrs Carmichael. And, while we're at it, the goal posts regarding Alex.'

'Shit, that's a large collection of goal posts,' Dan chuckled. 'Sounds serious. Guess I'll have to put a hold on solving the city's crimes.'

'Does anybody know?' Eve asked, enigmatically.

'Know? About what?' Dan answered warily, unsure of where the conversation was heading.

'Um . . . you know, about us?'

'Christ, that was years ago.'

'I know, I know, but does anyone know about it?'

'No, no one.'

'You sure?'

'Sure I'm sure. I told nobody.'

'No, of course.'

'You were only seventeen, for Christ's sake.'

'Fifteen, Dan. I was fifteen.'

'No, it's impossible. You told me you were seventeen, going on eighteen.'

'I lied.'

'You lied?' Dan rose from his chair, turned in a circle and sat down again, running a hand through his hair as implications of every dimension crowded into his head. 'Jesus, Eve. *Chri*st.' He was lost, going round in circles and mixing-up names. 'Fif*teen*?'

'So that's why it has to remain a secret.'

'Too damn right! Jesus, it's a fucking nightmare. Shit, if this got out . . .'

'It can't get out, not ever.'

'No one knows, honey, it didn't last long enough.'

'One semester, Dan, one crazy summer. Christ, it'd be a disaster . . .'

'A fucking catastrophe is what it'd be.'

'So no one knows, then?'

'It's dead and buried.'

Eve leaned forward, her head disappearing behind a curtain of hair as she concentrated on pouring hot water into the glass container. 'It has to stay that way, for everybody's sake.' Fitting the plunger into the top of the *cafetière*, she looked at Dan and said, 'You were my first.'

'I should say I was.'

'It was your uniform, all those shiny buttons and everything, and your voice, cool and full of authority. All the girls went silly.'

'Not you, though.'

'Huh, I was the silliest.' Eve forced the plunger through the dark brown liquid, the movement causing a ripple of coffee to spill over the container's rim. 'But also the happiest.'

'So none of your friends was aware of what was happening?'

'They probably guessed! Hell, I was scooting around like the cat that got the cream.'

'But you didn't tell them, you know, in girly conversation?'

'Um . . .'

'It's important, goddamn it.'

'I don't know, Dan, maybe I did. Jesus, I was a teenager, foolishly in love with an older man. The other girls were jealous, asking all kinds of stuff, you know, kids stuff? So, yeah, maybe one or two cottoned on but, shit, we were horny as hell.'

'What does that mean?'

'Aw fuck, we were all out to get laid.'

'At fif*teen?*'

'Fifteen, thirteen . . . a gang of Lolita's hungry for the real thing, a collection of little time bombs all primed and charged and waiting to explode.'

'But . . .'

'Oh, c'mon, it's not long since people got married at that age and started dropping kids. Shit, in some countries it's still customary. When we women start growing boobs we think we're ready for sex. I was, but this you already know. It's a primaeval urge, it's natural, it's a fact of life.' Eve grinned as she poured the coffee. 'Also,' she continued, replacing the pot onto the table, 'when your body has been contorted into just about every position in the book, you discover muscles in the strangest places. Hmm, the doorstep of sexual awakening.'

'You mean your ballet?'

'Of course my ballet. I started dancing when I was five and began serious training when I was eight. Christ, I was probably up for it at the age of twelve.'

'*Twelve?*'

'Maybe younger.'

'*Eve!*'

'I know, I know, it's totally forbidden and everything, but when you stand with one foot on the ground and the other stretched along the *barre*, you start to wonder at the sensations pulling at your groin. Shit, it's real, really real.'

'It's uncanny, it's not elegant.'

'Not elegant? What's the matter with you? Ballet dancers are the most elegant people in the world. We're taught poise and control and we're as fit as gymnasts, and, unlike all those catwalk people, we smile while we strut our funky swan-like stuff.'

'True. So where do you want to start?'

'Start?'

'Charley or Alex?'

'Oh, right, um . . . Alex.' Eve took a sip of coffee and peered through wisps of aromatic steam. The situation was delicate. Despite the fact that they'd been intimate it was ridiculous to think of Dan as a former boyfriend; he'd been, what, ten years her senior? She smiled as she recalled the heat of the summer and the candescence of her young body. Masterfully, she'd tutored her parents into believing she'd been going to meet a group of classmates, one of whom was celebrating his birthday. Agnes would be there, she'd informed them, as would Carol and Johanna; and Tom, whose birthday it was – in reality, 'cos that was something that could be checked – would be bringing Gary and Steve and somebody else and had gotten permission to drive his dad's car.

The confusion and bewilderment had been pretty intense and of course there had been the added tension of making sure she didn't get pregnant. It was the number one rule, dictated on their first date, a frolic through the attractions of Coney Island, with its famous coaster, hot dogs and aquarium. They'd held hands and giggled, although now, thinking about it, Eve seemed to remember that she'd been the one who'd done most of the giggling. The ride home had been an orgy of kissing and edgy petting whenever the traffic lights had been against them, or, in Dan's opinion at the time, with them. It had all been so easy, just like being a grown-up, and she'd known that Dan had been impressed. But later, when he'd tried to slide her panties over her bony hips, she'd panicked and slapped the intruding hand. Outside her parent's house she'd unglued herself from a tight embrace, straightened her skirt and oozed out of the car. Bubbling with excitement, she'd remained standing outside the front door for an eternity while trying to contain her feelings.

'Alex?'

Eve blinked, took another sip and set the cup onto its saucer. 'Yup, Alex. Well, I've sent him on a mission to meet his ex.'

'I know.'

'Excuse me?'

'We met, Alex and me, on the ferry.'

'What? When?'

'Oh, a few days back, you were still in hospital. He was worried. And as it happened to be Mandie's birthday, we all went out together.'

'*He* was worried? About what?'

'Well, about you, obviously. He didn't know what to do.'

'And did you tell him what to do?'

'No, you'd already done that. You told him to go and meet people.'

'Yes, damn it, I did.' Eve got up and advanced towards a bank of kitchen cupboards. 'Would you like some brandy? I think we have some. Anyways, I need some, I'm beginning to feel weak.' She discovered an unopened bottle of Rémy and passed it to Dan, saying 'Open.'

Dan looked at the bottle and started unscrewing the cap.

'Well, do you think I've been silly?' Eve crossed the kitchen and took a couple of glasses from another cupboard.

'Do you?' Dan responded.

'Don't be a fucking psychologist, that's what she was.'

'What, Jessica?'

'Yes, Dan, Jessica.'

'Shit, of course she was. Up her own ass, just like the rest of 'em.'

'Yes. But do you think I can trust him?'

'Alex? He's in love with you.' Bottle in one hand and cap in the other, Dan poured decent amounts of cognac.

'He used to be in love with her.'

'That was then, this is now.'

'Dan?'

'He had no problem about meeting with Mrs Carmichael, he was okay about that. It was just that he was a little dubious about your other suggestions.'

'London and Munich and stuff, I suppose?'

'About Jessica. He was pretty reluctant.'

'Was he?'

'Until I put him right, until I told him he might as well use the time profitably.'

'Profitably? Shit, Dan, what were you thinking?'

'Yeah, wrong word. What would be the right one?'

'No, it's okay, profitably is good, exactly right, sums up the situation beautifully.'

'I think he thought you were testing him.'

'Testing him? How?'

'Well, he didn't exactly say . . .'

'Dan, what *did* he say?'

'Very little, but he was definitely not happy about leaving you.'

'Really?' Eve took a mouthful of Rémy and swilled it around her teeth.

'Absolutely. He was like a little boy lost, didn't know which way to turn. Before meeting up with Mandie, we went to a bar, downtown, someplace I go with the boys from the station house, you know, to chill? Anyway, he started to unwind, opened up a bit. He spoke about Jessica, spoke about her quite a lot, saying how the whole thing had screwed him up, put him on edge. Spoke about you as well, said how much you'd done for him, how you helped bring his confidence back, that sort of stuff? He also said there were so many things he didn't know about you, your history, your relationships, your . . .'

'Our history, yours and mine.' Eve swallowed the brandy. 'And what about Mandie?'

'What a*bout* Mandie?'

'Well, she could spill the beans, upset the applecart, dislodge the Pope.'

'No, I told you, nobody knows. Dislodge the Pope?'

'Yeah, well I'm nervous, I don't feel too good.'

'The brandy'll help.'

'Not s'posed to be drinking, taking too many drugs.'

'Aw, honey, you'll be fine, both of you.'

'You think?'

'I know it, I know people. It's my job.'

'Dan, the people you know are all criminals! Shit, s'pose we are, too! Or were!' Eve picked up the glass of brandy and touched it against Dan's. ' 'S'funny, you know, us talking about something that happened all those years ago.'

'Funny? Why funny?'

'Because Alex and Jessica are probably doing exactly the same thing; and their relationship was more intense.'

'Really? Why?'

'They were older.'

'Yeah, but not intense, honey, not like us. *We* had intensity. Bloody hell, it was incredible.'

Eve giggled and used both hands to pull at her hair, rear-ranging it so it draped seductively forwards over her right shoulder. 'Yes,' she agreed, 'it was.'

Dan leaned back and clasped his hands behind his head. 'But now you've got Alex, he's a good man, really worried about you and really in love with you. He was going crazy when you were in that hospital, it was all Mandie and I could do to keep him from attacking the doctors and nurses. I had to give him a serious talking to on that first day, telling him there was nothing he could do and that it was pointless for him to hang around getting under the feet of the hospital staff. I took him home and Mandie put him to bed.'

'Yeah, he told me. Said it was really strange to wake up and find Mandie staring at him, it kinda got him to wondering if the whole thing had been a dream, you know, the relationship and everything?'

'Mmm, and now you have to put the experience behind you.' Dan raised his glass and smiled. 'But, you know? this drama will have pulled you closer together, it's the way it is. A life-threatening situation is a great way of strengthening a relationship, especially yours which is pretty solid in any case.'

'Yeah, I guess.'

'So what about Charley? What strange secrets are you going to reveal about him?'

'Well . . .'

'No, no, on second thoughts, wait, you should tell us both, me and Mandie. Come and have dinner, tonight, and, as Marvin Gaye said, "Move on up".'

'You weren't joking,' Eve announced as she and Dan entered the apartment. The music of Marvin Gaye was playing at one or two decibels above the background ambience.

'Hey,' Dan called through funk-filled space, 'I've brought home an extra mouth to feed.' He smiled at Eve and helped her remove her coat. 'Sit,' he told her, 'I'll go find a bottle of something.' He ambled across the living room and embraced Mandie, who was on her way out of the kitchen to meet the surprise guest.

'Eve!' she exclaimed, 'how are you? It's great to see you. How's Alex?'

Eve stood and the two women kissed and Eve presented Mandie with a small bouquet of roses she'd collected from a tiny but well-stocked florist, somewhere between Queens and Manhattan.

'What are these for?'

'They're for you.'

'Me?'

'And Dan, for all your kindness and attention.'

'Don't be silly, you're part of the family. Alex too. Where is he?'

'Europe.'

'Europe? So he's gone?'

'Yup, meeting people.'

'One of whom would be Jessica?'

'Also.'

'Um . . . okay, you know what you're doing.' Mandie returned to the kitchen and Eve followed. 'Dan, open a bottle of something with bubbles, we need to celebrate. Look in the fridge.' She turned to smile at Eve. 'What *are* you doing?'

'Don't ask!'

'No, no, I'm sure you wouldn't have sent your man to meet his ex, unless you had good reason.'

'Hmm, I had my reasons but I'm not so sure they were good.'

'Sweetheart,' Dan interrupted, peeling foil from the neck of a bulging bottle, 'leave her alone. We've talked it through, inside out and sideways, and it's going to be okay.'

'I wondered where you'd got to,' Mandie remarked, looking at Dan whilst handing a dish of layered potatoes to Eve. 'Put them on the table, anywhere you can find space. So, you had a secret rendezvous with my man?'

'I didn't know about it, he just sort of turned up,' Eve replied, smiling, slight flutters creeping through her stomach.

'Just joking,' Mandie grinned, looking radiant. 'Peas.'

Eve took the steaming dish and placed it on the table, next to the potatoes.

Mandie opened another section of the oven and removed

a tray of lumpy brown things, light and dark, sizzling and shiny. She set the tray onto the table at the same time that an explosion announced Dan's success with the bottle. 'Okay everyone, sit, anywhere, tuck in.'

'It looks great,' Eve said admiringly, selecting a chair near the vegetables. 'What is it?'

'Mexican, one of Dan's favourites, chicken and chorizo, all spicy and loaded with garlic and peppers.' Mandie spooned an enormous helping onto a plate and passed it to Eve. 'Help yourself to the veg, hon, it's really good you're here.'

Fiddling with a couple of spoons, Eve arranged sliced potatoes, grilled with cheese and milk, and steamed peas around the chicken-chorizo mixture. 'Mmm, smells incredible,' she said, smiling at Dan as he poured a glass of Spumante. Lifting the glass, she toasted the chef, 'Happy days and . . . thanks.'

Reciprocating, Mandie raised a glass that Dan had just finished filling. 'To the best of friends, and to Alex, wherever he is.'

Dan sat himself at the head of the table, slurped at his drink and announced, 'Eve has something to tell you.'

'She does?' Eve asked.

'Certainly, she does,' Dan smirked. 'Something about Charley.'

'Charley?' Mandie asked. 'Your grandfather?'

Eve chewed on chicken and contemplated her plate of food, wondering how to admit her indiscretion regarding honest answers. She sipped at the bubbly stuff.

'Eve?' Mandie coaxed.

'Yes, Dan's right, I have something to say on the matter of my grandpa. Sort of goes back to just after he died, when you and I met, remember? When you came asking questions about the paintings and about my relationship with him.'

'Yes, I remember. What about it?' Looking first at Dan, then at Eve, Mandie tried to read the suddenly serious faces. 'Jesus, what is it with the both of youse? You're as thick as thieves.'

'Well,' Eve answered, blushing furiously, 'I was a little economical with the truth. Thing is, I lied. There, I said it.'

'Lied? But there was nothing to lie about, was there?' Mandie looked at Dan. 'Hey, what's the matter with this girl?'

'Mandie, I knew nothing about the paintings, their history or where they came from, that much was true. But as for grandpa, well . . . I kind of knew about um . . .'

'Christ, girl, you're among friends, spit it out.'

'He rescued her.'

'Her? Her who?'

'Mrs Carmichael, during the war, from the Nazis.'

'What?' Mandie and Dan both asked the question, almost at the same instant. 'Why?'

'I don't know the details, he never went into it. People, you know, of his generation? they don't like to talk too much about what they did in the war. I suppose they spend their lives trying to forget.'

'But he must've told you more?'

'No, not really, just that he helped her after the Nazis had taken her husband and child.'

'*Jesus!*'

'That's it, that's about as much as I know. I'm sorry.'

'Didn't Alex go and see Mrs Carmichael, before he went to Europe?' Dan asked. 'He told me he wanted to talk with her.'

'Yes, but he told me nothing.'

'But he saw you after the meeting, before he left?'

'Yep, but maybe he thought the hospital was not an ideal place for deep discussion. Or maybe he thought I was too poorly.' Eve smiled, 'He just stood at the bedside, eating my chocolates.'

Chapter Seven:

Munich

1

The streets were full of *Fasching*, burgeoning with ideas of fiesta, fashion and freshness of the soul; and, as Wolfgang sedately motored through Schwabing, the inevitable question rose up and found itself in mid air, wobbling in front of the dashboard. 'Vhere is the Jessica?' The words trembled a little to the right, where the letters unscrambled themselves in a jet stream of warm air issuing from a plastic vent.

Alex turned and looked at his friend. 'Voolfy, there's a lot I have to tell you.'

*　　*　　*

The Anglo-German friendship had started about seven years previously, when Alex had been roped-in to attending a stag party, a boisterous affair conducted in the very same artistic quarter of Munich through which he was now gliding. The revellers had been pretty much out of control, and after the obligatory dance across tabletops following the sweaty footsteps of an obligatory stripper, the team of hotfooted Lotharios, daringly led by Nick, had unknowingly descended into a gay bar. Elegant-looking cocktails took the place of beer steins, while a tall blonde, resembling Marlene, swooped upon an anxious Alex. Thus began a game of musical chairs with Alex moving steadily from one bar stool to the next, hotly pursued by a man on high heels. Relinquishing the last available stool, Alex had stood miserably at the end of the bar, watching apprehensively as a hero stepped up to the avenging blonde and asked, '*Hermann, was machst du?*'

Inebriated though he was, Alex realised that this was not directed at him, and he looked on in hazy acceptance as Marlene was cornered and induced to sit passively in front of an exotic drink. Alex just had time to appreciate an exploratory sip from his own drink, when the man who'd saved the day proceeded to introduce himself. '*Ich bin der Wolfgang,*' he'd said good naturedly. '*Es tut mir leid, aber mein Freund Hermann ist ein bisschen . . .*'

'Loco,' Alex had suggested unambiguously.

'*Genau.*'

'*Und ich spreche kein Deutsch,*' he added as a last resort in a desperate attempt to dampen any lusty ardour that the newcomer might possess.

'*Ach so, tut mir* . . . Sorry, sorry . . . from vhere are you coming?'

'London.' Trying to stand more upright, Alex had used a deeper voice in an effort to display his heterosexualness. 'England.' The word issued from the depths of his stomach, a threatening rumble designed to keep intruders at a distance.

'*Ach so, und* vhy are you being here?'

'Good question,' Alex answered, wondering the same thing.

'No, not here,' the German said, smiling and swinging

an arm as though encompassing the club, 'but here, in München?'

'Ah, well, I'm here with some friends . . . it's a stag party.' Alex peered through dimness. 'Over there, my friends,' he gestured, using a small umbrella that had been protecting his cocktail. Thinking that this explained everything, he relaxed, just a little.

'Ah, yes, stag party,' Wolfgang had nodded sagely. 'Vhat is this?'

Resigned to the fact that the German was here to stay, and aware that there appeared to be no imminent threat from unwanted advances, Alex had started to tread the lengthy path of explanation.

* * *

And now, as Wolfgang swung off the street and nosed into an underground garage, Alex began to unwind, confident that the benign Bavarian would be only too eager to join in with his plans regarding the paintings. After all, he reflected, Wolfgang had been present at the inception, the moment of discovery when he and Jessica had been on their quest to locate the two missing *Prentiss Poses*, the title that had been applied to the risqué pictures.

'Alex, is *gut* that you are being here at this time.'

Their footsteps echoed loudly in the vast expanse of empty concrete as Wolfgang ushered them towards a lift. 'The city is full of fun and everyone is celebrating *Fasching*. There are being parties everyvhere and tonight is one. It'll be different, I am haffing friends here . . . *und* I can be introducing you to some of them.'

'Great,' Alex laughingly responded. 'Can't wait.'

'No, no,' Wolfgang added hastily, 'you vill be seeing. Some of them are straight . . . a little bohemian maybe, but straight. They are nice people.'

'Yes, my friend, I'm sure they are,' Alex agreed.

'So,' Wolfgang smilingy concluded. 'Ve are haffing a date.'

The lift, silent and efficient, sped them to the sixth floor and opened onto a large lobby. 'Here is the apartment of Heidi,' Wolfgang announced, unlocking a solid-looking door. 'Ve vill stay for a couple of days. Is okay?'

Narrowly avoiding collision with a sexy, leather-clad Le Corbusier chaise longue, Alex stepped across the modern living room and gazed at the panorama spread out before him – Munich in all its glory. 'Is okay, Voolfy,' he answered, using his friend's nickname, while his roving eyes located the twin domes of the famous Frauenkirch, 'it's very much okay.' Peering through a smudgy reflection of himself, he smiled at Wolfgang's difficulty with the letter "w". It reminded him of Jessica and her suggestion that werewolves and wigwams and especially the name Edward Woodward would be words that should be avoided by the German-speaking fraternity. The sound of an opening door caused him to turn round.

'*Heidi, servus*,' Wolfgang said, greeting a tall woman whom Alex thought seemed vaguely familiar. With a large smile, Wolfgang placed an arm around Alex's shoulders and introduced him. 'Here is Alex of London, but of course you haff met already.'

'We have?' Alex asked, struggling to recall where he might have met the woman called Heidi.

'You haff.' Wolfgang's smile widened into a grin. 'I am saving you vhen she vas a him.'

Alex stepped back in amazement. 'But you were . . .'

'Yes, yes, she vas the Hermann,' Wolfgang announced delightedly, almost proudly.

'Dressed as Marlene,' Alex added, remembering the awkward situation.

'Underneath ze arches,' the newly transformed Heidi sang, wistfully and huskily.

'And from chair to chair,' Alex intoned, supplying an improvised second line to the wartime ditty.

'Indeed,' Wolfgang guffawed, 'it vas enchanting to vatch.'

'Scary it was, Voolfy, scary.'

'Yes, my friend, but all in *gut* fun. We saw that you English were . . . how you say . . . "out your deeps"? So we decided to make your visit a little more vibrant.'

'Depths. We were, we were, we certainly were, but we were so pissed it didn't really matter where we were or what we were doing.'

'Yes, *Schatzi*, that's vhy I vas rescuing you. Eventually.'

'Thanks Voolfy. It was a narrow escape.'

'Yes,' Heidi giggled. 'You vill never know how narrow.'

'So, come Alex, ve vill go find coffee *und* you can be telling me everything about Jessica.' Still with his arm wrapped around Alex's neck, Wolfgang led the startled Englishman past the smirking Heidi and out of the apartment.

2

Although aware of the form of their relationship, Wolfgang was surprised when he learned that the split between Jessica and Alex was irrevocable. 'But you were perfect together; made for one another, I should be saying,' he said.

'I know,' Alex agreed.

'And you were great as a team. I am remembering vhen ve are finding the paintings . . .'

'I know,' Alex repeated, manfully trying to stem the tide of Wolfgang's reminiscences.

'And she loved you, Alex, it vas obvious . . .'

'On and off, Voolfy. When it was on, everything was great, perfect, but . . . Well, let's just say she had her moments.'

'Ve are all haffing moments, it's being the same for everyone, even for us.' Wolfgang used his eyes to indicate the groups of men engaged in happy conversation at the half-dozen or so tables squeezed into the small café. 'I was thinking it strange, your phone-call, you remember? When Jessica vas coming to collect Rembrandt *und* you are saying to tell her you are already haffing it.'

'I know.'

'*Und* ve vere talking about everything, afterwards, vhen you vere arriving to collect it. You were telling me about the problems, but . . . but we are sometimes haffing to be patient.'

'Yes, but my patience just ran out. I tried, Voolfy, believe me, I tried. You know what Jessica's like, she's up and down, she's feisty; it's her mien.'

'Mean? Mean vhat?'

'No, no, *mien*, with an 'i' and an 'e', even though it comes from "demeanour". Anyway, it means, um . . . Well, it's her way.'

'Okay, but still we are all the time needing to be patient.'

'I know, Voolfy, you're right, but now there's Eve.'

'Eve? Vhat is Eve?'

'I suppose you would pronounce it 'Eva'. She's American.'

'I see.' Wolfgang beamed through his heavy bifocals.

'And she's . . .' Alex stopped, wondering if in fact he should be informing the world about Eve's connection to the man who'd intercepted the paintings on their secret passage out of Europe. '. . . Fantastic.'

Wolfgang nodded and the spectacles slid down his nose. He used thumb and first finger to shove them back to the bridge. 'But, Alex . . .'

'No, she really is. She's incredible. She doesn't have an ounce of jealousy. She encouraged me to come on this trip while she's recuperating.'

'Recup . . ?'

'Um . . . getting better. She was involved in a motor accident. Actually, it was pretty bad and for twenty-four hours it was touch and go. I was going crazy and everyone was saying there was nothing to be done, we just had to wait. Terrible, terrible, and then she turned the corner and started to improve and lay propped up on a heap of pillows and told me to go to Europe. You know, there she is with tubes running in and out of her and she just sort of smiles and tells me what to do, even though she knows all about Jessica and stuff. Sort of had me on edge for a while, wondering if there was any kind of hidden agenda behind her thinking. Shit! Sorry Voolfy, I'm running on, talking too fast and you probably don't understand anything I've said, except . . . Well, she's quite remarkable.'

'So it would seem, my friend. You haff to tell me everything, how you met and where you met, and . . .'

'I will, Voolfy, but let's order some more coffee and a couple of beers. There's other stuff I want to talk about as well.'

'Hmm . . . remember the last time you were here and we are going to the general's house to collect a crate for the putting in of Rembrandt? And on the way you are telling me that you hadn't gone completely mad?'

'I did?'

'You did, you are saying "It's okay Voolfy, I haven't gone completely mad. Not yet." '

'Okay. So you think that now I have, huh?'

Wolfgang smiled. 'Perhaps it's the coffee, too much of it.'

'Yeah, perhaps, but this woman is something else. She used to be a ballet dancer and now she teaches. You'll have to meet her.' Alex paused and thought about the scheme he'd come up with, the one that would entail a return to southern Germany. 'You know what? You will meet her, Voolfy. And in the not too distant future.'

Stubby bottles of Paulaner arrived on the table and were soon joined by two fresh cups of coffee. Wolfgang stared at the collection of beverages and toyed with a paper tube of sugar, waiting for Alex to continue. A group of five or six people entered the café and swarmed round an adjoining table, like wasps descending upon a dollop of ice cream dumped on the pavement from a child's careless cornet-carrying hand. They were speaking some Germanic type of language, but looser and uglier and sickly, and Alex watched as huge asses were deposited onto spindly-legged metal chairs. Almost immediately, as though at some prearranged signal, packets of cigarettes were removed from pockets and handbags and placed in religious ritual onto the table. In the manner of acolytes, clamouring at the rail waiting for the Lord's small white connecting devices to be placed on slavering tongues, the new arrivals broke into a clicking frenzy of impatient though well-rehearsed application of flame to cigarette, almost military in execution. After providing successful ignition, the plastic lighters were placed in imperial importance atop the individual stores of tobacco, while lazy clouds of exhaled redemption, collected by slightly less lazy coils of air, were transported unerringly into Alex's nostrils. It was an invasion, a group attack on private air-space – disgusting, skin-crawlingly nauseating and right up there with the selfish attitude of unthinking bastards who rejoice in the belief that pavements are constructed solely to be consecrated by their over-fed, under-exercised rats on strings.

'Anyway,' Alex continued, batting at smoky wedges of frustration and glowering at the gathering of conceited foreigners, 'I came up with this idea.'

Wolfgang raised a tiny coffee cup to his generous lips,

downed the bitter contents and waited for revelation.

'I need your help, Voolfy, with something that goes back to the conversation we had when you told me about that big house next to the lake. I need you to find out all you can about the character that lives in it.'

Wolfgang, his face relaxing in fleshy fashion, a collection of padded muscles floating loosely around bespectacled eyes, set the empty cup on its saucer, adroitly placing it in the centre of a flimsy paper doily which, in harmony with the cup, was happily broadcasting the fact that the coffee belonged to someone called *illy*. Alex, finding some sort of security in the friendly framework that peered across the table, attached his mouth to the neck of a beer bottle and nodded, hoping the movement might suggest to Wolfgang that he should explain his smug all-knowing look. 'You know?' he coaxed, disconnecting the bottle, 'the mysterious mansion that seems never . . .'

'To be occupied,' Wolfgang cut in. 'So, my friend, I am haffing news for you. I haff found who is being the owner.'

'You have?'

'But of course!' Wolfgang was enjoying the role of being the bearer of good news, of being able to answer a question that had been raised on Alex's previous visit. 'One day I am motoring past the house and I am noticing a man in the garden.'

'The general?' Alex prompted hopefully.

'The gardener,' Wolfgang continued without a flutter. 'So, I am stopping and talking to him. I am pretending to be a northerner from Hamburg or somewhere and I am interesting to buying something on the lake.' He looked up. 'You can say "on the lake"?'

'Um . . . yes, "on the lake" is fine.'

'Or maybe it is better saying "by the lake"?'

'Either, Wolfgang,' Alex advised. 'Both are fine.'

'Oh, okay . . . but "on the lake" sounds sort of funny, don't you think?'

'Really, Wolfgang, it's fine, you can use both.' Having come up with a plan that more or less depended on the German's news, Alex was in the position of a hotfooted Dudley Moore on the beach in *"10"*, hopping from sizzling footprint to sizzling footprint. He'd set himself a bunch of hoops to jump through, most of them being wielded by people whom he'd have to control in the manner of an eccentric Ring Master. Bugger, he was on a roll, faced with a challenge that carried a good possibility of payback, and all Wolfgang was worried about was whether a property should be on the lake or next to the fucking thing. '*Voolfy!*' he cried, exasperated, banging the bottle onto the table for effect and watching a host of golden bubbles froth out of the top in fizzy agitation. '*What?*' Alex glared at the smoke-haloed faces that had turned to investigate the sound of the bottle.

'Vell, ve vere talking about hedges and how to stop the bank from collapsing vhen vashed by giant vaves from the speeding skis of the jet set.'

'And?' Rich kids and water sports could be mulled over at a later date.

'*Und* this elderly gentleman on a vheelchair comes from behind the hedge *und* . . . Do you say "on a vheelchair" or "in a vheelchair"?'

'*Voolfy! In!*'

'Ah, "in" is *gut*. Anyway, he is wanting to know who I am.'

'You didn't tell him?'

'No, remember? I am pretending to be from the north. He was kind of charming, the old school, you know? An elderly gentleman at rest, haffing . . .'

'Leisure, Voolfy, an elderly gentleman at leisure.'

'Leisure . . . *ja, natürlich, Muße*, is better.'

'Yes, yes. So did you find out who he was? Is?'

'He is the General, Alex. The general who owned the kindergarten before it is *be*ing a kindergarten. But today he is calling himself Geisler.'

'Shit, I always had my suspicions. Voolfy, this calls for more beer, we have to celebrate.'

'Exactly, Alex, *Scheiße*, as we say. The world is not being so small, huh?'

'Big.'

'*Ach so*, big. It is a small place.'

'But do you know for sure?'

'Of course I am knowing. In conversation the general is using the word *Kinderstube*, which is being a room for small children, and this I am thinking is connecting him.'

'*Kinderstube*, kindergarten, it's all the same to me; kids are kids, big or small. It's a bit strange though . . . *Stube*, isn't that German for pub?'

'*Ja*, nowadays it is, especially in Bavaria and usually added to the end of a name. But in the old days it is simply meaning "room".'

'I suppose those would have been the old days when the general was last in residence.'

Alex stopped talking while two additional bottles of beer were lined up alongside their exhausted relatives and the four coffee cups, the latter drained of nervy liquid but retaining on their insides a telltale dirty brown ring just below the rim. The air-polluting crowd, reckoned by Wolfgang to be Netherlanders, rose as one and pocketed their life-support systems. With much scraping of slender metal legs on a series of unyielding terracotta tiles, they rearranged the chairs into a haphazard formation, exited the door and trooped away down the street.

'Maybe in those days it *was* just a room,' Alex mused, watching the swaying of the bums, 'although a big one, a place reserved for the offspring of the general's friends and colleagues. Maybe only after the war did it evolve into a kindergarten. And that's another thing that's weird, why on earth did he mention the kindergarten? From his point of view, surely it's a bit of history that's best kept secret?'

'Maybe, Alex, maybe. But, since he wasn't one of Hitler's thugs, he's probably not being too worried. Also, he doesn't know that I am being almost a neighbour, so maybe he was being a little on guard.'

'That'll be "off guard".'

'*Ja.* He was probably off guard.'

'True, Voolfy, true.'

Banging together the necks of the fresh bottles, they sucked beer.

'But then, Voolfy, he was involved in removing all those works of art and goodness knows what else. Surely that would . . .'

'Of course, but there's no reason why anyone from around here would be knowing this. We are only knowing because ve vent searching and are becoming lucky.'

'And how.'

'Oh,' Wolfgang started to explain, 'because we are finding the paintings, the . . .'

'No, no, I didn't mean that, it wasn't a question, it was just sort of . . . Well, an agreement to your statement, an agreement that carries some form of . . . not exaggeration exactly but more like, um, amplification. Yep, you said, "We got lucky", so when I said, "And how", I meant that we got very lucky. And, Voolfy, now that you seem to have unearthed the general, we appear to have got even luckier. More lucky, another amplification.'

'Alex, my friend, you would make a very good English teacher.'

'And you would make a very good detective.'

'So, as they are saying, vhere do ve go from here?'

'We tread carefully, Voolfy, very carefully. We tiptoe around, staying out of the way, but keeping the general firmly in our sights so that we know his whereabouts at all times.'

'But what if he is seeing me? Bad Wiessee is being a small place.'

'Well, you met only because you ventured into his neck of the woods . . . um, his territory. You'd never seen him before and he'd never seen you. When he's at home, home is where he stays. And I remember you saying that he seems to be absent for most of the time, so I don't think there's much chance of bumping into him.'

'No, but if I did?'

'You're property hunting. Stick to the story.'

'Alex, you're being mysterious. Vhat are you planning?'

'Something big, Voolfy, something dynamic that can succeed only with your help.'

'*Ach so.*'

'So are you in or are you out? With me, or . . ?'

'*Mein Gott!* You sound just like Husain ibn Ali.'

'Yes, other people have to be involved.' Alex paused and thought about what Wolfgang had just said. 'Who?'

'Husain ibn Ali. He was being Muhammad's . . . how you say? Grandson? Around the end of the seventh century, at Karbala, he is asking the army of Yazid I if they wanted to be with his forces or if they were against.'

'Christ! What was the answer?'

'Vas being the wrong answer! They are saying, "Of course against you!" and this brought about not only battle and the death of Husain, but also everlasting hatred between the Sunni and Shiite brethren.'

'Voolfy, that's amazing. How do you know such stuff?'

'It's interesting stuff, Alex, and I am reading much books.'

'Bloody hell, you'd make an excellent history teacher. So, knowing all this, be careful how you answer!'

'I am being in, Alex, of course I'm in. But vhat am I haffing to be doing?'

'I'll tell you when I've worked out the final details. But for now, just keep tabs on our friend.'

'Tabs? Vhat are tabs?'

'Eyes.'

'Eyes are tabs?'

'Yes, eyes are tabs,' Alex smirked. 'At least, here and now they are.'

'Tabs.' Wolfgang paused while he assimilated the new-found fact. 'I am not knowing this. You English, you are strange in your ways.'

3

Everything was green, including the drinks, although some were blue. The atmosphere was stuffed with Spandau Ballet and The Communards and the buoyant crowd was spectacularly colourful, ordained as iconic variations of characters from *The Rocky Horror Picture Show* along with a smattering of Trekkies. Alex grinned inanely and began drinking lurid cocktails.

In an amazingly short space of time everyone became beautiful and he fell into a side-together-side camp version of the cha-cha. Sandwiched between an athletic Uhuru and an exceedingly large, exceedingly elegant jelly baby, he shimmied left and right, unconscious of the spectacle until he thought of the prospect, and the excuse it offered, of peanuts.

'I need peanuts,' he informed his gyrating companions. 'They're good for alcohol.' He grabbed his moment when the music changed rhythm and the bpm's became a worry to his respiratory system. Shaking hands with his bouncy comrades, he looked around for Wolfgang and saw him in earnest conversation with a tall, thin, dark-skinned alien. Threading his way to the garishly decorated bar, Alex collected another cocktail, dispensed with the baby umbrella and downed the drink in one thirsty gulp. Scooping a handful of peanuts from a convenient dish, he leant against the bar and gawped at the outlandish proceedings.

Apart from the drunken spree, when no one had known what they were doing, Alex had never been to a gay club, the idea never having crossed his mind, and, were it not for the predilection of his German friend, he wouldn't have considered the necessity to cross the threshold. To be fair, Wolfgang hadn't been pushy when he'd suggested an evening in one of his favourite haunts, not at all, and Alex had been honestly vague about complying with the idea. Lazily surveying the patrons of the swinging establishment he noticed their demeanour, the relaxed manner in which they engaged in easy conversation. It was one big family, dancing, laughing, drinking and chatting, everyone seemed to be familiar and no one was judged. The more he looked, the more he understood. Here, aside from their costumes, everyone was equal, there were no false pretensions. And then he noticed that the crowd included several women, most of them sitting in small groups at tables edged around the petite dance floor. To his inexperienced eye they looked like normal women, wearing normal women's apparel and engaging in normal women's conversation, and probably sipping at normal women's drinks. All of a sudden, Wolfgang and the lanky alien were at his side.

'These women,' Alex asked. 'Are they normal?'

'*Alex!*' Wolfgang exclaimed in mock horror. 'Vhat sort of question is this? And vhat is normal?'

'No, no, I don't mean normal, not really. I don't know, but they don't look gay, not particularly, not all of them.' Alex felt his feet digging rapidly towards Australia. 'You know?' he finished lamely and annoyingly squeakily.

'Some are, Alex, and some aren't. And some are men. We don't make distinctions between people. They are who they are and they are what they are, and here they are having the freedom to be themselves.'

'So it's all very liberal?' Alex asked, nodding his head in anticipation of the answer.

'But of course, like the horse. What else? People come here to be free of inhibition and free of prejudice.'

'Shit, Voolfy, absofuckinglutely. What a great attitude, pity the rest of the world doesn't follow suit. Um . . . what horse?'

'It's vhat ve are learning at school to remember the phrase "Of course." '

Wolfgang turned to the alien and laid an arm on green Lurex shoulders. 'Here is the Kurt. Used to hang around with the Heidi when she was being a he.' Wolfgang peered closely at Alex's face to witness any reaction. There was none, nothing radical, perhaps just a blink of an eye and the trace of a smile. 'Come, come, Alex, shake hands. Kurt wants to buy you a drink.'

This did elicit a reaction. Alex shook hands with the alien and clapped him on the back, hard. 'Good idea, Kurt. How about a beer?' He kept his voice low, as gravelly as possible, and grinned like a lunatic.

'So, I'll leave you two to it,' Wolfgang announced, returning to the dance floor as K.C. and the Sunshine Band launched into strains of familiar irrepressible happiness.

Someone was knocking at the door. Shit, someone was *opening* the door! Bugger, Alex thought, deciding it must be the middle of the night.

'Alex, vake up. I haff been talking with the station.'

Emergent intelligence groped through all the possibilities. 'Radio station? Space station?' he enquired in a feeble voice.

'Train station. I haff booked a ticket.'

'Oh, good,' Alex responded. Then, 'Where are we going?'

'London. You, not we.'

'Me? Just me? Me alone?' A sweet gooeyness of stale cocktails made Alex's teeth seem the size of tombstones and he had difficulty in speaking properly. Vague memories of last night's loud music massaged his aching head into something the size and cruddiness of a volcano on the verge of eruption, and anything more energetic than lying in a darkened room was not an option.

'You are going to London. You, and nobody else but you.'

'Christ, sounds like a romantic song a crooner would croon.'

'Crooner?'

'Sinatra, Voolfy, that type of thing. You know, a ballad in a nineteen-fifties smoky night club? A little like that place last night, only different.' Alex, by now, had woken up and was thinking of breakfast, something to soak up the viscosity that was swilling around inside his guts. And then he began to wonder why he was going to London. 'Voolfy, why am I going to London?'

'Because you are haffing things to be doing, remember? You haff been telling me that you are wishing to stay in the States with this lady, no? So, you must be organising and packing for your trip.'

'Oh, yes.'

'*Und* you must be speaking to the Indian.'

'Indian? What Indian?'

250

'The landlord man of your house.'

'Shit, yes. What time's my train, then?' Alex looked at the inside of his left wrist, at a couple of blue veins that normally reside invisibly beneath his watch, and had a momentary panic until he remembered he'd put the timepiece in his jeans pocket before taking a shower at some ridiculously late hour.

'Don't worry, Alex, we are haffing the time for breakfast. The train is not until eleven.'

Shoving his legs across the bed, Alex spent too long trying to force them into his jeans. When he'd managed to pull the denims as far as his thighs, he fumbled in the pockets, located the watch and moodily strapped it onto his wrist. He picked his shirt off the floor, worked his arms through the sleeves and stood up, thinking of Mr Banergee. Then he started thinking about Terry and the fact that he'd have to call him, better, visit, and speak to him urgently and set the plans in motion.

And then he was on the train to the Hook and following his former self. Level crossings with jangly bells reminded him of the exact same journey he'd made with Jessica, a passage through paradise with the girl of his dreams and one of the newly discovered paintings.

He was in the dining car when the train pulled into Stuttgart. He was still in the dining car when the train pulled out of Stuttgart. As if in a daze, he watched the station signs pick up speed in their backward motion across the window. It was all too familiar. He ordered another glass of wine and turned his mind to the future.

He was greeted by Mr Banergee himself, beaming widely in eager Indian apology. 'Ah, Mister Alex, how fortunate,' a set of gleaming white teeth informed him as he approached the front door. 'It is being too long since we are speaking. But now you are here, you see? It really is most fortunate.' The Indian's head started moving from side to side in a display of excitement at the possibility of receiving some rent.

'Yes, I see,' Alex said, shaking the hand that had been proffered. 'Here I am.' He spent a few moments unlocking the door and invited the landlord to follow him into the house, thinking how strange it was to be inviting someone into a building that was already his. Depositing his holdall on the living room floor, he turned to confront the hand-wringing gentleman.

'Your boxes are still here,' Mr Banergee observed.

Alex looked at the packing cases neatly filling the area under the bay window and realised he'd have to go through them. Soon. There was so much stuff, a whole lifetime of stuff that had to be sorted, and a lot of it, hell, most of it, should probably be thrown away. He looked at the landlord and said, 'Yes, so they are.'

'But Mister Alex, you must be unpacking everything. A home is a home, no? Is this not what they are saying?'

'This, indeed, is what they're saying,' Alex agreed, thinking of New York rather than Southgate.

'It is a wonderful thing, a wonderful saying. You must get a little sign to hang on the wall, there,' the Indian suggested, pointing through the open door, 'in the hallway.'

'Yes, yes, but . . .'

'It will definitely be making your home more better. More a home.' The Indian's enthusiasm was powerful.

'Mr Banergee,' Alex started, taking a deep breath and lowering his tone a register or two so as to sound authoritative, 'I'm leaving.'

'But you can't! I mean, you are only just arriving.'

'I know, but I have to go to America.'

'America!' Mr Banergee's voice bounced into realms of incredulity. 'America?' The place was across uncharted oceans and more dangerous than the Indian subcontinent. It was modern and full of Gekkoes, two-legged animals more ferocious and troublesome than any cobra or tiger. And then another thought crawled into the landlord's mind. 'You are not liking the house? Maybe I can find another, better, bigger.' Truckloads of baksheesh passed in front of his eyes as he gleefully imagined more rent. 'Yes, yes, I know a place. In Tottenham, very nice and being very suitable for Mister Alex.'

Alex peered at a series of large photographs that were blue-tacked to the walls of Terry and Christine's living room, and then he inspected a notice board that was virtually hidden behind a sea of close-up photos of sections of the human body: an arm, elbow, a nose, a pair of eyes, hair; clothing too: a jacket, velvet trousers, shoes, buckles, etc. A desk, situated in front of tall French windows overlooking a square, was arrayed with yet more photos taken from a multitude of angles, all of the same object which, it appeared, was being reproduced on a large canvas in the centre of the room.

'Looks like you're making a copy of something,' Alex posited, quite intelligently, as Terry came into the room carrying a tray bearing a jar of paintbrushes and a bottle of gin.

'Yes, yes, it's all very exciting,' Terry replied, manoeuvring stuff around a cluttered tabletop to make space for the tray. 'It's excellent for practice.'

'Practice? You need to practice?'

'Absolutely, absolutely,' Terry answered absentmindedly.

253

'Glasses, we need glasses. Christine's never here when needed.' He fussed around in a corner of the room, opening and closing squeaky doors that belonged to an impressive cabinet. 'Ah, success.'

'But I thought you were a professional?' Alex asked, slightly confused, slightly embarrassed and thinking that perhaps he'd come to the wrong place.

'Professional? Me?' Terry began pouring gin.

'Yes,' Alex responded. 'Aren't you? I mean, you did all that work for Michelstraub, you know, uncovering those *Prentiss Poses?*'

'Ah, yes, the *Prentiss Poses*; great fun, very enjoyable. You were right, Alex, Michelstraub does like to eat, almost as much as he likes to talk. Quite a character.' Terry handed Alex a glass. 'Um, sorry, what was the question?'

'Do you have any tonic?' Alex raised the glass and smiled encouragingly.

'Oh, yes, sorry. Of course, tonic.'

'And . . . are you a professional?'

The question snatched at Terry's ears as he walked across the room and fiddled in the cabinet. 'Yes, actually, to both questions.' He started giggling, 'Tonic and professional. Whilst being a professional picture restorer, I'm a bit of an amateur when it comes to painting.' He unscrewed the top of a discovered bottle of tonic water and managed to direct some of the pent-up liquid into Alex's glass. 'Why? What's so important?'

Alex waited, while Terry added some tonic to his own drink, before suggesting they sit.

'Problems?' Terry asked.

'Problems, no, just plans. A wild scheme that revolves around you.'

'And will I be travelling to the States on account of this scheme?'

'No, I don't think any travelling will be necessary,' Alex smiled, recalling the reception he and Terry had received when they'd flown to New York together. Terry had been summoned by Michelstraub to work on the *Prentiss Poses*, and Alex had accompanied him across the Pond to meet Dan and Mandie who'd become Alex's best friends. And Eve. 'But I must say I'm happily impressed to see the way you attack the problem of making a duplicate painting.'

'Ah, so you want me to copy something. What?'

'The *Prentiss Poses*.'

'All of them?'

'Minus the Rembrandt and the Vermeer.'

'Right. And there'll be a reason, no doubt?'

'There will, but I don't want to tell you what it is. Not yet.'

'Aha.'

'I want you to copy the originals that you found beneath the *Poses* and then cover them up again.'

'The orig . . .'

'Mmm, the masterpieces.'

'That's a whole different ball-game.'

'But you can do it?'

'No.'

'No?'

'In themselves the *Poses* wouldn't be too much of a problem, they're sort of naïve, easy to replicate. But the Masters! Huh, Alex, I hate to say it but they're a little beyond my humble capabilities.'

'Okay. Bugger.' Alex sipped thoughtfully.

'But I know someone who could, a formidable artist

who'd relish such a challenge.'

'Would he relish keeping it secret?'

'Why?'

'Because.'

'Alex, what are you planning?'

'I'll tell you everything you need to know, but I can't divulge the endgame.'

'So you're hoping to duplicate Michelstraub's collection. Does he know?'

'He doesn't. Nobody does. And this is one of the reasons for all the secrecy.'

'Hmm, and how soon does all this need to be done? You understand it's not the sort of work that can be hurried.'

'Yes,' Alex laughed, 'I remember. "Infinite patience, consummate concentration!" '

'And the rest,' Terry agreed, raising the gin bottle and topping up the glasses. 'To make a genuine copy,' he continued, twisting his face into a wry smile, 'one has to dabble in forensic science. Everything has to be perfectly matched – oils, dyes, fabrics – it's an art in itself.'

'And you think this man is capable of coming up with the goods? Good goods, top quality articles that'll pass close inspection?'

'If you've got the money, he'll create perfection.'

Returning to Southgate, Alex remembered the message from the boys in blue, the uplifting news that Jessica's bag had been discovered. Changing Tubes at Warren Street, he emerged at the Barbican and stepped into a downpour. Devoid of umbrella and coat, he shelled out for a broadsheet and used it as makeshift protection as he hurried past Smithfields on his way to the police station. Apart from a handful of isolated people huddled miserably in doorways and bus shelters, the streets were deserted. Alex thought about diving into a chippy, but time was not on his side. Having made the decision to collect the bag, he knew he'd have to get a move on if he was to catch the evening flight to New York. He skidded through the station's front door and stood dripping in front of the desk sergeant.

'Yes, sir. Good afternoon, sir. How can I . . ? Oh, it's you. Come about the bag, have we?'

'Yes, absolutely. The bag, the blue one.'

'Yes, sir, the blue bag. The blue bag that was left in the car.' Shaking his head in silent protest at humanity's stupidities, the officer paced his way to a cupboard behind the desk. 'She was most fortunate, you know, it doesn't always turn out like this,' he informed Alex, turning round, bag in hand. 'Of course, there's no money inside. Well, there wouldn't be, would there?'

'Been through it, then, have we?'

' 'Course we've been through it, sir, else how would we know whose bag it was?'

'Description. Blue, raffia, long blue cord. Giveaway.'

'Sir?'

'Can't be that many blue raffia shoulder bags in your cupboard?'

'No, sir. Just the one.'

'There you go, then. That'll be Jessica's.'

'Yes, sir, the young lady's.'

'Thank you,' Alex said, feeling quite tired and wondering what he was going to do with the bag now he'd collected it. The sands of time were running out and there was no way he could get it to Jessica before he left the country. Bugger, bugger, bugger. He turned and walked towards the door.

'Excuse me, sir?' the sergeant called across the room, lifting a biro off the desk and holding it in mid air. 'If you wouldn't mind signing for the bag? Thank you, sir.'

Alex sped back to the desk and scrawled his name, narrowly missing the officer's stubby finger that was indicating exactly where his signature should be written.

'Much obliged, sir.'

'Um, listen,' Alex said, looking up from his handiwork. 'We were most impressed with the help we received from your colleague. Would you be sure to tell him thanks and that it was much appreciated?'

'Yes, sir, of course, sir. Will that be all, sir?'

'Yep, guess so. Bye.' Alex hurried out of the door and filled his lungs with the sweet air of freedom.

Chapter Eight:

Measures

1

'The trouble with all this parquet stuff is that it makes too much noise,' Alex complained, while Eve shucked off her shoes and collapsed onto the sofa.

'No it doesn't,' she contradicted.

'Yes, it does,' Alex responded, adamant.

'It's not the flooring, you crazy Englishman,' Eve giggled, 'how can a few planks of wood make noise?'

'Well, I'm just not used to it. We keep everything covered in carpet.'

'We do?'

'In England, we do.'

'And Europe?'

'Europe? Parquet everywhere.'

'There you go, then, that's where you've just come from so of course you're used to it. Anyway, English, are you pleased to see me? Are you, are you? Did you enjoy your travels? Have you brought me another sexy present?'

'Blimey! I'm just a little jet-lagged, but yes . . .'

'Kiss me, then, you little jet-lagged person. Kiss me like you mean it.'

Alex's tiredness melted away as their mouths locked together. He tasted Eve's saliva, sucked in lungfulls of Eve's breath and felt her body urgent against him, or maybe it was his body urgent against hers. Making her stand, he twisted her body around and pulled her onto his lap so that she was sitting facing him. 'I missed you, you know?' he confessed.

'Of course you did.'

'No, I mean really missed you.'

'Really? Really, really?'

'Next time, you'll have to come with me.'

'Next time?'

'Yes, when I go back to Germany.'

'And what will my students do? They'll stop exercising and become fat and lazy.'

'Well, what do they do when you take a holiday?'

'I don't.'

'Well . . . what did they do when you were in hospital?'

'They stopped exercising and became fat and lazy,' Eve answered, laughing. 'So why do you need to go back to Germany? What do they got that I don't?'

'Retired Nazi generals.'

'And what do *they* got that I don't?'

'Greed.'

'Ha, you think I'm not greedy? What's the matter with you? Take your clothes off, English.'

'Now?'

'Absolutely now.'

While Alex set about peeling off his clothes and scattering them everywhere, Eve stood up and removed her jeans and an overlarge, reddish-purplish and grey striped rugby shirt, another Christmas gift she'd received from Alex.

Alex looked at the taut, slender body in front of him, and at the bruises that marked the otherwise unblemished skin. Holding her by the hips, he moved his head forwards and brushed his lips across the flat stomach. He kissed her bellybutton, small and tightly puckered, and used the tip of his tongue to trace gentle spirals until hampered by the band of her panties. Using both hands, he edged the flimsy material downwards until it uncovered her sex. 'Open,' he ordered, pressing his fingers against Eve's thighs.

Fully compliant, Eve parted her legs, breathing deeply when she felt the gentle explorations of Alex's tongue. After a few tantalising seconds, she pushed her body forwards, impaling her wantonness onto the busy muscle. Alex pulled his head backwards and smiled up at Eve's face. 'Turn round and bend over,' he commanded.

Eager to please, Eve did as she was told, bending forwards until she was able to peer between her legs and watch as Alex moved his face towards her ass. ' "Turn round and bend over", is this what your housemasters used to say?'

'Mmm, but it's not so common these days, unless of course we're discussing religion. Especially the Catholic variety.'

'Ah, yes,' Eve murmured dreamily, 'the gateway to church-approved, pope-protected pederasty.'

'Pardon?' Surprised at Eve's outburst, Alex momentarily ceased nuzzling crevices.

'Well, it's true, it's like open season.'

Alex peered at the beautiful upside down face.

'And what do the high priests do about it?' the upside down mouth asked.

Alex grinned and raised his eyebrows. 'What?'

'Nothing.' The upside down eyes widened into a smile. 'Oh, sometimes one of the holy brothers gets his ass hauled before a court and perhaps a cardinal, canon, priest or primate, or whatever they like to call themselves, might give a little speech of disapproval; but nothing actually happens. The Vatican closes its ranks and the abuse continues. Like I said, church-approved, pope-protected. Whatever, I'm getting tired, I'm not as supple as I used to be.' Eve unwound herself and straightened her body. Removing her knickers, she leaned forwards and glued her mouth, right way round, to Alex's.

Having spent too long lying in a hospital bed with nothing to do but exercise her mind, Eve had circumscribed the envelope of sex and had come up with some new ideas. 'Pretend this appendage of yours is not actually yours,' she said, pushing him sideways onto the sofa and sliding her torso above his quivering member.

'Whose would it be?' Alex enquired, wondering where the conversation was going.

'Mine.'

'Yes. But you're a woman.'

'Exactly.'

'Then . . .'

'Use your imagination, honey. Pretend the stalk joining us together is nothing to do with your body. Think of it as an intruder, something invading the space between your legs. Feel it prodding against your lower belly . . .'

'But it's prodding against yours.'

'Alex, play the game! Role reversal, it's sexy.'

'Okay, okay.' He lay back and opened his mind to suggestion, opened his body to the imagined penetration.

'Can you feel it? Can you feel me entering your body?'

'*What?*'

'Now, sweetheart. Now I'm inside,' Eve whispered huskily into a convenient ear. 'I can feel your heat enveloping me.'

'*Jesus!*'

Managing to work one of her hands beneath him, Eve used her fingernails to scratch at the small of his back. Strong powers of persuasion, combining with strange ripples of sensation, infiltrated Alex's mind and caused him to start believing weird imaginings. It was true, his body *was* being invaded, everything was upside down and inside out, but it was okay, different and quite fascinating.

'*Fuck!*' he cried, as inverted sensibilities pulled at his entrails. 'How do you *do* that?'

Eve inserted two fingers into his mouth. 'Keep quiet,' she instructed, 'just lie there while I fuck you silly.'

Alex lay back and succumbed to the woman sprawled all over him.

'Open up to me, experience my body inside you.' She kissed him on the side of his neck, ran her tongue upwards and around the back of his ear.

Alex began to respond, pressing his hands against Eve's tight behind, pulling her in towards him, actually believing he had a warm receptacle for her to penetrate.

'Where does your darkness come from?' he asked later as they lay united in the stupor of exhaustion.

'Excuse me?'

'Your exotic olive skin tone, where does it come from? I told Jessica that you were a bit Indian.'

'A bit Indian? Which bit? Why?' Raising herself on one elbow, Eve fixed Alex with a steady gaze.

'She asked me.'

'About my darkness? How does she know about my darkness?'

'No, not about your darkness; about you. She asked about you.' Alex looked up, expecting to see worlds on a collision course.

'And you told her I was a bit Indian?'

'Well, yes. Aren't you?'

'My father was from Israel.'

'Israel?'

'Yes, you know, small country, full of people hated by everybody.'

'I don't.'

'Yes, but you're not everybody. Anyway, I'm just a bit Jewish; the clever bit.'

'Israel.' Alex was stranded in the Negev desert.

'Yes. There are a lot of people like me living in New York, I think we make up a quarter of the population; maybe more, maybe less. Some even have exotic olive skin like mine, and others, would you believe, are coloured the same as you. It depends.'

'Depends? On what?'

'No idea. Say, are you gonna start moving, or what? Your ardour is wrinkled. Actually, your ardour is deflated.'

'I've never been out with an Israeli.' The desert was wide and the sand was deep; and the mirage, confounding.

Alex withdrew his failed warrior and regarded it dismally.

Rearranging her sinuous limbs, Eve aligned her mouth within range of the reluctant muscle, informing it 'All your life you've been mollycoddled by Englishness. Well, my friend, your lord and master has left the island and now you have to explore the depths of exoticism.' Eve started laughing as she caressed him with her lips. 'You will find me a harsh mistress, expecting obedience and rigid attention; but a fair one, knowing no bounds when it comes to mutual satisfaction.'

'Amen,' said Alex. 'Things are beginning to shape up.'

'Yes, my little Ollie,' Eve agreed, admonishing the impressionable organ, 'they need to. Otherwise, you ship out.'

'Ollie? Ollie? Who the fuck's Ollie?'

'A colonel who stood up in court and made a mockery of the indictment against him,' Eve answered, twisting her body around and arranging her stomach into an intoxicating position above Alex's head.

'Ah.' He drew his fingers across hovering nakedness and allowed them to wander into a valley of shadows. Darkness descended, slowly, rapturously, until his lips encountered softness and his tongue tasted the musty warmth of heaven.

'There you go,' Eve murmured happily. 'Little Ollie stands to attention.'

'I know what I've been meaning to ask you,' Alex said during a wine break between bouts of energetic randiness.

'There's more?'

'How do you mean?'

'Above and beyond my olive-coloured skin.'

'Oh, yes, sorry.'

'And?'

'And . . . well, you know when you go to the bathroom?'

'Yes.' Long and drawn out, the answer held a question in its tail. Eve was growing accustomed to Alex's enquiries, his convoluted chains of thought.

'So when you're sitting there, you know, like women do . . .'

'We do?'

'Yes, of course, you pee sitting down.'

'We do?'

'Don't you?' A mixture of confusion and disbelief hovered behind the question.

'Don't have to. Some of us can pee standing up.'

'You can? I've never seen you; or any woman for that matter. I'd like to, though.'

'Ask me next time we shower together.'

'Really?'

Eve laughed, 'Simple things, Alex. We women evolved to amaze you.'

'Wow!'

'So, there I am, peeing and sitting down. A conventional female.'

'Ah, yes.' Alex's mind was floating through a world of fantasy. 'Anyway, when you look at the floor do you see things?'

'Dust, and pieces of gravel from Simon's box.'

'Yes, but nothing else?'

'Alex, you're starting to worry me. Where are you at?'

'It's just . . . just that I see things, you know?'

'Not really.'

'Stuff, figures, all different things.' Beginning to wish he hadn't opened the door on this confessional, Alex ended on a lame suggestion. 'Shapes and stuff?'

'Aha.'

'In the floor, you know, those tiles with the patterns on them, random and sort of squirly.'

'O - k - a - y.' Eve stretched the word magnificently, completely unsure of where the leitmotif was heading.

'No, straight up, I see things. And everyday they change

and it's fascinating and they never seem to repeat. Well, sometimes they do. Don't you see them?'

'They? Them?'

'Yes, they them, exactly! You have to use a lazy eye.'

'Or a bottle of wine, I should imagine.'

'You have to try, next time you go to the loo.' The excitement in Alex's voice was alarming.

'Sitting down,' Eve added, nodding sagely.

'Of course, of course. Tell me if you see anything.'

Eve raised the duvet and pulled it to one side. '*Niente*, I see
nada. He's all a-folded up on heemself like a baby concertina,'
she replied in an accent from somewhere stuck on the Italian
heel. 'Eh, Eengleesh, I am a-theenking he's a-gonna to sleep.'
Releasing the cover, she turned over and giggled into a pillow.

*   *   *

Simon was pissed-off. He'd spent the evening thinking about
life. In fact, he spent most of his time thinking about life.
He'd also given thought to other cats and about the probable
world that existed outside apartment 4b. Feline intellect told
him that things would be different out there and his subconscious speedily filled in all the blank spaces. Sometimes he
had vivid dreams about chasing wild things in the dark, charging through damp undergrowth like a fully-grown tiger and
climbing trees with the agility of a monkey. He was pissed-off
because his paws had never touched real ground, earthy stuff
at which he could scratch. And those small squeaky things
that his mistress kept buying replicas of – mouse, mice, whatever label the humans gave them; he'd never had the opportunity to sink his claws into one. He imagined leaping out from

behind a shrub, leaping out and landing on such a thing, or a bird – he'd seen those flying through the air, the fresh air that was attached to the balcony. He'd pin it to the ground and put it through its paces, maybe play with it awhile before pulling it to pieces and presenting choice morsels to the boss.

He sighed and lifted a paw, shook it awkwardly and returned it to the floor, his front legs parallel, up and down like elegant columns at the entrance to an Egyptian mausoleum. And then he started musing about sphinxes, although in reality he had no idea that that's what they were called. The mistress owned one, and on several occasions he'd taken the trouble to leap onto the back of the sofa, then the table, and then the top of the bookcase, to stare at the cat-shaped model. It was black and shiny and stared back annoyingly, and Simon would prod it with a tentative paw. But the reclining animal never responded, never uttered so much as a miaow and never blinked one of its exquisite eyes. Simon couldn't see the point, he couldn't understand the logic about having a cat or a miniature lion that never did anything. Again, he lifted his paw, looked at it and licked it, and set it down. But then, he thought, at least it doesn't give me any competition and it never eats anything. How stupid is that? But what if it's some sort of cat god, he began to wonder; a lesser, miniature one? Maybe that's why it doesn't eat anything? Maybe cat gods don't need food? Maybe they're too busy contemplating stuff we mortal cats don't understand? He glanced up at the bookcase and glared at the tips of the pointed wooden ears that were all he could see from his lowly position on the floor. Then he stopped thinking about lofty matters and returned his mind to mundane though important stuff, such as food.

What was going on, he wondered? The humans had been

occupied with that animalistic stuff ever since the man-person had returned; and that had been hours ago. What could be more essential, Simon asked himself, than placing food in my bowl? He stood and stretched, lazily, front legs, back legs, and then his spine. Tail erect, he walked into the kitchen and inspected his food bowl, clean and spotless, licked to shiny porcelain smoothness by his raspy tongue. He moved to the other bowl, the gleaming stainless steel bowl, the one that usually contained water, and sometimes milk. Sniffing at the surface he remembered he was thirsty and began daintily to lift the clear liquid into his mouth. After a few half-hearted laps he wandered into the living room, leapt onto an arm of the sofa and, with tail curled around his legs, sat and stared in supreme contemplation at the sphinx.

It had been a time of strangeness. Unclear about periods of days or weeks or weekends, to Simon a day was a day and a night was a night. One was light and one was dark, it was as simple as that, and one followed the other. Which way round they went wasn't important, just like the chicken and the egg; and Simon liked both. He wondered about the man with the strange accent, wondered why he'd been away. He found it hard to understand humans, couldn't fathom them out. First they come and hang around a while – daytime, night-time, no difference – then one of them disappears, then comes back, and, after a short while, goes away again. What sort of a life is that? It's just as well my mistress is here to fill my bowl every day, he grumbled to himself, otherwise there'd be trouble. Life should be easy, he reckoned, eat and sleep and occasionally try to escape. Once he had. He remembered it had been when some workmen, all dressed up in blue overalls, had been trying to squeeze a huge cardboard box through the front door. Sniffing freedom, he'd shot through the open space in the manner of a speedy panther. It had been a journey of discovery, exciting and laced with mysterious smells of other entities and, he seemed to remember, there'd been something that had spoken to him. '*Ding*' it had said, and then, annoyingly, had shut itself up before he'd had a chance to investigate the small world contained within the strange cubicle. And then, having found a large plant with huge shiny leaves, he'd been on the verge of digging his paws into the intoxicating brown stuff out of which the vegetation was growing, when he'd been captured.

Simon had learned not to scratch the furniture or pluck the cushions – apart of course from the Special Cushion, soft and fluffy and sort of squidgy and having a feel to it that he fancied was pretty akin to that of another cat – a type of behaviour disliked by humans and which he supposed was fair enough, understandable even. On one of his birthdays he'd been presented with a scratching post and he loved to sneak up on it, attacking it with gusto and all the ferocity of a jungle beast and making the silly yellow round thing that was attached to it swing around like a drunken canary.

*   *   *

'Look what I found!' Eve trilled, excitedly waving an important-looking document under Alex's nose. It was the following morning, breakfast time, after a night of debauchery and a little too much celebratory wine.

Alex raised his eyes from minute inspection of a bowl of cereal and reached for the flapping sheet of paper. 'It's a will,' he announced, trying to focus on the formal print at the head of the document. 'It's your will,' he added. 'Why are you showing me your will?'

'Not the will so much as what's attached.'

'Hmm,' Alex grunted, not too sure he wanted to be reading someone else's will, let alone a bunch of legalese, when he'd rather be fast asleep. He flipped the document and looked at a sheet of handwriting that had been stapled to the reverse. Across the top of the page the title of Michelstraub's company, Meyer, Michelstraub, & Meyer (Attorneys), stood out in firm business-like print. Suddenly, Alex experienced a surge of energy pulsing through his torpid brain. Suddenly, his tiredness and an unwelcome gathering of morning blues washed away and the day became a thing of beauty. 'What's this, then?' he asked. 'It's got Charley's signature at the bottom.'

'Read it, English, and then I'll explain everything as best I can,' Eve answered, sort of bobbing up and down in a ballet-based form of ecstasy.

'What's got into you, it's as though you're on drugs or something?'

'Something,' Eve admitted enigmatically, smiling widely like the Grand Canyon. 'Read.'

Alex shook his head in amused uncertainty and spooned a heap of cornflakes into his mouth, hoping that the act of chewing would assist the necessity of concentration. The lines were few, the letter short, and the information was straight to the point. His eyes grew into saucers and transferred their focus from document to woman. 'Wow!'

'Too damn right, wow,' Eve agreed enthusiastically.

'But why didn't you tell me about this before, why did you keep it such a secret?'

'I didn't, I only found it the other day.'

'But . . .'

'It was when I got home from the hospital, after the accident. They sort of make you think, accidents. It made me think.' She placed a kiss onto Alex's left cheek, just as he was filling his face with another load of flakes. 'I got to thinking about the hereafter and whether it was all organised, you know, all that stuff about finance and who to leave it to, not that I have any. And then I recalled that Charley had helped me prepare a will, a year, maybe two, before he died. He was great like that, saying how he'd always be there for me if ever I got into trouble, any kind of trouble. So I spent hours trying to find it. I looked everywhere, like you do when you know you've put something in a safe place but can't remember where that place is. Desperate! Eventually I found it in a shoebox full of photos, including some of me and Charley. Buried at the bottom it was, so as you can imagine I spent ages trawling through a cascade of memories. Anyway, I skipped through the will and came across this letter, Charley's letter. He must've snuck it onto the back when I wasn't looking. I was probably floating around his office, you know, practicing dance routines or something. All that legal shit isn't exactly the most interesting stuff in the world.'

'And this was two or three years ago?'

'Mmm, maybe five.'

'And you hadn't looked at these documents since sticking them into the shoebox?'

'No, why should I? It's not the sort of thing you think about every day, life's too short. And that's something you get to realise when you get hit by a car.'

'Blimey! So your grandfather left you his collection of paintings.'

'Yes, English, blimey. The paintings are mine.'

'Christ, George is going to hate this, he thinks he's the one and only rightful owner.'

'You think he'll accept this letter?'

'He'll have to, honey, Charley would've made sure of that. It's a statement in black and white, binding and all that sort of stuff. Hmm, can't wait to see George's face when he learns he's going to lose his precious collection.'

'I kinda feel a little sorry for him, you know? It's gonna be real hard after all this time, all the while thinking he's sitting on a fortune.'

'You shouldn't be too sorry, after all, he hasn't exactly thought too much about you. Anyway, he's a lawyer, and you should read what Shakespeare had to say about them. They're not the most gracious of people, but then I suppose they can't afford to be, not when they have to defend a convicted murderer.'

'Murderer?'

'For example.'

'A murderer! I can't imagine someone like George defending a murderer.'

'No, perhaps not. Whatever, now you have to start making decisions about the future and what you're going to do with these works of art. It's amazing, isn't it, how rapidly things change? This morning, life was just a fuzzy head and a bowl of cornflakes.'

'What about me? Where was I?' Eve complained, sliding her arms around Alex's torso.

'You were fetching the brown sugar.'

'Okay, deal. I'll fetch the sugar, you tell me about Mrs Carmichael.'

'What about Mrs Carmichael?'

'About the paintings, about Charley, about *für Elise*. You know, all the stuff you forgot to tell me when you came to see me in the hospital?'

'I did?'

'You certainly did. You were too happily occupied in eating my chocolates, as I seem to recall.'

'Ah, yes! They were tasty.'

'And? Mrs Carmichael?'

'Well, there's definitely a link between her and your grandfather and although she didn't actually say as much, I'm pretty sure that *für Elise* was written with her in mind.'

'You mean the painting was a present for her? From Charley?'

'Yes. I think so. She was clever, you know? always sort of skirting around my questions by slanting onto different subjects. Unable to keep control of the conversation I had problems trying to remember if my queries had actually been answered. But, hey, she proved to be a mine of information and actually ended up telling me oodles of stuff.'

'Oodles?'

'Amazing, a life full of tragedy! And then Charley turned up. He was there to help her in her hour of need.'

'And this happened in Czechoslovakia?'

'This happ . . . How do you know?'

'He told me. Charley. Used to tell me stories about his life in Vienna and Prague.'

'Why didn't you say?'

'Oh, I don't know, I suppose I thought it was something special. Childhood secrets between me and him.'

'And you knew about the rescue and everything?'

'Everything?'

'About the Germans taking away Mrs Carmichael's husband and daughter?'

'Yep, I knew about that. In fact while you were away I confessed as much to Mandie and Dan.'

'And you knew about them falling in love?'

'Grandpa? And Mrs Carmichael?'

'They were lovers.'

'Lovers?'

'Yeah, can you believe it?'

'Shit, no, he never mentioned anything like that.'

'You sure?'

'Sure I'm sure, I would've remembered. Christ!'

'Yeah, well, it was secret and sacred, something they obviously wished to keep to themselves. A friendship forged in impossible times.'

'Bloody hell! But, shit, that'd definitely explain the writing on the picture and why he wanted it to go to her.'

'Yep, that and the fact he was known as Karel.'

'Karel?'

'The Czechoslovak version of Charles.'

'Karel! Karel Meyer. The K.M. on the back of the frame, not Charley but Karel. Of course, it's so simple. Shit, English, well done, incredible! See? You did the right thing.'

'Yeah, but you pushed me, told me to go.'

'Maybe, maybe, but it was your idea in the first place.' Eve launched a kiss across space. 'Now, tell me about your escapades around London and Europe. What about Jessica, how did that go? And Wolfgang, what about him?'

2

'So we're going to Germany?' Eve was involved in the tricky business of making cheese sauce – milk and flour and arrowroot, all mixed up and heating in a small pan, while she grated a sizeable block of cheddar. 'Why?'

After relating details of his visit to Mrs Carmichael's, Alex had dropped hints about the necessity of returning to Europe. 'It's all to do with my master plan.'

'The one you haven't told me about.'

'Yes, the secret plan, the one I can't talk about.'

'But I'm your girlfriend.'

'Yes you are.'

'And so why can't you tell me what you're up to?'

'It's a matter of timing, it's all relative.'

'And you want me to come to Germany with you?'

'Yes, honey, of course. I missed you on my last trip and, besides, I'd like you to meet Wolfgang.'

'Ah, Voolfy.'

'Yep. And Jessica.' Alex dipped a curious finger into melting cheese.

'To get the Vermeer?'

'Well, I don't think it'll be that easy but we have to try. And then, if Terry's done what he's supposed to have done, we'll motor to Bavaria.'

'Where we'll do what, exactly?'

'I'll let you know when we get to London.'

'Wow, London and Germany and Jessica. When?'

'Um, probably in the summer.'

'Did you speak in riddles in your previous life?'

'Which one?'

'The one you spent with Jessica?'

'No, that was one of her traits,' Alex smiled at the super chef. 'Anyway, I think we should go see Michelstraub, as soon as possible.'

'Ah, that'll be fun.'

'Yes. Difficult also. He's not going to be too happy.'

Alex spent a great part of the journey north of New York recounting the story of the Scotsman's kilt. Reliving the moment, he giggled helplessly at each juncture of the unfolding yarn. 'It's so funny,' he laughed, looking sideways at Eve's unsmiling, uncomprehending face. When he came to mention the ginger nuts, he almost steered the car off the highway. Controlling himself, he then made the mistake of trying to explain the joke, outlining the history of Scottish fashion: the hairy legs, the long socks, the sporran and the dirk, and the strange sight of men wandering around in pleated skirts.

'And you wonder why we Americans think you're peculiar?'

'Them, not us. It's banter, honey, a little tit-for-tat between the Brits and the Scots. But it's nothing important, not the sort of stuff that comes up in everyday conversation.'

'Evidently.'

'Well, why would it? We make jokes about it because, hell, it's unreal. Have you ever seen a man in a kilt?'

'Tell me again,' Eve said, pushing at the boundaries of patience. 'Start at the beginning.'

Binghamton was blossoming, burgeoning forth in edgy belief that the winter months had at last come to an end. The spring day was green and brilliant and, despite an enormous pale yellow sun in a freshly washed blue sky, cold. The fields on either side of the approach road were all spingly and spangly with droplets of moisture clinging to slivers of young grass, and the hedgerows heavy with young buds. Looking at the immaculate fields and fences, Alex was reminded of his first trip to these quarters, indeed his first trip to America, eighteen months previously. He'd been on his own then and had had no idea of what he was letting himself in for. It had been a voyage of discovery, a circuitous route that had led, eventually, to the apocalypse with Jessica and the meeting with Eve.

Smirking widely, he shuffled the hire car backwards and forwards until he'd lined-up in perfect position, plumb centre between a pair of white lines. Whistling a happy tune, he jumped out of the automobile, walked round to the passenger door and helped Eve manoeuvre her bruised legs over the sill and onto the ground. Sauntering into the offices he came face to face with a tight-faced secretary, whose hair had been hauled towards an efficient bun that sat proudly on the back of her head.

Looking Alex up and down, the woman shook her head and sucked air through her teeth. 'Can't leave it there,' she said peevishly, 'you'll have to move it.'

'What?' Alex exclaimed. 'Why?'

'You've parked in Mr Michelstraub's slot,' came the smug reply.

'That's who we've come to see.'

'Yes, well, he isn't here.'

'So it'll be okay to leave the car where it is, then?'

'No, 'cos when he comes back it'll really annoy him and put him in a terrible mood. So, if you wouldn't mind.'

The sound of an approaching car speeding towards the group standing in the centre of the reception area, caused three heads to look out of the window. They watched as the vehicle entered the car park and came to a halt in the bay next to the space in contention. They watched Michelstraub haul his body off the leather seat, slam the car door and advance towards the office.

'What are you all looking at?' he asked, closing the entrance door behind him. 'What's the matter?'

'Um, I was just about to move my car,' Alex replied in a hesitant sort of way.

'Whatever for?'

'Well . . .'

'Come on, don't worry about it, it's fine where it is. Neat parking, too.' The lawyer's face creased around a friendly smile as he took hold of one of Eve's elbows and guided her towards his office. 'How are you?' he asked, his eyes bestowing genuine concern. 'Is Alex looking after you properly?'

The reception area had received a makeover, a reformation which included a ceiling-to-floor window next to the entrance door, wall-to-wall shiny floorboards, and plain white walls featuring a couple of brightly coloured paintings by the hand of . . . Alex had no idea. A collection of *National Geo-*

graphic magazines, which had kept him amused on his first trip to Michelstraub's domain, had elevated itself from the floor to bask in splendid display in a modern cabinet. Dark, glass-fronted and sleek, the unit blended well with the overall trans-formation, lifting the room out of its previous dowdiness.

'I see you've made changes,' Alex commented as he fol-lowed Eve's ushered footsteps.

'Yes, yes, changes,' the lawyer agreed, helping Eve lower herself into a large leather armchair. Alex swung on his heels and closed the door, grinning at the deflated secretary as he did so.

'So, what have we?' Michelstraub asked. 'I do hope there aren't going to be any more hold-ups while you gad about Europe making unnecessary discoveries?'

'Hardly unnecessary, George, I unearthed some interest-ing information.' Alex plonked himself into an armchair next to Eve's.

Michelstraub edged himself behind his giant desk and remained standing, thinking it would give the impression that he was in charge. 'What could be more interesting than selling the things?' he stated bluntly. 'What could be more interesting than making money?'

'Don't you have any feeling towards the paintings?' Alex asked, plaintively. 'You know, what's it called . . . empathy?

'No, not really.'

'None?' Eve asked, astonished. 'None at all? George, they belonged to your colleague, and your memory of him must at least make you wonder at their history.'

'No, no, they belonged to the firm,' Michelstraub argued, sidling into his chair and fiddling importantly with some papers that lay on the desktop. 'I have no wonder.'

'Then I guess you had no idea that one of the artists had been locked up by the Nazis?' Alex asked, sidelining the statement and bravely attempting to rouse curiosity.

'Really?' The response was flat and noncommittal.

'Yes, Fila. Actually it's his painting that has the two words written on the back of its frame.'

'Ah, and did you unravel any secrets as to whom those two words might be ascribed?'

'Maybe,' Alex answered, fidgeting squeakily in his seat as he evaded the direct question. After his lengthy meeting with Mrs Carmichael, he'd made a decision to honour her privacy, the stuff concerning her wartime relationship with the deceased lawyer. There was, after all, no reason for anyone to know. The affair had been closely guarded, it had happened a long time ago, and Alex had no intention of betraying the woman's confidence in him.

'Alex, sweetheart, could you fetch me a cup of water from that machine in the lobby? I'm feeling a little dehydrated after the journey.'

'Okay, sure.' Alex pulled himself out of deep thought, crossed the office and went out into reception. He closed the door behind him and prickled when the secretary asked him if everything was alright. 'Yup,' he replied, 'everything's dandy. Me and George, we're tight.' He racked his brain trying to remember if the woman had been in evidence when last he'd paid a visit to Binghamton, a visit that had spawned comic connotations due to Jessica's being in town on the very same day. Michelstraub had been hysterical, refusing to believe that Alex had been totally in the dark and unaware that his other half, ex-other half, had also been in the States, let alone here in upstate New York.

Backing into Michelstraub's office, a cup of water in each hand, he asked, 'Who's the artist, then?'

'Excuse me?'

'Out there, bright squares and circles and patches of paleness. Colourful stuff, modern, I think.'

'Oh, um, Klee.' Michelstraub seemed a little distressed, unsure of exactly why the meeting had been called.

'You don't recognise Klee, when you see one?' Eve chided, looking a little mystified as she tried to work out whether her question actually made sense.

'Nope, the arty stuff was more Jessica's forte. At one stage she even tried to stay one step ahead of Terry, swatting up on dozens of Baroque artists. But the plan sort of backfired.'

'Seems Jessica was an intellectual lady, you should have stayed with her. Think of all the stuff you could've learned.'

Alex twisted his face into a strange expression and handed Eve a chilly cup. 'Um, Eve has something to share with you,' he announced, turning towards Michelstraub.

The lawyer peered across his desk, first at Eve, then at Alex. 'She does?' There was some sense of hope, embers being stoked by unknown forces. At last, he thought, I'll be able to get rid of these things and get on with my life. All this stuff about artists being imprisoned during the war was depressing and he didn't really need to hear any more. Admittedly, Alex and that Jessica woman had been helpful, useful even. Hell, if it hadn't been for them, he wouldn't be in possession of the two extra paintings. Then he remembered that the English woman, damn her, had waltzed off with the picture by the man who called himself . . . what was it, Veneer? It was frustrating, extremely so, and he'd even considered ordering Alex to go after her and get it back. But now the boy was here, fooling around with Charley's granddaughter. He shook his head, placed his chubby hands onto the soothing sheets of paper, and waited.

'Why don't you finish telling George the story about the Czechoslovak artist?' Eve suggested. 'I'm sure he'd find it interesting.' She smiled at the lawyer, 'And then I'll share my secret.'

'Oh, okay.' Alex returned to the armchair and took a sip of water, then looked for somewhere to put the cup. There was nowhere, so he held it between both hands and concentrated on the artist's short life. 'Born in 1882 in Moravia, Emil Fila was the leader of the avant-garde movement in Prague. Though he painted mainly in the Cubist style, his later work began to incorporate influences from the world of Surrealism. At the outbreak of the war, the second one, he was arrested by the Gestapo . . .'

'Why are you telling me this?' Michelstraub butted-in. 'I don't have time for it and I'm really not interested.'

'Well you should be, George. You ought at least to have some knowledge regarding this collection of stunning paintings.'

'It's a commodity,' Michelstraub protested, 'nothing more, nothing less. In and out, just like a supermarket, and the quicker the turnaround, the better.'

'Don't be such a philistine,' Eve said, squaring up to the lawyer.

'No, no, it's okay, it's not a problem,' Alex said with a twinkle in his eyes. 'If he doesn't want to hear my story, tell him yours.'

Eve looked at Alex, then, reaching into a pocket, she regarded Michelstraub. 'So, George, I think this is one story you're going to have to take notice of.' Opening an envelope, she removed some papers and slid them across the desk.

'What's this?' Michelstraub asked suspiciously, unfolding the weighty documents. 'Why, it's a will,' he observed, thankful he'd found something he could deal with. 'Oh, it's your will, my dear.' He looked up and smiled at Eve. 'Why are you showing me your will? Is there a problem, do you need to change something?'

'It's not the will, George, it's the letter that's attached.'

Michestraub flipped the documents and stared at the letter with its all too familiar heading. 'Why, it's . . . it's from Charley,' he stated, quickly scanning the signature at the foot of the page. 'What does he want?' Wondering about tenses, he became embarrassed and coughed. 'Um . . .'

'He wants you to give me the paintings,' Eve answered succinctly.

'He what?'

'Read the words.'

In the silence of the room all that could be heard was the nervous rustling of paper and the heavy breathing of a cornered man.

'But, he can't . . . this means nothing,' Michelstraub exploded, slamming the papers onto the desk.

'He can, and it does,' Eve responded equably. 'I believe you call it a . . . living will, something written by a person while he's still *compos mentis*? And Charley was certainly mentally acute until the moment he died.'

'But this, but this . . .'

'Is preposterous; I know,' Eve smiled at the lawyer. 'But it's a fact.'

'I'll have it checked out,' Michelstraub countered, 'to make sure it's authentic.'

'Check all you like. In fact, I expect you might find a copy in Charley's files, he was meticulous in keeping copies of everything. But this you know.'

'But why?'

'I suppose he realised you'd have no interest in the paintings. Perhaps you never asked him about their history?'

'I had no idea they existed,' Michelstraub fumed, angry eyes flitting between his two antagonists, 'until Charley died and we moved out of the city.'

'Exactly. And when you discovered them,' Alex asked, 'well, six of them, in Mrs Carmichael's house, you didn't wonder at their heritage?'

'No.' Michestraub smacked his lips together. 'Anyway, at that stage they were different, they were titillating, easy on the eye.' He looked at Eve, awkwardly. 'You can't have them, you know. You won't get them.'

'Oh, come on, George, don't be selfish; 'specially when you keep admitting to having zero interest.'

'I'll sell them, give you some of the money.'

'George!'

'No, I mean it, it's . . .'

'It's not going to happen, they're not yours to sell. Read the words, then read them again. Legally, the paintings belong to me. There's no wriggle factor.'

'But how long have you known about this? When . . .'

'Not long. After my accident.'

'Uh-ha.'

'It shook me up, really shook me up, and got me to thinking . . . 'bout life.'

'And wills,' Michelstraub suggested.

'Yes. And when I came across Charley's letter, I was as surprised as you. Believe me, George, it was out of the blue.'

'And, er . . . what about the words on the back of that painting?'

'*Für Elise?*'

'Yes, who's that?'

'Alex discovered the persona of the mystery woman,' Eve answered, looking happily at the man in the chair next to hers.

'Mrs Carmichael,' Alex stated simply. 'Ellie.'

'Ellie?' Michelstraub repeated softly. 'Really? Ellie? How?'

'It's a long story, George, and very personal. I was highly privileged when she took me into her confidence.'

'But . . .'

'I made a promise.'

3

The summer storm had been short, sharp and sudden, and as Alex and Eve walked around the square's perimeter, they could hear the pitter-patter of latent drops of water dripping from the trees. Leaves, grass, benches, streets, pavements and cars – London was bright and shiny, slick with nature's free lubrication. Full of ozone, the air was fresh and earthy, a brief respite from the normal toxicity of oily exhaust fumes. And the streets were empty, almost, the pallid natives crowding instead the beaches of foreign climes.

'This must be it,' Eve said. 'Look, yellow door.'

'You do the talking,' Alex urged, as he pressed a buzzer adjacent to the name "Hastings".

'Hastings.' The voice, all crackly, came out of a hidden speaker.

'Hi, Mr Hastings, it's Eve.'

'Eve?'

'The owner of the paintings.'

'Paintings?'

'Eve, paintings, Alex. Am I helping?'

'Ah, Eve. From America.'

'It's my voice, it's a giveaway.'

'No, yes, no, come on up. I'll press the button and you can open the door.'

'Hmm . . . he sounds just like you, all confused and English,' Eve laughed as she pushed at the buzzing door.

'We haven't met,' Terry announced, ushering the visitors into his apartment. 'I'm Terry.'

'Terry, very good to meet you. Alex has told me a lot about you, how you discovered the lost works of art.'

'*Un*covered, maybe,' Terry agreed. 'It was Alex and . . . um, Jessica, who made the discovery.'

'It's okay,' Eve smiled, 'I know all about Jessica. In fact, we'll be seeing her tomorrow. We're doing the rounds.'

'Um . . .' Terry stalled, a little uncertain. 'Coffee?'

'You know,' Eve continued, explaining merrily, 'meeting Alex's European associates? After Jessica, we're off to see Wolfgang. Yes, please, coffee.' Turning to Alex, she asked 'Does he know Wolfgang?'

'Of, but they haven't met.' Alex was in a strange sort of mood, restive and slightly nervy. Although everything seemed to be proceeding as planned, he was anxious, apprehensive about the forthcoming meeting with Jessica. He was beginning to regret not informing her about the presence of Eve. It had been one of those toss-a-coin-in-the-air decisions, and the coin had told him to keep shtoom. He reached out and took one of Eve's hands into his own. 'The paintings, Terry, the originals, are, um, actually . . .'

'Mine,' Eve said brightly.'

'Pardon?' Terry halted his mission to the kitchen.

'They're mine, but don't let that stop you making the coffee. I'm parched.'

'I thought they were, er . . . Michelstraub's?'

'Yes, as did he. But we reckoned they belonged to Charley, Eve's grandfather, something that Michelstraub was loath to countenance,' Alex explained.

'Until I discovered a document,' Eve added delightedly, 'stating that my grandpa had left them to me. Coffee?'

'Um, coffee, yes,' Terry repeated in the manner of a stunned fish. He regrouped his legs to march him towards the kitchen. 'Um, carry on into the living room,' he said over his shoulder, 'the pictures are in there.'

'Terry, they're brilliant, remarkable.'

'Well, yes, maybe. They're not bad.' Terry placed a tray of cups and saucers, sugar bowl and milk jug, onto a table.

'But I can't tell the difference.'

'You're not meant to, Alex. No one's meant to.'

'No, of course. But really, Terry, you've done a fantastic job.'

Terry picked up one of the framed pictures and laid it reverently on top of his desk. Opening a drawer, he rifled through a collection of photographs, selected one and handed it to Alex. It was a snapshot of the painting in front of him, an exact copy of an erotic image created in wispy shades of pastel colours, an image that swept Alex's mind to another place – a small hotel in the mists of southern Germany – and another time, almost eighteen months ago, when he and Jessica and Wolfgang had crowded around a similar object.

'So what lurks beneath?'

'A copy of the original Master that was hidden beneath the original of this particular Prentiss.'

'I have to take your word for that.'

'I have to take your word that you're going to give me one of the original Masters as payment,' Terry countered. 'Although, now you tell me they belong to Eve, perhaps this'll be a little easier for you to achieve?'

'Perhaps,' Alex retorted, smiling at Eve. 'So, the Prentiss definitely passes muster, but what about the works of art that lie beneath this and the others?'

'They're good, Alex, they're excellent. My colleague came up trumps.'

'Yes, but good enough to fool everyone?'

'Certainly good enough to fool most people, even the so-called experts.'

'Really? That good?' Eve asked, peering over Alex's shoulder.

'It's an exact copy of the original, honey, well, you know, beneath this?' Alex explained, indicating the *Pose*. 'And look how good it is. No one's going to realise it's a copy, let alone think about what might be lying underneath.'

'So this photo, which looks like the ones back in the apartment, isn't . . ?'

'Yes, it is, it's taken from the same film. But, look . . . see? The match is perfect – colour, texture, dimensions, everything. Christ, Terry, it's superb, the whole thing, identical. Nothing jumps up and announces itself out of place, not to me anyway.'

Terry allowed himself a sliver of a smile. 'Yeah, I have to admit I'm quite proud of the new *Poses*, but it would've been nice to have re-created the Masters as well. They took a lot of work, everything's genuine – oils, mixtures, brush strokes, canvas, frames, and so too is the mastic-varnish of the *Poses*. I don't think there's too many people who'd notice anything out of place. Hell, the original fakes themselves can't've been seen by more than half-a-dozen people. And anyway, if the "experts" don't know for certain whether or not the *Mona Lisa* is genuine, there's definitely room for latitude with the rest of the world.'

'The *Mona Lisa*? A fake?' Eve stared at Terry in amazement.

'Nah, he's joking,' Alex said, half laughing. 'It can't be fake, not with so many people queueing up to stare at it.'

'Would you know?' Terry asked, suddenly all serious. 'If you were to stand in the Louvre for an hour, just staring at it, would you know?'

'No, probably not. But, hell, it has to be genuine, doesn't it?'

'Why?'

'Well, it's on display in a renowned gallery, and . . . and surely it's what the gallery tells us it is. I mean, they should know what they've got.'

'Yes, and like everyone else, you believe them.'

'Don't you?' Eve asked.

Terry looked at the American woman and smiled. 'If I tell you there's a Savery hiding beneath this display of eroticism, would you believe me?'

'Absolutely.'

'Even though you can't actually see it?'

'Yes, though this is a little different. For a start, I have no idea who Savery is. But even if I did, I know it's not the genuine article because you've just told us about its re-creation. And yes, I believe what you tell me since you seem to be an honest man.'

'It's like the ancients,' Terry responded obliquely, 'who said the world was flat and that everything else moved around it. Everyone believed them and so the theory became fact.'

'But about the *Mona Lisa*?' Alex asked. 'Is it a fake? Honestly?'

'Who knows? No one's certain, not absolutely. Over the years several copies have been produced and at one stage one of them was put on display while the original was locked away for protection. And there's a possibility, actually quite a good one, that the picture hanging in the Louvre – the "smile" that the world queues up to gawp at – was painted by Salai, an apprentice to da Vinci. A copy, excellent and accurate in every detail, but, a copy. On the other hand, yup, maybe it's the original. The authorities obviously like to think it is.'

'Blimey! How many people know about this?'

'How many people know if the steak they're eating is actually from Argentina?'

'But if it says so on the menu?'

'How are you going to prove it?'

'Well, I suppose you have to trace it back to the butcher, and then . . .'

'Or don't ask too many questions and just enjoy it with a glass of Argentine red.'

'A bottle of Argentine red, perhaps,' Alex chuckled. 'It's incredible, I'd never thought about the possibility of a painting hanging in a gallery not being the genuine article.'

'Exactly,' Terry concurred, 'no one does. People generally believe what they're told, and the more convincing the telling, the stronger the belief. Apart of course from cynical people like me.'

'So do you have doubts about every painting you see?' Eve asked.

'No, I just enjoy them the way we're meant to, unless

there's something so obviously out of kilter it simply has to be a fake.'

'So with the Savery we're okay?' Alex asked, prodding moodily at the gaudy image under which it was hiding. 'I mean, um, you know, it'll look like the real thing when eventually it gets to be seen?'

'It'll be okay, Alex, relax. Even when the person you're going to show it to gets an expert, as he will, to examine it thoroughly, this painting and all the others will pass the tests with flying colours. But tell me, what are you going to do about the Vermeer that Jessica has decided is hers?'

'Haven't decided yet,' Eve answered.

'Let her keep it, it can only go two ways.'

Eve raised her eyebrows in unvoiced enquiry.

'She can sell it, or she can keep it. If she puts it on the market, it'll raise a lot of questions. People will want to know its pedigree and she'll have to invent some story, something believable such as being bequeathed to her by a distant relative.'

'Couldn't she just tell it like it is?' Eve asked. 'The press would have a field day with tales of Naz . . .' She stopped herself, suddenly realising there'd been no mention of the general.

'Yes, she could, but without the provenance no one would believe her.'

'No. True.'

'So it's my guess she'll keep it and show it off to unbelieving friends, it'll certainly make a great conversation piece. Anyway, it probably doesn't matter what she does with it, not really. And this brings me to something else,' Terry added. 'Why didn't you want a copy of it? Or, for that matter, of the Rembrandt?'

'It'd've been overload. It's one thing to fool someone into believing the discovery of six paintings, after all, according to the documentation they were dispatched together in one shipment. But numbers seven and eight would have kiboshed the credibility.'

'But what's to say they didn't also make their way to the States?'

'Nothing, there's no certainty, nothing tangible. It's best to let sleeping dogs lie, let people think they were stolen by opportunist burglars.'

'Goodness!' Terry exclaimed. 'Now it's beginning to dawn on me just what you intend doing with these things.'

'Yeah? Well, keep your emergent thoughts to yourself. Please? I can't afford to have wild rumours flying around the art world. Not now, probably not ever.'

'It's okay, Alex, my lips are sealed, but . . .'

'No, no, no way, I'm not saying anything. Christ, Terry, even Eve doesn't know the full story.'

'Mmm, okay, I guess you're right. Clever. Here, let me help you load them into the car.'

4

'You're back, then?' Jessica asked eagerly as soon as she'd opened the door.

'Yep, all fired up and raring to go.'

Jessica stood to one side and swooped an arm, regal-fashion, inviting Alex into the house.

'And I'd like to introduce you to Eve.'

Time stood still and witnessed silence descending from the heavens. The moment didn't last long.

'Eve? The American?' Jessica asked dubiously as a tall slim woman trailed Alex through the open doorway.

'Yep, Eve the American from America.'

'But . . . why?'

'Because she wanted to meet you.'

'Well, this *is* a surprise.'

'Yes. And you'd be one to know all about surprises.'

Jessica arched her eyebrows towards the ceiling, an indication of silent interrogation.

'Scotland?' Alex prompted, and, thinking about matches and touchpapers, immediately regretted doing so.

'Ah, yes, the Highland Fling. Even managed to surprise

myself!' Jessica grinned and gulped in a sort of strangulated laugh.

'Perhaps, but we're not actually here to talk about past events.'

'So what does that leave?' Jessica asked craftily, sneaking a glance at the slinky American, giving her the once over. 'Not much, I should imagine.'

'Quite a lot, as it happens. Um, well, you see, Eve . . . turns out she's the rightful owner of the *Prentiss Poses* – all of them, including yours.'

'But . . . I thought they belonged to that lawyer? No, not *that* lawyer, not Michelstraub, but one of his cronies?'

'Charley . . .'

'Yes, that's him, Charley.'

'Well, firstly, Charley was a partner in the firm, and secondly, he was Eve's grandfather.'

'Eve? That Eve? This Eve?' Jessica sounded confused.

'The very same, the Eve that became a friend of Mandie's.'

'And went on to become your American girlfriend.'

'Yep, Mandie introduced us.'

'The hell she did. And you thought you'd bring her over here?'

'I exist, I speak, and I brought myself over here, albeit attached to Alex.'

'So I see.'

'So, let's get to basics,' Eve suggested. 'What have you done with the Vermeer?'

'Christ, you're worse than he is,' Jessica stated, shooting venomous glances through embarrassed space. 'In fact, he probably taught you.' Thrown off balance, she was stunned and resentful of the intrusion. There'd been no warning, no phone call to pave the way, no chatty conversation to prepare her for the tornado that had decided to wreak havoc on the wrong side of the ocean. She racked her brain trying to remember everything she knew about this woman, and quickly realised she knew very little. What was it that Alex had told her during the stilted conversation earlier in the year? Something about being Indian, was that it? Indian! Jessica peered at the face that was positioned too close to Alex's. Hmm, the woman's skin was definitely of a hue darker than the average Caucasian, yet didn't seem particularly Indian. Instead it had the appearance of being inordinately radiant, well toned and well cared for. Realising that everyone was standing inside the hallway, Jessica closed the door and regarded her pale hand as she turned the latch. Damn it, she thought, tall, attractive, assertive and full of bouncy health. Shit, maybe this *is* the girl from Ipanema.

'No, he didn't need to, it's an American thing.'

'Sorry?' Jessica had lost all trace of the here and now and briefly considered opening the door and shooing out the unwanted visitors. And then she remembered the question and her undignified response. Fuck it, she thought, deciding to stand her ground. 'Well, here's an English thing. I'm going to keep it.'

'Okay.' The reply was airy, the accompanying smile genuine. Salubrity whizzed through narrow confines. 'Cool.'

'That's it?' Jessica queried, unbalanced by the suave response. 'You're not going to start producing bits of paper proving this and that?'

'No.'

'What's she up to, your friend?' Jessica poked at Alex,

switching her attention away from the up-front New Yorker.

'Nothing,' Eve answered. 'I asked a question, you answered it. We move on.'

'Okay.' Jessica was perplexed. Ready for a fight, a crossing of the swords, a catty-type brawl, she felt denuded, like a beach when the tide goes out. 'Um . . .'

'You got a pub anywhere near?' Alex asked.

'No, yes . . . well, about ten minutes away. Five, if you walk quickly. Why?'

'Eve wants to have a drink in a typical English pub.'

'She does? Is she crazy?'

'You can come, too,' Eve smiled at Jessica. 'We can discuss Alex, if you like, all his foibles and stuff.'

'I don't think I want to discuss his . . . foibles,' Jessica grimaced. 'You have that word in the States?'

'We do,' Eve grinned, 'amongst others.'

The Coach and Horses, which had seen neither for seventy years, was experiencing a lull in trade. Between lunch and the end of the working day, its doldrum-filled corners were stirred only by the passing of any of the sun's rays that chanced to penetrate the grimy leaded windows.

Jessica was stuck, marooned. The tide showed no sign of returning. She felt all uptight and bitchy and her rudeness towards the attractive dark-haired woman had landed her on the wrong foot. Bollocks, she thought, it's all Alex's fault. Why hadn't he told me he was travelling *à deux*? Again she cast her mind back to his last visit, when they'd Barbican'd together and squabbled over the fusion dinner in Soho, and she remembered her suggestion that they sleep together. Shit, shit, shit. And then, recalling her remarks about Americans, her skin began to crawl in hot sweaty circles beneath her suddenly scratchy jersey dress. From deep within her down-turned face, she looked at the slender apparition annealed to her former lover. Minimal make up, healthy complexion, longhaired and leggy and wearing un-fussy clothes; there was nothing to dislike about this woman. Or maybe there was everything. Years of psychological training hadn't prepared her for this meeting. Learned print, consumed in eye-watering, elongated nights of lonely study, meant nothing when, finally, the big crunch landed on the doorstep. And here it was, only it wasn't big and there was nothing crunchy about it. Bugger, Alex had been right in his philosophy about her profession – a world of crotchety people hiding their munificent problems behind heavily panelled doors until someone with the same problem comes along. And then, bravely attempting to work out the stranger's problem, and at the same time their own, all the plastered-over cracks and crevices crumble into yawning chasms of despair. Walls start moving inward, slamming the psychologist's desk – along with its primly sharpened, precisely positioned pencils and green-hooded, brass-based, low-wattage lamp – into the low-lying couch upon which so many broken souls are rendered useless. Rule number one: Take the money, lie brazenly and smile convincingly. Rule number two: Repeat rule number one, over and over, in the manner of a well-trained politician. It's so easy, like taking candy from a baby. Easier. Equally gullible, fragile adults gurgle in gratuitous baby-fashion as they reach out to grasp the words of the prophet, the smart doctor whose salary they will fork out at the end of the session before eagerly setting up next week's appointment. Glancing at Alex, Jessica recalled the way he always used to ask her if she ever got tired of never having an answer.

In the same way that a game warden, too late in life – communing with his conscience and beginning to appreciate the wanton destruction he has visited upon Nature – seeks forgiveness, Jessica sipped at her lager-and-lime and quietly trawled through the sponginess of ethics. She needed something to grasp onto, a chink of purposeful destination, the touch of a hand upon the shoulder, anything that would seemingly grant redemption and take away the sins of a lifetime. Floating in a world of shadowy introspection, she was seething at this infringement of territorial boundaries. Alex and the American had fashioned an impenetrable balloon of gaiety upon an ancient settle that, in the evenings, was the hallowed perch reserved for the local hack, a tweed-coated curmudgeon who, periodically crossing and uncrossing thin spindly legs, would spend hours gazing into the near future. God help them, she thought, should the rightful owner of the straight-backed seat enter before his appointed time.

Jessica was brought out of her deliberations when the door rattled open, an unusual occurrence at this slack time of day, and in stepped Eileen, prancing like a pony on stilettos. 'Fuck, I've been looking for you everywhere!' she exclaimed, her vision dragging Jessica's familiar form out of a gloomy niche. 'Whatever are you doing in here, before the sun sinks over the yardarm?' Eileen's new high-heels bounced her into closer vicinity. 'Oh, Alex, what are *you* doing here? And who's this with her arm around your shoulders?'

Alex stood up and made the introduction. 'This is Eve.' He sat down again and grinned at Eileen. Turning to Eve, he said, 'Eileen is the woman that Jessica lives with. She's not backward about coming forward and she likes a drink. I discovered all this the first time I met her, the day . . . Shit, the very same day that Jessica informed everyone she was going to keep her Vermeer.'

'Yep,' Eileen concurred warmly, 'that's me.' She smiled, 'So, what's going on? What have I missed?'

'Nothing.' Jessica sounded surly and wished she didn't. She began to feel like an alien on her own turf. The others seemed so bright and breezy, probably under the influence of that damned Yankee, she decided, before remembering that Eileen had entered the pub as though on a cloud of her own. 'So what's with you,' she said, turning to her friend. 'What's put that smile on your phizog?'

'Pay rise,' Eileen chirruped. 'Only been there two weeks and the boss comes up, taps me on the shoulder and says, "You'll be happy with your pay packet". Then he winks, all slimily, you know, the way they do? and the white stubble on his chinny-chin-chin parts as though he's trying to pass a giant turd out of his mouth.'

'Ei*leen!*' Jessica shrieked. 'We're in mixed company.'

'Are we? I don't see any children. You don't mind, do you?' Eileen asked Eve.

'Um, no, we Americans can take most things.'

'See?' Alex commented. 'Not backward about coming forwards. Eileen doesn't stand on ceremony.'

'Eileen doesn't need to,' Eileen agreed. 'No point.'

'That was something you always used to say,' Alex observed, nodding towards Jessica. 'Remember? "If you're going to say something, say it". It was one of your favourite statements.'

'Still is,' Eileen remarked. 'We're a team, aren't we Jess? Straightforward, but maintaining dignity at all times.'

Alex winced at Eileen's use of the shortened name, but

noticed that Jessica hadn't launched herself into one of her tirades. Hmm, they must be really close, he thought. But how close? He didn't think that Jessica had any lesbian tendencies, but who knows? The times were seeing a lot of changes.

'So,' Eve explained, answering Eileen's question, 'after Jessica told us she was going to keep her painting, we decided to come to the pub. I've always wanted to sit in a real English pub and Jessica told us there was one around the corner. Sort of.'

'She's just like you, Jess,' Eileen stated. 'You have an American counterpart, it's unreal.'

'It's very real,' Jessica pouted. 'Alex ditches me and goes off to find an American version.'

Alex felt twitchy. He wanted to correct Jessica's statement regarding who left who, but, knowing it would inflame a delicate situation, refrained. He looked at Eve and admired her ability to remain calm under layers of brooding cumulus. She was sitting cross-legged, smiling, arms looped casually around her left knee. He couldn't help thinking how remarkable it was that only a few short months ago he'd thought he'd lost her to the grim reaper, the grinning voodoo who'd caused temptation to float in a blue balloon above an icy Manhattan street.

'Yes, but I'm here now,' Eileen responded, squeezing one of Jessica's legs and looking suspiciously radiant.

'Yes,' Jessica agreed, looking up as if from the depths of a deep blue ocean, uncertain of her whereabouts and dubious about her emotions. Steadying herself, she collected her nerves together, extracted a long breath from the difficult atmosphere and then slowly exhaled it, ridding her mind of the army of pick-wielding devils. 'So what are you going to do?' she enquired through gradually relaxing jaws.

'Do?' Alex asked. 'About what?'

'About the paintings. I mean, you know, you must have a plan or something, otherwise why would you come looking for me? Although I suppose I should be directing the question at Eve.'

'Alex has a master plan, but he won't tell anyone what it is,' Eve beamed at the two women sitting opposite. 'Not exactly.'

'He hasn't told you?' Eileen asked, eyebrows raised like the hackles on a distressed ridgeback. 'Blimey, must be a monster plan.'

'I'm going to sell them all,' Alex stated, suddenly wondering if he should be dropping this pebble of information into the airwaves swirling above the table's integral collection of indelible rings, heirlooms deposited by generations of perspiring bottles and glasses. 'On Eve's behalf.'

'All but mine,' Jessica responded, smiling like a guilty Cheshire Cat, one that had polished off a carton of cream.

'Yep,' Alex concurred, 'all but yours.'

'But, who to?' Jessica asked. 'To whom?'

'I can't tell you, there are too many loose ends and until I've got them all under control my lips are sealed.'

'A man of mystery,' Eileen purred. 'I like that, but it's a pity you're a man.'

'Why?' Eve asked.

'Well, let's put it like this. If he was a woman you might find yourself with a fight on your hands,' Eileen answered, her smile saintly.

'If he was a woman,' Eve parried, 'I'd be Stateside.'

'Yes, I suppose you would.'

'So . . . you and Jess . . ?' Alex asked ponderously.

'Me and Jess?'

'Are you, um . . ?'

'Come on, Alex,' Eileen said encouragingly, 'it's not like you to be bashful. You're among friends.' Seeking confirmation, she looked at Eve and Jessica. 'Isn't he?'

Eve smiled in brilliant affirmation. Jessica, caring neither one way nor the other, nodded her head in pensive acceptance of unwanted girly bonding.

'Goodness, Alex, step right up and announce your intentions,' Eileen instructed forcefully, yet smiling at the same time. 'What exactly is it that you think you need to know?'

'Okay, you and Jessica. Are you in a re, re, relation . . . ship?' He had a problem with the word, couldn't really pull it together. He tried again, slowly, one syllable at a time. 'Relationship?'

'Of course we're in a relationship.' Eileen's eyes were beguiling, pools of mystery inviting challenge.

'Really? But . . .'

'We live together, Alex. Under the same roof. In the same house. The one with Vermeer hanging on the wall.'

'Really? But . . .' The groove was deep and the needle sharp.

'But not in the same bed.'

'Oh . . .'

'Although if it were up to me . . .' Eileen left the supposition hanging in misty imaginations.

'By the way, Jessica, I've got your bag,' Alex announced, wading out of dangerous waters.

'Bag? What bag?' The response was short and sullen.

'The blue squidgy thing, you know, that the police found?'

'Oh, right.'

'So shall I send it to you, or what?'

'Whatever,' Jessica answered, summarily dismissing bag, Alex, Eve, and just about everything.

5

Simon sat and stared at the alien. Another alien, although this one seemed a little more familiar than the one with the strange accent. And then he twigged it. This alien always appeared whenever the mistress disappeared. Simon never knew where she went – the mistress – he never asked. How could he? he was a cat. These people, he thought, they're so strange. They disappear and reappear, disappear and reappear, usually for short spaces of time, but occasionally, like now, they float off for what seems an eternity. Sometimes one of them, sometimes both. He looked up as the visitor reached down to pat him on the head. 'It's okay, Simon,' she told him, 'they'll be back soon.' And he watched as the woman shuffled herself into a coat and let herself out of the apartment.

He prowled through the deserted quarters, pausing to sniff at familiar objects and wondering when the temporary alien would come back to give him some food. Food! That'd be nice! He returned to his eatery to see if there'd been a visitation, one he'd somehow missed. No, there hadn't. He sat for several minutes and stared at some miserable leftovers, crusted and quite unappetising. Disgusted, he scratched at the floor with a front paw, trying in vain to hide the offensive sight beneath an immovable tile. He mewed and changed paws. It was equally useless, the congealed mess stayed in stubborn perpetuity. Just to be on the safe side, just to be sure he hadn't missed anything and because he was curious, he lowered his breathing apparatus to make a final appraisal. The situation was beyond salvation, even for a hungry mog. He couldn't understand why the alien, but not really an alien, had entered his domain and not fed him. She'd stood in the kitchen and done some ironing; with no music! Simon had had to sit in front of his empty dish, hinting madly, while listening to some sort of crazy humming. It had gone on for ages and had driven him mad; the high-pitched hiss of the angry iron and the squeaky, out of tune stuff that issued from the part-time alien's mouth. And then she'd left; gone, went, disappeared, without the courtesy of leaving tasty morsels, not even the weeniest of crunchy things, in his dish.

Tail lifted in high disdain, Simon marched purposefully out of the kitchen. At times like this he liked to jump on his mistress, wherever she was, and plant kisses on her face and lick her nose with his little pink tongue. He quite believed she enjoyed these bonding sessions and sometimes he'd find the courage to visit her when she was taking a bath, up to her neck in bubbly stuff. He'd sit himself on the rounded edge of the tub and flick at the soap bubbles with a tentative paw. And then, in an act of foolish bravery, he'd stretch his body across the strange stuff that kept expanding and contracting and occasionally going "*pop*", until he could place his front legs on the mistress' chest. Strategically positioned, he'd elongate his neck towards Eve's face and commence nuzzling, until she started laughing, which was nearly always. Suspended above water, the tremors produced by the mistress' heaving body were something pretty terrifying, and he'd open his eyes to their utmost maximum and stare into those of Eve in horrific fascination as his small island of safety became quickly waterlogged. With his paws sliding beneath the surface he'd be speedy in reversing his previous manoeuvres, usually managing to back onto the edge of the bath, twist himself in midair and leap onto the floor, joyously regaining the safety of dry places. Sometimes, but thankfully not too often, his timing lacked perfection, his planning went all wrong and he ended up in poor imitation of a cat fish.

There were times, however, when he knew his mistress was not in the mood to be kissed. He knew this because she would pull her head back, suddenly, and accuse him of having terrible breath. Simon was clueless about this problem and had no idea what he should do to rectify it. Because it normally happened after his meals, he guessed, kind of slyly, that it might have something to do with his diet. However, he was by no means certain about this and whenever he was shunned and rudely pushed away from close proximity to Eve's face, he'd sit in thought mode and stare at the floor, trying to ignore the peculiarities of humans.

Now, thinking about life and all its mysteries, especially those concerning humans, he realised that the peculiarities had become weirder. The mistress and the strange person were continually jumping into bed and doing strange things to one another, things which invariably left them in a groaning heap of sweaty limbs. He had to admit though, from a cat's point of view, some of the things actually looked quite interesting.

Simon shook his head and looked up at the ceiling, at a fly which was buzzing in a demented sort of way in an up and down movement, as though drunk, that pitched it noisily into the white satin-finished surface. Stupid thing, he thought, wondering quite intelligently why a fly should be so active at this time of year. Like all the other annoying bugs and insects it should be asleep, or, better still, dead. The summer though, was okay, when the big glass doors were opened and fresh air and stuff wafted through the rooms bringing with it the occasional flying thing, which Simon chased with gleeful impunity as though it had been created solely for his amusement. It provided him with exercise, a feline assault course which batted to and fro over everything and sometimes under everything until the winged intruder had been knocked unconscious by a well-aimed paw. At this stage, he'd gather all his legs together and sit still, grinning like an Olympic champion while the vanquished insect spun round in ditzy circles. Then he'd eat it. Sometimes. But really these little creatures were too small, too fussy; child's play, until of course they wised up and realised it was safer to walk upside-down on the ceiling. When this happened there was nothing Simon could do, so he'd lope off in disgust and wish there was something larger, a mouse, say, or a stupid bird, that would provide more of a challenge.

He looked up at the black entity that was performing a lazy loop-the-loop, only the downward loop didn't end, or perhaps it was a case of an upward loop not materialising. Whichever, the fly, out of gas, out of energy and out of season, fell to the floor right at Simon's feet. His head had followed the flight from up to down and now he stared at the object as it spun around on its back, its legs scratching the air in some frantic futile dance routine. He thought about stamping on it and raised his right paw in readiness. And then he changed his mind and walked away from the situation.

Chapter Nine:

Dénouement

1

Wolfgang was all beams and chuckles and Bavarian benevolence. 'So, you are back,' he said cheerfully, taking hold of the visitors' elbows.

'So everyone keeps telling me,' Alex commented.

Stuck as he was between Eve and Alex, Wolfgang didn't know which way to turn. He put an arm around Eve's waist and encountered another, Alex's, already in position. He couldn't contain himself. 'Eve, welcome to Bavaria!' It is so good to be meeting you! Alex has told me much about you!'

'Not too much, I hope?'

'No, no, I mean only good things.' Wolfgang grinned in his ecstasy. 'The sun is shining *und* ve vill sit on the terrace. Alex, take this lovely woman *und* be putting up your feet while I am getting beers.'

'We'll come with you, Wolfgang,' Eve suggested, engaging their host with her large American smile. 'Don't regard us as guests, but rather as co-conspirators in Alex's grand plan. Lead on into the kitchen and show us the beer.'

'*Gut, gut, sehr gut.*' The large German padded happily through his home, his enthusiasm contagious. Alex and Eve flowed in the wake of good vibrations and helped with the provisions – a spread of cold meats, cheese, olives, bread and beer.

Relaxing on the terrace in an abundance of late afternoon sunshine, the threesome gazed at the magnificent view, a wide panorama across legions of pine trees and rocky crags, waves of crinkly ridges marching steadily, majestically downward to the cool reflective waters of Lake Tegernsee.

Leaning back into a deckchair, Alex raised his legs, extending them in front of him in an effort to ease muscles that had all but seized up after the long drive through a corner of France, a cross section of Belgium, and plenty of Germany. He couldn't help thinking back to the last time he'd been here, the genesis of this elongated adventure and the beginning of the end of his relationship with the woman whom he'd imagined to be the love of his life. How fickle it is, he reminisced, life and all its leaping changes, its crazy ups and downs, follies, fantasies and phenomena. Someone, he'd forgotten who, had concluded that it was all a game, a giant variation of *Twister* laden with all the intrigue of *Monopoly*. Such are the vagaries of life, its endless contortions of sleepwalking through a vast maze, exhausting and challenging and uncertain.

Secluded from a suddenly chill northern breeze, the verandah formed a perfect platform for earnest discussion. Apart from a slight buzz, caused by rising bubbles of carbon dioxide, the silence was profound while Wolfgang, and indeed Eve, waited for Alex to shed light on the complexities of his mind.

'It's called payback,' Alex announced decisively into the pristine mountain atmosphere.

'*Ach so*,' said a relieved Wolfgang, happy that the silence had at last been broken but clueless as to the word's meaning.

'Vhich is vhat?' He leaned into his chair and waited for clarification.

'We're going to sell the paintings back to the man who initiated their coming together.'

'We are?' Eve asked. 'How?'

'They're in the back of the car,' Alex answered somewhat confusingly, 'waiting to be returned to the Nazi burglar.'

'They are?' Wolfgang asked. 'I thought they were in America?'

'Yes,' Alex concurred ambiguously, 'there are those, too.'

'So you are saying there are being two sets of paintings?'

'Exactly,' Alex replied. 'The originals and the copies manufactured by Terry.'

'*Ach so*, copies?'

'Yes, Voolfy, and it's these that we are going to sell back to the dear general.'

'Shit!' Eve exclaimed, beaming with delight. 'Now I understand all the secrecy. It's a masterpiece; if it works.'

'It'll work,' Alex said reassuringly.

'But . . . but what if the general insists on an inspection?' asked a worried Wolfgang. 'What if he is haffing suspicions?'

'It's only natural he'll have suspicions, Voolfy, but an inspection shouldn't be a problem. The fakes are excellent. Terry assured me that his work would pass muster even if paraded in front of a panel of the world's so-called art experts.'

'Muster?'

'Inspection.'

'Ah, so he's good, this Terry?'

'Very good,' Alex confirmed, 'he and his accomplice.'

'So, vhat is being my part of the job?'

'Your part of the job, Voolfy, is to be your honest, convincing, amiable self.'

'Okay,' Wolfgang said, smiling widely. 'I think I can be managing this.'

'Of course you can. You must meet with the general and make him believe that I am an art dealer from London, that I was alerted to the collection when it surfaced in New York.'

'This is being easy, Alex, but how do we make him believe everything is genuine? We and the paintings?'

'We mention Eve's grandfather, and then we introduce Eve.'

'Shit, English, you've got it all worked out. It's perfect,' said an enchanted Eve.

'It is,' Alex agreed happily. 'It's as though the whole thing was delivered into our waiting palms, some form of God-sent providence.'

'Except you don't believe in God,' Eve pointed out.

'True,' Alex acceded. 'That problem aside, we have you and we have your passport. And the name Meyer, specifically Karel Meyer, will leave Herr General in no doubt as to authenticity.'

Wolfgang was still a little hesitant. 'But how do we account for our knowledge of the general, how do we make the connection between him and the paintings and New York and everything?'

'The letter from London's National Gallery, of which we have a copy.' Alex opened a slim briefcase and fumbled amongst a forest of papers. 'Here,' he said after a few rustling seconds, 'documentary proof.'

'Hey,' Eve asked, 'did you work this out all by yourself?'

'With the assistance of a little Jack.'

'Who's little Jack?' Wolfgang asked, confused at the dazzling speed of verbal badinage.

'Big Jack, actually. Big happy Jack, lives in a bottle.'

Two pairs of furrowed eyebrows glared at Alex.

'Daniels,' he explained under the combined onslaught from four rays of questioning vision, 'in Prague. I couldn't sleep, so I went to a bar, drank a few shots of whiskey and stumbled across this concept.'

'In the wee small hours,' Eve acknowledged, 'your moment of epiphany arrives out of alcoholic darkness.'

'Yep, my moment of enlightenment.' Alex leaned forward, drank from a stubby bottle of Paulaner and studied Wolfgang's face. 'Tomorrow,' he said, 'Voolfy, you visit the general and engage him in conversation and ask him if he's interested in art. Whatever his answer, you give him this photo.' Alex handed over a photograph of one of the *Prentiss Poses*.

'And this will be all that's necessary?'

'He'll be hooked,' Alex nodded sagely. 'He'll be amazed, shocked, and confused; but he'll be hooked.'

'And where do I fit in?' Eve asked. 'When do I get to meet the Nazi monster?'

'Maybe in a couple of days, honey, it sort of depends on his reaction. After he's seen this photo, he's going to want to see the genuine article. So we'll take it to him.' Alex smiled.

'Just like that?'

'Of course just like that, we have nothing to lose. We know the painting is a fake but the general will want to believe otherwise. His imagination will be pointing in the other direction, furnishing his stunned mind with a complete history spiralling all the way back to nineteen forty-five.'

'Alex, this is a *gut* plan, *sehr gut*. I can't vait, I vant to go now

321

to talk with him.'

'No, no, we wait until tomorrow. When we spoke on the phone, Voolfy, you said it was expected that he'd arrive back in Bavaria today, so we'll give him a few hours to settle into his lakeside way of life. Let him relax before we present him with an unbelievable truth.'

'So, Alex, we must celebrate this thing.' Wolfgang was all agitated and emotional. 'Vhat vould Jessica be thinking?'

'Jessica wasn't interested,' Alex informed the German.

'She wasn't?'

'Jessica has the Vermeer,' Eve explained. 'Jessica is content.'

'*Und* if the general gets to hear of it?' Wolfgang asked, anxiety climbing out of the unknown. 'He'll become suspic . . .'

'It'll be too late, he'll have his paintings. And because he'll have paid good money he'll be well and truly attached to them. Belief is a funny thing. And anyway, since we're offering only the pictures from New York, their copies, he'll continue to presume that the disappearance of the Vermeer and the Rembrandt was someone else's doing.'

'To think this is all beginning in my little guest house,' Wolfgang mused, 'is very satisfactory.' Rising to his feet, he trotted happily into the dark interior of the house. A handful of seconds later, he reappeared. 'But, Alex, for how much are you selling these paintings?'

'Market value, Voolfy. Market value.'

'But . . . how much?'

'Neither too much, nor too little, just the right amount, an affordable amount that won't deter a scheming Nazi.'

'Ex-Nazi, English.'

'There's no such thing, darling,' Alex responded. 'Once a Nazi, always a Nazi.'

2

The day was fresh, one of those when the sun plays hide-and-seek with sheep-sized clouds piling interminably out of the western horizon. Here, the horizon was high, formed by a range of enclosing hills, a line of baby mountains supporting a splendid array of spiky pines. At the foot of the steep slopes, Lake Tegernsee, rippled by agitated Renoir-fashioned wavelets, sparkled in intermittent sunlight.

For the hundredth time, Wolfgang slid his hand into his jacket to make sure the all-important photograph was nestled in the inner pocket. Running a fingertip along the reassuring ridge of card, he stepped up to the door and knocked loudly, stepping back in surprise when it was opened almost immediately. '*Guten Tag*,' he said. '*Herr Oberstürm?*'

'*Wer?*' came the curt reply.

'*Herr Oberstürm*,' Wolfgang repeated, undeterred. Although he knew about the general's pseudonym, he wanted to observe what happened when he used the man's real name. Nothing.

'*Ich bin der Geisler*,' the general announced, drawing himself up to his full military height, although, due to advanced age, this was a little diminished.

'*So, kein Problem,*' Wolfgang said, smiling his best genial smile. 'You see, I have come to talk to you about art. You are interested in art? But of course you are interested in art, everyone is interested in art, especially intelligent persons.' He held his breath, everything depended on the general's response.

'Art?' A ray of sunshine glanced off the general's head of fine white hair, short, fashioned almost in crew cut style. 'Art? What art?'

Wolfgang released his lungs, he could wrangle this one. The question had caught the general off guard and, though the answer had taken the form of a question, Wolfgang had a toe prodding at the opening gambit of an important game. 'Well, all sorts.' He held his arms open wide as though encompassing the entire art world. The general scratched at an irritation a couple of centimetres below his left eye, his shifty left eye. 'But specifically, the world of paintings,' Wolfgang added, masterfully reducing the world of art to one genre.

'Paintings? What paintings?' The general's other eye became shifty, though perhaps it was just a natural reaction to a sudden brightness of vacillating sunlight. 'Who are you?'

'I am nobody,' Wolfgang answered. 'Just a go-between.' He smiled again to show there was no inherent danger in being confronted by a go-between.

Clearly, the general was not out of sorts with this impromptu interview. His reply was direct and came straight from the hip. 'Between what?'

Wolfgang took his chance and presented the precious photograph. 'Between you and the man who has possession of this article.'

'But, wait a minute, you were here before.' Both eyes flickered in distressed recognition. 'Yes, I remember, you were talking to my gardener.' The general took hold of the photograph and tapped it against the edge of his close-shaven chin, while he pushed his mind to remember more.

'Yes, yes,' Wolfgang hurriedly agreed, 'of course, and this is how I am knowing where you are living.' He desperately wanted to escape from this line of conversation which, though going nowhere, could lead both men up the garden path.

'But why were you talking with my gardener?'

'Gardeners know everything, and not just about gardens,' Wolfgang joked in a half-serious manner.

'Yes, yes, this is certainly true,' the general agreed in sociable manner, nodding his head in sage vagueness. 'But . . .'

'And you remember of course that I am coming from Hamburg?' Wolfgang asked, hoping to add to the confusion.

'Hamburg? Yes, know the place. Cold and windy and full of northerners all speaking *Hochdeutsch*.'

'*Richtig*,' Wolfgang acquiesced, quickly switching to the harsh dialect and wondering why he hadn't already done so.

The general stopped tapping and lowered the photo to his side. Then, remembering that he was supposed to be looking at it, he lifted the picture to his face, adjusting the angle of the shiny surface so that he could see beyond the sun's reflections. His features became taut, and then became strained. 'What is the meaning of this?' he cried. Then, scaling back his emotion, he asked, 'What *is* this?'

'It's a photograph of a painting,' Wolfgang answered, in a manner that Alex would have been proud of.

'Yes, yes, but . . . there is . . .' Herr Oberstürm turned as quickly as his bad leg would allow and stormed into his house. Hurling his body into his wheelchair, parked next to a heavy oak table just inside the doorway, he employed the style of a

Paralympic champion and energetically wheeled himself along an echoey wooden corridor. Exploding into a cavernous sun-lit living room he spun the chair, almost on one wheel, into a wonderfully magnificent halt. 'Get my glasses. Over there, over there,' he directed a wrong-footed Wolfgang. 'Quickly, man, quickly.'

Wolfgang located the glasses, neatly folded on an arm of a deep leather armchair, and handed them to the retired military officer. Through a mixture of nervous excitement and too much haste, the general fumbled at his attempt to open the spectacles and dropped them onto the floor. 'Quickly, quickly,' he ordered. 'Pick the damned things up.'

Wolfgang, all a-flutter with anxious uncertainty, picked the article off the floor and once again handed the glasses to the general. Now what do I do? he asked himself in trepidation. Things were moving too quickly, he should have left immediately he'd put the photograph into the general's hands. What would Alex do, he wondered? Then he began to wonder what Alex would say if he blew the deal. *Scheiße*, he thought, this is too much responsibility. He regarded the general who, ensconced in his wheelchair, seemed to have somewhat shrunk in stature. He didn't seem so tough, so astute . . . so aware.

'Where did you get this?' the general barked. 'Where? From whom?'

'From an art dealer,' Wolfgang answered promptly, know-ing he had to stand up to the man sitting down. His assump-tion had been wrong. Though the general's eminence might indeed have diminished, his demeanour had sharpened, con-siderably. Perhaps, now that the concentration necessary to keep him on his pins had been removed, his power of thought had been increased.

'Art dealer? What art dealer? Where did he get this picture?'

Tzak, tzak, tzak – the questions flew like bullets from a machine gun. Wolfgang pictured the man in his heyday, ordering subalterns hither and thither like out-of-control Dodgem cars supplied with too much electricity.

'He's from London, England. Um, I don't know where he got the picture.'

'What? Speak up.'

'The picture, I don't know where it came from,' Wolfgang replied, utilising greater volume.

'And this man, the art dealer. Who is he?'

'He has the original painting.'

'No, no, it's not possible. It cannot be?'

'Maybe yes, maybe no,' Wolfgang stated enigmatically. Relaxing slightly, he lowered his tense shoulders. He reckoned the general had taken the bait, swallowed it all the way up to the float, but he knew he had to be careful; there was still a long way to go.

3

Alex slammed shut the boot, slammed shut Eve's door, slammed shut Wolfgang's door, jumped behind the wheel and slammed shut the driver's door.

'Steady on, English,' Eve warned, patting Alex's leg, 'do try to stay calm. Remember your Englishness.'

'I know, I know,' Alex frothed, turning the ignition key twice, ignoring the fact that the engine had roared into life at the first spark.

'He's not going anywhere,' Eve continued, 'he's going to be all keen and eager. And, if anything and if possible, more wound up than you. He's gonna be Mr Grabby, a ball of energy waiting to leap out of his chair and fondle his long-lost painting.'

'I'm all being nervous,' Wolfgang informed everyone.

'Why?' Eve snapped, turning to address their friend. 'You've already met him.'

'Exactly, *und* therefore I am knowing him. He is not silly.'

'Neither are we,' Eve responded forcefully. 'It's a great plan and we just have to stay cool, pretend it's the sort of thing we do everyday.'

'Okay, okay,' Alex said, sort of half over his shoulder as he pushed the car round a series of perilous bends, 'we all know what we're doing. Wolfgang, your rôle is translator, just keep ahead of the conversation and do the best you can. Eve, your rôle is one of authenticity relating to Charley and . . . Shit, we have to remember to refer to him as Karl.'

'Karl?' Eve asked.

'Of course, of course, the German version of Charles,' Wolfgang volunteered. '*Gut, gut*, well done, Alex, *gut* remembering.'

'And what will your job be?' Eve asked, smiling at Alex.

'I have to play the part of the expert salesman.' He banged the palm of a hand against the steering wheel. 'We can do this. We can.'

'Okay Voolfy?' Eve grinned over the seat. 'It'll be plain sailing, a breeze.'

'Breeze? Plane? Sailing?' Wolfgang shook his head in amusement. 'You English, you are crazy.'

'I'm American,' Eve reminded him, 'but that's okay, we're crazy too.'

Obviously in need of back up, the general had marshalled his troops in singular shape and form: the gardener. In the manner of an obedient soldier the man was standing to one side of the wheelchair, his body crammed into a suit, light grey, creased and outgrown. And, no doubt at the behest of his employer, he'd endeavoured to secure a tie around his neck. Holding onto one of the wheelchair's handles, he cranked himself into a semblance of vertical control and grinned widely as he recognised Wolfgang marching towards him. The general remained seated, erect and huffy, his face seriously trying to control seething emotions. Clenching his teeth and narrowing his eyes, he crossed his hands, resting them in his lap while his brain flip-flopped between hope and despair. He was tired and tetchy and short of sleep, his mind having spent the night in a sea of torment between sandy beaches of reclamation and rocky outcrops of trickery. The visitors came to a halt at a respectful distance from the wheelchair.

'*Guten Tag, Herr Geisler*,' Wolfgang said, acknowledging the alias and greeting the general's stare with straight-faced honesty.

'*Guten Tag*,' The general replied curtly, allowing his face to summon up a narrow smile. 'My gardener, Dieter, you know already.'

'*Guten Tag*,' Wolfgang repeated, nodding in friendly manner at the gardener, who managed to look excited and uncomfortable at the same time. '*Geht's gut?*'

'*Ja, ja, danke. . .*' Dieter responded jovially, happy to be addressed in the second person format and happy to be included in his boss' calculations, whatever they happened to be.

'*Und?*' the general growled, causing casual conversation to cease.

'This is the man from London,' Wolfgang announced in High German, introducing Alex. 'He is the man with the painting, the one you saw in the photograph.'

Bending forward and almost clicking his heels in the process, Alex held his hand out, forcing the general to unclasp his hands and reciprocate. '*Guten Tag, Herr General*,' Alex said pointedly.

The man in the wheelchair held Alex's hand in a tight grip and studied the Englishman's face. '*Stimmt*,' he said, his tone gravelly, '*wie Sie möchten. Und?*'

Listening to the timbre of the general's voice, Alex understood he was dealing with a man who'd brook no sophistry, a man who'd see straight through anything that wasn't watertight. He recalled the emotions that had been generated when standing at the locus of the general's wartime operations in Prague. The vision of countless valuables being taken from subjugated citizens served to tighten his resolve. 'Herr General, I take it you have studied the photograph that was presented to you yesterday?' He looked at Wolfgang and nodded, indicating that the sentence should be translated into German.

'No need,' said the general, intercepting the glance. 'I am speaking good English. French and Spanish, also.'

'Perhaps,' Alex acknowledged, 'but we will use German so that there can be no possibility of misunderstanding, for both of us.' He waited while Wolfgang dutifully said the same thing in German.

The general nodded, accepting the arrangement. 'And where exactly is the painting, the one in the photo?' he asked. 'The original, of course.'

Alex listened to the accuracy of Wolfgang's English version of the easy sentence. This is going to pan out, he thought, already the general is asking about the painting. 'In the car,' he answered, turning to walk the short distance to the driveway.

A silence of expectation hovered above the small gathering of people as Alex returned with a cloth-covered package. Placing the object into the general's hands, he noticed the man chewing his lower lip in anticipation.

'No, no!' the general exclaimed, thrusting the painting back into Alex's hands. 'You take it, carry it into the house. I wish to make a thorough inspection.'

Registering surprise, Alex barely managed to grasp the article that was being pushed towards him. He looked at Wolfgang, listened to the translation, and nodded when he understood what was being proposed. 'Of course, of course,' he agreed, holding onto the painting and following in the wake of the speedy chariot being expertly propelled by the multi-talented gardener. He looked at Eve and winked, as though to say *so far so good.* She rewarded him with a smile of encouragement and stepped into line behind the caravan of oddly assorted people. When the cavalcade reached the house, Wolfgang, as chief of operations, stepped ahead to open the door and then stood aside as the general was wheeled into comparative darkness.

'We'll go to the kitchen,' the general announced, wheeling himself to the left, 'big table, plenty of light. Dieter, find my magnifying glass, should be on my desk in the study.'

Positioning his chair in front of the table, he drummed the fingers of his right hand against the well-scrubbed wooden surface and gazed into an unknown horizon. Alex watched the man and wondered at the history that must be coursing through the elderly corridors of retrospection. The drumming stopped and the general hauled his vision back into the room. 'Well?' he said, shaking his head in miffed interrogation. 'Shall we put the painting on the table?'

Without waiting for the translation, Alex placed the painting on the tabletop and folded back the protective cloths.

'*Unglaublich,*' the general stated. '*Ich hätte nie gedacht, dass das möglich ist.*'

'Incredible,' Wolfgang repeated faithfully. 'I am neffer thinking this possible.' He grinned at Alex.

Leaning forward, the general called to Dieter. 'Hurry up,

man, where is the magnifier?'

Heavy steps paced into the kitchen as Dieter rushed to his master. '*Herr General, ich kann die Lupe nicht finden,*' he reported breathily, looking at the general and then at the painting. He gasped as his eyes focused on the erotic study. '*Herr General, was ist?*'

'It's a painting, Dieter,' the general answered calmly. 'Now, where exactly did you look?'

Dieter informed the general that he'd searched everywhere, but, when asked if he'd looked in the desk drawers, his face slid towards the lewd figures depicted on the canvas. '*Nein,*' he admitted, crestfallen.

'*So, Dieter, geh und sieh in den Schubladen, und mach schnell!*'

Dieter trotted out of the kitchen like an obedient spaniel, while Wolfgang brought Alex up to speed on the gist of the German dialogue.

Alex moved closer to the table and stared at the painting, trying to imagine why the general should need a magnifying glass. Although familiar with the photos supplied by Terry, the erotically charged painting, close up, was altogether of a different dimension. The picture portrayed four characters, all of whom were naked, and two trees, to which two of the characters, one male and one female, had been bound. Their arms, drawn above their heads, were fastened by means of some silky-looking material to convenient branches supplied by the deft hand of the artist – in this case, Terry. Their legs, pulled apart and upwards, were bent at the knees so that their feet, supposedly tethered behind the trunks, were not visible. The other characters, each standing to one side of the captives, had been depicted holding fig leaves, which they held in such a way as to shield the victims' genitals. The character standing next to the female captive was male, and vice versa. Alex recalled that another of the *Prentiss Poses*, also featuring the theme of bondage, portrayed the captives as being administered to by tormentors of the same sex. Mr Prentiss, whoever he was, must have been a connoisseur of unfussy pornography – titillation, as Michelstraub had correctly termed it. As with all the *Poses*, the picture had been executed in pastel colours and feathery brushstrokes, and because there was little detail of anything overtly sexual, much was left to the observer's imagination.

Sweating profusely, Dieter rushed back into the kitchen and placed a long-handled magnifying glass into the general's waiting hand. He then backed himself to the sink, turned on a tap and filled a glass with water, at which he slurped with extreme enthusiasm.

The general spent a few moments regarding the strange antics of his gardener, then, edging forwards, brought himself into closer proximity with the long-lost painting. He raised the magnifying glass and awarded the picture minute inspection. Alex watched as the man laboured left and right and up and down, moving the glass over every inch of canvas before inspecting the intricacies of the gilded wooden frame. After several minutes the silence was broken by Dieter, who once again turned on the tap and ran himself another glass of life-sustaining liquid.

'Dieter, come, lift the painting and turn it over so I can look at the back.'

Standing between the table and the sink, Alex unfolded his arms and swallowed hard as he listened to Wolfgang's translation. Moving out of the way, he watched Dieter carrying out the general's instructions. Shit, he thought, what now?

What could be so important about the back of the painting? Recalling the message, *Für Elise*, inscribed on the reverse of the Fila, he began to panic, wondering if there had been any other telltale marks, secret or otherwise, that had been written, scratched or stamped onto any or all of the other frames. Fuckity-fuck, he thought, swallowing again and discovering that his throat was drier than the Sahara. He risked a quick glance at Eve and noticed that she, too, was closely following the operation that was halfway through flipping the painting onto its back. He cleared the sand out of his throat. 'Herr general, while you're looking at your painting, may I use your phone?' Alex stood, solitary, like a wilting palm in a storm of pandemonium, while Wolfgang earned his credit.

'Of course,' Wolfgang smiled widely, supplying the English answer. 'In the study.'

Alex sidestepped around the group of avid spectators and made a beeline for the general's sanctum, following the course earlier taken by the diligent gardener. Entering the room, he closed the door behind him and hotfooted it to the phone. Angrily stabbing at outsize numbers, he cosseted the receiver against his left ear. '*Quick!*' he hissed loudly, when he heard that the respondent was Christine. 'Get Terry, it's Alex.' He flapped his free hand in frustration and flexed his knees, bobbing up and down like a swan dying badly.

'Alex!' Christine purred in her soft Scottish accent, 'how are .. ?'

'No no, no time, quick quick, get me Terry. Now.'

'Really!'

'It's *ur*gent!' Alex perspired into the mouthpiece. '*Quick!*' On hearing the reciprocal piece of equipment being smacked heavily onto a hard surface, he moved the receiver away from his ear. Then he brought it back, pressing the perforated plastic as close to his ear as possible. He could hear footsteps marching across the wooden London floor, footsteps accompanied by Christine's lilting vocals, '. . . sounds all panicky, like as though he's gone mad.' And then there was a scrabbling sound as the distant receiver was lifted from its temporary place of residence. 'Alex?'

'Shit, Terry, tell me if there were any marks or features on the backs of the paintings, the originals.'

'Marks, features?'

'You know, like the *Für Elise*?' Alex inserted his right index finger into the curly phone cable and started twisting the flexible stuff around his digit.

'Oh, yes, didn't I tell you?' Terry asked. Then, ponderously, 'I'm sure I told you.'

'No, you didn't. What the hell did you find? *Je*sus!'

'Oh, well, it was really interesting . . .'

'What? For fuck's sake, Terry, hurry up.'

'Where are you Alex?'

'*Terry!*' Alex squawked into the phone. 'Just fucking tell me!'

'Oh, um, straight lines, short, as though made with a knife or something . . .'

'And?'

'Filled with paint and smoothed over.'

'Paint?'

'Yes, paint, a different colour for each painting, like some sort of . . .'

'Code,' Alex breathed softly, almost inaudibly.

'Exactly, a code.'

'*Je*sus*fuck*ing*Chri*st, *Terry!*'

'No, no, it's okay . . .'

'What do you mean, "it's okay"?'

'I copied them, re-created them.'

'You did?' Alex almost peed with relief. 'Really?'

'Of course, colour for colour, painting for painting, exact matches.'

'Terry!' Alex hissed. 'You're a fucking hero.'

'I am?'

'A fucking life saver.'

'Well,' Terry chuckled in reply, 'that's the . . .'

Alex fiddled the receiver onto its cradle and walked towards the door. Placing his hand on the doorknob, he paused and took a deep breath. Then he let go of the door-knob and returned to the desk. Picking up the phone, he dialled his own number, allowing the system enough time to ring two or three times in the emptiness of his living room. Replacing the instrument, he spotted a business card resplend-ently positioned to one side of a large notepad. Squinting, he managed to decipher the logo, squirly stuff advertising the existence of a restaurant. One by one, he punched the numbers into the phone and let it ring, once, twice, and then replaced the receiver. 'Just like a real spy,' he muttered to him-self, opening the door and walking back to join the others.

The general looked up and nodded as Alex entered the kitchen. '*Vortrefflich!*' he said, eyes wide in genuine surprise. '*Alles in ordnung ist. Sie haben die anderen?*'

Although he reckoned he understood what the general was asking, Alex waited while Wolfgang went through the motions of translation. He nodded his head, 'Yes, I have the others. They are in the car.'

'*Und wie viel?*'

'Five, six in total,' Alex answered, even as Wolfgang was spinning out the words.

'This is calling for a drink, I believe,' the general announced, pulling himself into an upright position in his wheelchair. 'Dieter, brandy and glasses, outside in the fresh air. But first, young man, you will tell me how you are coming into possession of these pictures.'

'Outside,' Alex suggested, standing on firm ground but sweating all the same. 'In the fresh air and with the brandy.'

'*Wie Sie wünschen,*' the general agreed, grabbing his wheels and spinning himself around. 'We will sit by the lake. Dieter, bring also some ice.'

The general's estate included a small patio, situated between the house and the lake and surrounded by a low wall assembled out of rustic bricks. In the centre of the paved area a delicate fountain issued from the mouth of a dolphin, the fish sculpted into perpetuity and balancing on its tail atop a pedestal. Alex, Eve, Wolfgang and the general, sat around a white-painted wrought iron table and waited for Dieter to appear with the drinks. Steadying a slim briefcase on his lap, Alex opened it and removed a sheet of paper which he handed to the general.

'*Und? Was ist?*' the general asked, glancing at the page of English words.

'This is the documentation that links the paintings,' Alex replied, waiting for Wolfgang's translation, before adding, 'To you.' He nodded at himself, pleased with the way he was handling everything, pleased at the way things were turning out now that the hairy moment of inspection had passed, now that the hectic conversation with Terry had added weight and credence to elegant subterfuge. 'The paintings were found in

New York,' he continued slowly, 'in the home of a lawyer.'

'*Ein Rechtsanwalt?*' the general asked, whiskery eyebrows arched high. '*Wie so?*'

'I don't know how, I don't know why,' Alex lied. 'However, the lawyer has since passed away.'

'Passed away, Alex?' Wolfgang asked. 'Please, what is passed away?'

Looking across the peaceful patio, Alex shook his head, sadly, before nodding at Eve and screwing his face into a tight smile. 'Dead.'

'*Ach so, tot,*' Wolfgang relayed the information to the general. '*Der Rechtsanwalt ist tot.*'

'*Ja, so ist das Leben,*' the general nodded in agreement.

Believing the general had lost his mind and had said something about love, in the same sort of way that Kennedy had confusingly called himself a doughnut, Alex grinned inanely. '*Ja, ja,*' he agreed, almost clicking his heels again. And then Wolfgang made the translation and Alex understood that *Leben* actually meant life.

'Ah, yes indeed,' Alex concurred, realising the man hadn't lost his mind. Soberly, he directed his vision onto the general's face. 'And his name was Meyer.'

'*Wie?*'

'Meyer,' Alex repeated levelly. 'Karl Meyer.'

'Karl?' The general dropped the document and seized the arms of the wheelchair. 'Karl? *Mein Gott! Was ist los mit dir? Was meinst du?*' At the sudden use of the second person singular, all pretence of civility disappeared. '*Das ist unmöglich! Das kann ich wierklich nicht glauben!*'

'I know, Herr General, but it's true,' Alex smiled tightly.

'No, no, you haff no proof. And you haff told me the

man is being dead.' Wolfgang was sweating, his head swivelling back and forth as he kept up with the rapid dialogue.

'Yes. Though his granddaughter is alive,' Alex stated unequivocally.

'But . . .'

'And she is here,' Alex continued, unmercifully hammering truths into the general's reeling brain.

'She?' the general asked weakly, dragging his gaze from the verbose Englishman and refocusing on the dark haired girl who'd said nothing. 'You? Why would I believe you? Why should it be of . . .'

Wolfgang had paused, while considering the options of translation. 'Consequence?'

'Consequence,' Alex said slowly, relishing the word and smiling at the general like a leery mikado. 'It's of consequence to you.'

'To me?'

'It's proof,' Alex explained, getting to his feet, 'that connects everything together. Forty-five years of history linking Prague to Marseilles and Argentina to New York.' He strode across the lawn and passed out of sight behind a corner of the house.

'Dieter,' the general snapped. '*Gehe nach ihm.*'

Like an obedient though reluctant German shepherd, Dieter stopped pouring himself a drink and set off in pursuit of the Englishman.

'What is he talking about?' the general fired at Wolfgang.

Wolfgang shook his head and shrugged and said nothing.

Sensing conspiracy, the general pursed his lips, picked up his glass and swirled it in petulant circles, morosely watching the ice cubes spinning with the golden liquid. Despite the hassles of translation and the mocking tone evident in the Englishman's voice, he believed himself still to be in charge of proceedings. His knowledge of the English language, sufficient to allow him to follow most of the to-ing and fro-ing, had given him time to consider what was actually being said, and by the time he'd been presented with the alternate version of the English sentences, he'd been able to formulate an effective response. Until now. He took a gulp of brandy and set the glass onto the table. He didn't know whether to be overjoyed at the sudden appearance of these relics from the past or, *Donner und Blitzen*, pissed off that his identity had been so easily traced. Easily? He smiled at the notion. Forty-five years is a long time to remain incognito, he realised, tapping the armrests of the wheelchair, and he'd done well to return to the motherland after all those years of enforced exile. Then he started to wonder about Argentina and New York and the man called Karl who, he well remembered, had been the efficient go-between 'twixt the German high command and the diffident Czechoslovaks. They had been good days, he reflected, an era of parties and parades and truckloads of European splendour. How the hell had Karl managed to end up in New York, a lawyer of all things, an American one? '*Kruzifix!*' he muttered under his breath, thinking about the world and how it had been screwed several times over since the heydays when it had seemed that nothing could stop the advance of German military might. Well aware of the Fuhrer's insanity, the general had seen the end coming and had managed to slip away in the confusion of the Allied occupation. It had been a nightmare, Russians and Americans and Brits swarming all over his country, dividing the spoils and ensuring that English would be the dominant language. He glanced up as Dieter and the Englishman reappeared, each with out-stretched arms carrying bundles of well-wrapped paintings.

Wolfgang leapt from his chair and helped position the pictures, leaning them against the low wall and folding back their protective cloths. Within seconds, the patio was home to a gallery of erotic art.

'Here,' said Alex, selecting one of the paintings and bringing it over to the general. 'Look.'

If these people only knew what was hiding beneath these pictures, the general thought, taking hold of the painting being lowered into his hands. He began to survey the image in front of him, his eyes following the swirls of the artist's vivid imagination, and then, suddenly, the painting was removed from his hands and turned over. 'Here,' Alex repeated, stabbing a finger at an edge of the wooden frame. 'Look, read.'

The general looked and read. '*Für Elise*,' he said in perfect German. Then he repeated himself, in English. 'For Elise. It is the name of a piece of music by Beethoven.'

'Yes,' Alex agreed. 'Quite so. It also happens to be the name of a woman who was known to Meyer. In fact,' he added, his smile inscrutable and once again resembling that of a corpulent Japanese emperor, 'it is the name of a woman who lost everything to the inhumanity of swarming Nazis.'

'But this is haffing nothing to do with me,' the general protested in near perfect English. 'That was *der Führer*.'

'Yes.'

'*Und* I was not admiring of the Hitler,' the general elaborated, staring at the name inked onto the back of the frame.

'No.' Alex sighed. 'It seems that towards the end of the war, most people gave up on the magisterial power of the leader.'

'Exactly,' said the general, somewhat relieved that he appeared to be approaching common ground. '*Genau.*' He looked up as Alex dragged a chair across the tiles and sat next to him. '*Und?*'

'And,' said Alex, 'these are the connections that brought the paintings back to you. Well, perhaps not Hitler, he didn't have much to do with it, except of course for enabling you to purloin the pictures in the first place. Purloin, Wolfgang,' Alex explained, 'steal, take, pinch – when you're looking for the correct meaning to translate.'

Returning his gaze to the surface of the frame, the general searched for the secret mark that told him the painting was . . . He racked his memory, yes, it was the painting by that Czechoslovak artist, Fila, the one we locked up for the duration of the war. 'Yes,' he said, nodding heavily, 'it was bad what we did.' And then, suddenly wondering why these people were returning the paintings as though in forgiveness, he asked the question. 'Why?'

'How much do you think these paintings are worth?' Alex asked.

'Vurth?' The general looked at the pictures ranged around the edge of the patio, the lewd portraits that were worthless, and thought about their camouflaged secrets, the priceless works of art contained therein. 'Vhy?'

'Because I'm offering them for sale, and before I state my price it'd be interesting to hear what sort of value you think they might have.'

All eyes were on the general as the onlookers wondered how he was going to respond to this noble question. Collecting the upside down painting from the general, Alex placed it alongside the five *Prentiss Poses* leaning against the wall. He stood quietly for a few moments, regarding the paintings and thinking about their recent creation, and then, thinking he'd give the general a little space, he stepped out of the patio area and walked across the lawn to the edge of the lake. Gentle waters, lapping at the grass verges, became a sudden flurry of activity as a flock of ducks paddled about in urgent disarray, complaining noisily at the antics of one of their brethren whose beady-eyed mission seemed full of sexual intent. Towards the centre of the lake, a small flotilla of yachts floated in suspended animation, waiting for something to fill their listless sails, while bored helmsmen trailed suntanned arms through a series of slack bubbles surfacing from gloomy depths. Peering at the far shore, Alex thought he could make out the restaurant where he and Jessica had stopped, two summers ago, before they'd headed into the hills to find Wolfgang's private hotel. Shaking his head in the perceived wisdom that everything goes round in circles, he turned to look at the general's house, a complex mixture of brick, wood and sun-reflecting glass – two stories squashed beneath a gently sloping alpine roof, each side ending in a profusion of flower-filled baskets. Slowly retracing his steps, he came back to the patio, sat on the chair next to the general and picked up his glass. The scene was like a chessboard, the pieces immobile, waiting for the *coup de grâce*. Alex took a swig of brandy and swirled it around his mouth while looking across the table at Eve, who was staring at the tiles and studiously rearranging her hair. Draping it first over one shoulder, then over the other, the movement of dark tresses came alive beneath the sunlight and resembled a glistening cascade of treacle.

Wolfgang was beginning to feel a little unnecessary. No one was speaking and his job as translator seemed to have been terminated. He took a handkerchief from a pocket and dabbed at his sweating forehead, removing his glasses so he could apply the operation to the rest of his face. Sitting at the same side of the table as Eve, the sun was behind him, so that his face was more or less hidden in deep shadows. Even so, the ruddy glow emanating from his skin was easily discernible.

Regarding him from the other side of the table, Alex could almost feel the coils of panic that were causing his friend's feathers to become ruffled.

As though waiting simply for the order to move, the gardener seemed ready to launch himself in any direction. Neither young nor old – perhaps, Alex deduced, looking at the man's tanned face and earth-ingrained hands, around the half-century mark – Dieter's body appeared to be in a constant state of flux, yet hesitant, puppet-like and somehow incapable of moving on its own accord. Powerful muscles of the Teutonic variety lay dormant, uneasy, bunched and tensed in eagerness to get on with the weeding or the mowing, or pouring the general's brandy.

'*Nur sechs?*' The general's sudden question took everybody by surprise. He twisted his head to the left and stared at the man who'd dared to bring the pigeons home to roost.

Cranking himself into action, Wolfgang replaced his spectacles on his nose, hooking them over his ears as he voiced the easy translation. 'Just six?'

'Six,' Alex replied, nodding in agreement with the short statement.

'But this document you are showing me is saying eight.'

'I know,' Alex countered, quickly alert after a slightly hesitant translation. 'The National Gallery told me the same thing.' *Fuck!* he thought. Fuck, fuck, *fuck!* How could I be so

346

stupid? He cloaked his ineptitude in silence, hoping for the best, hoping it would throw the ball back into the general's court.

'And what did you think?' Sitting bolt upright, the general was on the attack, a king surrounded by circling pawns.

'Think?' Alex riposted. 'I didn't need to think. I was called to New York, I was handed six paintings, and I brought them to you. And here they are,' he smiled, a sweep of his right arm indicating the reclining *Prentiss Poses*, 'all yours, for a price.'

'So you are thinking they are of value to me?' The general was breathing fire, anxious beyond measure to keep the precious bounty that had miraculously been returned, doubly anxious not to open any lines of enquiry as to its true worth. Gazing at the trophies that lay almost within reach, his vision bored through the flimsy artifice – layers of paint, thin as a breath and shrouding each gem. Once again he was ensconced at the centre of operations, his mind opening portals in the manner of that television programme in which a never-ending stream of objects is paraded on a conveyor belt in front of a greedy-eyed contestant. And it was true, the line of stolen treasure brought to the house in Prague had been infinite – goblets, plates, chandeliers, furniture, paintings, engravings, ornaments, gold, silver, trinkets – anything and everything that was deemed valuable had been examined by the general. And now, here, by the shores of Lake Tegernsee, six of the most important articles were sunning themselves in tantalising proximity.

'Of course,' Alex responded, finding a narrow path through treacherous constructs of clever conversation. 'Your obvious desire to spirit these paintings to Argentina at the end of the war, as evinced by the document you just referred to, gives rise to the question: why? The obvious answer, indeed the only answer, would be security. A new life . . .' Witnessing the energetic waving of his friend's arms and the worry outlined on his face, Alex stopped in mid-flow. 'Wolfgang, what?'

'Words, Alex, words,' Wolfgang cried. 'Vhat is "evinced" *und* vhat is "spirit"? It is being a ghost, no? Or maybe a drink?'

'Ah, yes, sorry Wolfgang. No. Um, "evinced" is, um, proof . . . the proof contained in the document, and, er, "spirit", in this case, means to move something secretly from one place to another. Okay?' Alex waited while Wolfgang tussled with the strange vocabulary. After a short while and after what seemed like far too many German words, he watched, satisfied, as the general nodded his head. 'Okay,' Alex continued. 'Now, where was I?'

'In a new life,' Wolfgang reminded him, happily translating in reverse.

'I was? Really?' Alex paused and collected his thoughts. 'Oh yes, a new life. Anyway, Herr General, having escaped from the motherland you'd have had to set up home in a new territory, and to do this you need funds. A new life in a new dominion requires money, wealth, some form of support.'

'*Und?*' The general could feel something nasty pulling at his entrails.

'And,' Alex answered, gesturing with both hands, 'I reckon this little collection is worth a lot of money.' He watched the general's face, looking closely to see if there was any sign of betrayal, any sign of impending doom. There wasn't. The general, outwardly at any rate, had his emotions firmly under control. Alex grinned and released the punch line, the idea that would supply the general with an easy out. 'But of course, I expect you were due to receive payment from the connoisseur.'

'Connoisseur,' Wolfgang echoed. 'Yes, I know this word, it is coming from French after it is coming from Latin.'

'Connoisseur?' the general queried. 'What connoisseur?'

'The gentleman, General, to whom you were shipping this collection of erotic studies. I'm pretty certain this sort of stuff is not particularly to your liking, not your speciality. Not exactly your cup of tea?'

'Cup of tea,' said Wolfgang, raising his face towards the sky. 'Yes, I am knowing this also. It is one of your strange English sayings, no?'

'Yes,' Alex assented. 'Can you translate it?'

'No need,' came a growling response from the general. 'I also am familiar with this Englishness; and yes, you are correct in your assumption.'

Alex stood and shoved his hands into his pockets, and waited for elucidation to pour forth from his opponent's lips. He shook his head, a gentle movement, barely perceptible as he thought about parallel processes, the chains of thought that were rumbling through both his and the general's brains. Both were aware of the falsehood they were skating around, but only he, Alex, knew the story from all aspects, from the origins to the present seesaw situation. Cognisant of the double deception, he breathed deeply and masked his deepest fears.

'Dieter,' the general barked. '*Kaffee.*'

The gardener almost snapped in two as he energised his body into compliance with the master's request. Leaving the clutter of the brandy bottle and used glasses arranged in splendid disarray on the tabletop, he trotted across the lawn and entered the shadowy interior of the general's home.

'I cannot afford to have witnesses to the value of these paintings,' the general announced, shifting about in his wheelchair while trying to make himself less uncomfortable. 'Now that they are here, in my home, they must be hidden . . . How you are saying? – Out of sight, out of mind? until I am able to have them transported to my contact.'

'He is still alive, then?' Alex asked, genuine concern apparent on his face. 'Your buyer?'

The general's head spun so rapidly that Alex was sure he heard a chorus of bones and muscles ripping apart. He thought about jumping into the position of third slip, just in case the elderly pate suffered detachment.

'Of course, why not? I will be ringing him tonight,' the general answered, sliding under the cover of Alex's convenient suggestion. His mind was racing, grabbing at intelligent computations with regard to the amount of money he wanted . . . No, not wanted, but needed, and was being forced to part with in order to secure the collection. 'Yes, you must be coming back tomorrow and I will be giving you the money. I presume cash?' He looked up, squinting through the sunlight at the tall Englishman. He'd regained his confidence in the knowledge that the paintings, magically – barring unknown and unforeseen calamities – were once again under his control.

'Yes, cash.' Alex walked across the patio and began covering the paintings, wrapping them with the protective cloths.

The general watched moodily as the packages were collected together, ready to be trundled back to the car. He was on the edge of a precipice. The paintings were his and he had to have them. Lifting his head from sombre speculation, he beckoned Alex towards him and whispered into the Englishman's ear.

Alex pulled his head away and looked at Eve. 'Twenty . . .'

'Shhh,' the general hissed, holding a finger up to his lips. 'Our agreement must be . . . secret.'

Alex returned his head to close proximity with the general's. 'Per painting?'

'Yes,' came the whispered response.

'No,' Alex replied.

'No?' the general's voice registered shock. 'No?'

'No,' Alex repeated.

'But they are being only a small collection. Twenty thousand is much money for an unknown artist.'

Alex smiled. 'Yet you took a lot of trouble to ship the unknown artist's small collection to Argentina.'

'Yes, but . . .'

'And it would have cost a small fortune and a great deal of organisation.'

'Yes, but . . .'

'And therefore, Herr General, I think the "small collection",' Alex used his fingers to indicate the apostrophes, 'is worth more than the figure you have stated. Especially,' he continued, 'now that the world has progressed through fifty years and everything carries considerably more value.' Pleased with his speedy rationalisation, he checked himself, realising he'd have to be careful not to push too hard. 'I might be wrong,' he added softly, opening portals. Looking at Wolfgang, Alex smiled and leaned his head sideways, indicating that he and Eve should leave the vicinity so that the general's wish, regarding secrecy, could be respected.

'Now,' said the general, observing the go-between and the young woman wandering towards the lake, 'we are having the fields to ourselves.'

'Playing field, General, as we say in English.'

'Of course, playing field,' the general acknowledged. 'So, tell me, you have some sort of figure in mind?'

Shit! Alex had dreaded this moment and this particular question. Of course, he'd shoved several figures around, carefully balancing those of the astronomical variety – which quite possibly could be attached to the genuine Masters – with lesser amounts, which might reasonably be realised by the *Prentiss Poses*. He chewed at his lower lip for a couple of seconds, and then took the plunge. 'One hundred thousand,' he stated. 'Each.'

'What? Preposterous!'

'It depends,' Alex calmly replied. 'It depends on how much you want to regain possession. I certainly imagine these paintings would attract attention from other collectors of this type of art, and there must surely be many such people.'

'You are an astute young man,' the general said, smiling at his adversary, 'I could have used your talents in days gone by. You and Karl, huh, a formidable team!'

'Mmm, though Karl, evidently, was even more astute. After all, if he hadn't found these pictures in New York, you and I wouldn't be here talking about them,' Alex responded, skimming around the actual truth. He had misgiving premonitions about the way the conversation was going. It'd be better to stay clear of the Karl connection before the general discovered exactly how astute the man had been.

'Seventy-five thousand,' the general barked.

Alex quickly realised that no one had mentioned currency. Shit. Seventy-five thousand Deutsche marks were not exactly the same as seventy-five thousand pounds, or dollars. Bugger. 'Eighty,' he said. 'Eighty-thousand dollars.' Momentarily, he'd thought about sterling, until a split-second decision latched onto the American currency – more universal and perhaps a little more conducive to the general.

'Agreed.'

'Cash, as mentioned.'

'Of course, the trademark of the dealer.' Inwardly ecstatic at having rescued his camouflaged collection for such a reasonable price, the general smiled, reservedly, and offered his hand to shake on the agreed contract.

Inwardly ecstatic at having sold the bogus collection for an enormous sum of money, Alex smiled tightly as he grasped the outstretched hand and shook it firmly. 'We'll be back tomorrow.'

'The evening is better. I will need time to find the money.'

Wandering back from their impromptu stroll around the garden, Eve and Wolfgang plonked themselves onto the chairs at the same moment that Dieter returned with the coffee.

4

The following day was dull and rainy, a thick layer of cloud hovering tenaciously above the lake, mistiness seeping at the edges of everything. After a late lunch in one of the town's hostelries, Alex, Eve and Wolfgang, motored leisurely around the expanse of water, arriving at the general's residence at the early onset of dusk.

Welcoming the sales party into the kitchen, the general graciously suggested *Kaffee und Kuchen* and libations of a specially procured schnapps. 'Well, here we are,' he said in English, waving aside Wolfgang's surprise at not having to translate. 'I haff spoken to Argentina and I haff verified that the other two paintings are . . . gone.'

'My, my, you have been a busy general,' Alex commented, relishing the aroma of fresh coffee being brewed by an apron-garbed Dieter.

'Exactly,' the general agreed, sinking into his wheelchair having exhausted himself with a profusion of cheerful *Guten Tags*. 'The pictures were stolen while alterations and improvements were being made to a house that once was mine. Hah, it seems you cannot being to trust anybody.'

'Indeed no,' Alex agreed. 'The world's a tricky place.'

The general seemed to be having a problem with the statement, so Alex suggested to Wolfgang that he should translate.

'But, Alex, vhat is "sticky"?'

'Tricky, Wolfgang, tricky. Um . . . bugger, um . . . Difficult, use the word "difficult", it'll do.'

'*Ach so, genau,*' the general agreed, 'very difficult.' Placing an elbow onto one of the wheelchair's arms, he supported his head on the elevated palm of his hand and pondered the confusions of an altered world.

'London's National Gallery knew about the house,' Alex confessed, breaking into the pensive silence. 'In fact, they sent a man to investigate. Apparently, in the years after you were called to Prague, the house was converted into a kindergarten.'

'Yes, yes,' the general nodded irritably, 'they were not slow in making changes.'

'And you believe the two missing paintings were actually there, in your old house? Did you have them on display?' Alex had decided to ask as many questions as possible, to flood the man with excess information regarding the past in an attempt to make him forget the present. 'But why didn't you take them with you? Did you leave everything behind? Or did you take it all? Surely you must have had a batman or two to take care of all the packing?'

'Of course, everything was packed and taken to Czechoslovakia. The German army was very efficient, precise in the control of logistics.'

'So it could have been them, General, the batmen.' It was a statement, short and sweet and guaranteed to thicken muddy waters.

'They vould neffer . . .'

'No,' Alex quickly agreed, 'I am sure they were most loyal.'

'They vould haff been shot,' the general stormed. '*Und* I vould haff done the shooting.'

'Yes,' Alex said quietly, 'of course.' A cup of coffee was placed in front of him and he had to move quickly, indicating to Dieter that the milk the German was on the verge of pouring was not required. '*Schwarz, Dieter, danke.*'

'*Zucker?*'

'*Nein, danke.*'

'*Ohne Zucker, ohne Milch? Ist der Kaffee nicht zu stark?*'

'It's okay, Dieter, I like strong coffee. Wolfgang, please tell him that coffee of this quality is not so easy to find in London.'

Listening to the convivial conversation being fielded by his gardener, the general smiled in abstract reflection. If life were only so easy, he thought, if the world's greatest problems revolved around the question of sugar and milk, it'd be a far better place. Grasping Alex by an elbow, he pulled himself closer to the Englishman. 'Don't be mentioning the money,' he whispered, 'it would not be good for Dieter to know about the value of these things. He's local to the area and knows many people. And gardeners? Well, shall we say they like to talk.'

Grinning widely at the motley collection of people scattered about his kitchen, the general ordered Dieter to pour the schnapps. 'We are having agreement,' he announced proudly. 'After forty-five years, I am having my paintings.' He turned to face Alex. 'You did bring them with you?'

'You have the money?'

'But of course.'

'Then the paintings are yours.'

Suddenly effusive in what seemed an easy though costly victory, the general leered at Eve. 'So, my dear, you are being the granddaughter of the Karl?'

'I am indeed the granddaughter of the Karl,' Eve replied succinctly, copying the German mannerism of inserting a "the" before someone's name. 'Except I called him Charley.'

'Of course, of course, the American name. And you knew him well?'

'Yes, Herr General, I did.'

'And did he tell you what he was doing during the war?'

'A little, but like most people who lived through that dreadful era, he wisely kept most of it to himself.'

'He was a good man, my dear, working hard on liaison between the Czechoslovaks and the Germans. He was a go-between, a little like the Wolfgang.'

'Uh-ha, so I understand.' Eve smiled inwardly, knowing the truth that lay behind Charley's wartime endeavours. 'He was very much like the Wolfgang.'

'He was my right-hand man, the Karl. Indispensable.'

'Yes, I can imagine. And of course he must have thought a great deal of you,' Eve lied, smiling sweetly, 'to have been so persistent in tracing the paintings.'

'Yes, yes,' the general gushed happily. 'It really is quite amazing.'

Chapter Ten:

Ne plus ultra

1

Because it took place in bed, the celebratory homecoming was more of a pyjama party, except no one was wearing pyjamas. Two of the participants were naked under the covers, while the third was curled up on top of the duvet.

'So tell me again about the strange people, you know, the one's who have a multitude of names?' Eve asked, popping her head into daylight and breathing comparatively fresh air.

'Sorry?' Alex said, his voice muffled by the bag of goose feathers.

'Come out of there and explain. You were trying to tell me how they change the endings of their words, even their names, so that, what was it . . . Lenka becomes, what?'

'Oh, yeah, crazy, Lenko. I even noticed a video, a *Dirty Harry* movie, which referred to three different Eastwoods.'

'Really? Does he know?'

'It's to do with the words "by" and "of", or something like that. They don't use them, they change the names instead.'

'That's ridiculous! How can you expect to have a serious conversation with someone who keeps changing his name.'

'S'pose you have to learn the language,' Alex answered

thoughtfully.

'And did you? Go on, I bet you did, just a little. Speak to me some Czechish.'

'No, it's impossible, and anyway supposing I could I'd have to speak like this without modulation and without enthusiasm cramming in as many words as possible until I run out of breath and my voice tumbles through several registers and grinds to a halt.'

'Jesus!'

'Ex-*act*-ly. And, after drawing-in a planet-sized gulp of air I'd probably gallop through another four or five sentences of meaningless tosh until me lungs collapse like a pair of squeezed bellows.'

'Sort of like juggling, keeping all the balls in the air?'

'Mmm, sort of. Anyway, since it seems to be question time, I don't understand why you let Jessica keep the Vermeer?'

'Goodness, English, you've been silent about that for a long time. Been brooding have we?'

'No, it's just that I wondered at your reasoning.'

'Well, basically, she was right. If you and she, and Wolfgang, hadn't gone foraging in foreign fields, we'd still be two paintings short. And, what's more, we probably wouldn't be any the wiser.'

'What do you mean?'

'About the forgeries, about the *Prentiss Poses* being a red herring. Herrings.'

'What do you mean?' Alex knew he'd missed something. He knew also he had no idea what it was.

'Well, it was only because one of the paintings had been slightly damaged . . .'

'Shit!'

Eve raised the duvet, allowing light to shine on Alex's head. 'And because of that damage the three of you went poking about and came up with the theory that something was being covered up. Go on, smile. I love it when you smile.'

'Shit.' Alex was stuck in verbal feculence. He sat up and propped himself against the bed head. 'Amazing. You're absolutely right, I'd forgotten what a fluke that was. And then, and then . . .'

'And then you gave the painting to your buddy Terry, who scraped away and revealed the hidden Vermeer, the painting that Jessica's got hanging in her living room.'

'Eileen's, yes. Shit.'

'So, I think maybe she deserves to keep it.'

'But what about you? I mean all the paintings were left to you, were they not?'

'Indeed, but I think I can spare one,' Eve grinned above the rumpled bedclothes.

'Or two,' Alex remonstrated. 'Don't forget the Fila you decided you're going to give Mrs Carmichael.'

'Aw, Alex, that was hers from day one. It had her name on it.'

'But . . .'

'And she definitely deserves it. What an incredible story.'

Alex nodded his head in pensive agreement. 'She must have known about them, you know, those paintings?'

'You think?'

'She must've. Hell, they were in her house for years.'

'Along with a load of other stuff. You told me the place was like a museum.'

'It was, it was. Her husband, her second husband, was a

363

collector . . .'

'Unless of course Charley made a deal.'

'Deal?'

'Turns up with the paintings and says he's looking for secure storage, somewhere out of the way where they wouldn't be noticed. You know, a quiet understanding between him and the husband?'

'But why would he do that?' Alex asked, still nodding gently.

'Who knows?' Eve answered, sliding herself out of bed. She walked across to a chair and picked up a pair of jeans. 'But then, hey!' she cried, stepping back to the side of the bed, jeans dangling from her hands in uncertain suspension. 'He'd've known that if anything were to happen to him, the paintings, including the one he'd selected for his wartime lover, would be closeted under her roof, Mrs Carmichael's, Ellie, Elise.'

'*Je*sus! Yes.'

'He was clever, sharp as they come. He'd've had it planned down to the last detail.'

'And?'

'And what?'

'And . . . there's someone else who's as sharp as they come,' Alex laughed, pulling Eve on top of him. 'That was a cool move of yours, praising Charley's perseverance in track-ing down the paintings.'

'Yeah, I thought so.'

'Hell, you should've seen the general's face, you had him eating out of your hand.'

'Ah, yes,' Eve giggled. 'Hey, what's this?'

'What?'

'It seems my little friend has been crying,' Eve announced, sliding a fingertip around the oily head of a rampant dick.

'Well, I was getting all excited down there beneath the covers,' Alex explained, enjoying the sensation that was spreading throughout his body.

'So it would seem,' Eve agreed, grabbing one of Alex's hands and guiding it to a secret place of warmth and moist sanctity. 'Me too.' Leaning in towards Alex's member, she began to dab gently with her tongue. 'Secreting your own lubrication, huh?' she asked between exploratory licks. 'No need, honey, I got plenty of my own.'

Manoeuvring into better position, Alex allowed his tongue to wander lightly through the valley of genitalia, before using two fingers to pinch and hold the fragile edges together. Bringing his other hand into operation, he ran his index finger teasingly to and fro along the length of the clam-like groove.

'Ah, *fuck!*' Eve yelled.

'What?' Alex asked, alarmed, thinking either he'd done something heinous or, doubtful, Eve had climaxed.

'It's Simon,' Eve gasped, 'sank his claws into my calf.'

'Probably thinks he's riding some tempestuous sea.'

'Yeah, but . . . Hey, don't stop, that was great.'

'Really? Where's the cat?'

'Don't know, probably jumped ashore.'

'Okay, so turn around and face away from me. Yeah, like that. Now, down, gently.'

'I can't see your face.'

'No, but you can see what's happening.'

Eve lowered her head forwards and watched her body impale itself on the rigid shaft. Moving a hand between her thighs she brushed her fingernails across Alex's scrotum, up and down and beyond. Fascinated with the conjunction of their bodies, she used her other hand to part her lips, wide, wider, and leaned further forwards so she could witness every detail. Alex placed his hands on the tiny cheeks of Eve's taut ass, spreading then squeezing them together – sweet temptation, hallelujah – now you see it, now you don't, now you see it . . . Sort of on a par with a believer's vision of God the Father, God the Son, and God the Holy Ghost, nowandforeverworldwithoutendamen. Madness. Maintaining a steady manipulation – open, closed, open, closed – he used the tip of a thumb to press against the wrinkled button whenever it winked at him. Then, reeling under Eve's delicate exploration of his fundament, he felt himself near the brink and willed his stomach muscles to work harder.

Thrilled and excited, because she'd never really viewed it from this angle, Eve stared at the small opening of her urethra, enthralled as it widened and contracted against the constant movement of male intrusion. Everything felt so good, so right, perfect and . . . '*Fuck!*' she cried, witnessing a few drops of emergent urine. 'Hey, English, you've made me pee myself,' she exclaimed, unsure of whether or not she was going to pee some more. 'Huh, *that* hasn't happened on too many occasions.'

For Alex, it was all too much, the very idea of shooting his semen into a woman while she was peeing. Christ! it was like Christmas and Easter and everybody's birthday, the whole lot coming together – now, especially NOW, as he sensed his bollocks being bathed under a trickle of warm liquid – in one huge orgasm.

2

It was the following morning, late, and brunch was being prepared with useful assistance provided by a bottle of Cabernet Sauvignon from the sunny hills of California.

'When I woke up this morning . . .'

'Are you going to burst into song?' Alex asked gleefully.

'Me? Hardly. It's just that when I woke up, it was raining.'

'Yeah? Are you going to wash that stuff, then?' Alex asked, suspiciously watching Eve empty a bag of salad into a bowl. 'Aren't you going to check it to make sure it's not full of marauding Lithuanians?'

'What? Damn! Simon, leave it alone, you won't like it,' Eve instructed the cat as it pounced on an escaping piece of greenery.

Responding with a loud miaow, roughly translated as 'Might do!' Simon speared the errant verdure with a handy claw. Then, irritated, waved it in the air when the leaf refused to let go.

'You know,' Alex continued, 'those germy things that make you ill?'

'You mean listeria?'

'Do I?'

'Yes, but you get that from eggs.'

'You do? Well, what do you get from lettuce?'

'Nothing.'

'Not much point in eating it, then,' Alex reasoned.

Simon retreated from under the busy feet of the talkative chef and the man with the funny accent. He needed to sort out the problem with the thing that had tangled itself around the rest of the claws of his front left-hand paw. Besides, he was feeling slightly nauseous after wheeling his body through a series of figure of eights between the four legs of the humans. And, nausea or not, he had to work out whether his pleasure at seeing the return of his mistress and the alien outweighed his annoyance at not being fed. Life, he thought, eyeing the small piece of lettuce, is a never-ending series of hassles. Bringing the article to his mouth he bit it and found it tasted of nothing, so he bit it again, just to make sure. Intuition informed him that stuff of this colour, especially the stuff known as grass, was beneficial to the feline digestive system. Sadly, ceaseless roaming around enclosed spaces had unearthed nothing that remotely bore any resemblance to the image conjured up by his imagination. Why, he asked himself, hadn't his keeper thought to fill a shallow tray with earth and plant it with the seeds of this magical substance? Given the impossibility of nature convening at such an altitude and spontaneously providing oases of gently waving grasses, it seemed such an easy and obvious thing to do.

Glaring from under the table he listened to his stomach, which had begun to gurgle in an alarming fashion, and reckoned he'd better stroke it with his tongue in an effort to make the hunger go away. Lying on his side and sort of balancing himself on his left-hand front leg, he held his right-hand front leg out of the way and folded his neck forwards until he was able to attend to the grumbling belly. He couldn't understand it, what were the humans thinking of? Last night, when they'd returned, crashing and banging around the apartment, laughing and chattering fit to bust, they'd picked him up and petted him for a couple of minutes, maybe less, then, after opening a bottle of something, they'd zoomed into the bedroom and immediately forgotten about important stuff like food.

Aw, shit, this is really uncomfortable, he decided, bent all over himself and straining every muscle in order to reach his abdomen. He stopped for a breather and peered across the floor to where his food bowl should have been. Another green thing had managed to escape, so he deemed it might be worth investigating. Uncurling his body, Simon rose to his feet, padded across the tiles and elevated the lettuce into his mouth.

'Look,' said Alex. 'Simon's become a vegetarian.'

'The hell I have,' Simon answered via a series of miaows, while manoeuvring the flimsy leaf around his mouth.

'Do you think he's hungry?' Alex asked.

Simon looked up at the tall alien and awarded him a withering look.

'Didn't we feed him?' Eve asked, unfolding rashers of bacon into a hissing frying pan. 'I'm sure we fed him.'

Simon edged forwards a couple of paces and sat upright, statue-like, in front of his eatery. 'Come on, come on,' he willed the forgetful guardians.

'Shit,' Eve exclaimed, 'I don't think we did, did we?'

'Bingo!' Simon thought. 'Now.'

'Simon, Simon, my little man, I'm so sorry,' Eve said, bending down and collecting the animal into her arms. 'What a stupid mummy you've got.'

'Don't worry about all that,' Simon protested, miaowing determinedly, legs pointing in all directions like a broken bagpipe, 'just put me down and *feed* me.'

'*Jesus!*' Alex announced, hurrying into action and opening and closing cupboards, 'he must be starving.'

Simon glared at the alien through half-closed eyes. 'You think?' he miaowed.

'*Now I've got a job to do . . .*' Alex sang to the tune of the military training ditty – the one which has the first line, shouted by the commanding officer, being repeated by a squad of raw recruits.

'*. . . Feed the cat some chicken stew.*' He sang the second line while reading the legend on the can of cat food.

'Have you been drinking?' Eve asked suspiciously.

'No, well, a sipette, maybe two, but I feel like I have, you know, full of oxygen, bouncy and exuberant?'

'Bouncy?'

'Yeah, bouncy, like I'm about to explode with an over abundance of life.'

'It'll be the rain, honey, negative ions zipping through space.'

'I thought that only happened with thunder and lightning?'

'Whatever.'

'Anyway, isn't that what you were talking about before we realised we'd forgotten to feed his lordship?' Alex asked, placing a well-filled bowl onto the floor in front of Simon.

'I was? Yes, I was. It's just that I love it, being all cosy and warm and listening to the elements.' Eve went to the fridge and collected an assortment of extras for the salad.

'Hmm, sounds sort of jazzy,' Alex observed, wandering towards a shelf supporting Eve's collection of CDs.

'It's wonderful,' Eve went on, unfazed, 'cuddling up to the man you love, feeling the warmth of his body while the sound of rain drums ceaselessly against the window panes.'

'Or . . . funky.'

'Raw and earthy, elemental, romantic.'

'Ah, romantic jazzy funk . . . perhaps something by Mr Jarreau?' Alex busied himself at the controls of the hi-fi and then wandered over to place his arms around Eve's waist. 'I feel the same, honey,' he said, turning her around to face him. 'You've turned my life around.'

'So, sweetheart, with all that energy bursting through your veins you should be capable of lifting a knife and chopping these green onions.'

'Yep.' Now that Al was launched into *Closer To Your Love*, Alex felt capable of anything.

'And this pepper,' Eve said, rolling a red variety along the worktop.

'Yep.'

'You're not on drugs, are you?'

'Don't need to be.'

'Okay, just checking.'

'Not, never, nohow.' Alex was on a roll. 'Tomatoes?'

'Here.'

'Cucumber?'

'Yes. Blimey, English, what's got into you?'

'Carrots?'

'Hmm, you get vision from carrots.'

'Vision?'

'Night vision. They contain something that improves your ability to see in the dark.'

'Wow, perhaps if you'd eaten more carrots in your youth, you'd have seen that car coming.'

'Night vision, English, not rear vision.' Eve broke some eggs into a pan of frothing butter and leant her hips against the worktop. Taking a sip of wine, she became pensive, methodically stirring the yellow mixture with a wooden spoon and adding a little milk until everything took on the right consistency. 'Four,' she said, scraping scrambled eggs onto two plates.

'Eggs?'

'Yes, but paintings also.' Eve used her fingers to pick six strips of nearly burnt bacon from the sizzling frying pan and laid them artistically, three apiece, on top of the eggs.

'Excuse me?' Alex was slowly assimilating the American way of speech.

'I think we should let George keep one.'

'George? The man who went into near frenzy when you told him the paintings were yours? Why? Are you crazy?'

'No, I just think . . .'

'He wouldn't do the same for you, honey.'

'No, probably not.' Eve transferred the plates to the table and sat. 'But in a similar sort of way to Jessica, if it hadn't been for George . . . Oh, pepper, honey, and the salt. If he hadn't got in touch with you, none of this would have happened.'

Alex brought the condiments to the table and collected the glasses of wine. 'No, this is true,' he agreed, pulling out a chair and sitting down. 'Certainly true.'

'And,' Eve said, raising her glass in readiness for a toast, 'you wouldn't have had your moment of epiphany about returning the pictures to the Herr General.'

'Mmm.' Alex was having a problem trying to decide if he had time to load a forkful of egg and bacon into his mouth before picking up his glass. He chose the latter.

'And, we wouldn't be . . . Um, well, nearly half-a-million dollars richer. Cheers, English.'

'Cheers, sweetheart. Yeah, you're right, we can afford to be nice to George. And, who knows? maybe one day we might need a lawyer, a friendly one.'

'And what about Wolfgang?'

'What about him?'

'Well, he was pretty instrumental.'

'He was indeed.'

'I seem to remember you telling me that it was Wolfgang who first recognised the Rembrandt.'

'Yes, you're right. Good old Voolfy. Although actually he wasn't too sure about it, not at first.'

'Well, I think we should let him have it.'

'The Rembrandt?'

'Yes, English. Why not?'

'They're your pictures, honey, to do with as you want.' Alex took a thoughtful sip of wine. 'It might be a little dangerous, though, you know, sending one of the paintings back to the vicinity of the general?'

'No, I don't think so. Anyway, we'll let Wolfgang decide.'

'So, Mrs Carmichael, George, Jessica, and Wolfgang. And Terry of course, to pay for all his work. In your new-found wealth, you brave young American, you've become quite a philanthropist. You've also put quite a dent in the kitty.'

'Brave?'

'I should say so, either that or mad. It was a courageous thing to do, letting me trollop off to London to confront my old flame while you were languishing in hospital.'

'Just so long as it wasn't rekindled.'

'Me? Jessica? Rekindled?'

Eve opened her eyes wide and stared at Alex, questioning, searching.

'I don't think so,' Alex stated as Eve parted her lips and brushed them against his.

'It's a strange story, though, you and Jessica. She's okay. I mean, you know? it can't have been easy, her having to confront me standing on her doorstep, all unannounced.'

'No, I suppose that might have been . . .'

'But she handled it. Yeah, at first she may have been thrown by the suddenness but, in the pub, she did manage to sort of get herself together. I don't know, honey, it must've been a good relationship, most of the time?'

'Initially, like all relationships, yeah, it was great and everything was rosy. That period when you fool around discovering one another, it's fun, like it was with us. Um, still is.'

'And? Be careful.'

'Well, black clouds were hovering on the horizon, internal struggles that were hard for her to control kept bubbling to the surface. And then of course I discovered she was a psychologist, and these people have major issues.'

'They do?'

'Yeah, most of them have more problems than the people they claim to help. Anyway, the English aren't too good when it comes to talking about shit, you know, the deep emotional stuff? We tend to step around it, cover everything with our stiff upper lip and let it fester.'

'Oh, we don't avoid anything and we don't let stuff fester, we just crash straight in.'

'Yep, and then get to visit your shrinks. Anyway, it was like living on a roller coaster, riding round in happy land until, suddenly, down it all goes. And there were some pretty scary moments when she'd do weird sort of stuff, like disappearing into the night.'

'Really?'

'Yeah, really. One evening she just took off, left dinner stewing on the stove.'

'And what did you do, English, pour a glass of wine and eat the food?'

'No, I went in search. Trailed all over north London.'

'And you found her?'

'No, well, yes. She went zipping past in a taxi. After I'd been all round the houses, there she was, blonde hair flying in the wind.'

'Must've been difficult?'

'The mood swings? Yeah. Like . . . Well, you know how it is when you change your toothbrush?'

'Oh, shit, I hate that. Nothing fits, it's like you're trying to clean someone else's mouth.'

'Yes.'

'So how does that relate to Jess . . . Oh, I see. Shit!'

'Well, perhaps not as sudden as a toothbrush change. But I didn't see them coming, the swings. Out of the blue they were, indiscriminate, on and off like a mask, the sort of thing a clown does with his face. Or an actor.'

'And what about you? There are always two sides to a story.'

'Yep, and you'd have to ask Jessica.'

'You know, honey?' Eve said slowly, 'if you want to keep in touch with her, on the phone, like a long distance sort of communication, that'd be okay with me, I'm not a jealous kinda girl. Christ, we all have a past, makes us what we are.' She stopped rambling, suddenly conscious about her own past and the amoral secrets of youth.

'Yeah, but . . .'

'Anyway, when it comes down to it there's not a lot you can do. If someone wants to be with you, they will. Hey, English, we have to live for today, for who knows what tomorrow might bring?'

'Blimey, you're not going to go all peculiar on me, are you?'

'Don't think so, not just now.'

'Thank fuck for that. One weird woman is quite enough.'

'But maybe in the future,' Eve suggested, grinning salaciously.

Alex toyed with the stem of his glass and pondered awhile, thinking about the meeting he'd had earlier in the year, the crazy evening in London which, in all truth, had been exhilarating but had also proved the accuracy of the adage about leopards and spots. Jessica would always be Jessica, the lovable, helter-skelter thirty-something with a bundle of issues. 'Nah,' he said, answering Eve's earlier question, 'no need. New life, new love.' Realising anyway it was a no-brainer, he picked up the glass and took a large mouthful of crisp sunshine. 'Besides,' he added, 'all my friends are here.'

'Your friends?'

'Of course, Mandie and Dan.'

'Oh yes,' Eve acknowledged, perhaps a little pensively.

'Mandie, and Dan.'

'Yup, and there's a great big ocean that agrees with me. And, having been cooped up in a car with you, trundling around Europe . . .'

'Yes.'

'And having witnessed you counter the conjectures of the English coterie . . .'

'I just love it when you alliterate.'

'Not to mention the amassing of a fortune . . .'

'Ah.'

'And watching you give it all away,' Alex grinned.

'Me?'

'Okay, then. Us.'

'This'll be going somewhere, then?'

'I'm going to give you an answer.' Alex looked directly into Eve's blue-grey eyes.

'To what?'

'To a question you asked me when first we met.'

'You mean you didn't answer then and there?'

'No, I was drifting through heaven and all confused.'

'So?'

'The answer's yes.'

'And what was the question? Remind me.'

'You asked me if I was going to stay.'

'I did?' Smiling, Eve reached out and caressed Alex's hand as it clutched the glass.

'You did, and the answer is yes.' Elevating himself, Alex leaned across the table. 'Here I am and here I stay,' he said, hovering inelegantly, one hand placed either side of his empty plate. 'Stand up and let me kiss the lips of an angel.'

Author's note
(June 2013)

Circumstantial evidence.

To a certain extent, and certainly within the remit of literary license, the proof of a painting's authenticity is somewhat dubious. After all, how many of today's "experts" actually witnessed those magical brushstrokes at the moment they were being applied to virgin canvas? None. As a result, everything is hearsay, or at best attested to via documentation that, similarly, may or may not be genuine.

Today's experts have a wealth of tools at hand, including chemicals that allow them to test oils, pigments and fabrics, and high-powered microscopes and infrared that peer more closely than perhaps necessary. And, naturally, today's master forger also has access to this modern paraphernalia. Being a superlative artist is not enough. Nowadays, a forger has to double as a forensic scientist, a chemist *au fait* with all aspects of modern analysis.

So, where does this leave us?

Well, perhaps it's best not to ask too many questions. Ever since mankind first decorated his cave with inspired art, the rest of us have stood and stared and generally admired. Landscapes, seascapes, portraits, battlegrounds, blobs and circles, dots, squares and weird imaginings – all have been allotted wall space for our eager vision. Are these images real, or fake? Do we, the observers, care? We like to think we do. We like to believe what we see, we like to imagine that the work of art in front of our eyes actually was created by the accredited artist. Or do we? Do we just admire the painting for what it is – the play of sunlight on a distant mountain range; the wind-filled sails of a galleon; or the lifeless body of a hare on a kitchen table? Or is it the whole caboodle – artist, genre, method and subject? What is it that actually interests us? As they say, 'one man's heaven is another man's hell', so is it correct or even possible to label an article as being "good" or "bad"? This is the beautiful thing about art, whether it be music, literature, photography or painting – we are all individual observers, each with our own requirements.

Another interesting question revolves around interchangeability – could, for example, a Turner seascape have been executed by Constable? Could a landscape by Canelleto have been depicted by Turner? And, taking it further, could any of these wonderful Masterpieces have been produced by any of the artists' accomplished students? Recently, (2013), a collection of drawings housed in the British Museum and attributed to Italian artists, was found to be of Spanish creation.

Two or three years ago, in Prague, the *Mona Lisa* was included in an exhaustive exhibition of Leonardo da Vinci's famous inventions. Supposedly, the painting on display was a replica – understandably so, since it's believed that the hallowed version in the Louvre is never allowed to leave the country. In fact, the painting has led an interesting life, travelling between Fontainebleu, Versailles, Napoleon's bedroom, and the Louvre. And then, in 1911, it was stolen by Vincenzo Perugia, allegedly on behalf of an arts dealer from Buenos Aires. However, because the dealer already possessed several copies of the painting, each of which he was happily managing to sell for $300,000, he never bothered to collect the 'genuine' painting from Perugia. When the theft became public knowledge, *Mona Lisa* forgeries began emerging from everywhere, most of them being offered to the Louvre as the real thing. But it wasn't until 1913, when Perugia tried to sell his picture to Florence's Uffizi gallery, that the stolen painting came to light. Was this the genuine *Mona Lisa*? Who knows?

There is documented proof that the original *Mona Lisa* was once owned by the French king, Francis I. Further documentation, however, reveals that in 1518 – one year before da Vinci's death – a gentleman called Salai (one of da Vinci's apprentices), sold a painting to a representative of Francis I. Although the painting is not named, the amount of money received by Salai leads one to suspect that he sold it claiming it to be one of the Master's.

In his will, da Vinci bequeathed Salai half a vineyard, but no paintings. This, however, doesn't appear to tally with Salai's will, which happens to list various paintings by da Vinci – including the *Mona Lisa* – and suggests that the paintings in Salai's possession were no more than bogus copies of the Master's work. Further, due to the fact that in 1517 da Vinci suffered a stroke and was unable to move his left hand, there is a definite possibility that his paintings were effected or completed by one or more of his apprentices.

And, there's another story, also claiming that the *Mona Lisa* at the Louvre is not the original but a very good copy bought by the gallery sometime between 1911 and 1913 – interestingly, the time of Perugia's theft. The original, so the story goes, is stored in a Swiss vault, safe from vandalism and supposedly safe from theft.

These are interesting theories and, since Leonardo isn't around to give verification, that's all they will ever be. So, in Terry's words, eat the steak, drink the wine, and don't ask too many questions.

Glossary of German words and phrases
as used in *Revelations*

Page   4   *Cojones (Spanish)* - Balls

Page *186*   *dobrý, děkuju (Czech)* - Good, thank you

Page *231*   *Fasching* - Carnival

Page *232*   *'Hermann, was machst du?'* -
                   Hermann, what are you doing?

Page *232*   *'Ich bin der Wolfgang.'* - I'm Wolfgang

Page *232*   *'Es tut mir leid, aber mein Freund Hermann ist ein*
      bisschen...' - Sorry, but my friend, Hermann, is a little...

Page *232*   *'Genau.'* - Exactly

Page *232*   *'Und ich spreche kein Deutsch.'* -
                   And I don't speak German

Page *233*   *'gut.'* - Good

Page *234*   *'Heidi, servus.'* - Heidi, hello (Bavaria only)

Page *235*   *'Schatzi.'* - Sweetheart

Page *243*   *'Natürlich* - Of course

Page *243*   *'Muße.'* - Leisure

Page *243*   *'Scheiße.'* - Shit

Page *245*   *'Mein Gott!'* - My God!

Page *317*   *'Gut, gut, sehr gut.'* - Good, good, very good

Page *323*   *'Guten Tag.'* - Good day

Page *323*   *'Wer?'* - Who?

Page *324*   *'So, kein Problem.'* - So, no problem

Page *325*   *'Hochdeutsch.'* - High German ('Correct German'
                   spoken in the north of Germany and in cities)

Page *325*   *'Richtig.'* - Correct

Page *331* *'Geht's gut?'* - How are you doing?

Page *331* *'Ja, ja, danke.'* - Yes, yes, thanks

Page *331* *'Stimmt ... wie Sie möchten.'* -
Correct ... as you like

Page *333* *'Unglaublich. Ich hätte nie gedacht, dass das möglich ist.'* -
Unbelievable. I'd have never thought it possible

Page *334* *'Herr General, ich kann die Lupe nicht finden.'* -
Herr General, I can't find the magnifying glass

Page *334* *'Herr General, was ist?'* - Herr General, what is it?

Page *334* *'So, Dieter, geh und sieh in den Schubladen, und mach schnell!'* -
So, Dieter, go and look in the study, and hurry up

Page *338* *'Vortrefflich! Alles in ordnung ist. Sie haben die anderen?'*
Excellent! Everything's okay. You have the others?

Page *338* *'Und, wie viel?'* - And how many?

Page *339* *'Wie Sie wünschen.'* - As you wish

Page *339* *'Und? Was ist?'* - And? What is it?

Page *340* *'Ein Rechtsanwalt?'* - A lawyer?

Page *340* *'Wie so?'* - How so?

Page *340* *'Ach so, tot.'* - Okay, dead

Page *340* *'Der Rechtsanwalt ist tot.'* - The lawyer is dead

Page *340* *'Ja, so ist das Leben'* - Yep, such is life

Page *340* *'Mein Gott! Was ist los mit dir? Was meinst du?'* -
My God! What's the matter with you? What do you mean?

Page *340* *'Das ist unmöglich! Das kann ich wierklich nicht glauben.'*
This is impossible! I really can't believe it

Page *341* '*Gehe nach ihm.*' - Go after him

Page *342* '*Donner und Blitzen!*' - Thunder and lightning

Page *342* '*Kruzifix!*' - Good day (Expression used in Bavaria)

Page *346* '*Nur sechs?* - Only six?

Page *349* '*Kaffee.*' - Coffee

Page *355* '*Kaffee und Kuchen.*' - Coffee and biscuits

Page *357* '*Schwarz, Dieter, danke.*' - Black, Dieter, thanks

Page *357* '*Zucker?*' - Sugar?

Page *357* '*Ohne Zucker, ohne Milch? Ist der Kaffee nicht zu stark?*'
Without sugar, without milk? Isn't the coffee too strong?

Page *359* '*Ne plus ultra.*' (*Latin*) - The perfect place

384

R i p p l e s

Richard C Pizey

Alex and Jessica live in north London and, like many young couples, lead a problematic life. Now, unbidden, an extra dimension lands on the doormat and adds to their troubles.

Set in the 1980s, this ingenious story flirts with humour, music, art history, Nazi machination . . . and sex, as Alex and Jessica delve into the secrets behind a set of paintings recently discovered in upstate New York.

Linking past to present and attempting to unravel the intricacies of art fraud, this whirlwind adventure combines mystery and intimacy and hurtles through London, New York, Bavaria and Scotland on a quest concerned not only with works of art, but also with the struggles of an in-your-face relationship.

Bold, brash and upfront, *Ripples* tantalises, teases and transports you to places and situations previously confined to your imagination.

Ripples (prequel to *Revelations*), is the first novel from
Richard C Pizey, author of *Echoes of Andalucía*.
Available from bookshops or at www.augfifth.com

AUGMENTED FIFTH
ANOTHER DIMENSION
www.augfifth.com

Ripples

Echoes of Andalucía

Richard C Pizey

José is seventy-nine years old and there isn't much he doesn't know. He is short and stout, has strong beliefs and is regarded by many as the fount of all wisdom.

María is José's wife. She is short and stout, faithfully supports her husband in everything, and is blissfully happy when surrounded by her immediate family.

Echoes of Andalucía is set in the week following 9/11 - a time of world crisis, a time when the future is held in suspense.

Detailing twenty-four hours in the life of José and his family, the story subtly encompasses seventy years, as José - dipping in and out of habitual frequent siestas - comes to terms with episodes from his colourful past and grapples with the aftermath of the attack on America.

Bloody and brutal, beautiful and tragic, *Echoes of Andalucía* dances with the fiery sensuality of this haunting country and reveals the hidden way-of-life still to be found in the mountains of southern Spain.

Echoes of Andalucía is the second novel from Richard C Pizey, author of *Ripples* and its sequel, *Revelations*.
Available from bookshops or at www.augfifth.com

AUGMENTED FIFTH
ANOTHER DIMENSION
www.augfifth.com